About the Author

D0532552

Eamon grew up above th_____ents
in an area of central I_____ttle
Jerusalem'. His early exp_____gave
him a deep sense of connection to his native place. After a series
of short-term jobs in motorcycle servicing, courier deliveries,
boiler maintenance, bar work and community development,
he joined a window installation company where he held
variety of posts. While there, he became a campaigner in the
fledgling gay liberation movement, serving three terms as
spokesperson for Ireland's National Gay Federation. He moved
to London in the mid 1980s following the collapse of the
window company. After two years working with Haringey
Council's Lesbian and Gay Unit (including the anti-Clause 28
campaign) he became involved in social housing development,
which became his chosen career.

Eamon began his lifelong interest in learning about
storytelling with classes at the People's College in 1970s
Dublin, before going on to study at London's Goldsmiths
and later Birkbeck College, attending summer schools at the
Irish Writers' Centre, and more recently joining masterclasses
with admired American poet Diana Goetsch (via Paragraph
NY). Eamon's short stories have been published in literary
magazines including *Tees Valley Writer*, *Automatic Pilot* and
Chroma. *The Journal of Truth and Consequences* nominated his
'Fear of Landing' for a Pushcart Prize, and 'Nataí Bocht' was
included in *Quare Fellas*, a collection of LGBT+ fiction
published by Basement Press in Ireland. He is currently

working on revisions to his novel *A Very Foolish Dream* (the name will change) which was Highly Commended in the 2019 Novel Fair sponsored by the Irish Writers' Centre in Dublin. *Dolly Considine's Hotel* is his debut novel.

Eamon is the happy father of three wonderful children. He and his civil partner Tomás are proud to be called Papa and Papi by their two lovely grandchildren, Daragh and Alva. Eamon and Tomás increasingly divide their time between London, Dublin, and other parts of Ireland.

Dolly Considine's Hotel

Eamon Somers

unbound

This edition first published in 2019

Unbound
6th Floor Mutual House, 70 Conduit Street, London W1S 2GF
www.unbound.com
All rights reserved

© Eamon Somers, 2021

This book is a work of fiction and, except in the case of historical fact, any resemblance to actual persons, living or dead, is purely coincidental.

ISBN (eBook): 978-1-78965-130-0
ISBN (Paperback): 978-1-78965-129-4

Cover design by Mecob

Printed and bound in Great Britain by Clays Ltd, Elcograf S.p.A.

Super Patrons

Carol Albertyn Christie
Alva Ali
Irum Ali
Paul Allen
Guervork Antonian
Joselyne Aroda
R. Ashe
Michael Aylwin
Andrew Baker
Farhan Bari
Jodi Bartle
Richard Beard
Elizabeth Bennett
Ros Bentley
Michael Bergin
Mary Berry
Richard Bird
Arno Blumhofer
Michael Booth
Stella Brade
Paul Bradley-Cong/ Out on the Page
Andy Brown
Rizzel Bryce
Tomás Campbell
Tony Campbell
Bob Cant
Donal Carey
Chetan Chowhan
Alexander Christie-Reardon

Tommy Coady
Noreen Corlett
Jenny Corrigan
Paula Costello
Damian Cullen
Glenn Cumiskey
Tom Curtis
Patrick Devlin
Catherine Doogan
Margaret Doogan
Neelam Dosanjh
Cathy Dunning
Lucia Errity
M Etherton
Helen Finch
Fergus Finlayson
Charmaine Francis
Mark Gardner
Patrick Gates
Anne Gravesen-Hepworth and her uncle
Praveen Greedharry
Teeny Grier
Geraldine Harrington
Martin Hazell
Mary Wilhelmena Patricia Healy
Pol Heaney
Paul Henry
Ramona Hillier-O'Hara
Sally Hodgkinson

Angus Hudson
Gemma Jackson
Jennifer Jess
Liam Johnston
Jacqueline Jolley
Alistair Jones
Aidan Kelly
Bernard Keogh & Josquin San Luis
Daanish Khan
John Kiely
A Kiernan
Della King
Sebastian Kinsella
Gill Kirby
David Kneale
Nicola Labuschagne
Nigel Lane
Mary Lavelle
Gerard Lawler
Angela Le Peuple
Arthur Leahy
Shaun Levin
Mark London
Steve Lunniss
Edmund Lynch & Martin
John MacIsaac
Ed Madden and Bert Easter
Gabrielle Mander
Isabel Manley
Gina Manning
Julie Markwell
Alison C. Mathias
Joseph McAuliffe
R. John McBratney
Mamie McCarthy
Neil Mckeich
Ciaran McKinney
Elaine McLaughlin
Mary McLoughlin-Campbell
Seamus McMenamin
David Monks
Jeremy Mooney Somers
Daragh Mooney-Somers
Julie Mooney-Somers
Martin Morrissey
Carl Mulkern

Terry Munyard
Aveen Murray
Brian Murray
Fionn Murray
Rory Murray
Peter Nevins
Senator David Norris & Ezra Yizhak
Caitriona O'Donnell
Eoin O'Donnell
Orlaith O'Donnell
Rory O'Donnell-Bird
Siobhan O'Donnell-Bird
Mary O'Malley-Campbell
Paul O'Dwyer
Gavin Pearson
Zeh Prado
Irene Quinn
Mary Quinn
Luca Rado
Stewart Rafter
Kim Randall
Eilish Rawson
Katherine Reardon
Addison Redley
Mary Rochford
Betty Rockwell
Jonathan Sanders Pizarro
Kim Sangster
Aki Schilz
Lesia Scholey
Pam Scott
Milan Šelj
Simon Sellens
Sarah Smith
John Peter Somers
Peter Somers
Ruairi Somers
Turlough Somers
Mary Somers-Kelleher
Antanas Spokas
John Stafford
Kaye Stout
Annie Tayler
Kath Tayler
Paul Tibbles
Donal Traynor

At the dances I was one of the most untiring and gayest. One evening a cousin of Sasha, a young boy, took me aside. With a grave face, as if he were about to announce the death of a dear comrade, he whispered to me that it did not behove an agitator to dance. Certainly not with such reckless abandon, anyway... I did not believe that a Cause which stood for a beautiful ideal, for anarchism, for release and freedom from convention and prejudice, should demand the denial of life and joy.

– Emma Goldman *(Living My Life, 1931)*

Prologue

AN EARLIER SUMMER

Eight-year-old Paddy Butler's mother gave up wearing tights and began to dress in floral tops and long patchwork skirts when his father went off to live in London. So whenever he and his friend Johnner hid in the bushes of next door's front garden, it was Johnner's mother who donated the laddered tights they cut and pulled over their faces to spend an afternoon spying. They wanted to be like Napoleon Solo and Illya Kuryakin in *The Man from U.N.C.L.E.*

Next door's garden was overgrown with hedges, and grass, and dandelions, running wild, and they could crouch down there all afternoon, listening to and watching the bush-filtered passers-by, safe behind the vegetation and the stretched nylon so long as they maintained total silence. They learnt to mime shock, or point at the state of a neighbour's shoes; but a stretched, distorted or itchy face couldn't communicate a subtle observation about the chatter they overheard, and every spying session ended when the frustration became so much that words threatened to spill out by themselves like from an overfull bladder. It was always Johnner who gave in first, and Paddy

1

who smiled inside the foot of Mrs Johnston's tights and allowed himself to be led next door to Johnner's front room, where they would speak with only the ears of walls listening and laugh at the things they'd seen and heard.

Although Paddy had his junior detective's notebook with him when he was in the garden, it stayed rolled up in his coat pocket, and it was only later, in bed, that he flattened it out to record the observations made during their afternoon stakeout, and would fall asleep, perhaps wondering whether the woman from the bread shop cared that the hem of her skirt could be seen beneath the red coat she always wore, or why the owner of the corner house sometimes had a limp, or, on the Saturday after the British Embassy was burnt down, what Johnner's father meant when they heard him telling a man they didn't know: 'She might be the prettiest women in Cabra, but no self-respecting husband should have to put up with that kind of thing.'

Johnner never asked to read his detective's notes, and Paddy never offered to let him.

Dolly Considine's Hotel

AFTER THE DANCING STOPPED

8th September 1983, 21:45–24:00

Pro-Life champion Mrs Eileen Mitchell studied the artificial orangeness of her squash drink as the youth was ushered out of the hotel lounge, his nakedness partially covered by a cape taken by Mrs Mitchell's assistant from one of the dancers that had participated in the shameful skit on Irish motherhood. Two other performers squeezed the seven-foot-high papier mâché Mother Ireland figure through the door behind him, her skirts lowered over her permanently distended belly and hiding the void from where the 'baby' had been disgorged. Another bundled up the bloodstained caul that had accompanied the fully grown infant out onto the lounge carpet, careful to ensure the trailing umbilical cord did not trip any of the referendum victory party crowd as they swarmed into the space vacated by the departing troupe.

Dolly McClean (née Considine) had hoped to enjoy the evening as a guest rather than as the hotel's landlady. But here she was, in a delicate red dress in place of her day-to-day black culottes and matching top, needing to push through the throng to order the hotel's dogsbody to collect the dancers' swords and bring them to the first-floor sitting room, and to make sure the Mother Ireland prop was pushed into the vestibule between the ladies and the stairs down to the gents. Partygoers on their way to their respective toilets would have to squeeze past the figure's exhausted grey face until it could be returned to the theatre where it belonged.

On any other Thursday she would be feeling the exhilaration of having just finished a tough three-setter and be anticipating the white wine spritzer waiting for her in the tennis club bar. She prayed that, with the shenanigans over, the referendum victory party would settle back into a normal late-night drinking session in the Curragh House Hotel.

Over the next two hours, Mrs Mitchell donned her 'ready to leave' look, several times. But whenever she mimed putting on her coat towards her assistant, Giolla-Íosa McClean TD beamed his gleaming politician's grin at her, making her shake her head and say, 'Perhaps I'll have a fresh orange squash.'

The evening had started with Giolla-Íosa, the opposition party's sitting representative for the Dublin South-East constituency, in which the hotel was located, making a presentation to Mrs Mitchell in recognition of her valuable contribution to the Pro-Life victory. His elder brother Cathal McClean had been standing behind him, and heard the words Giolla-Íosa loud-whispered as Mrs Mitchell acknowledged the dying applause with her well-known self-effacing smile. But it wasn't until he saw the effect his brother's grins were having on Mrs Mitchell's attempted departures that he realised it was Giolla-Íosa's whispered promise that made her go on to suffer an evening of mass drunkenness, perhaps in the hope that if he explained himself before she left the outcome he'd predicted could be forestalled. 'My brother Cathal tells me that the Pro-

Life Amendment is so badly worded,' Giolla-Íosa had said, 'that almost any legal challenge to it will be upheld. The people of Ireland have been sold a pup.'

But no such explanation had been offered by the time Giolla-Íosa's two young lackeys began rounding up any dancers they could find for a reprise of the performance. 'Who fucked Mother Ireland?' a voice was heard to shout when the theme music faltered, having initially hushed most of the shouting, singing and even snoring drunks still at the victory party. Dolly pushed through to where a man was wrestling the papier mâché figure towards the Porchester Lounge. 'No more nakedness,' she said.

'It's okay Dollys,' Mikhail Mayakovsky said in his dubious Russian accent. 'This time it's the phantoms pregnancy. We have no baby. Mother Ireland is swollen with nothings but the hot airs.'

'And no swords. They're dangerous. Do you hear me? A lot of drink has been taken.'

But the swords were already being held to the lips of the remaining dancers and the lips of Giolla-Íosa's lackeys, now sporting tossed hair and unbuttoned shirts after an evening of forming alliances with Pro-Lifers and anti-abortionists over beer and neat Jameson.

The mongrel troupe conga'd randomly rather than circle-dancing Mother Ireland, the shape dictated by drunks newly arrived from other referendum parties (and wakes) who were seeing the performance for the first time. Swordless dancers improvised with umbrellas and even the ice tongs grabbed from behind the bar. It was four burly men from the new crowd standing like defensive rugby players just inside the lounge door who took up the previously shouted question, and perhaps because they'd been chanting in spontaneous groups all evening they continued now – 'Who fucked Mother

Ireland? Who fucked Mother Ireland?', timing the chant so it was in step with the music, stamping their feet because clapping their hands was impossible with nowhere to put a glass except between the crooks of their arms and their chests, when clapping would cause spillage, and no chance of a refill now that Dolly had managed to push past them into the room and was shouting that service was finished; no last orders. And when the music reached its crescendo this time, even with the relative balance of the dancers guaranteeing Pro-Lifer superiority, each one in turn plunged his or her sword or umbrella point into the papier mâché belly of Mother Ireland, as if the shame implied by the chanting crowd's question outweighed the importance of either of the two lives notionally involved.

Shouts of 'good on ya' and 'fine girl ya're' replaced the music when it stopped.

Whatever Mrs Mitchell had thought of Giolla-Íosa McClean's predictions, when the swords began clashing over the head of Mother Ireland for the reprise, she was finally reaching a sensible shoe from the lowest of the front steps down onto the footpath and waving at a passing taxi. And while the demands of the music and the rhythm of the crowd were controlling the timing of the plunges into the papier mâché belly, the taxi man was asking Mrs Mitchell if she'd had a good evening, and as the final wound was inflicted on Mother Ireland and her phantom foetus, she replied with her famous smile.

When Giolla-Íosa's lackeys had begun to redistribute the swords, his older brother Cathal had become conscious of having a bad feeling and wished there was a way to get his brother out of the room without anybody noticing. Giolla-Íosa himself was staring at Dolly. She was waving her arms and trying to get into the lounge, but seemed to be barred from doing so by two men in suede jackets whom Cathal did not recognise, one on either side of her, her hair tumbling as they jostled her between them, together looking like the back three of a rugby scrummage getting ready to drop down onto the second row of four in front of them.

Dolly Considine's Hotel

MAKING PLANS: ST PATRICK'S DAY

17th March 1983

'You could have changed your clothes.'

Johnner began his rant as soon as they met up outside Quinnsworth in Phibsborough. It was he who'd arranged a day of flyer distribution ('Good News for Happy Families') at the St Patrick's Day parade. Not that there was any point in telling Paddy he was jeopardising their holiday fund by sporting his brother's tomato sauce- and beer-stained ex-army jacket and torn jeans instead of the neat clothing demanded by the flyer company. Turning into Mountjoy Street, Paddy's clothes blended with the abandoned buildings crying out to be bulldozed, the Black Church poking out into the streetscape like a neighbour wanting to shake its head at the lack of civic pride, and in turn encouraging Johnner's rant: the state of Irish politics, the paucity of national ambition, and the lack of prospects for the youth of Ireland.

The drumming they could hear, but not yet see, was getting louder as they advanced, the competing rhythms beginning to

colonise Johnner, his feet surrendering first, then his clicking
fingers, followed by his waving elbows. Even his heart seemed
eager to have an outside force take control of its beating. But
it didn't stop him announcing the absolute necessity for them
of getting out of the country, if not for the rest of their youth,
then at least for the summer before their last year of secondary
school.

Rounding Mary's Corner with the Black Church looming
over them, they were confronted by fume-spewing coaches
unloading American college bands into the space between the
sooty church and the fractured skeletons of dead buildings. The
roadway was crammed with pristine white uniforms and blue
uniforms, flashed with epaulettes of gold and red; instruments,
white, silver and brass, coming out of their cases to be
tentatively stroked for the performance ahead; spittle and
fingers, moistening and warming.

It wasn't the crush of the gawking enthralled, or Paddy
being unable to hear him over the noisy scales, that made
Johnner suspend his rant. But the cacophony and confusion
of rhythms were hijacking his feelings, making it impossible
for him to speak. Only when they reached the top end of
O'Connell Street with the noises receding was he liberated
enough to resume. 'We could spend the summer as Redcoats
in Butlins... I could teach the children drumming, and you...
Or... or driving cars from New York to Florida... Route 66...
Join all those people looking for America. Or go interrailing
across Europe... courtesy of American chicks... on their final
fling before they settle down to... domestic goddessity.'

Johnner stopped as they reached Clerys's shop window, and
snatched at Paddy's arm to halt him too, but then let go in
a show of surrender. The first eager families were already
lining the middle of the street, waving hand-sized tricolours
and protecting their places against the metal barriers ready for

the best view of the parade. They would appreciate a flyer explaining how insecure their homes were without a burglar alarm.

Johnner touched the sprig of muddy shamrock his mother had pinned to his lapel before he'd left the house. 'Say something,' he said, and pushed Paddy against the glass protecting Clerys's display of crockery and table lamps behind a foreground of monstrous green crêpe paper versions of the national emblem. 'You are so fucking opaque,' Johnner said, confident that the shop front had resisted heavier bodies than this titchy scrap, so he pushed him again, with more force; a shamrock secured to the inside of the glass quivered. 'Tell me what you want.'

But instead of answering or bouncing back for another push, Paddy slid down the window to the footpath and toppled over onto his right side, his hands joined together under his chin and his knees curled up into spooning position, his whole body shaking like a person having an epileptic fit or a peculiar orgasm. His black woolly hat squeezed off to reveal his home-hacked haircut.

'Fuck you,' Johnner spat as he tore at the flyers' packaging, dropped half onto the footpath, before beginning to walk away. 'Like it or not,' he said, stepping back, 'we're getting out of this godforsaken city for the summer. I will not work in my father's factory, and you will not mope about the streets in your mystical twilight. We will transform ourselves into stylish, free, out-of-Ireland internationalists. I, to become Drew, son of Ginger Baker, and you, to make up your mind if you're to be Julius or Julian, journal keeper, fictionaliser, liar. You have three days to start honing your new identity, and to come up with ways to find the funding.'

And then, God help him, he kicked his best friend, twice,

if only on his bony little arse, before forcing a smile for the woman who grabbed his arm to pull him away.

'Ah now son, leave the lad alone,' she said. 'Isn't it the feast of St Patrick?'

'Just a little domestic situation,' Johnner said, and she released his arm and nodded, as if she knew all about such things.

Dolly Considine's Hotel

DOLLY STANDS UP TO THE NAYSAYERS

April 1953

When her Aunt Ellen's will was read out and the extent of the debts run up during the year-long closure were known, Dolly Considine's father announced publicly that the twelve-bedroom hotel up in Dublin would be sold at auction. His daughter might have inherited the business, he said, but she was only eighteen and her place was with her family in County Offaly. Everyone knew he had to look decisive in public, but to his constituents, party managers and the pro- and anti-Fianna Fail newspapers it would be the outcome of the coroner's inquest that decided his political future, and not the decisions he made about his under-age daughter's hotel.

Dolly had been persuading her mother to take her Christmas shopping in Dublin for years before the scandal. On her very first stay in the hotel, towards the end of The Emergency, with war rationing still affecting everyone else, and while watching a couple of American soldiers in mufti in the visitors' lounge, she had made a promise about her future. And as if to seal it, she let go of her mother's hand, brushed a fleck of glitter from the front of her long brown coat, and shook her head to make the two pink rosebuds pinned to the rim of the hat her mother had bought her that afternoon in Brown Thomas quiver with certainty. She smiled at the American soldiers to let them know they were invited to come back to the bar to sip celebratory drinks with her on the day she moved into the hotel for ever.

The manageress, Mrs Burns, always in black and white like the waitresses in Bewley's, had her own opinion about the hotel owner's sister and favourite niece occupying beds she could have filled twice over in the days on either side of the Feast of the Immaculate Conception, the traditional opportunity for country people to come to Dublin for their Christmas shopping. But it was December 1951 before she said anything.

'Dolly is getting to be such a grand lady, she might be more comfortable in the Hibernian next year,' Mrs Burns said as the pair of them stood at reception fretting over suitcases and Christmas-wrapped parcels, and waiting for a taxi to take them to Kingsbridge station. She might have said something similar the following year, but by the time the decorations went up in the shops, Josie Geoghan was dead, the hotel was closed, and Mrs Burns herself dismissed and living with her sister in Birmingham; and the shame which would finish off Aunt Ellen two days before Little Christmas had already begun its work.

Far from it being the Hibernian Hotel, a week after the inquest into the death of the chambermaid recorded a verdict of misadventure Dolly and her mother were sleeping in Mrs Burns's old bed, and, despite Mrs Considine's speaking to auctioneers, Dolly was making plans for a grand reopening: washing, scrubbing, dusting, and making beds like a professional. She even painted the hall ceiling when the man she'd engaged to do it was scared away by Mrs Considine's warning that he would have to join the hotel's long list of creditors. Invitations to the Curragh House reopening were issued and her mother had no choice except to attend, and pretend it was an opportunity for the auctioneer to familiarise himself with the business.

A couple of trustees attended from the Porchester Theatre, which occupied one basement of the two-building hotel, and expressed their personal satisfaction at the prospect of the interval drinks bar being open again. The remaining trustees boycotted the event, claiming that association with the scandalous hotel was sullying their artistic integrity. Dolly presented them with an invoice for rent arrears, but that didn't stop one of them remarking that her lipstick reminded him of the woman who played Arte O'Neale in the production of *The Shaughraun* that had brought him into theatre.

Mr and Mrs Hannafin, who had continued to live-in while the hotel was officially closed, also attended, and when Dolly gave them a welcoming sherry each, she issued them with a bill for their arrears. The other long-term guest, Miss Guilfoyle, did not appear, so her invoice was slipped under her door.

Dolly introduced everyone to her late aunt's solicitor, who confirmed that selling the hotel without Dolly's full agreement would be against the spirit of the bequest. Mrs Considine was in bed by midnight, and thinking about her poor sister Ellen, entirely innocent of wrongdoing and yet dead of shame. She was still wondering how best to protect her daughter when Dolly joined her just after two.

Dolly Considine's Hotel

OUR HERO'S DEPARTURE SUFFERS A SETBACK

18th June 1983

He is no longer Paddy. He is Julian. Julian is decisive. Julian knows what he wants. And right now he wants Johnner to become Drew and get them out of Cabra. But his so-called friend is not the alpha Drew he'd made himself out to be when he tantalised Paddy with visions for their summer adventures.

'All you have to do is surrender to the programme. You know how to do that, don't you?'

But now, when turning back is impossible, at the very instant of implementation, when Julian has already shouldered on and buckled his backpack in response to the doorbell ringing, here is Johnner's baby brother standing on the front step with a note.

'*Me ma won't let me go. I have to start work in Da's office on Monday…*'

Julian held the backpack straps and watched the messenger cycle away, the news sinking in and not sinking in at the same time.

Paddy Butler would still have been in bed at seven-thirty on a Saturday morning, whereas he, Julian Ryder, is up, shaved, and dressed, with the 'torportudity' of which Johnner's mother accused him banished, along with his black hair, thanks to a bottle his mother abandoned when she turned 'natural' for her womanly politics.

He kicked the door closed, released the shoulder straps, and stomped down to the kitchen. 'Normal service is resumed,' he shouted, and fished through the dustbin for the Virgin Prunes tape he'd ceremoniously dumped earlier in a ritual to mark the commencement of his new world-embracing life.

'Maybe I don't need Johnner,' he said as he wiped brown sauce off the cassette. 'I can go by myself.' Except the devastating sting was in the final sentence of baby brother's note: '*She's cut up the BABA cash-card.*'

Julian shared his bedroom with his brother Christopher's collection of jazz records, and Johnner had persuaded him ('He's been bumming round Greece for years, he's never coming home') to sell carefully selected 78s to a man with a stall in George's Street Arcade, and to hand over the proceeds to be lodged in their Big Adventure Bank Account.

She's cut up the BABA cash-card.

He would go back to bed and let his mother drag him out when she came home, hyper, and looking for a fight, after a day at the GPO talking about abortion rights. Except his mother had sent Christopher the fare home after he'd promised not to miss her birthday for a third year in a row. Julian needed to be well away from Cabra when Christopher discovered his records were missing.

'Fuck.'

Johnner's baby brother had been on his way to fulfil his altar-boy duties at eight o'clock Mass at St Pippin's when he delivered the note. Julian could see the spire from the bedroom window. Maybe he could piggyback a prayer onto the altar-boy's innocence to prevent Christopher from returning. Otherwise it would only be a plane crash that would save him from a beating, and maybe it would be better not to wish for that. But if it happened anyway, it wouldn't be his fault. The Virgin Prunes blared 'Decline and Fall' into his misery, its dreams and flying- away lyrics doing nothing to cheer him up.

The note he'd written to his mother flew onto the floor as he swept back the blankets. The best thing he'd ever penned, and now she'd never see it. In earlier versions, he'd blamed his departure on her plan to spend the summer spouting politics, but in the published version he'd softened his accusations, and respected any feelings she might have about him going off without telling her. '*See you Mam*,' he'd signed off. '*I'm going over to London to see Uncle Arthur. Sorry to miss your birthday.*' He'd thought about signing it Julian, but his name change would have taken too much explaining, especially as she had banned Enid Blyton books from the house when he was ten. He was nothing like the bossy twit in the Famous Five. It was Johnner who named him Julian after Paddy'd written an essay praising the Roman Emperor in his Latin class. But he liked being Julian, he wasn't going back to Paddy, and one day his mother would have to get used to it.

The grapevine said that Uncle Arthur was doing okay, although he refused to answer his sister's letters or forgive her for whatever dreadful secret she'd betrayed. The great thing was Arthur would never contact her to say he hadn't turned up.

Me ma won't let me go.

She's cut up the BABA cash-card.

What a fuck up. No wonder he was cold. He pulled the blankets over his fully dressed self, *If I Die, I Die* in perfect tune with his mood. And yet something sent his right foot out from under the blankets to kick the stereo system up in line with the top of Christopher's Dave Brubeck poster. Too much planning had gone into their summer for it to change so easily. Baby brother's note was just a test of Julian's loyalty. Johnner would be at the bus station, they would laugh when they met up and slap each other's backs with mutual self-belief.

He reached for a 'just in case' boxed set from his brother's collection, put the letter to his mother back on display, and set his free hand burning against the handrail down the stairs before flying his jacket horizontally off the newel post and bouncing his backpack through the opened hall door. He slowed briefly to push the records down between his changes of clothes and the pristine journal waiting to record the adventures that were lining up to welcome him.

Dolly Considine's Hotel

IF DOLLY HAD BEEN A BOY, THEY'D HAVE PUT HER THROUGH UNIVERSITY

April 1953

'Listen to me, young lady,' her mother said the morning after the grand reopening. 'You are a child without any experience of business. The hotel's reputation will never recover from the scandal. That's why the National Bank is refusing to provide further credit.' She closed the lid on her suitcase and pressed the two catches down with a click each. Dolly's empty suitcase sat on the bed, the open wardrobe exposing the clothes she was refusing to pack.

'Aunt Ellen got—'

'My sister ran the hotel for forty years without ever borrowing a penny. But in a month's time, the debts will be greater than the value of the building. And then the bank will own it. We have no choice but to sell.' Mrs Considine had put on her hat and coat before she rang for the taxi. Now she adjusted her hair in the mirror and pursed her lips at the reflection of her daughter's frustrated face.

'Your father has decided, the auctioneer has been instructed, and the date is set.'

'The least you can do is tell the manager to freeze Aunt Ellen's loans, and get Daddy to guarantee a new overdraft.' The rolled-up sleeves of her striped pyjamas, the sliver of morning sun on her bare arms and the lace curtains blowing against her back insisted she stand her ground.

'I came here to help get the hotel ready for auction. I've calmed your creditors, told the permanent guests and Paddy the Porter they must make other arrangements, and held my tongue while you indulged in reckless spending on a pointless party.'

'Please, Mother. Just one year. And if the books are not balancing by then, they can do what they like with the place.'

'The taxi will be here in a minute, please get dressed and do your packing.'

'If I'd been a boy, you'd have put me through university.' She didn't dare mention her dead brother by name, or the savings account they'd set up on his first birthday. Aunt Ellen had been trying to even things up when she named Dolly in her will.

'That's it,' her mother said. 'Your duty as a daughter is to come back to Birr to prepare for your future as a wife and mother.'

'You mean, to be Daddy's trinket, paraded across the constituency to show the voters what a normal happy family we are.' She swept the tangling curtains away and shook her head at the taxi man waving up at her.

'I don't know what you're suggesting,' her mother said. 'Your father has done everything for you, and if he brings you to party functions it's because he's preparing you to be a suitable wife for an up and coming politician.'

'I'm not going home,' Dolly said. She slammed the lid closed on her empty suitcase, pushed it to the floor and kicked it under the bed. 'I'll never go back. Never.'

Dolly Considine's Hotel

COULD THIS BE A MIRACLE?

18th June 1983

Julian was barely inside the crowded Busárus when he heard 'Hey Paddy' behind him, the voice more purring than Johnner's, unless his friend was messing with him. Besides, his name was now Julian: decisive, witty, creative, slightly flamboyant Julian. Even so, he tried to reconfigure each of the faces around him into Johnner's, ready to say, I never doubted you, I knew you'd make it, have you got the tickets?

But there was no Johnner, only Peter Sweeney from school whom he and Johnner had nicknamed Mr Collins because of the way he pursued Julian, wanting to be friends, and more, ostensibly because their fathers had been drinking buddies.

'Are you off on your MWT?' Peter asked.

'Nah, that was all just gas. Help us through the winter.'

'Drew told me all about Micro World Tour.'

'Drew? What a name.' Why had Johnner told him? It was no one's business but their own.

'I think Julian suits you,' he said. 'There's something totally Julian about you. And the hair, blond, yeah, just perfect.'

He'd heard stuff like this before from Peter. Next he'd be on about how their fathers were friends, so they should be too.

'You inspired me, Julian. Honest. That's why I'm going to London, although my parents thought changing my name would only attract attention from the anti-terror squad. And I won't have to work unless I want to because they gave me enough money to last the summer.'

Was this what Johnner intended? That Peter would tag along? Or even worse, go in his place? No fucking way. He didn't want to be cruel, but he'd pick his own friends.

'That's great for you,' Julian said.

'So, are you on this bus then?' Peter nodded towards the ferry shuttle and turned for him to fall into step. A mass of teenagers with backpacks and army surplus clothing crowded around the ticket inspector before casually throwing their bags into the luggage compartment.

'This bus?' He needed time to think. Getting the fare out of him would be easy, and there would be drink all the way to London. But Mr Collins would never let him go. He'd latch onto him, taking their friendship so much for granted that Julian would explode with frustration, and then there would be plaintive faces, and begging, and tears. Maybe if Johnner was still on his way... No. No. The possibilities! Endless. Play for time. He looked round in case Johnner was watching, testing him.

'Naw, I'm here to meet my uncle Arthur. He's sorting out some problem with his ticket,' Julian said, and released the straps from one shoulder and then the other. 'This is his backpack.'

'I'm staying with my uncle Richard,' Peter said. 'He has a

house in Kilburn. My own key and the run of the place 'cause he's never there. You'd be welcome if you wanted.'

He was begging, already. Fiddling with the side pocket of his own backpack, his XXXL Glastonbury T-shirt, even bigger than he needed, billowing as if inviting Julian in to share it, bringing on shivers at the thought. It could not happen.

'I promised my uncle. It's his first time home in twenty years. I have to be here for him.' He'd been praying for a miracle to save him from his brother's wrath and now he was talking himself out of it. *Just say yes, you twat*, he could hear Johnner shouting from his bedroom in Cabra.

'Well, if you change your mind the next bus is at half past,' Peter said. 'I'll wait if you like.'

'For what? Think of me frustrated in Dublin when the chicks in Soho are sucking your dick.'

Julian waved back at him as the bus pulled out of its bay. Johnner would laugh at him, and call him Elizabeth Bennet for abandoning their adventure just because he couldn't bear to be under a compliment to poor old Mr Collins. Except Johnner would never even know. And, if Julian hadn't listened to Johnner, he'd have been free to spend his summer people-watching in Phibsborough shopping centre and getting in the odd tanning day among the sand dunes at Dollymount Strand. Instead, he'd have to find a way to hide from his brother, and worst of all he didn't even have the money from selling his brother's records. If he were braver, he'd go home, kick in the back door, and call the Guards to say the place had been burgled.

But at least it would be his version of events that would go into his journal and stand as the definitive 'Summer of '83' record, his *Summer of Unrequited Love*. *S.O.U.L.* Johnner would be consigned to a footnote. Served the fucker right.

Dolly Considine's Hotel

NO TIME TO BE SQUEAMISH

October 1956

Dolly was cleaning room eleven when she found the box in the bedside locker. She recognised the name printed on the side from hearing it whispered in the bar and knew what the contents were for. The box went straight into the waste basket carried from room to room, and slid beneath the jumble of empty shampoo sachets, bits of cotton wool, train and cinema tickets, and the long blue wrapper from a bandage (as well as the old bandage itself) left by the woman in room six.

'I've lived and worked in England for nine years,' the man who'd occupied the room for four nights had told her as he'd settled his bill. 'In Ballyliffin, County Donegal, my fiancée has waited these six years, a model of Irish womanhood, and the house her father and brothers built for us has stood forlorn for nearly four. It needs a woman's touch and the patter of tiny feet.'

Dolly was tucking in the bottom sheet when she recalled him even earlier, at breakfast, tucking into his rashers and

25

eggs, and being just as florid in describing his fiancée's nut-brown hair and comely figure to another guest. Had he already abandoned his condoms by then? Or did he wait till he returned to the room to collect his suitcase? A symbolic marker between his temporary existence in Birmingham and his real life in Donegal? Legal in England, an offence in Ireland, but sinful everywhere.

When she retrieved the box from the basket, she found that one of the greaseproof envelopes had been opened. Had the contents been used and washed for reuse, or been abandoned after the paper was torn? She imagined his partner asserting herself, maybe at the sight of him fiddling with the wrapper, balking at the idea of committing a compounding sin, with even worse consequences than pregnancy.

Dolly used her duster to clean streaks of shampoo from the cardboard, and slipped the pack into the pocket of the apron shielding her full-skirted burgundy dress. A frisson of some sort ran through her at the thought of offering them to a nameless man, trying to balance a sophisticated casualness in her manner with the need to prove she was not a loose woman.

Hours later, while registering a married couple from County Tipperary, she wondered why the Donegal man had risked the danger of customs officers searching his luggage and publicly shaming him only to wilfully abandon the condoms in the Curragh House Hotel, when he could have offered them to a friend, or made a little profit.

There was only the briefest question of the opened condom ever coming into intimate contact with Dolly before she flushed it down the second-floor toilet. Would she regret her squeamishness when legal replacements were impossible locally? She smiled at the Tipperary man being clutched by his wife as he signed the register, and wondered if he was the sort to put an unwrapped condom back into the box. She wasn't sure how it was going to happen to her, and she didn't have any man in mind, but she felt a longing, not just in her head, but down below also. The unopened companions would be the agents to her own unlocking. Behind her smile, she giggled at her silliness, and handed the wife the key to room eleven.

Dolly Considine's Hotel

JULIAN MAKES AN ALTERNATIVE PLAN

18th June 1983

'I can't finish me coffee,' a woman pulling a strap attached to a suitcase with wheels said, pointing behind herself to the seat Julian had just reached. 'I thought I had more time. I put in two sugars, but I didn't get a chance to stir it before they called the bus. They won't let you take hot drinks on board.'

He nodded and smiled. 'Thank you. Just what I needed.' A seat for himself and another for his backpack. A sweet coffee, and enough time to record a few succinct observations about travel and travellers before heading over to George's Street and the record man's stall. He looked towards the woman in the back seat of the bus and waved, putting Uncle Arthur back into his head; he'd do as he'd written to his mother, and go to him, courtesy of his brother's last few records.

'Adventures begin in bus stations,' Johnner had told him, filling his head with images of Beat poet- and musician-filled Greyhounds heading across America and Magic Buses leaving Amsterdam for Greece in a cloud of hashish smoke. The list of small-town destinations above the departure bays conjured up nothing but more of the Gombeen shite Johnner said they had to get away from. Yet all around him European and American accents were lovingly mangling the names of those same Irish towns.

He put his coffee on the floor between his hand-me-down Portwests and took his journal from his backpack to record his thoughts on the fifties décor, the country people up to the big city for shopping, the young foreigners looking for the authentic Irish experience. But his own situation came first: '*Living the spontaneous life can be hard when your best friend takes all your money,*' he wrote, pleased with himself for the compactness of the sentence. Although the *can be* was weak. It had to be more direct. '*Money–stealing friends stifle the spontaneous life,*' was better, except he wanted the sentence to start with *living*, not *money*. Johnner was over. Julian had to embrace the triumph of life, not the power of betrayal.

'You don't mind if I move your haversack, do ya?' The north of Ireland accent came from beyond his backpack, which was moved to the floor and its place on the chair taken by a bigger, fuller bag. 'I need to check the address I'm going to.'

The boy was maybe a year older than Julian, his dark suit a match for the suits Julian saw outside the funeral home on the Old Cabra Road. Except this boy's tie was school-striped, not black. He sat down on the next chair along, his bag now between them, and took a newspaper and a street map from the bag, talking as he went. 'See me, I'm going for a job,' he said, 'at Miss Dolly Considine's, the well-known hotelier.' His hair was longer than Johnner's. Julian would want it cut.

'I was told to be there at eleven,' the boy said, stretching his legs out in front of him, and moving his finger along the lines of paper streets, twisting and turning his ankles as if he were following the traced-out route. He had small, even dainty feet, and Julian could see him dancing, or ducking and weaving around a football field leaving bigger men behind frustrated. 'I was up at four and my mammy was up before that, if she slept at all. She admitted to half past three when I came down and found her making sandwiches and fretting about me missing the bus. My older brother didn't even get out of bed to say goodbye. What sort of leave-taking was that?'

Julian picked up his coffee and looked back at the sentence in his journal. His own mother would be outside the GPO all day, encouraging people to sign a petition in support of a woman's right to terminate her unwanted pregnancy, and his own brother, now over the Irish Sea, expecting a midday meal on the table and a younger brother who respected his collection of precious jazz records.

'I suppose you've just arrived in Ireland,' the boy said, his finger pressed to the map but his eyes looking at Julian, 'so no point in asking you for directions. Let me guess. You're blond, like a German. Or Swedish? Do you even understand what I'm saying?'

Julian shook his head, then nodded, excited that his hair made him look foreign. But if he spoke, he'd be a Dubliner again, so he smiled and widened his eyes. The boy wanted him to be exotic.

'I see you have the notebook to record your experiences. My mammy is very fond of a notebook. Very fond.'

A bus station attendant began herding people towards the shuttle bus. He should find out the times for the later ferries, but the boy's soothing one-sided chatter was relaxing the hard plastic seat into a deep body-hugging beanbag. It had been listening to Johnner that had got him into his present trouble; he was not going to be distracted by this boy's seductive lilt.

Miss Dolly Considine. He would write it down before he

forgot. He would focus on her, record her name, imagine her frustrated spinsterhood, her excitement at the forthcoming interview with the young man.

'My mammy refers to her notebook as her *Cuntas an Lae*. It's Irish,' the boy said. 'I suppose you wouldn't be able to pronounce it; it'd be foreign in your mouth.'

Julian knew the Irish for diary well enough from school, and was leaning the coffee towards the floor when two black shoes intruded. Monstrous compared to the dancer's. Brown corduroy thighs almost touching Julian's stooping head, jolting him upright, the coffee still clutched. A man of his mother's age, his knees bent, shirt button undone at the navel, two fists clenched, and puffing.

'Right Malone,' corduroy man said, leaning down, spitting into Julian's face, 'we want a word with you.'

'No, not the blond bombshell,' a voice behind Julian said, and corduroy man stepped sideways, kicking Julian's backpack as he did so. He reached one hand for the shoulder of the north of Ireland boy who started to rise from his seat. The owner of the second voice also offered restraining hands. Big men, not to be messed with, respectable enough to be plain-clothes detectives.

'This beautiful specimen is the Malone we want,' the second man said, and he leaned over the north of Ireland boy's shoulder to grin at him, and passed a pair of handcuffs to corduroy man, whose spit was tickling Julian's face.

Julian didn't trust his fingers to let him sip his coffee, or his legs to get him away. Besides, his backpack had ended up between corduroy man and the north of Ireland boy's chair; it was surrounded, and retrieving it would mean pushing between the policemen and their prisoner, his actions taken as an attempt to facilitate escape. Best to look disinterested.

To treat it like a private matter between Malone and Dublin's friendly coppers.

He swept his eyes upwards to the destinations board, checking on the way to see if anyone else saw what was happening, and then downwards to a crowd of people responding to the announcement about their bus's departure bay. He hoped that the coffee-clutching hand on his knee, and his left elbow resting on the boy's bag, would make him appear absorbed in his own business. He couldn't resist straining his eyes sideways when the man behind him forced the boy's arms into his sight-line, the open handcuffs hovering over the exposed wrists, or surrendering fully when the boy levered his whole body towards corduroy man, and tried to dance his way under the reaching hands. The man pitched forward to stop him, kneeling on Julian's backpack, the crunch of his brother's prized 78s felt more than heard as the man's forehead connected with the boy's nose and bounced him back into the seat. Unable to look away when the cuffs snapped on Malone's slender wrists and he was dragged to his feet.

'Is this all you have?' the man who'd so newly scuppered Julian's final chance of getting the ferry fare sneered as he picked up Julian's backpack and pushed it into Malone's crotch.

'My mammy packed it herself,' the boy said, his nose bleeding and tears streaming down his face. He half-turned as if he was going to look at Julian but stopped.

'Please take very good care of it,' he said into the face of the policeman, 'or my mammy will be very cross with you.'

Julian pressed his elbow down on the bag beside him and hoped it was a fair swap. His journal was on his lap and he was wearing the best of what he owned. His brother's broken records were worthless. He watched the men walk the boy towards the exit, a blue light flashing through the glass doors, until the coffee dripping onto his leg made him notice the paper cup squeezed out of shape.

He reached for the boy's newspaper and tore off a page to mop up the spilt coffee. A red inked circle around an ad in the vacancies offered section and a handwritten address in capital letters all down one margin demanded attention.

Trainee hotel barman wanted. Live-in, it read.

He dropped the rest of the paper on the coffee puddle, folded the torn page inside his journal and took his new bag to the gents to check for another pair of trousers.

You stood by and let that boy be lifted, his mother's voice, half a mile away at her GPO stall shouted as he passed the urinals and the men staring sideways at each other's dicks in the piss- and bleach-smelly gents. Her words vying with the water gushing out of cisterns or into sinks. Going on about them coming for the communists and the Jews and there being no one left when it was her turn, hysterical with her favourite poem. *You should have shouted and caused a scene. A boy was lifted in a busy bus station and no one noticed.*

But he didn't care what she thought. He had his own feelings. The boy's name was Malone. Malone. He rolled it around his chattering teeth and wrote it on a clean page, and then put '*Cuntas an Lae*' above.

Malone. It felt good. Malone. It fitted into a gap somewhere like an important jigsaw piece. Malone. The coppers dragging him to his feet, lifting him by the cuffs raised above his head, a modern-day Sebastian, in a bus station, taken to be stripped and dealt with out of public sight.

The toilet cubicle was too cramped to search the bag properly, but just inside the zip was a copy of a republican newspaper and beneath that a pair of trousers he could change into. In a side pocket he found a P45 from a previous employer.

He couldn't read the handwritten name, but it didn't look anything like Malone. Anyway, he was not changing his name again. Julian Ryder suited the person he would become; he did not need an identity already occupied by someone associated with whatever awful things were suggested by the attendance of the plain-clothes squad.

He stood back from the washbasin mirror to see how he looked. Malone's trousers were looser than he was used to, but the legs were about right, and the belt he'd found would hold them up. He rinsed the last of the coffee from his hands and shook them before looking around for a drier.

'Are you coming or going?' a man said, pretending to wash his own hands at the next basin.

'Going,' he said, smiling. 'Going for now, but I might be back.' He would find Miss Considine's hotel and try for the job. He'd wear the clothes with the respect he expected Malone to show to his. And when he turned up in a few days with bruises and broken ribs from his holiday with the heavy gang, Malone could have his job, and Julian would begin his adventure in earnest. He swung the bag onto his shoulder, smiled at the man still pretending to dry his already dry hands, and left the fluorescent glare of the basement toilet.

A place of refuge, safe from his brother, and maybe a job, at least for a few days. He stopped at the bus station doors and touched the side pocket snuggling his journal to make it a promise: 'I swear that whatever happens, you will be the first to know.'

Dolly Considine's Hotel

DOLLY HAS AN UNEXPECTED ENCOUNTER WITH HER PAST

November 1956

Even before Dolly had entered secondary school, her father began dressing her up and taking her to the annual Fianna Fáil conference, the Ard Fheis. But in 1952, with the scandal that closed his sister-in-law's hotel still making headlines, he'd stayed away, and when he heard rumours of enemies in the party conspiring against him, he'd made her swear never to attend another 'bloody witch-hunting Ard Fheis'. But in November 1956 Dolly braved her fear of being recognised, keeping on the frumpy hat and coat abandoned by a guest who'd come to Dublin to shop for her going away outfit, and spent the day near the edges of the crowds milling in and out of the Round Room in the Mansion House. It wasn't until late afternoon, as she was just about to leave, that her arm was grabbed by a regular guest from the hotel.

'It's Dolly Considine! Is your daddy here?'

And who should overhear this question being asked but Cathal McClean, his younger brother Giolla-Íosa standing back. Cathal then shook her hand and asked after Dolly's father, although their mother would surely provide the brothers with regular updates on all the neighbours whether they wanted them or not.

'He gets very agitated at conference time,' Dolly said. 'Last year he set the kitchen on fire. My mother won't be able to leave him alone in the house until he settles down again.' She was surprised to hear herself slipping back into the Offaly accent. At least she hadn't said *my mudder*.

It was Giolla-Íosa who nodded then, but neither of the brothers commented.

Outside on Dawson Street it was raining, and Cathal insisted on holding her umbrella over her while she waited for her bus. Giolla-Íosa was formal, and polite, and allowed Cathal to stand closer to her, Dolly's poor father's 'unfortunate error of judgement' ensuring that he was not seen to engage more than was necessary in public. But she was exhausted from the conference, the smoke, the noise, the sight of the either careful or exuberant glad-handing, and the fiery intensity of the older men sporting War of Independence medals on their jackets, as if it was a Wolfe Tone commemoration in Bodenstown cemetery they were attending rather than a meeting of constitutional democrats. These old men frightened her with their bitterness at the compromises imposed by politics, although the same men were generally pliable and well-behaved when they turned up at the hotel looking for a late drink.

'Did you hear GI's speech?' Cathal asked. 'I think it was well received. De Valera himself looked impressed.'

'Should I expect a credit for some of the ideas?' The debates of their shared youth in Birr were being turned into party policy.

She felt left behind. 'I hear the dance tax is to be abolished,' she said. But neither of them appeared to know about that.

'If you've got a notion, GI's got an election.' Cathal looked proud and slapped his brother's shoulder.

'My mother says you're very much at home in Cork,' Dolly said, looking at Giolla-Íosa. 'No time at all now and you'll have a nomination and a seat in the Dáil.'

'There'll be nothing from that quarter,' Cathal said. 'Too many buckos standing in line looking for old debts to be paid off. No, this boyo is for Dublin. More suited to Dublin politics, aren't you, GI?'

Giolla-Íosa smiled and shrugged as if election campaigns were all a mystery to him. 'Whatever my agent says. I'm just the eejit who does what he's told.'

No idiot, Dolly thought, but said, 'You'll be on a late train back tonight then?'

'Ah, sure he'll never have Dublin support if his face isn't seen by the right people. Sean Lemass is expected at a fringe meeting this evening and we'll go along to that.' Cathal closed, shook out and handed her the umbrella as she boarded the bus. 'You'll have lunch with us tomorrow,' he said, 'before Giolla-Íosa goes for his train?' His cheeks were quite flushed as he waited for the nod, which she gave him from the platform of the bus, after a suitable pause.

In her anxiety to get away from the McClean brothers and their excitement about fringe meetings, she'd taken the first bus that came along. She would almost have been better to walk all the way. But this one took her past the Swiss Chalet which was displaying a poster for Humphrey Murphy and his Band. She wanted to go dancing. Her mother's voice reminded her of the Fianna Fáil delegates staying in the hotel, but she didn't care; they would still be drinking when she got back. Maureen in the Russell Hotel, her friend, and reputedly out dancing three nights a week, would know the liveliest venue for a Wednesday outing. She tapped her feet on the floor of the bus and got a look from the woman beside her.

Dolly Considine's Hotel

EVERY OPPORTUNITY, A WELCOME OPPORTUNITY

18th June 1983

'Who are you? You're not from, from—'

'Derry... I'm here for my interview,' Julian said. 'For the job.' But his attempt at Malone's northern accent was not convincing the young woman who'd found him standing in the middle of the hotel's front lounge when she pushed in the door with her back to avoid dropping the two large loaves of bread and the stack of plastic containers occupying her hands. Her hair was the same colour as his own, but she was taller in her heels, and several years older. He smiled up at her.

'You? No way. We have no vacancies.' Her lips were pressed into a thin challenge. The green of the carpet and the fussy hunting pictures on the wall gave her face a big-house skivvy look.

'Yes you do. It's in the paper.' He held the page towards her. 'See for yourself.'

She turned away to put the containers on the bar counter and then turned back to shoo him out into the hall.

'I was told be here at eleven,' he said. 'And I'm early. I wrote down the time and the address. This is the Curragh House Hotel?' He looked about the room for confirmation. The four round tables and assorted stools ignored him. The backwards letters of 'Porchester Lounge' etched diagonally into the reeded glass door quivered slightly in the breeze but remained silent. He couldn't claim to be Malone, but he could legitimately claim to be his representative, at least for as long as Malone was detained elsewhere.

'We don't have a vacancy. And if we did, it is now filled.' She was no Dubliner, neither northsider nor southsider.

'This is a quite a small lounge,' he said, changing his approach. 'I'm used to working in bigger places.' The tiny bar counter was almost invisible under the containers and the sliced bread. There were corporation houses in Cabra with bigger bars in their poky front rooms. 'It looks to me that you need a sandwich maker. Someone to turn those basic ingredients into a taste sensation.'

'I'd like you to leave, now,' she said, on the move again, 'or I will call the Gardaí.' Her hand reached towards his chest and she began to push Julian backwards towards the door. 'Try Manpower on D'Olier Street,' she said, sounding like a culchie fresh up from the bog. 'Manpower always has a list of vacancies.' She sneered as she pushed.

His step backwards tripped him over Malone's bag the way boys were propelled by bullies over their crouching friends in his old schoolyard, his hands meeting sticky carpet instead of the gritty concrete of those days.

'Malone won't be coming…' He might have said more, but the closeness of her skinny legs and the taut edge of her skirt's hem, which looked ready to be hoisted up to allow a sharp kick to be delivered, stilled his words for a second. Then he said, 'He told me to work his shifts for a few days, keep the job open for him, then he'll be here.' How would Malone know where to find his bag if Julian didn't wait until he got away from the special branch?

'You two, in behind the bar. Now.' A small wiry guy wearing a green balaclava pushed over two tables as he sidled towards the window, where he and his knife were silhouetted against the light. He was dressed in jeans and ex-army boots, and a jacket that was darker, more ill-fitting, and bore more campaign badges than Julian's. His thin face-covering moved like a glove puppet when he spoke. He arced the knife back and forth between Julian, still winded and helpless on the floor, and the woman who was standing rigidly, her fists twitching by her sides as if they wanted to seize the knife, say thank you to the silly creature, and put his weapon in a place of safety.

'The bar is closed,' she said.

'In behind the counter. Now.' He used the knife to point, and then kicked the bag between Julian's spread legs to encourage him upwards. 'Move.' He almost offered his other hand but reached to roll one of the fallen-over tables instead.

'The bar is closed,' she said again. 'I can't get in without keys.'

'Well, climb over the counter, darling.' He transferred the knife to his left hand and circled Julian to get closer to her. He pushed her towards the bar, the knife extended back towards Julian.

'I'm not climbing in this,' she said, shaking her head while staring at him, sweeping her hands downwards over her tight skirt.

'Well, shrimp here can,' he hissed, and he kicked a stool to show he meant business. 'Now. Chop chop.'

'She's the boss,' Julian said. He'd seen knives when gangs came waging war around the playground in Ventry Park. Cornered twice when his curiosity made him dally. Steak knives nicked from Peg's Kitchen in the shopping centre. *Are you from Carnlough? Are ya? Answer me.* The agitated hysteria making it difficult to predict when the slash would come. Only clothes, both times – his lower arm, and across his chest. The chest tear in particular adding history to his army jacket.

He was bouncing from side to side like a boxer. Julian might have to defend himself if he lunged, but otherwise it was better to let him stay in charge.

'Is it money you want?' Julian said.

'Just get in there now.'

'What are you waiting for?' the woman asked. 'It's not my place. See if I care.' Her lips pressing together as if she'd tasted something sour.

Julian moved the stack of food containers to the nearest table, and climbed over. The inside was more generous than it looked from the drinkers' side, and continued on into an adjoining room, twice as big really. Malone would be at home here, in a white shirt and pink dicky bow, prowling between the two halves of the bar, keeping everyone happy. It would be easy to escape through the other lounge, let the glove puppet and pursed lips fight it out. But he had to have a bag to swap with Malone, and more importantly he was not abandoning his journal with its account of his morning so far.

Malone's hands would instinctively reach for the shaker and the ice to offer glove puppet a cocktail. He'd be surveying the bottles for likely candidates, his upper arms already taking up the rhythm needed for the shaking.

'Where's the cash register?' Julian asked the woman.

'It's a drawer,' she answered.

He found the brass finger-pull and gripped it. A note inside: '*Sylvia, come and see me. I have a bag of change for the float. DMcC.*' A red panic alarm button invited him to press. More importantly, an inviting pint glass half full of coins, tips maybe, seemed to be compensation for his trouble.

'In a minute.' He winked at the silver coins.

He tilted the drawer up so it could be seen over the counter.

'There you go. Just some cash bags and a French franc. How about a drink?'

'Are you making a laugh of me?'

Julian shook his head. 'I'd be rightly pissed off if I was in your shoes.'

'Don't fuck with the 'RA, mate. Turn out your pockets.'

'You're not IRA,' said the woman, Julian supposed she was the Sylvia of the note. 'The state of you.'

'Have a bottle of brandy. Go on. Any bottle you like.'

'You'll give him nothing. If you were a man at all you'd have run him out onto the street by now.'

He probably didn't mean to cut her, but she waved her right arm very close to his covered face as he advanced, and the knife sliced through her cardigan.

'Now look what you've made me do.'

They all waited for blood, but she gripped the gash tightly with her left hand and stepped back behind a table.

'You're scum,' she said. 'Nothing but scum.'

Julian put a three-quarters-full bottle of whiskey on the counter and placed his finger on the red button. He delayed pressing until the glove puppet's hand was wrapped around the bottle's neck as if it was his very touch that set off the alarm. Then he reached behind for another bottle, the lime cordial draining into his sleeve as he lifted it into clubbing position.

'I'll get yous for this. The 'RA has a long—'

The wail of the alarm from the hall drowned out his fleeing screech.

Julian looked to the silver in the tips glass to tell him if there was enough for his fare to London, and more importantly how he could get out without pursed lips noticing the sagging bulges in his jacket pockets. If there was no job then the original plan was back on. He would write to the hotel from London, explain about Malone and the mix-up with the bag. Let them sort it out.

He licked his sticky hand and the sharp lime taste demanded a war cry.

'Fuck the begrudgers.'

Dolly Considine's Hotel

November 1956

Inviting Dolly to the Civil Service Club instead of the Dáil restaurant allowed Cathal to treat her to the dish of the day, safe from party hacks or elected members who might have recognised her, and caused Giolla-Íosa to be taken aside by a friendly party elder before he left the building. 'It's not just her father's error of judgement, but his flirtation with Fine Gael, and before that the fascist Blueshirts. This would not be a good alliance for a young politician on the way up. Charity is well and good, but...', the pause inserted to enable the subject to be changed to the state of the train the young hopeful would endure back to Cork, but returned to if Giolla-Íosa showed anything less than wholehearted contrition.

'Remember the fucker didn't even have the decency to die in office. Sympathy alone would have brought the vote out for us, but he stayed in bed and let Fine Gael take the seat as if they'd had it for a hundred years.' The man's face changing suddenly: 'He's not gone and snuffed it? Is that why you're being friendly with the daughter?' Waiting for a shake or a nod from Giolla-Íosa. 'Ah, that'll be a great funeral. You wouldn't want to miss that. Might even be fisticuffs. But promise me you'll be putting distance between yourself and the Considines.'

Except that when Cathal returned to his desk, Giolla-Íosa escorted Dolly and her bicycle through St Stephen's Green and back to the hotel. All the while letting her know, through his enquiries after her mother, his description of Cork women as 'such boring dressers', and the smile she recognised, exactly what he was expecting of her. And she drank in the trees and the ducks squabbling over the bread thrown for them all the more, because she knew she would capitulate, and enjoy herself.

Dolly was not a virgin. But the confident way Giolla-Íosa transported her through his various steps towards getting her into bed made her realise someone had worked on his technique since their walks together by the river after Sunday Mass when she was still in secondary school, he clean in his white shirt and tie, and she in one of the outfits her mother felt obliged to kit her out in from the local shop in Birr. Sitting on the bench, her hair down around her shoulders and the hat she'd worn to Mass on the seat beside her, the pair of them taking turns to read headlines from her *Sunday Independent* and his *Sunday Press*, listening to the running water in any silences, until she put an end to his waiting. The newspapers raised and her hand withdrawn if anyone came past, but generally it was quiet until the late Mass was over. He kept his eyes closed and moved his hands as if miming his thoughts for the swans looking up from the water, the *Sunday Press* rustling as his fingers traced over the contours of his fantasy woman. Dolly did what was expected, fascinated that it could mean so much.

Now here in the hotel, still hyper with excitement the day after his speech at the Ard Fheis, the seven years had not slowed his hands. They had become more purposeful in their determination to hold onto her. She admired his pragmatism; today in the bed where he hadn't needed her condom, and yesterday in the Mansion House, flushed at the podium, his gaze sweeping over the entire audience, gesturing, smiling, grimacing; every inch the go-ahead young accountant and soon to be elected TD, but sounding like a clergyman with his talk about never forgetting the old people's contribution to the foundation of the state. His whole body seeming to express passion, but when his hair fell forward onto his face, he was careful not to get Brylcreem on the fingers that nudged it back. They had to be kept clean in case he got to shake De Valera's hand as he returned to his seat among the delegates from the Cork cumann. He was the Cork cumann's boy and they cheered for him, although they hesitated about whether to stand up or not until Dev himself looked away from his notes and nodded in apparent approval.

Summer of Unrequited Love

JULIAN IMAGINES MALONE'S MISS CONSIDINE EXPECTING A DERRY BOY, BUT GETTING A DUBLINER

Jun '83

On another changeover morning she might have been amused by Sylvia's irritation at having to clean William's bedroom. But today, the noisy re-stacking of Dolly's son's books and the returning of shoes and clothes to the squeaky wardrobe next door was disturbing her attempt at an after-breakfast nap on the living room couch. It was a full twenty minutes before the merciful slam of the bedroom door signalled the end of her ordeal for another week.

'Sylvia, can you come in?'

'Yes, missus.'

'I'm expecting a new boy shortly.' Dolly spoke from her reclining position. 'From Derry.' She brushed away the creamy fringes of the Foxford rug itching her face but did not open her eyes.

'That's not much notice,' Sylvia said. 'I have twenty-four

crates of porter due, and Brendan has to be watched or there'll be breakages.'

'Thank you, Sylvia. Please see to it that the boy is settled in. I want no confusion.'

'Mrs McClean, I'm entitled to reasonable notice when arrangements—'

'Yes, yes, yes. Sometimes we just have to muck in.' She pulled the rug back up to her face to dismiss the girl.

'I run the two bars single-handed and manage Brendan.'

She gave the girl the satisfaction of opening her eyes and elbowed herself half-up. 'If it's your notice you're looking for...' Then waved her away with her whole arm.

'I've got a new waif for you,' Giolla-Íosa had said when he phoned just after breakfast, and she still in her nightdress. He made it sound like he was doing her a favour.

'Oh Giolla-Íosa. Does it have to be today?' He never asked whether having a psychotic lunatic in her hotel for six months would interfere with her life.

'This is not a conversation for the phone,' he said. 'I'll see you this evening.'

The call ended before she could remind him she'd been putting up with his waifs for ten years. But the thought of another arrogant, belligerent face lurking on the stairs or cluttering up the kitchen sapped the energy out of her.

'Oh Dolly, Dolly, Dolly, listen to yourself,' GI would have laughed had he kept talking. 'In fifteen minutes, you'll be drinking coffee and pleasuring yourself at the boy's nervous speculation as to what you know and don't know about him.'

One of William's abandoned textbooks dug into her side as she lay back. She tried to wriggle herself comfortable. But the picture of the boy as he stepped down from the coach watching out for signs that he might have been betrayed and trying to turn the pinched faces in the bus station into welcoming providers of refuge made further rest impossible. She rose and kicked out at the couch. If she didn't want another boy, Giolla-Íosa should just accept it. Talk about her pleasuring herself was just unpleasant.

The sideboard mirror reminded her that attendance to her grey roots was overdue. She ran her fingers over her skirt to ensure her stretch on the couch had not creased it. Was she looking a bit shabby, or was it the anticipation of having to see their tic-ridden suspicious faces watching her as she moved through her own home that was wearing her down? Much easier to send money to a republican defence fund than have to deal with their pent-up furies distracting her from her business, especially now, with the economy slipping into collapse.

'You're like a mother to them,' GI had patronised after the last one. Not easy to be maternal when she knew the sort of things they'd done or were planning.

'Half the bloody youth of the country unemployed and you take on the shiftiest little weasels you can find,' her husband Cathal always said, thinking she'd advertised for a trainee and selected from a dozen applicants.

'And whose fault is it that the country is in its present state?'

'My brother Giolla-Íosa is the politician.'

But it's you who manages his thinking and doings, she might have said, and Cathal would have responded with: And who puts the thoughts into my head? Shifting it all back on her. Neither of the McClean brothers had much time for her views since she'd married into the family, but, if Dolly were given charge of the world, it would soon be a very different place. Her foot was reaching for the first step down the stairs when a sliver of bacon stuck between two back teeth since breakfast made her aware of how uneasy she was. No doubt her tongue had been trying to dislodge it since Giolla-Íosa's call. The boy would notice her irritable lips, and think he was the cause. The defiance clear on his face as he calculated whether she'd already betrayed him to the Gardaí.

Someone shouting downstairs, a Dubliner, the words indistinct with the nasal slurring that, with them, passes for speaking. Such an unpleasant accent, she said to the pinkie nail failing to dislodge the bacon. It would be Brendan having trouble with the deliverymen. They went on about breakages as if it was their money. Sylvia needed to sort it out.

But then the panic alarm in the bar began to hurt her ears.

'Built for comfort more than speed,' Dolly's father had often said, but she managed two steps at a time, her head bent to watch her low navy-blue heels engaging the stair carpet securely.

'Brendan,' she shouted towards the basement stairs. 'Brendan,' her hand on the Porchester Lounge door handle before she realised he would not hear her over the piercing bell. He'd better be on his way.

Sylvia was in the middle of the room clutching her arm, blood dripping onto the carpet. A cur of a youth behind the bar, smiling like he deserved a reward for his work. The brat gone wild already and not yet welcomed into his place of refuge. Well, it had to happen some time. And maybe it was better on the first day before he got settled. That's it. He's finished. And no more of them. GI would have to find another safe house.

'Get out,' she shouted. 'Get out now,' her raised voice hurting her throat in its attempt to outdo the alarm. And then Brendan almost knocked her over as he launched himself at the counter. Not the most athletic of men, it took him a second run to clamber over it, but he did take the ruffian down and they both disappeared from view. Which mobilised Sylvia to lean over the bar and fiddle with the alarm, the sudden silence as shocking as the noise.

'Sylvia,' Dolly said, 'you're bleeding,' and gave her a bar towel to wipe up. 'A curse on you,' she shouted as she leaned over the counter. 'A curse on all men who attack defenceless women.' And she spat to seal her words, and with Brendan covering almost everything except the urchin's face she was unsure where the spittle landed. But then his left hand appeared and reached up and swept fingerfuls of mixer bottles against hard surfaces, smashing glass and splattering the pair of them with thick juice and splinters.

'Sit on him Brendan. Sit on him until I—' She wanted to say, until I call the Guards. But she couldn't do that.

'Never ring me,' GI always said, 'no matter what happens. The phones are all tapped.'

But she had to do something. One of his boys had gone wild. And poor Sylvia. Except Sylvia was lifting the counter flap to join Brendan inside the bar. Panic rising, that Sylvia and Brendan were planning revenge. Dolly's hand going to her mouth when it should have stayed away to allow her words to be heard loud and clear: 'No Sylvia, no. Just throw him out on the street. No violence,' a jumbled mutter which she might afterwards have to claim had been a direct order to her staff. It wasn't the courts she was frightened of. It would be the other crowd; this ruffian was one of their own, and they'd be immune to a self-defence plea. The very least she could expect would be her hotel burnt out, and it might not stop there.

But Sylvia said, 'Let him up, Brendan.'

And Dolly nodded. 'That's right, Brendan. Into the understairs cupboard with him till the Guards come. Hurry now.' Not that she would call the Guards, or either of the McClean brothers. It was all too complicated. Let Sylvia deal with it, was what she wanted to say. But it was her hotel, and they expected her to take charge. She spat into his face when he

52

was dragged out from behind the bar and repeated her earlier curse. That took the smile off his face.

'Lock the little runt up, Brendan, and stand over him while I see to Sylvia's injuries.'

Dolly Considine's Hotel

ARRANGEMENTS WILL HAVE TO BE MADE

November 1956

On the morning after Giolla-Íosa's half-hour with Dolly Considine in room eleven, Paddy the Porter, retired for years but still allowed to live-in and help out, put the breakfast tray on the table outside room twelve and shuffled down to the Kickham Room. A red-faced farmer from Mayo had asked for a second helping of porridge and Dolly was spooning it from the pot into his dish when Paddy said, 'There's no answer from Miss Guilfoyle in room twelve.'

He'd shaken the sleeve of the bright kimono she'd taken to wearing while serving breakfast when he should have said excuse me, madam. Dolly's mother would tick him off in front of the guests.

'I expect Miss Guilfoyle has forgotten to put in her hearing aid,' Dolly said, although she wondered if Paddy's own ears were good enough to hear if Miss Guilfoyle had shouted at him to go away.

An hour earlier when her mother rang, she could still feel

Giolla-Íosa's weight pressing down on her, feel his breath on her face and smell his slightly sour underarms. The news that her father would never work again was hardly a surprise, but she hadn't expected to hear that the bank would no longer accept his acting as her guarantor. A little drama with Miss Guilfoyle would be a welcome distraction. She passed the porridge pot to Paddy, who put it on the table beside the Mayo farmer.

'She's dead, you know,' Paddy said, as he followed her up the stairs. 'As sure as eggs is eggs, she's dead.' And Dolly knew he was blessing himself as he spoke, but she didn't turn around to check. A dead woman in the hotel would be a drama; Miss Guilfoyle was old, but she was too irritating to die without a fuss.

Paddy hung back, but Dolly marched into the room and straight over to the bed where the woman was obviously sleeping, her hand outside the covers, as if ready to wake up. And yet she was dead, curled up like a wizened baby. The long-suffering sister of one of Ireland's heroes of 1916 had passed away quietly in room twelve.

There were people who'd say it was God's punishment for what she'd allowed Giolla-Íosa to do in the room next door, perhaps while the woman lay dying. Let them, she said as she went down to reception to report the death. Miss Guilfoyle had used her brother's reputation to avoid paying for her room or food for years, so maybe God was rewarding Dolly, but no one would suggest that. She tried not to dwell on whether Giolla-Íosa's grunts might have played a part.

Paddy the Porter paced the reception area while she waited for the operator to answer. He confirmed the news to each passing guest or member of staff. 'Arrangements will have to be made,' he said, looking at Dolly in some sort of judgement, as if 'arrangements' were not already under way. Then he began to light a fire in the Kickham Room, when it was never lit until the evening.

'Death might be inconvenient,' he said when he came back to share the news with the postman putting the mail on the reception counter. The envelopes invited Dolly to flick through them in the hope of finding further distraction amongst the usual bills.

'We have a dead woman in room twelve,' she told the operator. 'Should I have the Guards or the ambulance?'

The note from Cathal McClean was a surprise. '*It was so nice to be able to take you to lunch on Thursday,*' it began, before going on to apologise if Giolla-Íosa appeared standoffish. '*He has a lot on his mind,*' the letter went on, before closing and signing off with '*Your friend Cathal.*' She crumpled the paper into a ball, and, when her call was finished, went to lean over Paddy stoking the fire and dropped it onto the flames.

Two days later every surface in the Kickham Room was covered with sympathy cards and Mass cards. But at least the flowers were out of sight in room twelve, waiting on Miss Guilfoyle's nephews to organise themselves over from England for the funeral. 'Curragh House was her home,' the younger nephew told Dolly on the phone. He had wanted his aunt to lie in state for three days in the Kickham Room, with hotel staff in sombre uniforms, a book of condolence and members of the Cumann na mBan and the Old IRA keeping watch in hourly shifts. But thankfully the Gardaí had insisted on a post-mortem, which meant the remains would stay at the morgue until the day of the funeral. 'You should be honoured,' the nephew said, 'to have a role in my aunt's obsequies.' Dolly picked up the statement setting out his aunt's overdue payments. Only her mother taking the receiver stopped her demanding immediate settlement in full.

'Of course we're honoured,' Mrs Considine said. 'And we look forward to meeting you, even if the circumstances are unfortunate for you and for the Irish nation.' She put the receiver back and looked at the statement before she spoke. 'Now young lady, it's time you grew up. Your father and I have stood by you these past three years while you've wasted money on high fashion and displayed scant aptitude for running a successful hotel; and all the while your father has gone without the full-time care he needs. And now we hear that you've begun… entertaining.'

Dolly lowered her eyes to think of an answer. Her mother's head cocked as if listening for the sounds of her wild behaviour reverberating down from the bedroom.

'The insurance company next door needs to expand and has made a generous offer for the building housing the guest bedrooms, and will even permit the theatre to remain as tenants,' her mother said. 'That will allow you to keep the two bars, the staff and private accommodation and live comfortably until you find a husband. The alternative is that you come home and share the burden of looking after your sick and ageing father in his final years.'

Summer of Unrequited Love

JULIAN CONTINUES HIS JOURNAL ACCOUNT OF
MISS DOLLY MANAGING THE SITUATION

Jun '83

Dolly occasionally leaned on the counter in the Kickham Room to talk to visitors both seated and standing, but today she squeezed into one of the bucket chairs to hear Sylvia explain why her arm was bleeding and what she had to say about the intruder that Brendan had dragged out from behind the bar.

'Fetch some water for us both,' she said to Sylvia, hoping it might help her barmaid to stop shaking.

'I'm here about the job,' the boy interrupted, and Dolly held her hand up to stop him speaking. Brendan, bless him, kept the ruffian's arm pinned behind his back, ready to break it at her signal. But this was not a boy from Derry or Belfast looking for a safe house for a few months. And why would Giolla-Íosa send her a lowlife Dubliner? The shard of bacon still between her teeth encouraged her to suck at it while she tried to make sense of what was going on.

'Who sent you?' she asked. If he was the real thing, he'd have a cover story; if he wasn't, she'd run him out.

'I spoke to a woman on the phone,' he said, waving a bit of newspaper. 'She gave me the address. That's why you have to interview me. It's the law.'

Such an ugly accent. She could not bear to have it barking all day long. Giolla-Íosa, Giolla-Íosa, take him away.

'I don't need the likes of you to teach me the law, thank you,' she said. Why was he calling it a job? Giolla-Íosa had reassured her that the ad was only placed in the paper to let her refer to it if the Gardaí ever questioned her. None of the others ever called it a job. They were under orders to keep a low profile. Was he expecting to be paid? Wasn't it enough that she'd be feeding him for six months?

'And when I get here, I'm held at knifepoint by the IRA, beaten up by… by a… a… a…' He tried to turn his head to look at Brendan as if that would help him with a description, but a twist of his arm stopped that. 'Look at my clothes, torn, and covered in…' He picked a shard of glass from his jacket with his free hand. His trousers were ill fitting, borrowed-looking, the kind of thing issued to released prisoners. Maybe that was it. She looked to his knuckles and neck for signs of prison tattoos.

'Sylvia,' Dolly said.

Her barmaid had pulled up her cardigan sleeve and was dabbing at her cut with antiseptic and cotton wool.

'Sylvia.' She spoke louder. Was Sylvia in shock or feigning concentration to avoid answering? Had she and the ruffian concocted the story about the man holding them both at knifepoint? After all, why had Dolly herself not seen the scum running away when the alarm went off? She'd been on her way downstairs, with a clear view of the door.

'Sylvia!'

'Yes, Mrs McClean?'

'Was there someone else? Did he say he was IRA?'

'Yes. But he wasn't. Much too stupid. Anyone could have taken him. A junkie more like. Looking for fix money.'

'Junkies don't wear balaclavas,' the ruffian said.

He'd have learnt all about junkies and lowlife when he was in prison.

'I wouldn't have given him anything, but Mr Generous here... What is your name?' Sylvia didn't seem to like him. Or was this a part of their strategy?

'Julian.'

'Julian? Julian?' Brendan looked to Dolly as if the name alone was reason enough to break his arm.

This could not be one of Giolla-Íosa's refugees. More likely he'd heard about the hotel from inmates in whatever institution he'd been released from. She had to get him off the premises.

'Now Julian, I understand how you feel.' She reached for the armrests to lift herself out of the chair. 'A bit of a wasted journey. Unfortunately, we have no job, but thank you for helping Sylvia, and goodbye.'

'What about my shirt? I need a wash. Look at me.'

'There's a public toilet up on the canal bridge, and another in St Stephen's Green. But this is a private hotel, and it's closed.' She waved at Brendan to take him away.

'What about the police? My statement?'

'We'll sort all that out. No need for you to bother your head.'

'A robbery has been committed here,' he said. 'I was held at knifepoint and threatened. I witnessed a woman being stabbed. This is a matter for the Guards. I have an interview at another hotel –' and he wrenched his arm free from Brendan's grip and pushed up his sticky sleeve although he was not wearing a watch – 'at one. Just enough time to get my recollections down on paper.'

If he's just been released from prison, he'd hardly want to

speak to the Gardaí. But then neither would any of the boys who'd ever taken shelter in her hotel.

'Which is the nearest Garda station? I've seen Earlsfort Terrace Station on Garda patrol. And what about a launderette? I can't turn up at my next interview like this. I'll need thirty pounds for a new interview shirt and for laundry costs.'

This she understood. An offer to buy him off. A straightforward trade. But not the Gardaí. She took her glass from her little table and sipped water while she considered.

'Brendan, take the young man downstairs to the kitchen and make him a cup of tea while he cleans up. Hurry up now.' She waved her empty hand, and handed her glass to Sylvia.

'You can't open the bar in a bloodstained cardigan,' she said to her. 'Kindly go and change it.'

A plan was forming in her head. What if the knife-wielding boy had been Giolla-Íosa's intended guest? She was certainly not going to take him in. Not now. So why not go along with Julian's story? She could legitimately tell GI she'd assumed he'd been sent via the usual channels. I have no way of checking, she would say. And if you have any concerns about impersonation then you need to take that up with the boy himself.

If the ruffians of Dublin knew the hotel was being used as a safe house then the Gardaí special branch would also know. GI's friends would have to find alternative accommodation for Derry's troubled youth. She'd been too generous in the past; her own health and that of her employees, as well as her business, had suffered. It was time for the hotel to return to its proper function.

Dolly Considine's Hotel

THE MAN WITH THE MASS CARD

November 1956

As Miss Guilfoyle had been a Protestant they were not expected to attend the actual church service, but could wait outside with other Catholic mourners and join the emerging cortège on its journey to the Protestant graveyard at Mount Jerome.

'It's Daddy that has to be seen at every funeral in the county,' Dolly told her mother, 'not me.'

'Miss Guilfoyle's nephews are more likely to honour her debts if we pay our respects properly,' her mother said, looking down at her own black dress and coat.

'Someone needs to be here to greet the mourners with light refreshments when the interment is over. I've given the staff the morning off to attend the funeral,' Dolly said. She'd put up with her mother repeatedly removing the sale agreement from the sideboard drawer and displaying it where it could torture her. She'd accepted the need to sell part of the hotel, but she didn't need pestering. A few hours away from her mother would be welcome.

With everyone gone she was alone in the hotel for the first time in the three and a half years since she'd inherited. Even the one-legged Mr Hannafin, in spite of being on the opposite side to the Guilfoyles during the Civil War, struggled down the stairs using his wife's shoulders and one crutch, his empty trouser leg folded up and kept in place with a large safety pin of the type Dolly had worn on her pleated Irish-dancing skirt when she was a child.

The sandwiches she'd made were covered in greaseproof paper on tables in the Kickham Room. The water in the tea urn was heating slowly, and the jugs of milk were on the kitchen table with saucers on top to keep the flies off. The only job left was to measure out sherry into the tiny glasses sitting on trays in the front hall. Her mother had lined up teapots beside the tea urn for those who wouldn't partake of alcohol.

When the bell rang, she knew it would be a confused mourner, and tried to ignore it. But when they persisted, she was prepared to be cross as she approached the hall door.

'My minister sent me round with this Mass card.' It was Cathal McClean. 'He couldn't attend himself because he's speaking in the Dáil, but he wanted to be associated with the tributes.' He held the card out towards her but stood looking around the lobby of Curragh House as if he was appraising it for an entry in the tourist board brochure.

She wasn't ready for company.

'He wanted me to go to the church but delayed signing the card until fifteen minutes ago.' His appraisal of the hall finished, he began to look at the carpet in front of her feet.

'Well, you're here now,' she said. 'We'll put the card with the others in the Kickham Room and go upstairs for a sherry.'

He looked frightened when she began to help him off with

his coat. She draped it over a chair and picked up one of the smaller sherry trays and let him stand for a second or two before she moved and said, 'Come along,' and led the way to the family sitting room. She regretted not making him carry the tray.

Dolly Considine's Hotel

JULIAN MEETS THE KITCHEN, AND DOLLY ORDERS SWEET TEA

18th June 1983

A hundred years of cooking smells cloyed through the kitchen door towards Julian. He surrendered to Brendan's pushing to allow old fried bread and burnt black pudding to assail his nostrils; and beyond that a rich mist of cigarette smoke and boiling bacon and cabbage demanded his attention.

Brendan lifted him by his army jacket's shoulders and dropped him in front of a deeply chipped Belfast sink before rocking back against the dangerous-looking industrial gas cooker propped up on blackened yellow bricks. The floor was sticky with the same grease that was taking colour out of the flaking, sickly beige walls and adding colour to the once-white ceiling. He could taste the bacon rind Brendan scraped from the dirty plates, the congealed grease generously coming along, swallowed without being chewed, as he watched Julian.

'I could have snapped your neck. Easily,' Brendan said, as Julian moved three burnt pots out of the sink to rinse the sticky lime cordial from his arm. The barred window beyond the sink looked out onto a concrete yard littered with broken wooden crates. A rusted glass-fronted fridge stood with the open door hanging off and framing the stack of bar stools beyond, their broken legs like piled corpses waiting to be brought back to life. Echoes of a humming, saucy maid with clothes pegs between her teeth, stretching to hang sheets and pillowcases on a long-gone clothes line, were loud enough to rattle the window's cobwebbed glass.

'I know how to kill a man so no one knows he's dead for ages and the police can't prove anything. You could be cold on a slab now. And you'd deserve it for stabbing Sylvia and upsetting Mrs McClean.' He wedged Julian against the sink and began to feel him up and down. 'Where's the knife? How did you get Sylvia to say it was someone else? I was shifting crates from the street into the cellar and would have seen him. You are a fucking liar as well as a dirty robber and a girl slasher. If I ever see you round here again, you're dead. Do you hear me?'

Julian wriggled his bottom against Brendan and the man pulled away.

'Dirty queer. Fucking bum boy. That's what you are. Mrs McClean will never give you a job, never. She hates queers.'

'There's no vacancy. There never has been a vacancy,' Julian said, adopting the woman's own tone.

'She only said that because she hates you. You're too small to work in the Curragh House Hotel. Little shrimp. Little faggot shrimp.'

'Brendan, watch your language.' It was Mrs McClean. 'Have you made Julian a cup of tea? Sweet tea is best for a shock. Isn't that right? And a cup for Sylvia. Make a big pot and we can all have a drop. There's leftover marble cake in the larder. You should show Julian where everything is so he can help out down here when he's not needed in the bars.' She looked Julian up and down, her face neutral, denying that in whatever she was planning to do with him she might end up being the loser.

'Now, may I see your references, Julian?'

'It's all in my other suitcase. I left it at the bus station.' He'd give himself free rein to make up a story for every question. 'It's signed by Miss Lavern Williams, the manageress of The Blue Lagoon in Jersey. The cocktail lounge. Do you know it? I've been there all winter. But decided to spend the summer in Dublin.' He smiled at Mrs McClean. He could see she didn't want him to go to the police but was too mean to pay him off.

She continued to stare at him but said nothing.

'Fair enough,' he said, aloud.

'I beg your pardon?' Mrs McClean said, sounding arch and southside.

'I said fair enough. You know, that's grand. That sort of thing.'

She was calculating. Trying to get the measure of him. Wondering if she knew what she was doing. He'd need time to adjust to Johnner chickening out of their adventure, and a new plan. Plan B or maybe C. Enough time to raid the tips glass. The only certain thing was, he could not go back to Cabra while his brother was home, but more than a day or two in Curragh House would be a head fuck. He looked at the woman's powdered face and her muscle-bound sidekick and scanned the room so it could tell him why she didn't want him talking to the cops. The room seemed to smirk and say why did he care? Hadn't he talked himself into sanctuary? Gifted himself a Dickensian kitchen, and met three fucking nutters whose portraits were going into his journal?

She was nodding, her fingers combing through the fringe of the salmon-pink shawl draped around her shoulders. He tried not to look too pleased with himself. A fucking job. On his own, and against the odds. Without bloody Johnner. He was a fucking genius. Nothing short of a genius.

'And my room?' he asked.

'I beg your pardon?'

Was she reserving a right to change her mind?

'My room? You know, where I'll be sleeping.'

'Is there space in the boys' room, Brendan?'

The boys' room? That sounded like sharing. The baboon, hopefully not in the same bed, but at least close by. He was going to be David fucking Attenborough studying the animal at close quarters. He smiled at Brendan. He'd need a way of protecting himself if he was sharing, but he rubbed his hands together and nodded his head.

'Mrs McClean, I am very happy to have the opportunity to work in your hotel. I think I will be very happy here.'

'Where are your black trousers and white shirt?' She grimaced at his trousers and what she could see of his check shirt.

'The Blue Lagoon supplied a uniform,' he said. 'A fresh shirt every shift.' He liked the sound of that. He was turning into a poetic liar.

'Well, it's only that Russian and his troupe for lunch. But for the evening trade I insist on black trousers and white shirt. Is that understood?'

He wanted to say I'm wearing Malone's trousers, I'll check his bag for white shirts, but the stickiness of the lime juice cordial drying on his arms and shoulders was tormenting him, so he just nodded and smiled.

'Brendan,' she said. 'Go up to the Porchester Lounge and bring down Julian's bag so he can change out of his soiled shirt. Run along.' And she clapped her hands together like a little girl at her own birthday party.

Julian was in love.

Dolly Considine's Hotel

IF SHE'S GOOD ENOUGH FOR THE BETTER-LOOKING YOUNGER BROTHER...

November 1956

It would not be easy to get Cathal McClean to make love to her anywhere, never mind in the room next to where Miss Guilfoyle had so recently died and while the woman's funeral cortège was on its way to pause outside the hotel in recognition of the thirty-five years she'd lived in Curragh House. It wasn't that Cathal would resist Dolly's advances, but he would not understand what she was proposing. A simple 'no' would stop it, any time he liked, if that's what he wanted. But what was not to want? If she was good enough for Giolla-Íosa then she was good enough for his plainer, older brother. But to get to that point, she would have to take charge and lead him obliquely every step of the way, and risk humiliating herself if she appeared over-keen.

During the last summer Dolly and the McClean brothers had spent debating what they would do when they ran the country (once the Emergency caused by the war in Europe was finally over), it was only Giolla-Íosa who made any advances to her.

She'd often wondered what it would be like to give Cathal the relief she gave his younger brother so freely on the banks of the river after Sunday Mass. But he never showed the slightest interest in that side of her. Which convinced her that his role in life was to ensure Giolla-Íosa had all he needed rather than worry about himself.

Seven years later, here he was, in her funeral-darkened upstairs sitting room in the middle of the day, sipping sherry and giggling at their lack of reverence. But getting Cathal to have a sherry was a long way from getting him to freely lift her flower-patterned skirt and silky slip and make keen, if inept, love to her.

Dolly still thought of the sitting room as the exclusive preserve of the former manageress Mrs Burns. She'd always given Dolly ten minutes of her time on the second afternoon of her and her mother's Christmas shopping visits, fulfilling an obligation to entertain the niece of the hotel owner. But gone now were the articles of clothing drying in front of the fire, as were the clouds of smelly face powder that had trailed behind her as she moved from the cabinet protecting the glasses and bottles of squash across to Dolly to present the overly diluted orange drink, and then onward to stand with her back to the fireplace, her hands clasped in front of her green skirt as her heels rose and fell, with nothing to say until Dolly's mother knocked on the door to rescue them both.

Dolly and Cathal knelt in front of the window to peer under the drawn blind at the funeral cortège as it slowly passed the only home Miss Guilfoyle had known since her family was burnt out by the Black and Tans searching for her rebel brother in 1922. The second sherry was making Dolly a little tipsy and she leaned on Cathal's shoulder to balance herself. The cortège took so long to pass that her leg had gone to sleep when it was time to get up. Cathal had to help her back to the couch, allow her to keep her weight off the sleeping foot. And then they both sat down and began to giggle again.

'I've missed you,' she said. And he smiled just as she remembered. Everything could so easily return to how it had been when she, Cathal and Giolla-Íosa had sat together in the parlour in Birr arguing politics while her mother was shopping or laying out a corpse or doing constituency work for her father. Today they were sipping sherry and Giolla-Íosa was absent, except that Cathal spoke about his brother as if he was on the couch between them, or over by the window rolling up the blinds because the funeral had passed and there was no need to sit in the gloom. Every small silence filled with Giolla-Íosa.

How Giolla-Íosa likes Cork.

How Giolla-Íosa hopes for promotion in his accountancy firm.

How difficult it was for Giolla-Íosa to find a suitable constituency.

Followed by a series of questions.

'Dolly, do you think Giolla-Íosa should stay in Cork? Or should he move to Dublin?'

'Do you think that the South Riding constituency is his best bet? I mean, you know it better than any of us.'

'No more Giolla-Íosa,' she ordered. 'What about your own plans?' And she snuggled right up to him.

'They'll be at the graveyard by now,' he said, 'standing around waiting for the last post to be played. The diehards encouraging each other to start a decade of the rosary. Where would you like to be buried?'

'Jesus Christ.' Almost leaping away from him. But then she remembered the discussion tricks of the old days. 'By rights Miss Guilfoyle should have gone into the republican plot in Glasnevin.' Something inflammatory to change the subject.

'Dolly, that's just silly,' he said.

'She suffered more than her brother. He spent his time on the run taking advantage of the daughters who risked their lives hiding him and got a full military funeral when he fell in front of a train, drunk, at Limerick Junction.'

'Next you'll say the cemetery should have a plot for people who live for Ireland instead of dying,' Cathal said. 'We'd end up with no one in family graves except wasters and children.' He looked ready to launch into one of the idealistic speeches he'd indulged in during their Birr parlour days.

She'd listen if it got him going, but really she wanted fun. She wanted to be touched. Not to hear about death or heroes. Those were the conversations they'd had when they were children. Cathal and Giolla-Íosa reeling off the names of War of Independence people they'd seen on the street that day, reminding each other of the part their families had played. Sometimes shying away from the Civil War in case Dolly thought they were blaming her father for any involvement with the death of their grandfather.

'I sometimes wish things were back the way they were before I was sent up to Dublin,' he said. 'We worked very well together, the three of us, arguing, agreeing and disagreeing.'

'We could try for an argument now, so long as we make up before the mourners get back,' she said, 'if you'd like.'

He looked at her but gave no sign that her words had more than their own meaning.

'Dolly, do you think Giolla-Íosa should emigrate? Maybe to America?'

It was the last question she would allow, but instead of answering she leaned in to Cathal's face, and growled, the way she'd growled when she was thirteen and the McClean brothers were being silly. Now she pushed herself up onto her knees on the couch, took the nearest of his jacket lapels between her teeth, and shook her head like a ferret-killing dog.

The texture of the material was horrid against her tongue, and she curled the tip away to prevent it from making her retch. But she had to do something, or she would be going back to the boiling tea urns, and if she did that she would never get him into bed.

'There is Australia, but it's got unpleasant associations with convicts.' Cathal continued his speech as if snarling women attached to his jacket were an everyday occurrence. 'He has a plan to work abroad for say ten years, and then return in triumph to take his rightful place...'

The tea urn call was getting louder, but instead of answering it she released his lapel and leaned further over, perhaps she would kiss him, or grab his head as she was now doing, to lean it back and improve the angle, all the better to rub her lips furiously against his, daring herself until she brushed her tongue forward and eased one knee over so that she straddled him, swearing that she would not stop until Giolla-Íosa was banished from his silly mind. But now that she was there, Dolly limited herself to rocking slightly on Cathal's lap, anything more would spook him. Surely she could feel his response through her crumpled skirt. She'd have to change it before the funeral guests returned; it would please her mother to see the grey but flowery skirt replaced by the plain black when she found her daughter composed and ready with trays of sherry and tea and freshly cut sandwiches.

She'd known Cathal would be more allowing than participating in their lovemaking, but her exasperation to get him to lift his hands off the couch cushions and onto any part of her body induced her to spit 'Giolla-Íosa had a good time' into his gritted teeth as she kissed him. The transferred smear of lipstick made Cathal's innocent face look more like that of a schoolboy who's been at the raspberry cordial than a man just over the first hurdle in his seduction of the woman he's secretly loved since she was a schoolgirl.

She'd intended to manoeuvre herself to his other side where there was more room, but she overbalanced and tumbled, clutching at the air as she fell back towards the floor. And Cathal's immediate move after her was probably more to do with fear that she might be hurt than with any thought of taking advantage of her splayed, winded state.

But the brief shock did not divert her; she grabbed at his lapels, avoiding the spittle-wet area, and pulled sharply as he leaned over to minister to any injury. The surprise made him stumble, his good manners shooting his hands outwards beyond her outline so they landed on the carpet and not anywhere on her person. But it finally gave her the full body contact she wanted even if his weight winded her in ways she hadn't expected.

'Cathal Cathal Cathal,' she whispered. She wasn't sure what else to say. *Do it to me* would have sent him running, but that's what she'd have said to Giolla-Íosa, even though he wouldn't have needed any encouragement in the first place. 'Oh Cathal,' she said. 'At long last. We're together.'

Dolly Considine's Hotel

JULIAN PROMISES TO WRITE A STORY FOR BRENDAN

18th June 1983

Julian was still clinging to his triumphant feeling when Malone's bag, drop-kicked by Brendan from the half-landing, tumbled him backwards off his feet like a circus clown, making him bang his head against the basement hall floor's uneven quarry tiles. Malone's quality soft leather bag pressed into him like a light lover. He squeezed it to himself to relieve the pain, and looked up at the bumps and hollows of the ancient basement ceiling. The crumbling plaster was a chorus of distorted cracked faces sneering down at him.

Leave now, they sang, *before it's too late.*

'Brendan!' Mrs McClean shouted from further back along the corridor.

Julian rolled onto his side and pushed himself to his knees. Dirty daylight was coming through the half-glazed door behind her, the sunshine barely enough for him to see steps leading up to railings and the street beyond.

'Brendan!' called Mrs McClean more loudly, advancing past Julian towards the stairs. 'Get the stock in off the footpath.'

Brendan hesitated on the bottom step and her arm lifted as if she would slap him.

'Immediately,' she threatened, a tinge of Moore Street market in her voice.

Brendan began pulling on a loop of twine round his neck and extracted a key tucked down his shirt like a scapula, and unlocked a door beyond the kitchen.

Mrs McClean clapped her hands at Julian.

'On your feet,' she said. 'You're on duty in the Porchester Lounge.'

'The faces, the faces,' he whispered, pointing at the ceiling plaster. His head hurt, his eyes were blurry and maybe the faces were right, he should get out.

'Put that bag in the boys' room,' she said, pointing to the furthest door.

The bag, yes, the bag would tell him Malone's secrets. Explain what the detectives were looking for. Reveal more danger for him. Be the final decider. To stay or walk away, find a quiet park and record his adventure in his journal, and then... And then what? There must be a hostel somewhere for a homeless boy. A charity that would help him. He just had to be more imaginative.

But the smell of socks and farts in the boys' bedroom had a different story to tell: the frayed grey sheets and greasy stained blankets, the seven pillows on one bed, none on the other, the windowsill with its stack of tattered porn magazines. The bulging ceiling and patches of missing plaster, the exposed laths like ribs stripped of their flesh.

The boys' bedroom wasn't sneering at him; it wanted attention, maybe his. And Malone's bag wanted his clothes to be smelt and his story to be absorbed. It would ease itself open and allow Julian to ferret out clues, to look for the false bottom filled with heroin, or, or... He couldn't think of anything else that would be of interest.

He lifted the motherly folded bundles of clean crisp shirts, plaid shorts, black socks and blue trousers trimmed with tartan like his brother Christopher had worn ten years earlier. Everything smelt of flowers except for two pairs of Italian black shoes in brown paper bags that smelt of fresh polish. He counted out ten brand new T-shirts onto the soiled blankets, their new whiteness, their look of never having been stretched to fit over anyone's head, taking on extra starkness in the squalid basement bedroom. He could see Malone in his graffiti-carved police cell, the smell of shit and stale piss emanating from the coverless toilet, keeping strong with the thought of reunion with his fresh unspoilt T-shirts.

The T-shirts wanted to describe Malone naked in the morning after his shower, Brendan frozen in his bed as he watched a new one being pulled on, broken in, the hugging material smoothed along Malone's torso, to be worn only once before being dispensed to the adoring needy. Brendan mesmerised daily by the magic bag's seemingly endless supply.

And then Brendan was blocking the misty light coming through the bedroom window, three crates of beer shaking so the bottles rattled and sang like a chanting mob. Distortions in the glass giving him two mouths, simultaneously sneering and calling him bum boy. He kicked at the bedroom door as he passed Julian on his way to the beer cellar. 'You won't last a week,' he hissed. 'Not a fucking week.' Seconds later the crash of crates onto other crates; the monster in his lair patrolling, and bumping into things, in his blind fury.

The whitewashed breast above the open fireplace was covered in blocks of tiny Xs, seven wide, an army of Space Invaders advancing out of the smoke-stained mantelpiece towards the ceiling above. A record of someone's stay – a prisoner, a lover? The pencil marks told Julian nothing except that someone had put them there. The Xs and the person who'd scratched them were fair game, as was the hotel, Sylvia and Mrs McClean. His to take inspiration from and make meaningful. Like an investor buying up an ancient family business and stripping out the assets. He would suck in what he saw and spew out words any way he liked.

The crashing and rattling from the beer cellar provided a rhythm and a different plea for attention.

'You'll get your story too. You thick culchie shite,' Julian muttered. 'It's fermenting as you snort and paw.' And he zipped Malone's bag closed and pushed it under the bed.

Dolly Considine's Hotel

A NOTE FROM HER FATHER'S FRIEND AND INNOCENT NEMESIS

April 1957

Dolly never had to concern herself about Giolla-Íosa when he was doing her. And that's what it was: Giolla-Íosa did her. Never any need to worry, just allow herself to be transported away from the day to day by the rhythm, by the expertise, by his sense of entitlement.

Cathal, by contrast, anchored her to the lumpy mattress. It wasn't just his extra weight, but the way he stopped every few thrusts to ask if he was hurting her, or betraying her, or tiring her. Or to catch his breath or adjust himself in some way which she didn't understand. All of which made surrender impossible. Even when she rolled him over so she was on top, she continued to be anchored. The rattle of a delivery man on the street, a barking dog, even the squeal of brakes as cars approached the junction, all were brought into the room by his response to them, turning them into watching angels stationed around the bed.

At least when she was on her back she could tuck in her chin and look at his chest instead of his effort-filled face. Close her eyes to stop herself counting the thrusts until he asked if her back was okay, or if his beard was scratching her, his breath offending her, his embrace too needy. One wet Thursday afternoon he said, 'Not too tight for you?' Which made her think of corsets, and nooses.

What the brothers did have in common was that they didn't linger in her bed once they'd finished. With Cathal it was his guilt at having taken advantage of her. But for Giolla-Íosa it was the suddenly remembered meeting or the urgent appointment that had crept up on them when they were having such a good time. Once the brothers started to fidget, Dolly never thought to stop them, although she did try to reassure Cathal that she *was* okay.

John Toomey had been her father's friend since they'd been single men, although they were members of opposing political parties. But in the 1954 general election, the Fianna Fáil candidate who stood for her father's vacated seat was eliminated on the second count and the transfer votes went mainly to Toomey, resulting in the South Riding seat going to Fine Gael and leading Dolly to anticipate that he would stay away from the Considines, except perhaps to attend her father's funeral if her father died first. But coming up to six months after she started seeing the two McClean brothers, she was surprised to receive a note from him.

'*There is something I want to discuss with you,*' John Toomey wrote on the back of a postcard showing a view of Cumberland Square in Birr before it was renamed. He invited her to Leinster House to lunch in the members' restaurant.

The party machine blamed her father for not keeping the vote together, and some accused him of openly supporting

Toomey, and Toomey himself boasted of his friend's support. But by the time of the election her father was only months away from never leaving the house again. If the election was mentioned he shook his head and looked bewildered, perhaps no longer caring or understanding.

'You know I think of the South Riding seat as your father's.' John Toomey was watching his knife as he buttered his bread roll.

Dolly had been a slightly pimply sixteen year old in her Sainte Union uniform the last time he saw her. Now she looked down towards her spoon dipping into the mixed vegetable soup. She giggled to herself at the thought that she might have left undone the second button down on her blouse.

'When the Civil War ended,' he said, 'De Valera's boys strutted around the countryside like bullies; no one could stand up to them. They treated the rest of us as though we were the English. Elected representatives beaten up and murdered.'

She smiled at a waitress balancing a tray of lunches for two Fianna Fáil backbenchers at the next table. They were regulars in her hotel but would avoid eye contact while she was dining with a member of the inter-party government.

'Between their thuggery and Dev's non-payment of rents campaign starting to drive exporting farmers into bankruptcy, it was small wonder the Blueshirts emerged; and without men like Terence Considine they might have survived much longer, and the outcome been a lot dirtier.'

She'd heard all this before. In her own way, she was proud of her father, but what had he done but strut about with a different set of men, shaking hands and slapping backs? And just when he was ready for office, ready to exercise the peace, they passed him over. His cross-party friendships seen as a betrayal. The Civil War sides potent and alive, when it counted.

'And yet there are towns in Offaly where Fine Gael people still call my father "the hurler on the ditch" and "a turncoat". Accuse him of biding his time in the Civil War, as they'd done during the War of Independence, saying he wasn't a peacemaker at all, but was waiting to see who got the upper hand.'

'Dolly, that's all in the past.'

'It's thirty years. And they still look at me as if I'm to blame, when I wasn't even born.'

A silence then as she cut the fat off the meat on her plate. She felt sick. She loved bacon, and her father. So, either all this talk was making her sick, or Jesus Christ, God forbid, she was pregnant.

John Toomey's shirt was frayed around the collar, and his suit was shiny where the elbows touched the tablecloth. She would never let any man of hers leave the house looking like that. Previously white, the shirt was now nearly grey with bad washing, which caused her to check what the Fine Gaelers at other tables were wearing. A smattering of blues, a natural enough colour for farmers and elected representatives whether they'd ever flirted with fascism or not.

If she was forced to abandon her lunch, she would know she was pregnant. But if her upset was caused by thinking about her daddy, then she would breathe deeply, and smile, and swallow, and have dessert and coffee, and maybe even a brandy, if John Toomey offered.

'I have a few more years,' he said. 'Maybe two full terms. If you got involved now you could be ready to stand when I retire. You'll be in your thirties. Your children being at school will allow you time to devote to your duties.'

She felt herself blush. Could he see she was dithering over the bacon? Did he know about Cathal or Giolla-Íosa? *I hear you're interviewing for a husband* was something he would never say. And she wasn't. Was she?

'You think I should stand for Daddy's seat?' she asked. He was right. The seat was hers. But did she want it? She cut the bacon into small pieces the way her father had done for her when she was tiny. *Dolly McClean (née Considine) Teachta Dála.* The sound made even the rind and the oozing fat look appetising.

'You'll have to work for it. Make your home among your electorate. Put the effort into the constituency. Your husband would have to be happy for you to spend time in Dublin at least when the house is sitting. All these things have to be planned. Success won't happen by itself. But the party will support you.'

'You mean,' she said, 'I'd have to join your lot?'

'Fine Gael is your natural home, Dolly,' he said. 'And the seat is secure now. No need to make the compromises forced on your father. Besides, they should have stood by him. He had nothing to do with Josie Geoghan. He was blameless. FF betrayed him. He would be alive and well and holding high office today if he'd thrown his lot in with Fine Gael.'

'Daddy is not dead,' she said, and nodded yes to the waiter for coffee, shook her head no to brandy.

She lost interest after that. A brief flash of what might have been, until she understood. She could never join Fine Gael. No matter what Fianna Fáil had done to her father, she belonged with them. But at least Toomey's utterances proved he didn't know about Giolla-Íosa or Cathal.

'I might win the seat back for the FFers,' she said, smiling. She liked apple and custard. In the hotel kitchen she followed her mother's recipe, counting four cloves per portion into the stewing apples and removing them before dishing up for her guests.

'That lot will never nominate a woman unless she's a

widow,' he said. 'Even in Dublin, where a woman is respected a bit more.'

She called the waiter back and indicated that she would have a brandy to match her host's.

'*Time enough to look after the women when the men are all right* is the Fianna Fáil motto, and that's the liberal wing. Whereas all our lot want is good representation. I'm not saying you'll walk it, but with the party machine, and your own hard work…' He sniffed his brandy before putting the glass to his lips.

Was he savouring the apparent success of his plan?

'The country needs strong-minded women with opinions and commitment. The Considines are well known and loved. You shouldn't let all the work your father did go to waste.'

'The country doesn't always get what it needs,' Dolly said. But she was thinking about telling Giolla-Íosa that John Toomey wanted her to inherit his seat. Would she allow him to undress her, or wait until he was inside her, or indeed until he was rushing off to a meeting that he'd forgotten? She'd say nothing at all to Cathal. She smiled at John Toomey. 'Let's have another brandy,' she said, 'and I will think about your proposal.'

The leader of the Labour party passed them as she stood up from the table; he smiled at John, and said good day to her.

She nodded to the Garda on duty at the door of Leinster House as she shook hands with her host, and then made her way across the cobbled enclosure to Kildare Street. What would John Toomey or her father think if she joined the Labour party? And why shouldn't she? She was living in Dublin. She was her own woman. Who was to stop her? Certainly not either of the McClean brothers.

But it was John Toomey's mention of Josie Geoghan that came into her head and drew her back to herself. She was glad she'd had the second brandy; it made her able to lengthen her stride, pull her shoulders back and think about winking at the man in uniform and cap holding open the gate for her. But she relished how she looked these days, so she nodded, and walked on.

Dolly Considine's Hotel

JULIAN RISES FROM THE BASEMENT ONLY TO
FALL ON HIS KNEES

18th June 1983

The smell of turf-smoke from the black trousers transported
Julian to Malone's mother's country cottage with its single
light bulb and smoke-stained chimney breast, the woman sad
at his imminent departure but saying, those trousers need dry-
cleaning. The bunched-up waistband and tucked-in shirt
looked wrong in the gents' toilet mirror, but he pulled the
shirt tails out a little and let material flop loosely over his belt,
and flicked through glimpses of Malone's naked legs in the
same trousers, their skins touching, sweat mixing, and hairs
intertwining, becoming Malone for his ascent of the rickety
carpeted stairs, his shoulders back, his posture balletic and his
hands facing upwards like those of a welcoming pope. At
the ladies' toilet he turned to acknowledge the ill-fitting door
and creamy plastic handle before moving past the cramped
reception desk with its glowing Sacred Heart lamp. Then he
turned to choose between the Kickham Room and the
Porchester Lounge for his grand entrance, raising his left arm

in preparation for the acknowledgement of the waiting staff, and would have smacked Mrs McClean in the face as she left the Kickham Room if she hadn't raised her own arm to defend herself. She gripped his hand with both of hers and bent his fingers backwards. Had she been the school bully in St Peter's Julian would be on his knees already, the bully's spittle peppering his face as he leaned over him and forced his surrender.

'You have been hired for a trial period only,' she said, her accent back in south Dublin. 'If you cause any upset to the staff or customers, it will result in instant dismissal. Do you understand?' She bent his fingers further back to underline her words, forcing him to kneel right down. Mrs McClean: her feet apart, standing tall like a monument to herself. Her hands stretched out, still around his, like those of a matador about to drive his sword into the neck of a young bull.

'Oh Dolly McCleans, shouldn't you confine this kind of behaviour to the bedroom?' said a man with an exaggerated Russian accent behind him.

'Your sandwiches are in the Porchester Lounge, Mr Mayakovsky,' she said, still looking down at her kneeling victim.

'Assembled and cut with your own fair hand.' The man was about Julian's father's age. He had a shaggy beard and a full-length Astrakhan coat opened to reveal a red shirt and bottle green corduroy trousers. Behind him stood four women wearing tracksuit type clothes and leg warmers.

'By Sylvia, Mr Mayakovsky. That's what I pay her for.'

'And the young man on his knees Dolly McCleans, what do you pay him for?' He was staring at Julian. He looked hungry.

'I was intending to address that very point when I finished demonstrating the defenceless woman's self-defence technique. However, now that you and your entourage have arrived, I shall wait until after lunch.' She released Julian and made her way towards the stairs. She was reaching for the banister when she turned to him, his fingers out of sight behind his back being rubbed to ease the pain.

'Mr Mayakovsky is a revered visitor to Curragh House, Julian. Be sure to make him feel at home.'

Julian smiled at the group of women jostling past the Russian whose searching stare had now moved to his crotch.

'I am Julian Ryder,' he said. 'Curragh House's new barman. Your lunch awaits you.' He was holding the Porchester door for the oldest of the four women when he noticed a boy behind her pushing his feet forward almost in sync with hers, like a delayed shadow, the rear end of a pantomime horse but without the costume. The woman herself, as if unaware of him, followed the others to the window overlooking the street. They marked out their places around the plates of sandwiches with handbags, cigarette boxes and matches. Two of them completed the enclosure with glass ashtrays picked from a shelf to the left of the window. The shadowing boy slunk into the corner on the other side, draped himself onto a high stool against the wall, put his thumb in his mouth, and looked ready to burst into tears. A poster announcing the forthcoming production of *A Song for All Saints* at the Porchester Theatre framed his head like a wig made of words.

Julian put his hand out to lift the counter flap, but Sylvia pushed a damp cloth and a pencil and paper towards him.

'See what the ladies want to drink,' she said, and lifted her head at Mr Mayakovsky seating himself at the bar.

'What can I get you?' Julian asked the man, ignoring her, leaning inward, all the better to sniff the Astrakhan.

'Sylvia will look after me. Won't you Sylvia?'

She sneered and waved Julian away.

'Your new lounge boy is a bit of a rebel,' Mr Mayakovsky said. 'You'll have to keep an eye on him.'

'There's plenty of others will do that,' she said.

Julian didn't want to be a lounge boy. He'd done that when he was thirteen, filled in for Johnner while he went to Spain on holiday.

Sylvia placed a glass on the counter in front of Mr Mayakovsky. 'Vodka,' she said.

The man took the glass and swallowed the contents in one gulp. Julian moved towards the window. The women were already smoking and eating the sandwiches.

'Is it your first day?' the older woman asked, the sound of her voice whipping her thumb-sucking shadow's eyes to her face.

'Have you seen Josie?' the youngest woman asked. 'She lurks on the stairs waiting to touch up any passing man. Keep your privates covered.'

'Ah, leave him alone,' the older woman said. 'Can't you see he's nervous?'

'But I want to know if he's seen Josie yet.'

Mr Mayakovsky turned away from the bar with his second vodka and gave Julian several seconds to answer before lowering the drink in one gulp.

'How can I help you ladies,' Julian asked, 'drinks-wise?'

'Two Cidonas and two bottles of stout for us,' the older women said. 'And a milky coffee for Leroy.'

'Leroy?' Julian said, before he could stop himself. The boy was a skinny, sulking redhead with freckles. Straight out of a picture postcard featuring turf-filled creels on donkeys in a Galway bog. A Seamus, or a Patrick, maybe, but not a swashbuckling Leroy.

'It's not his real name.' The older woman smiled at Julian and sucked on her cigarette. 'Mr Mayakovsky has told him to follow me around all day in the character of Leroy, although in the play he's Howard, my son. I'm Estelle. Mr Mayakovsky is really Leroy.'

Julian didn't understand.

'And is Josie another character?' he asked.

'No, darling. Josie Geoghan died in a bedroom upstairs. And now she haunts the stairs and landings.'

'In the old days, people used to bump into the dead porter Paddy. But only Brendan sees him nowadays,' the youngest said.

They were making fun of him. He smiled and went to collect the drinks already lined up on the counter.

If Mr Mayakovsky swallowed his vodkas whole, Leroy and the women stretched out their one drink until the Russian stood up just after three o'clock and held the door while they trooped out into the hall. He'd eaten none of the sandwiches and bought the rest of the bottle of vodka to take back to the theatre. He used his free hand to wave Julian over and put his arm around his shoulders.

'Be sure to respect Josie,' he said, before pulling the door after him. The glass in the Porchester Lounge door allowed Julian to see the boy who was neither Leroy nor Howard waiting for his inspiration to return from the ladies' toilet.

'Wash up all the glasses and return the coffee cup to the kitchen.' Sylvia lifted the counter flap and spoke as she crossed the room. 'Mrs McClean wants to see you upstairs. Be here at five for the teas, if you still have a job.'

Through the front window he watched her put on her coat as she crossed the road.

'Where can she be going in such a rush?' he asked the strange-looking man in the poster above Leroy's empty coffee cup. 'Is it to see a sick mother? Or to get some afternoon delight with a married man?'

Mrs McClean was calling his name from the top of the

stairs. As he ascended, her tennis shoes, rounded calves and short white skirt under the open beige mac made him forget to watch out for Josie. She handed him an old envelope with a harp printed on the address side to indicate official state correspondence. She pointed to the writing on the back: '*Please give bearer one leg of lamb, and settle up Curragh House's meat bill,*' she read. 'Do you understand? The money is in the envelope. Thirty pounds. Bring back the change. Buckley's in Chatham Street. Do you know where that is?'

'Chatham Street?' he said. Thirty lovely Irish punts. Enough money to get to London. It would be hours before they missed him. How many more chances was he going to get? 'Of course I know where Chatham Street is.' He smiled at her. He could already feel the ferry swaying under his feet, and the rattle of the duty-free bottles. Another bloody miracle.

'Top of Grafton Street. First turn on your left. You do know Grafton Street?'

She was goading him into scarpering with the money.

'If you need the launderette, I suggest you go there first, so the meat is not out of the fridge for very long.' She was letting him take his bag, Malone's bag, practically instructing him to do a runner. Mrs McClean pushed open the nearest of the three doors; the envelope was urging him on, but the first-floor landing was taunting him to absorb its details before he left: the complicated brown and blue stucco around the ceiling, the peeling green and yellow wallpaper that stretched up the stairs to the next floor, and the deep beige carpet patterned with carved swirls.

The door opened again. She took the envelope back and spoke as she wrote: 'And a jar of La Malva olives from Magill's in Clarendon Street,' she said. 'In olive oil or brine or a mixture.' She slipped in another tenner before handing it back. 'I have tennis for the rest of the afternoon.'

A faded gold sign on Mrs McClean's pale green door announced 'Manageress', the paint above the knob worn away to reveal an older brown shade beneath. The middle door had a painted 'Private' sign and the one on the left a brass 'Room 11', and a flowery plate above the knob to protect the paint from pushing fingers. He could hear muttered whispers coming from behind each door. Two hundred years of secrets that he would never know. The trapped and leftover echoes resigned to his departure, already pulling their bodices and cloaks tightly around themselves in disappointment.

He was out on the street swinging Malone's bag over his shoulder when he realised the ghosts of Paddy and Josie had ignored him. Had the hotel tested him as a suitable chronicler and found him wanting? But his head was already filling with stories about it, and the ghosts' bad manners would not stop him thinking about them as he began his latest attempt to get out of Dublin.

Dolly Considine's Hotel

THE TESTIMONY AND PARANOIAS OF MIKHAIL MAYAKOVSKY #1

June 1983

'I'm not playing a girl,' the boy called Kevin had wailed. 'Just because my voice is still breaking doesn't mean I want to be a girl. I am Howard.'

And I said, 'Okay sweetheart. You don't need to play Estelle. Just read her lines. I want to hear what she sounds like. Play with me. Will you do that? Play with me. I like boys who play with me.' I put my arm around his shoulders to hug him, but he ran out of the theatre and sulked outside like one of those black aquarium fish that hide in the dark while all the colourful little blues and golds dart about being fabulous.

But a couple of hours later I'm presented with the edgy Julian whose every sinew screams, I want it, give it to me, it's mine, now. Could my Jerry have sent him? From beyond the grave? A little distraction because he knows something I don't know about *A Song for All Saints*? Bad reviews? My production pulled? A little fornication to take the edge off my soon to be bubbling-over hatreds? Probably not.

Still, I hadn't been in love since that cheap set designer from Jerry's funeral who'd strung me along for months, promising but not delivering. Eventually driving me to accept the Dublin gig, to get away from him. A backwater respite of peace and quiet.

'Maybe you should stay away from the avant-garde theatre. Stick to Cathleen ní Houlihan,' I hissed when the girls dragged Kevin in out of the rain, and when I stroked his damp shoulder-length hair all he did was shake my hand off his lowered head. But I let him stay, I needed to hear the script with Irish accents. The American words reverted to their peasant Irish roots. The girls were more playful. Eager to be boys or girls or young or old. Unfortunately, smooth, sickeningly smooth, too well trained, too well behaved; priming me to be ready when Julian was presented. 'That's the rough diamond this show needs,' I told my dead Jerry at lunchtime when I found Dolly McClean remonstrating with her new lounge boy's cheeky face. Of course, six double vodkas later, followed by the rest of the bottle during the afternoon rehearsal, and I was back before tea introducing my middle digit, right hand, into his fundament. That's a boy that wants to play, that wants a master of play to broaden his experience. Convinced I was right when I found he wasn't an actor on the make, at all. And obviously not a waiter either, in fact a silly chicken without a single reason to be stuck in that dump, and if he isn't now, he soon will be, stuck. I told him to get out, if he valued his life, his uniqueness, his ratness. Well maybe I didn't mention rats.

I'd seen his abused look before, and was torn between the certainty that it made him perfect for the part and an equal certainty that the ease with which he let me engage in anal digitalis screamed that I was dealing with a very scary unknown quantity. I knew that with grooming and management his Howard would electrify the audience, although without training it could also cost him his sanity, or me mine. But to my shame, in my fear of upsetting the theatre committee, I played safe.

'What do you want to be?' I asked him the second time I came into the hotel.

'You mean when I grow up?'

'Classic. Yes, when you grow up.'

'Nothing.'

'And when you were a child?'

He looked at me, his face serious, sneering, and holding a deep breath for an age. I thought he was about to say something... well... profound.

'The only thing I've ever wanted was to be a soda jerk,' he said. And although I've been around actors all my life, I couldn't tell if he was jerking me...

'With slicked-back hair, white shirt, rolled-up sleeves, and a pink dicky bow?' I asked. I recover quickly.

'Maybe,' he said, and shrugged his shoulders, dismissing me.

But I knew I'd have to see him again.

Dolly Considine's Hotel

HIS FINAL OPPORTUNITY TO ESCAPE DUBLIN, REJECTED

18th June 1983

One lime-cordial-sticky shirt was hardly enough reason to look for a launderette, but bringing Malone's bag with him would convince Mrs McClean that her plan was working. He was taking the bait; and if he went straight to the ferry booking office and spent her money on his ticket, he wouldn't be able to chicken out. He'd have to leave Dublin. But he was imagining Malone anticipating his reunion with his bag when the sign for Chatham Street dragged his attention towards it. And when he listened, he heard Buckley the butcher calling him to settle the hotel's meat bill, and, just as insistently, the voices of the Malva olives in brine and olive oil calling his name. At the very least he had to go and describe the shops to his journal.

Sylvia was leaning over the kitchen table reading a newspaper article about primary school closures when he got back to the hotel at five.

'There you go,' he said, and put the bag of fresh meat and the jar of olives on top of her paper. 'Will I take the change up to Mrs McClean?' He wanted to be up with the stories, hiding out behind the first floor's closed doors. He'd thrown away his latest miracle to come back and listen. He was entitled. They were his.

'The teas will be ready in two minutes. Give her the change then.' If Sylvia was surprised to see him, it didn't show. She moved away to poke at rashers spitting flaming grease from the high-level grill, leaning backwards so her face didn't get splattered. The smell of the burning bacon was warming up the cold greasy aura he'd been expecting in the kitchen.

'Don't just stand there,' Sylvia said. 'Put the trays out; cut the bread and butter it. Make the tea, two spoons in each teapot, don't forget the crockery or cutlery, they have brown sauce and tomato sauce in their rooms.'

She wasn't speaking to him, but to every boy who'd ever done the job.

'Chop chop,' she said. 'The Hannafins' tray first. One large teapot and two of everything else.'

The butcher had been hacking at a lump of meat in the worn-down dip of the chopping block when Julian put Malone's bag on the floor and took Mrs McClean's shopping list from his trouser pocket. The man folded his arms on his chest, still clutching the cleaver, and looked at him the way his father had done the night he'd left the house in Cabra. A sort of breathless anger shook Julian and made him put the envelope on the counter edge instead of reading out the words, and then he stepped backwards out of range of the cleaver.

'Give me the bloody thing,' Sylvia was shouting, pulling the full tray from his hands, visibly restraining herself in order to avoid spilling the tea or the cover plate that kept the bacon warm from sliding onto the floor. 'I'll take it up myself.' He'd need to concentrate.

'Mrs McClean's tray is ready except for the tea. Pour the water in when it boils. At least you know where her room is.'

He was halfway up the basement stairs when Sylvia stopped him. 'Mrs McC has gone out. Put the tray back on the kitchen table with a tea towel over it for William. He'll be home at seven. And Mr McC is having supper out.'

'What about my tea?' he asked, the smell of the bacon reminding him he hadn't eaten all day.

'Come straight up to the bar,' she said, reaching to take the shopping change from the tray.

The woman in the delicatessen had been wearing a blue shop-coat and told him that Mrs McClean had been her customer for more than twenty years.

'A great woman for a jar of olives after a morning browsing in Brown Thomas, occasionally with a single purchase clutched to her side.'

He'd resisted telling her his mother had nursed a desire to burn down BTs when she was a young one because of the spoilt princesses who shopped there. 'I hate olives,' he'd said instead.

'Ah, you'll grow to like them,' she said. 'You have the look of a connoisseur in the making.'

Julian's first customer was a large farmer type whose shirt was pulled so tight around his middle that the lips of his navel seemed to be stretching forward to suck on the cigarette burning in the ashtray. Three tiny women were looking at him adoringly, giggling and egging each other on. Despite their contrasting hair colours and clothes they really seemed to be one person who had only divided into three to take on the bulk of this farmer.

'Look at our little lounge boy,' the man said. 'Isn't he as neat as a suckling bonabh?' The women briefly allowed their eyes to flicker towards Julian before resuming their adoration.

'Bring us some fresh drinks like a good little bonabh,' he boomed at Julian, and the women giggled again. Johnner had gone through a phase of calling him a whippet, but no one had ever called him a piglet before. He looked at the farmer's tight shirt front for hints of squashed teats available for suckling. *Yugh.* He allowed his face to sympathise with the women, sniffing the air for the smell of manure.

'So, this is your new right-hand boy,' said a man sitting on the stool that had been occupied by Mayakovsky at lunch. He had a queeny voice and he looked Julian up and down just as Mayakovsky had done, but with more sneer than lust. Sylvia had swapped her lunchtime cardigan for a tight-fitting green dress. She was drying glasses and obviously trying to ignore the man whose elbows and hands were trespassing so far into the bar he could have rinsed his fingers in her washing water. Something about the two of them reminded Julian of an old married couple.

'I could do with a right-hand boy myself,' he said and waved an arm encased in plaster.

'Jack!' Sylvia said in a voice with warning in it.

'Now Sylvia. The plaster comes off tomorrow and I'll be back to my normal limp-wristed self after my six weeks of artificial stiffness.'

The farmer man shut up for the seconds immediately following the crack of Sylvia's teacloth very close to Jack's face.

Julian reached over the counter for the ashes bucket and backed away.

'Welcome to Curragh House,' Jack said, and raised his eyebrows at him before handing his glass to Sylvia. 'Be a darling and put another gin in that,' he said to her, and turned back to watch Julian empty ashtrays into his bucket and wipe them clean.

'I hope your credentials are up to scratch,' Jack said just after eight o'clock as Julian came to the counter with the glasses abandoned by the farmer and his lady friends. 'These detective boyos will find out soon enough if they're not.' Two burly-looking men in short coats entered the Porchester Lounge and looked at each of the occupants in turn. One of them, chewing something in his left cheek, nodded and pointed a finger in Julian's direction, a silent *stay where you are*. Were they following up on Malone's arrest? Looking for his bag? Coming for Julian? He gripped the counter to steady himself.

'Sylvia, I think your skinny lounge boy is not so keen on the boys in blue.'

The men turned back out to the hall and a slimmer, slighter man passed through and up the stairs.

'Or is he awed by the sight of the great Giolla-Íosa McClean, TD?'

When the two men re-entered they nodded at Sylvia and positioned themselves by the window overlooking the front steps and the street.

'Go down to the kitchen,' Sylvia said, 'and make a pot of coffee and two rounds of cheese and ham sandwiches for the detectives. Hurry now.'

His breath came back to him on the stairs and he rubbed his hands together. The feds would be fed, but it would cost. Sandwiches for the detectives would require a mini-gastronomic sensation for the plucky lounge-boy writer. A pot of watery coffee would pay for research without restraint, the run of the shabby kitchen, enough time to open every door, every drawer, listening for every story. Except he felt steered about the kitchen, guided from cupboard to larder to fridge to cutting board, the correct drawer seeming to open itself as the bread, the fillings, the condiments, the cutlery, the coffee, came leaping into his hands, first time, and in the order required.

The two detectives were continuing their surveillance of the street when Julian got back to the Porchester Lounge. But the coffee pot rocked, and liquid spurted out onto the table as he placed the round tray between them.

'Jesus Christ,' the younger of them said, and pushed his chair away to avoid the dripping liquid.

'You've had a lucky escape, young man,' the older detective said as he leaned his face into Julian's, spraying him with toffee-smelling spittle. Was he talking about the spilt coffee? Or had Mrs McClean reported his unexpected appearance at the hotel, demanding a job? Or had she suggested a link with the knife-wielding glove puppet? Or had Malone told the Gardaí about his bag and the boy who took it? Plenty of time for them to make a connection to the arrest in Busárus and dispatch two detectives to carry out observations. Any moment now they'd kick him to the floor and snap the handcuffs on before he could say, it's all a mistake – I don't even know him.

'A very lucky escape indeed,' the younger one said, delaying the moment, staring at the belt buckle holding up his trousers – Malone's belt, Malone's trousers – then lifting his eyes to Julian's face. He'd have used his training to deduce why the belt was drawn two notches tighter than the only visibly worn notch, Julian stepping back as the man's hand moved. Was he going to grab the belt and twist the buckle up for his colleague to see? *Our little suspect is not wearing his own trousers. Shall I ask him why, sir?*

But instead he put sugar into his cup and slowly poured the coffee, watching the grains melt. 'A nice how-do-you-do if my coat is covered in coffee stains when the Taoiseach-in-waiting has to be driven home,' he said.

Fuck Malone, Julian thought as he wiped the spillage, checking the younger detective's middle for signs of a holstered gun. He's turned me into a twitching *wreck*.

'Deputy McClean is very insistent: "The presentation of the parade ground is required at all times."'

He had to learn to take things in his stride, the way Malone did. It wasn't just the shirt and trousers he'd borrowed. He needed to have Malone's attitude as well. Show the world a calm exterior no matter what was going on inside. He flicked his cloth at the sandwich crumbs that had fallen onto the lap of the younger detective, making the man look ready to defend himself. Julian smiled cheekily at him. 'Remember the parade ground.'

'I hope you appreciate that the Taoiseach-in-waiting is in the house,' he said to a couple who'd arrived while he'd been in the kitchen. He lifted the woman's handbag to wipe under it and curled his lip slightly at the man, who looked familiar, maybe someone from the television. Over at the bar Jack was watching him and fiddling with the frayed edges of his plaster cast.

Summer of Unrequited Love

THE ERRANT CHAMBERMAID

'33 to '39

Josie Geoghan never noticed herself checking the stomachs of the ladies who came to see Nurse Cadden until she overheard the woman in red gloves accusing her of staring. Hardly a surprise if she did, when they stood on the doorstep of the Rathmines house letting her guess the reason for their visit, and she barely finished with Sister Dymphna but very pleased to be in Dublin and in charge of opening the door to visitors for the clinic.

'I'm here to have my dandruff treated,' a woman might mutter while Josie held the opened basement door. Or, 'Does the nurse do warts?' The braver ones would mouth 'women's trouble', while only a rare brazen thing would push the door in on Josie without a glance back up the basement area steps to see if anyone was watching. And why would Josie not check for signs that she had warts or dandruff or women's troubles, and Josie herself standing in the waiting room, helpless, looking as if it was she that should know what was to be done.

'I'm not Nurse Cadden, you know. But Nurse Cadden's assistant,' she would say, although her assistance was mostly provided outside the treatment room. She was in charge of the front door, the waiting room, and the kitchen to make a cup of tea for the ladies when their treatment was finished, or earlier sometimes if Nurse Cadden decided. But she wasn't a parlourmaid. And the woman with the red gloves shouldn't have called her that. She was a trainee midwife. Nurse Cadden had promised to get her into the maternity hospital to start proper training, and in the meanwhile she could help out with her visitors. Nurse Cadden was good to her. She liked being her assistant.

Josie had shown the woman in red gloves into the waiting room, invited her to sit down on one of the comfortable chairs and pointed at the magazines. But the woman ignored the chairs, and stood with her coat open, pulling at each fingertip on the left hand in turn, before sweeping the red leather off in a whip and starting on the other glove. All the while looking at Josie instead of at her hands, as if Josie was a naughty schoolgirl, and she the reverend mother, waiting for an explanation. It was she who wanted the service, so it would be natural for Josie to give an involuntary glance up and down the opened coat for a suggestion as to why she wanted to see Nurse.

'Your parlourmaid was staring at me,' the woman said to Nurse Cadden before Josie had closed the door of the ground-floor treatment room. 'Far too cheeky for her place.' She squeezed her red gloves together in one hand, the empty fingers wagging as she spoke.

After that, Josie made sure to look at every visitor's stomach. Not immediately the hall door was opened, because coats covered a multitude, and sometimes a woman would hesitate over her coat and Josie would have to step forward and say,

'Nurse Cadden can't see you with that on, now can she?' And help with buttons before allowing her eyes to sweep downwards. 'You're not showing yet, thank God' caused one or two women to burst into tears, but mostly it sent flattening hands to smooth out stomachs.

'I think you're too far gone,' she told a mousy woman wearing a corset, and gave her a little poke under her ribcage. Then she swept the woman's coat off and flung it onto a chair.

After some visitors, Nurse Cadden would say, 'The sheet in the treatment room needs changing,' and right enough there would be blood or other stains and Josie would steep the sheet in cold water for a little while before boiling it in a big pot over the Rayburn, having already mopped the lino clean of any drips. Her favourite job was bringing the instruments and the white enamel bowls down to the kitchen to boil.

It was a cold, late winter's afternoon the first time Nurse Cadden came into the kitchen and asked Josie to open the burner door. She held a paper bag out in front of herself and pushed it in on top of the hot coals. The smell from the Rayburn was usually no worse than burnt eggshells, and only noticeable if Josie had let the fire die down and the wetness and the size of the bag overwhelmed the coals, forcing smoke out of the burner into the kitchen to make Josie cough and to fleck any clothes drying on the line in the back area with black smuts.

After she'd closed the door, and while the woman in the red gloves was being examined, she'd waited, listening, and heard the woman say, 'Those don't look very clean. I could get an infection from dirty instruments.'

The ungrateful bitch.

Dolly Considine's Hotel

THE END OF HIS FIRST SHIFT

19th June 1983

The clock behind the bar was showing midnight when Sylvia told Julian to let the two detectives know: 'He'll be down in a minute.' Eager to get a look at the man who'd spent the evening with Mrs McClean, he was holding the Porchester Lounge door when the shouting and sounds of scuffles began in the hallway, only calming after Mr Mayakovsky was bundled onto the sticky carpet at his feet and the door snatched closed by the younger detective.

'Lounge boy,' Mr Mayakovsky said, 'kindly escort me to a chair, I need to rest. And bring me vodka, ice cold, no lemon. I suppose those delicious sandwiches from lunchtime are all gone?'

Sylvia had the drink ready and gave him three packets of crisps. 'Tell him it's all we have.'

'Do me a favour and open those. Ripping crisp-bags makes my teeth water.'

'I'll do one now and keep an eye on your consumption,' Julian said.

'To your shadow prime minister, better known as the Real Taoiseach, and to Ireland,' the man said as he raised the glass to his lips. 'It's a wonderful country, but the people need jobs, not referendums.'

'My mother's exact words,' Julian said, 'except she says referenda.'

'I look forward to meeting her,' Mr Mayakovsky said. He was drunk, and his eyes blinked as he stared. 'She sounds like a smart cookie.'

Like many Derry mothers, Malone's would have worried about her son being picked up and questioned. Might even have had numbers for solicitors at the ready, though probably none in Dublin. Had he used his permitted phone call to let her know? Julian's own mother carried a little card explaining what to do if it happened to her.

'Aye,' he said three times to test his recollection of Malone's actual accent, and not just those of the men he heard complaining on television. 'She's that okay,' but then there was the matter of putting the words into the way northerners spoke. 'My mammy is that. Aye, Mr Mayakovsky.'

'You can call me Max.'

'Is that what your mother calls you?'

'She called me Mikhail. But most Irish people find that a mouthful.' His empty hand reached for Julian's, his skin rough for a man who sat around theatres and drank vodka all day.

When Julian's father ran off to live in England, the man who owned the corner shop, and known locally as Grocer Jack, took to holding Julian's hand when he reached for the shopping money. 'How is your mother managing?' he would ask, his free fingers fiddling out of sight, but his eyes looking at Julian. 'You should tell her to call in and see me,' he always said, as he pushed a bit of broken nougat into Julian's mouth as if he was a sweet-loving child. The shopkeeper's hands had been soft and silky smooth compared to Mikhail Mayakovsky's.

'I am a troubled artist,' Mikhail said. 'Troubled and tortured.'

He tried to use his grip on Julian's fingers to rise out of the bucket chair, but Julian rejected the strain.

'I am hounded, and maligned, and treated cruelly, by your fellow country people.' He pulled on Julian's hand to stand up. His voice rose and his glass, drained of its vodka, shook in the air, the ice rattling against the sides.

'Julian,' Sylvia shouted. Both of them turned to look at her. 'Stop tormenting Mr Mayakovsky.'

Julian's fingers were released, and the man sank back into the chair. 'Get me another vodka,' he said. 'Do be a darling.'

When Julian returned from the kitchen with Irish coffees for an American couple who'd gushed into the 'quaint little hotel' well after two, Mrs McClean was clapping her hands and announcing that the bar was closed. Her make-up cleaned off now, she looked ready for a fight. Mikhail Mayakovsky had been asleep in his bucket seat by the window for an hour, his glass tilted in his hand, the ice melted and dripping onto the carpet.

'Wake that man up,' Mrs McClean said, and reached her hands out for the glasses clutched by the two nearest stragglers. 'If you'd been doing your job Julian, this man would be passing out at his own hotel, not in mine.'

Julian tried to look crestfallen. 'Wake up, Mr Mayakovsky. Time to go home. The bar is closed. Wakey wakey.' He reached into the pockets of the long Astrakhan coat to check for a hotel key.

'What are you doing, Julian?' Mrs McClean grabbed his hand and snatched it from the man's pocket.

'Finding out where he is staying.'

'Well, you shouldn't go fumbling through other people's pockets unless it's trouble you're looking for.'

'Yes, Mrs McClean.'

'He always stays at the Shelbourne. You'd better walk him round the Green.'

'How will I get back in?'

She turned away. 'Come along Sylvia. Close up the bar and go to bed. Brendan can clean up in the morning. It's nearly three; I have to be up at seven.'

'Mrs McClean, what am I to do with Mr Mayakovsky?'

'That's your affair, Julian. You should have kept Sylvia informed about his drinking, and she would have stopped serving him. Do your job. How dare you allow a man to fall asleep in full view of our guests? How dare you? Now goodnight.'

Sylvia left the bar through the Kickham Room, turning all the lights out as she went.

'Come on Mr Major Cockski, wake up. You can't sleep here.' Because shaking the man did not work, he first tried to lift him to his feet, which caused him to slip further down the chair, and then to jolt him back up with the help of his trouser belt. But the chair tipped over and the man rolled out and toppled the stooping Julian to the floor. The face of Mikhail Mayakovsky lit by the streetlight, leering down at him, and awake.

'What are you doing to me?' he said. 'What are you doing to me? What are you doing to me?' His voice getting louder with each utterance. He would be screeching in a second, Mrs McClean rushing back to investigate. Julian pulled the face down towards him. He couldn't scream if he was being kissed. The next 'What are you do… ?' tapering off into a mumble. The man's tongue in Julian's mouth before the mumble finished. And then amazingly he was not just awake, but was up on his feet, moving like a boxer limbering up for a fight, as if the act of twisting his tongue in Julian's mouth had rewound him like a depleted clockwork toy.

'Josie's room. That's the place. I have the key,' he said. 'Help me,' and he put his arm around Julian's shoulders and stumbled up the stairs to the first floor. There was a bit of bumbling with the lock, and then the pair of them were inside, and Julian slipped out of the man's crooked arm to record what he was seeing.

'Sylvia lets me stay here if it's been a long night,' he said.

The room was colder than the landing; it smelt damp, and a bare low-watt bulb over the bed made it look like a seedy black and white movie. The bed itself was a single, sunk in the middle like a cartoon bed. The pale quilt hanging to the floor covered the void beneath, but Julian hadn't checked under his bed for years.

The kissing had been repulsive. Now what was he supposed to do? Encourage the man to lie down, hope he falls asleep before anything else happens? All the quicker if he sat on the bed and tried not to look like he was bracing himself for Mikhail's bulk, or if he stretched out, all the easier to roll to the far side and off onto the floor.

But with the dusty Astrakhan coat dropped onto the carpet, Mikhail pulled Julian up off the bed.

'Not yet, not yet. We have to pay our respects to Josie,' he said, closing his eyes and joining his hands. 'Dear Josie, thank you for letting us use your room. We hope that wherever you are tonight you have found peace, and that your killers are being tormented.' He opened his eyes to look at Julian and nodded. 'Say it,' he whispered after several nods. 'Say it. You're Catholic, aren't you?'

'Say what?' They weren't at fucking Mass. What was there to say? Amen? 'Amen,' he said.

'Amen.' Mikhail said it too, and buried Julian beneath him on the dusty bed.

Summer of Unrequited Love

THE ERRANT CHAMBERMAID... SAYS A PRAYER

Jun '52

Woolworths in Grafton Street was closing for the day as Josie Geoghan stopped for a rest. Her arms were tired from carrying the hotel manageress's shopping. She'd had to go to a second Home & Colonial to find honey-in-the-comb for Mrs Burns. A porter was lifting shutter panels from a handcart and sliding them into the tracks and scowled to warn her not to cause an obstruction with her shopping bags.

'Please Jesus,' she'd whispered when she stopped for a prayer in Johnston's Court Church, 'losing a baby is a bad thing but it won't be his fault if he's born. If anyone is to blame, it's me for being taken in by Mr O'Brien or Mr O'Brien for not treating me properly. I would rather die than give up my baby. And I know that killing myself would be a sin, but I would never do it anyway. It's just a saying, but if you gave me the choice of dying or having my baby adopted, then I would prefer to die.'

She waited until the shutters were in place on Woolworths' right-hand door before she stepped up to lean against the jamb. She sniffed the air for Mr O'Brien's carbolic smell, more transported by the memory of the one dance they'd had, than she'd been when she was in his arms. She knew she was being foolish, particularly when she was suffering the consequences of what started that night.

She'd only stopped to take a stone out of her shoe, and only leaned against Woolworths' shuttered front doors for support. She hadn't known Mr O'Brien was behind her.

'Hello Josie,' he'd said.

One waltz around the Clerys ballroom and she'd thanked him, saying no to a follow-up, a quickstep. 'If the manageress found out I was dancing with you, and you a resident in the hotel, I'd be out of a job,' she'd said, and went back to her friend Maureen, who worked at the Central Hotel in Wicklow Street. Maureen was as fond of lecturing Josie about having more fun as she was of the dangers of fun. 'They think that because I'm a slavey,' Maureen was fond of saying, 'they can click their fingers and I'll do what they want.' Maureen could just as easily have said the opposite, but every sermon ended the same. 'No one is going to dump me in a hostel in Sean MacDermott Street with fifty other girls in trouble, thank you very much.' After which she was as likely to laugh as she was to look bitter.

'I'm not following you,' Mr O'Brien had said. 'This is my way home too. Have you hurt your foot? Twisted your ankle with all that dancing? I watched after you refused me. You hardly sat down all evening.' He reached out to take her elbow and lifted her towards him.

'Thank you, Mr O'Brien, I can manage very well. Goodnight.'

'Josie,' he said, 'your manageress can't accuse you of

fraternising with the guests when we're both going in the same
direction.'

'You don't know Mrs Burns.'

'A disappointed woman, I think,' he said. 'Hm?'

'Disappointed or not, Mr O'Brien, I need my job,' she said,
and walked on. In her haste to get away she hadn't removed
the stone from her shoe that had allowed him to speak to her in
the first place.

Clerys ballroom had been packed with girls laughing,
nudging each other and shaking their hair out of their faces as
they waited for the next dance: a ladies' choice, a snowball, or
a Paul Jones that gave everyone a chance and no one had to
feel left out. But when Mr O'Brien leaned into the doorway
of Woolworths to try and pull her towards him, the whiff of
his carbolic insisted she recall the warmth that had radiated
through his shirt, as well as the steadying embrace forced on
her when he'd tripped over his own foot. Even with the
swirling smoke and the drunken belches from other dancers,
it was the disinfectant of carbolic that had triumphed. Now,
here on Grafton Street with the few stragglers walking and
dawdling in shop doors, his virtuous Lifebuoy confirmed that
the slow misguided cycle around the ballroom had been the
dance of her life.

Thankfully his footsteps were a decent distance behind, but
his eyes would be watching her back as she moved, the lower
part of her calves visible below the hem of her coat. She could
feel herself leaning into him again to let his chest and arms
hold her upright. The stone was still digging into her foot, but
it would give him encouragement if she stopped again. Three
louts from the vegetable stalls on Camden Street recognised her
as she walked past the Dr Scholl's shop with her hair down and
her scarf in her pocket because she'd been too warm when she

left Clerys. 'Put your scarf on,' Maureen had told her as they parted at the bottom of Wicklow Street, but she hadn't.

The tallest of the louts blew smoke in her direction but she focused her eyes on the footpath and smelt more than saw it. Mr O'Brien was singing behind her. Had it been her singing, the louts would have jeered. But he was entitled, even on the street. She didn't recognise the tune at first, but then remembered she'd danced to it. '(It's No) Sin'. She didn't think the priest would agree because although she'd been concentrating on keeping him upright during his wobbling waltz, here on Grafton Street she'd turned him into a perfect dancer. His fingers pressing firmly into her back, not quite cheeky, but very low for a waltz. His chest, braced against hers, lifting and swirling her off her feet. His breath warm on her ear, his lips against her neck as she crossed the road towards the Shelbourne Hotel side of the Green, busier and better lit than if she walked around by the university.

The song's chorus, loudly proclaiming beating hearts and forever love, echoed through the street. Jesus, he'd shame her with his carry on. If she walked more quickly, she might lose him, but the stone was cutting the inside of her heel. She leaned her ankle over to avoid walking on it. Then she kicked the protruding bottom step of the St Stephen's Green Club to dislodge it, but wobbled enough to give him the right to run up and catch her around the waist, even after her equilibrium had been fully restored.

'Mr O'Brien, please cut that out now.'

'I thought you didn't see the step, Josie, and were going to fall.'

'I'm perfectly all right, thank you,' she said.

The door to the club opened and several laughing men emerged.

'Tally ho,' a man in a cravat and expensive-looking suit

shouted, and she was mortified to think it might be at her. Her father had embarrassed her, shouting outside her school, demanding to see Sister Dymphna the day after she'd slapped Josie. He'd sold a calf that morning, and been in the pub, which had sent him to remonstrate with the nuns instead of going home with a cardboard box of shopping. The head nun had made her take him away, and he kept saying that if Sister Dymphna had been a man, he would have boxed her ears. She'd returned to school for domestic science, and it was Josie's ears that were boxed, and her sponge cake hadn't risen.

It was nice being fussed over, even if he was making a show of her on the street. But thankfully kicking that step had sent the stone up between her toes and let her walk on.

'Are you okay, miss?' the Woolworths man asked after installing the final panel. 'You look faint.' He'd come stooping out of the low door set into the shutter, releasing the smell of the ice-cream machine just inside.

'No, I'm…' Her stomach remembered giving breakfast back that morning, but she hadn't eaten since, so there was nothing left except bile. 'I'm fine, thank you.' And she stepped out into the centre of the footpath. Mrs Burns's six tins of peas and a large jar of butter beans, as well as the grapefruits Josie hadn't been able to get at Camden Street that morning, were dragging down her arms. She followed the same route she'd walked that first night with Mr O'Brien, and just as slowly once he'd kissed her outside the auctioneers. He'd kissed her again opposite the bottom end of Hume Street as he pressed her against the railings surrounding the Green. And when she opened her eyes she saw, halfway up the street, a woman looking around as if to see if anyone was watching her before stepping up to a door and waiting to be let in.

'Someone for Nurse Cadden,' Josie had muttered, remembering Maureen's tales of women dying after being treated by Nursie, and she pushed Mr O'Brien away. It was not going to happen to her.

Summer of Unrequited Love

ALL MESMERISED WITH THINKING ABOUT THE ESCAPE FROM THE EVIL BEDROOM

Jun '83

'Don't take it personally. That's the way Mr Mayakovsky is. You mustn't let him make you angry. Especially when you're not settled into your new job yet.'

The voice was not in his head. But the room was empty except for Julian standing on the frayed green rug and Mr Mayakovsky, taking up the whole bed, snoring.

'I'm not angry,' he hissed as he groped about the floor for his trousers. He had to get out. Julian Bertram Ryder was not going to waste his life being angry, even if he was angry, which he wasn't. Unless maybe he'd inhaled anger along with the alcohol fumes from Mayakovsky's breath or was being buffeted by leftover anger stored in the room. Whatever was making him feel funny didn't matter. It would subside once he was outside.

'It was just sex.' Sex with a drunk who'd been briefly awake, then back asleep before his shudders of pleasure had subsided, curled into a self-protective recovery position after pushing

Julian out of the tiny bed. He'd remember nothing about it in the morning.

Julian was sick with the tiredness of being awake for nearly twenty-four hours. It wasn't supposed to be like this. Johnner's promises about their adventure had never conjured up visions of him washing his cock in a sink in a seedy hotel in Dublin and drying it on a dusty curtain, and making his hands gritty, and his nose itch. Nor had he imagined a disembodied voice saying: 'Pick up your shoes and make your way back to your room. Everything will be all right after a little sleep.'

Mayakovsky's incantation and yelps may have summoned the ghost of Josie, but had the noises coming from room eleven alerted Mrs McClean? There'd be pursed lips from Sylvia and thumps from Brendan, if they'd heard. Unless it was expected. Part of the service. *First dibs on the new lounge boy.*

'Fuck 'em. Fuck 'em all.' He'd only kissed Mayakovsky to stop him shouting for help and waking everyone in the hotel. And it would have finished there, except Mayakovsky had said, 'Upstairs, now. Come on.'

Being upstairs was what Julian wanted; to be escorted into the secret laden rooms, and allowed to hear the old voices, and to uncover the stories. Maybe even encounter a former occupant. And when Mr Mayakovsky had made him join in the 'Thank you Josie', like grace before meals, he'd thought, what happens now? Will Josie appear? And while he listened and waited, the man's tongue had forced its way into his mouth like a distraction.

The unearthly 'You've had an adventure now, sir, and you'll sleep all the better for it' was right: he'd never have slept without relieving himself, in the dark gents to avoid Brendan. He should be feeling gratitude, not whatever the feelings were that were raging in him now. So they must not belong to him.

And his fingers were not stuck to the doorknob, it was just that his brain had forgotten how to make them work.

'Now sir, it's been a long night. A corridor is no place for a tired young man. All mesmerised with recalling the escape from the evil bedroom, like the heroine in a mushy love story.'

He could hear noises coming from Mrs McClean's bedroom. In a second or two she'd emerge in her nightdress and discover his glued fingers, Mr Mayakovsky beyond, visible and audible.

Have you been in that room, Julian?

And yet his fingers were released, his elbow gripped, and his whole self moved along like he was on castors and didn't need to lift his feet, the smell of mothballs and musty clothes rising as he reached the top step. All pitch dark below, except for the light from the street coming through the glass in the front door and making a silhouette of the wrought iron foliage protecting it. 'Now young sir, let's get you back to your quarters. All over now. No harm done. Discretion: that's what's needed. Never did anyone any harm. Not at all.'

His foot was surprised at the firmness of the topmost step, the whispers so close to his ear he strove to feel the inevitable breath while dreading there might be spittle.

'Have you tucked up in your own bed in no time, sir. No one any the wiser. A little lie-in after your exertions is what you deserve. Followed by a big breakfast and some fresh air in St Stephen's Green to clear your head. That's the cure for everything, sir: a little fresh air.'

The fumbling at Mrs McClean's door warned it was about to open, but he was far enough down the stairs now not to be seen unless they leaned over the banister, the projected streetlight patterning his bare feet as he passed the hall door. He'd allowed himself to be distracted from listening to the stories in room eleven, but he would be back. He wanted them all, they were his, he was greedy for them. Less greedy for the taste of Mikhail's breath stuck in his nostrils like an alien membrane that would have to be scraped off and flushed down the toilet.

'You're not the first, my lad. Not by a long shot. And you won't be the last.'

A hacking cough could be heard from the bathroom above, and the sound of a man pissing. The light from its open door casting weak, grainy shadows.

His elbow fell as if it had been released. 'Thank you, Josie,' he whispered when he reached the Porchester Lounge. He stood for several seconds allowing something to drain out of him, then turned as if Paddy the Porter should be waiting to escort him onwards to the boys' bedroom.

Dolly Considine's Hotel

CAN WATER CROSS THE REAL WORLD/DREAM WORLD BARRIER?

19th June 1983

In a dream, it would be such a cliché; the basement hallway stretching into an endless prison corridor marked by a long rhythm of missing light bulbs, bird-stained concrete flooring, steel doors on both sides, one per stride, right left, right left, each of them resisting his tugs and shoulders until, like Alice falling down the rabbit hole, Julian finds himself swinging into Malone's bare brick cell. His new friend has his back to the high-barred, yellow-grimed window, is huddling in whispers with corduroy man and the other plain-clothes officer who arrested Malone in the bus station.

The door shudders closed behind him, and the detectives lift Julian without effort and drop him onto a green steel chair with a splintered plywood seat. Malone moves to stand in front of him, a table between, the green leather inlay decorated with carved initials. Malone is in green too, his uniform the cut and colour of the 1916 displays in the museum on remembered schooldays out. Even down to the buttons being leather, but the cap isn't sitting as jauntily as Julian thinks it should be.

Corduroy man hands him the broken pieces of Blind Willie McTell's 'Lord Have Mercy, If You Please', and the other one bumps a record player across the table towards Julian. The turntable is revolving, and the warm burning air is filled with static hum.

Malone puts one hand on the green inlay and leers towards Julian's face. Four other plain-clothes men arrange themselves in a symmetrical fan behind him before he speaks. 'I don't know this tune,' he says, and pulls the cap-peak down over his eyes. 'And my mammy doesn't know it either. But she wants you to play it. To show how you respect the people of Derry. Play it for us now, if you please.' His voice is menacing, and he spits each word into Julian's face.

Julian examines the broken bits of his brother's most valuable record. He wants to tell Malone about his mother throwing petrol bombs when the British Embassy was burnt after Bloody Sunday. But who is Malone working for? Whose uniform is he wearing? Why does he want the music? Does he want to dance?

He assembles the fragments on the turntable, but when he lowers the playing arm it skips and jumps and catches in a crack and drags a piece off the sticky rubber. It was the special branch man that knelt on his bag and broke the record. Blind Willie could still sing in their heads, but dancing without music would look silly. 'I can hum it if you like, and we could dance,' he whispers in a voice too low to be heard.

'Prove your respect,' Malone says, and sweeps the player onto the floor. There are sparks and the static hum dies. 'Tell us about your mother.'

His mother? Why? What about her? 'It's all in my short

story,' he blurts out. 'My first short story. I wrote it when I was eight.'

'What's this seminal work called?' Malone says. His voice is softer, and he leans away just a little, all the better for the friendly smile creeping over his face to be seen.

'"My Mammy was Throwing Petrol Bombs".'

There is a silence while Malone and the others seem to consider the title. None of them move.

'Right,' Malone says after an age. He turns his head to corduroy man. 'Send a car round for the woman. And search the house for the story. Then throw this one out. It's been eleven years but at last we know the truth.'

And to his shame Julian wants Malone to go on speaking; to go on towering over him in his uniform, leaning in and out as he moves between menace and tolerance. 'Can I have some water?' he asks because they're the only words he can think of. A plain-clothes man in jeans and a paint-stained T-shirt fills a tin mug from a green enamel jug and advances towards him. But instead of putting it into Julian's outstretched hand, he pours it over his lap.

'That'll cool your ardour,' the man says and smirks at Malone for approval.

It's not possible for water to cross the dream world/real world barrier, but it wakes him up as it soaks through to his legs, the evidence conclusive, like the time when his brother took him camping and the rain coming into the tent made him cry and beg to go home. He leaps from the bed, Brendan pissing on him while he slept easier to believe than that he's pissed himself.

Dolly Considine's Hotel

NORMAL SERVICE IS RESUMED

19th June 1983

'I've never wet the bed,' Julian announced to Mr and Mrs Hannafins' loaded breakfast tray as he climbed the stairs. 'Why would I start now?'

A squirt of tea flew from the teapot as he turned at the top of the stairs, and the upside-down plates over the two cooked breakfasts slid towards his stomach. He stopped to listen outside room eleven for any sound of Mikhail still sleeping. But shouting from the Hannafins' room encouraged him along there.

His older brother had wet the bed when their father went to live in England. Christopher claimed it was a leaking hot water bottle or the rain coming through the window, which was as believable as his mother telling them their father would be home for Christmas. But then one day his mother was shouting as she came through the front door, 'Get down here the pair of you.' Not even bothering to take off her coat or put down her shopping. Her words coming out in spurts with shaking breaths between.

'No more secrets... My husband is gone... Your father is gone... He's never coming back... I will never take him back. And tonight, you are not going to wet the bed.... Do you hear me?'

And Christopher said, 'It's all his fault,' pointing at him. 'He wrote the lies that made Daddy leave. Otherwise everything would be the same.' He didn't mention his own wetting the bed.

His mother sent him into the kitchen so she could have a grown-up talk with Christopher in the front room. He didn't mind. He might be only nearly nine, but he knew things Christopher didn't know. So what if the story in his copybook made Daddy go to England? He sent money home every week, and they never had to listen to him shouting.

His school bag was on the kitchen table, so he took out his copybook. '*The Leaking Hot Water Bottle*', he wrote at the top of a new page and was hunting for a first line of a story about a boy who wet the bed, when his mother came into the room.

'You have to help Christopher to be the man of the house,' she announced, gave him a hug, and asked what he wanted for his tea. He never finished the story about Christopher because in school the next day he found the page was torn out.

The Hannafins' door was opened by a woman in an orange dressing gown that needed washing.

'Are you new?' she asked.

'I suppose so.' His legs were clammy from the wet sheet. He didn't feel new. He held the tray out to her, unsure if she would take it or open the door wider to let him put it down.

'Do you have a name?'

'Pa–Pa–Julian.'

'Pa Pa Julian? Are you foreign?'

'No, it's just Julian. I – sometimes stutter in new situations,' and he smiled. He would have to stop forgetting about his new name.

'Where's my sock?' a voice shouted from behind her, and she opened the door fully and stepped backwards into the room.

'Put it down there,' she said, pointing at a table already set for two. The cutlery and dishes Sylvia told him to bring were not needed. His father had always ignored the cup and saucer his mother set for him and drank his tea from his own special mug. He took it with him when he went to England, or maybe his mother smashed it.

'Would you like me to…'

Julian hesitated. The weak bulb above the head of the man in the single bed facing him picked out the glowing white of one complete leg and the red tip of the other. The stump's angry face stared, and the cover plates clattered onto the Hannafins' array of condiments and the contents of a YR Sauce bottle trickled out onto the tablecloth.

'Get him out of here,' the man said, 'and then find my sock. I can hardly turn up at the castle saying I'm late because my wife didn't lay out my sock. Most women have to provide two socks. But all I demand is one. And even that is apparently too much to ask.'

'I'll pick up the tray later,' Julian said as he held the doorknob. But he lingered to suck the room into his head. It was a stage set: ready for a story from the 1920s. The wallpaper, the furniture, the ceiling, the three pictures of Michael Collins hanging over the fireplace, even the two elderly people; everything was moving towards the same shade of brown, except for the man's glowing one and a half legs. The room smelt of talcum powder and sweat. Sixty years of underarms and crotches that needed to be scrubbed with carbolic. He looked at Mrs Hannafin and tried to imagine her being turned on by her stale, angry husband. He pulled the door after him and turned quickly to ensure that Josie was not lurking on the landing, waiting to push him down the stairs for his bad thoughts.

Summer of Unrequited Love

THE ERRANT CHAMBERMAID... LOOKS FOR HELP

Jun '52

The house in Rathmines had always looked freshly decorated, but the Hume Street hall door had peeling paint, and several bars were missing from the railing meant to stop people from falling down into the basement area. Josie was faced by more than a dozen bells, round, square and rectangular, and scattered over the face of the door like black, white and brown acne, instead of the one bell she remembered that had rung in the grand entrance hall as well as in the basement below.

Until her first night with Mr O'Brien she'd always cut through St Stephen's Green on her way to or from the shops in Grafton Street. But since then she followed their walk of love, although because it took longer it was only when she was off duty that she lingered at the places where he'd kissed her. Her station opposite the end of Hume Street (*Josie is kissed for the second time*) was polluted by thoughts of Nurse Cadden. She would be ordered to visit Nursie, the way Sister Dymphna had ordered her to the head nun's office for her punishments.

129

Helpless at the bottom of Hume Street every day, knowing she needed to go, but made defiant by her fear of Sister Dymphna and Nurse Cadden, even as she wanted to surrender to the urgency, and to their instructions. Somehow hoping that if she became less fearful, they would resolve the matter between them. She'd missed a second period. There could be no doubt. She'd seen what it did to Nurse Cadden's women, and she wasn't going to be like them.

Some of the bells had names or flat numbers written on sticky paper or carved into the paintwork. Her finger was hovering over a nameless printed sign, 'Chiropodist', and she was wondering if she would be able to bring herself to push the bell when the door began to open. Please, let it not be Nurse Cadden, she only wanted to find out if this was the right address. Everyone knew she'd had to keep moving since she came out of jail; she might even have given up her work. Breathing again when a much younger woman in a bright green coat said, 'Can I help you?' The woman wasn't smiling, and Josie noticed her eyes flicker to her stomach. She lifted her head and set her face into a friendly smile before she answered.

'I'm sure you can. I'm enquiring after Mamie Cadden actually. I believe she treats dandruff.'

'This is a respectable house. If you persist in looking for "treatment" here, both she and you will find yourselves run out of the place.'

'Do I look as if I have dandruff?' Josie said, touching her hair. 'It's for my friend Maureen. She suffers terribly. She's tried everything, and then she heard about Nurse Cadden.'

'Do you think it was cures for scaly scalp that got Nursie five years' hard labour? And the chemist shops filled with patent ointments?'

'My friend Maureen will be disappointed if I don't locate her. She's tried everything, and Nurse Cadden is—'

'You've got a bun in the oven,' the woman said. 'I can always tell, although any man that's laid a finger on the likes of you must be desperate.'

'Thank you,' Josie said. 'Thank you very much. I'll pass on your information about Nurse Cadden to my friend. It might encourage her to discuss her condition with her doctor instead of the chemist,' and she stepped backwards away from the door.

'Off you go,' the woman said, pulling the door closed, but waiting for Josie to move away. 'Take your enquiries elsewhere. Or, God forgive you, go to the holy nuns in the Magdalene Laundry, admit your sin, and beg forgiveness.'

'Good day to you,' Josie said from the footpath, trying to sound like Mrs Hannafin who boarded at the hotel with her one-legged hero of Ireland husband.

She contained her shaking until she got back to St Stephen's Green, the bags of shopping dragging her down so much she thought she'd faint. Her head was steaming under her scarf, and a cold hand was creeping from her waist up her back to her shoulders, where it began to squeeze icy fingers, Mr O'Brien's turned cold, against her neck and behind her ears. The retch rose from her empty stomach and whipped her head over the painted iron chain suspended between bollards to keep the traffic from straying onto the footpath. It produced nothing, but the sensation was worse than if a pint of bile had been projected.

The coldness and the paint-clogged steadiness of the ring linking the chain to the bollard helped her to breathe and to ignore the 'Are you okay, miss? Will I call someone, miss?' from a schoolboy swinging on the chain suspended between the next two bollards, his hands gripping links on either side to balance himself as he swung.

It may not have been Mr O'Brien's icy hand squeezing

her neck, but surely that was him coming towards her, his evening paper tucked under his arm, his salesman's sample case swinging to a halt as he dithered, crossed the road towards the Loreto convent and headed away from her as if he'd forgotten something. Back to the hotel no doubt, to pay his bill and rush home to Longford for a family emergency.

God bless his eyesight for spotting her distress so far away, and her own for not protecting her from seeing her abandonment. 'The curse of God on him,' she said to the boy, 'the whore's melt.'

Mr O'Brien lifted his hat as he passed the convent. A signal no doubt that she should throw herself on the nuns' mercy, not his. Well, she wasn't going to. The memory of Sister Dymphna's stinging slap could still force her head upright.

'Will I carry a bag for you?' the young fellow said, and reached for one, striding ahead when she released the grips, but then stopping for her to catch up.

'I don't miss my sister,' he said.

Josie's 'What?' out of her mouth before she could even wonder if he were simple.

'She went to England, but I don't miss her. Even when she didn't come home for Christmas. Mammy says she'll never come home. What do you think?'

When they reached the spot where Mr O'Brien had crossed the road, she looked over at the nuns' house. 'Yiz lucky fuckers,' she said, including the simple boy's sister for good measure. Josie didn't know anyone in England, leastways not anyone who would help her. She was on her own. Mr O'Brien would find a new hotel for his fortnightly trips to Dublin, and another dance hall for a new slavey.

'I'm going the other way,' the boy said when she started to cross towards Leeson Street, and he stepped backwards but held the bag out towards her. 'Are you going to give me a half-crown?' he asked.

She reached for the bag. Her purse was in it. She'd give him something.

'A half-crown,' he said. 'I want to send me sister a birthday card,' and he shook the bag to tempt her.

She stepped closer and reached, and he stepped further away, causing her to shake her head. She'd have to check if she had sixpence, but more was too much when all he'd done was walk one side of the Green with her. She was still shaking her head and reaching when the bag began to drop in slow motion onto the footpath, the sides holding their shape like the skirt on a woman falling to her knees.

'I'm sorry miss.' The crack of the large jar of butter beans distracted her from his sarcasm. The scut turning away from her as the burst salty water spread out around the bag in a wavy circle. Mrs Burns would be furious, but if Josie hurried back to the hotel she could rinse any broken glass off the butter beans and have them sitting in a bowl when the woman emerged from her office to toss her salad for her evening meal.

Dolly Considine's Hotel

JULIAN MEETS THE MCCLEAN SCION

19th June 1983

'All I want is a shower,' Julian hissed at the portrait of the master of the Ormond Hunt that hung on the wall outside the women's toilet. 'Amn't I entitled to wash and to change into clean underwear?' But the hunt master looked more interested in whipping his horse over the fence than in Julian.

Julian lifted the last of the McClean breakfast trays like an offering to the god of bathing as he rose up the stairs.

'My, are you the lucky boy?' a fair-haired, taller, wider youth of about his own age said when the family living room door opened. He reached for his breakfast but then drew back. 'Mummy always employs such ugly, skinny urchins,' he said, examining Julian's face. 'I'm convinced it's to remind me of how well fed, how handsome I am. That not everyone gets the opportunities I have. What do you think?'

'Can you smell something?' Julian asked. 'It's like piss. Has someone been... ?' He looked round the hall, sniffing.

'I understand from my studies that fresh urine is odour free,' the boy said. 'The smell develops when it is permitted to go stale.' He shut the door with his foot as he backed into the room.

Stale smells were crowding the landing; acrid, matured, and nothing to do with Julian. Instead they represented the lingering presences of those who'd stood on this very spot... A stooped old man unable to release the breakfast tray without his arthritic fingers being prised off it. A younger man with his ear to the door, listening to the sound of the woman he loves, inside betraying him with another man. The man's lips still moving to the words of the Five Sorrowful Mysteries, his fingers marking off the Our Father and each Hail Mary, each Glory Be on the rosary beads out of sight in his pocket.

'Julian, have you brought William his breakfast?' Mrs McClean said from behind him. The appliqué roses down the front of her pink dressing gown reminded him of the gaudy bushes outside the front door of his mother's neighbour's house in Cabra. The newspaper she was clutching announced that the coalition government was divided over the wording for the Pro-Life Referendum.

'Is it possible to take a bath, Mrs McClean?' he asked.

'Staff are permitted to shower in the second-floor bathroom between ten-thirty and eleven. Kindly retain the soap and the towel Sylvia gives you for your own personal use.' She pushed open her living room door and waited until he had turned towards the stairs before she closed it.

'Mrs McClean says I'm to have soap and a towel,' he said to Sylvia when he was back in the kitchen. Brendan was pacing up and down like a cinema simpleton with a secret, rubbing his hands together and his fingers through his hair, grinning and shaking his head to stop himself from blurting out the substance.

Sylvia sniffed. 'Yes, you need a wash. But I'm first. And

what about you Brendan? Don't you need a shower?' His head moved from side to side, his eyes dreamy as if gauging whether being in the shower immediately after Sylvia would be worth the trouble of taking off his clothes.

'Maybe,' he said. 'Maybe,' and his sneer suggested the secret would be revealed soon enough.

Fuck you, Julian smiled back in silence. I'm going to have a shower and get into the clean clothes lovingly folded by Malone's mother. You can't touch me, you thick culchie.

Sylvia handed him a threadbare towel with the colours drained to grey. 'There's no soap,' she said. 'You'll have to buy your own. Come on Brendan. We don't want to delay the new boy.' Her turn to sneer.

Julian searched under the kitchen sink and found an old bar of soap veined with black lines. But his swagger across the hall into the boys' bedroom was halted by the sight of Malone's clothes scattered across the room. The previously pristine T-shirts showed the marks of grinding shoes, and, whatever the source of the wetness, of having soaked filth from the carpet. The reason for Brendan's glee, exposed.

He lifted Malone's now empty soft brown bag from the floor, put his face into it, sniffed at the leather and let his cheek brush against the textured inside. He was putting it down on the bed when he noticed that the stiff sheet lining the bottom was not sitting right. His fingers hesitant and eager as he inserted them into a gap and lifted it. There would be secrets, the reason for Malone's arrest. But it was just books, neatly laid down in two lines. He'd seen the movies; the pages would be hollowed out and filled with drugs. Would he flush the evidence down the toilet, or go back to the bus station, put the bag in a locker and telephone someone? *Check out locker thirty-six.*

But Malone's books were intact. No hollows, no drugs. Only

the titles. *The Death of the Heart, The Demon Lover, Look At All Those Roses, A World of Love.* Twelve books with their spines unbroken, their pages unmarked. No reason to be hidden, unless Malone was ashamed of reading what Julian's father called mushy fiction. He remembered his shower, he needed washing, he picked the cleanest of the clothes.

'Why did Malone have to spoil everything by having you?' he asked the innocent-looking young woman's face on the cover of *The Death of the Heart*. 'You can be cousins to Brendan's girly magazines. The thicko will find you on the windowsill and rip you up.' Outside, the sound of church bells seemed to seal his mood, but as he stepped out into the hall he tried to convince himself that the bells might be ringing with some kind of good news.

Summer of Unrequited Love

THE ERRANT CHAMBERMAID... FILLS IN THE LAUNDRY LIST

Jun '52

'Men will use you and discard you,' Sister Dymphna had warned, and if she'd got her hands on Josie now, she'd have sent her to the laundry nuns – the way she'd sent her to the headmistress – and her baby somewhere else. And as soon as Mrs Burns noticed Josie's tummy beginning to bulge, she'd do the same.

The form she was filling in, recording the numbers of sheets, bolster cases, tablecloths and aprons going into the hotel's laundry bags, had the convent address in bold print at the bottom. It was girls like her that kept the place going. What could the nuns do to her, except take her in? Of course, they'd make her confess everything, and beg forgiveness, although there'd be no need to mention trying to find out where Nurse Cadden lived. Thinking a bad thing wasn't the same as doing it. Even Jesus had allowed the devil to take him up on a height and show him the possibilities. The state of Josie's soul was between her and God, and if she went to confession it would be wiped clean. She supposed the laundry's pastor would be like the travelling Lenten priest, sneaking round looking for signs of forbidden dances, and giving the pulpit lectern a good old banging as he filled their heads with stories of hell, and later in confession demanding full details of any sins and shouting at girls when they got embarrassed or cried. But Josie was no mousy thing, or at all like the woman who'd burst into tears after she'd poked her under her ribs, the one who'd thrown herself under a train between Glasthule and Sandycove after her consultation with Nurse Cadden, God forgive her.

Had she been a boy, Josie would have been a beater, sharing the gushy shower of coins thrown up by the landlord for the pack of boys marauding through the copse's undergrowth competing to scare the most birds, even if it was the gang itself and not any individual that made the game flee from their hiding places.

If she didn't find Nurse Cadden soon, it would be too late. She had to try again. She kicked the bag of laundry and it rolled down the stairs forcing Mrs Hannafin to step to one side to let it pass. She held the completed form up to her face so her giggling would not be seen.

Dolly Considine's Hotel

JULIAN TAKES A SHOWER

19th June 1983

With ten minutes of shower time remaining, Julian rapped on the door to the second-floor bathroom. 'Brendan, it's five past eleven,' he lied. 'Mrs McC has turned off the hot water. She wants you downstairs, immediately.'

'No time for a shower now, pissy boy,' Brendan said when he emerged fully dressed with his hair in the same greasy unwashed state it'd been in an hour earlier.

'Maybe tomorrow,' Julian smiled, slipped around him, and locked the door. Already pulling at his clothes and using his instep to remove his shoes, his mother telling him to open his laces first.

'You're fucking dead. Do you hear me?' Brendan could be ignored because the warm water was calling him. But the sloping floor and the walls angling away from the back of the building were also demanding attention. Plaster chunks from the ceiling lay where they had fallen, like lumps of Grocer Jack's broken nougat. The triangle-shaped gaps stuffed with newspaper showed how much the room had moved. Four sickly-looking timber blocks, covered in black mould, were propping up the bath, and through a hole in a crumbled floorboard Julian could see the backyard directly below. 'You live in a rotting wooden box, suspended in mid-air,' he told the maid picking abandoned towels from the floor in the picture above the toilet cistern. 'It's only a matter of time till you go crashing down to join the broken bottle crates below you.'

Brendan's body odour and cigarette smoke overwhelmed any lingering hint there might have been of the toiletries consumed during Sylvia's shower, denying him help with the profile going into his journal. But as soon as he stepped under it, the hot water beating down distracted Julian from them all. The old-fashioned laundry-smelling soap from the kitchen made foam where there had been sticky piss and eased apart the hairs above his cock, matted with Mikhail's or his own dried spunk from the night before. The cock itself was insistent, and suggested he think about the men who'd stood under this shower and done the same, their orgasms heightened by the fear that the dangerous bathroom was about to pull away from the building and tumble onto the yard below. Mikhail poked his smelly breath into his face and Julian banished the image. Malone on the other hand wanted to hold hands and talk, which threatened to soften him.

'The allocated hot water has been used,' Mrs McClean shouted from outside the door. 'Finish up now.'

He imagined hard Upper Cabra lads, Finglas lads, Artane lads, all skinny-white and naked, spraying each other with cold water, and ejaculated into his hand.

'I'm finished,' he shouted, and rinsed his cock before he grabbed the threadbare towel and stepped out of the bath, careful to put his feet where he hoped supporting joists would save him from falling through the rotten floor.

Dolly Considine's Hotel

JULIAN IS REMINDED OF HIS MOTHER'S KNITTED SKIRT

June 1983

'My next project will be to put the Jews of Dublin on the stage,' Mikhail Mayakovsky told the woman from the Porchester Theatre committee. She'd arrived just as the cast were finishing their sandwiches and he his vodka lunch. His words a response to her announcement that the committee was investigating the relevance of his productions to the Irish nation. 'I want to showcase these ancient people to the non-Jews of Dublin; I want to tell the stories of the Irish Jews who died in Auschwitz.' His look towards Julian suggested he was pleased with himself.

'Last month it was tinkers in Ballyfermot, and the month before it was the unemployed of Tallagh,' she said. 'You've spent your tenure putting on plays that attack and denigrate our great Irish traditions.'

'I commission Irish writers to tell me stories about Irish travellers, the Irish unemployed and Irish Jews.' His feet twitched as if they wanted to move around the room to add weight to his words. 'And my current production is American.'

'Why don't you stage plays that show how we have shrugged off the shackles of seven hundred years of occupation? Or go back to England and show London's West End what their taxes and their army are still doing in the occupied part of our country?'

His fingers stroked the chair-back as if recalling his private performance with the little lounge boy. A week had passed since he'd woken alone in Josie's old room. He couldn't remember if anything had happened, only that when he was back in his hotel he'd transferred a pack of condoms from his toilet bag to his jacket pocket.

'It's the Irish I love. The Irish I want to be a part of. Only you Irish get it up for me.' He thrust his groin forward to illustrate and looked over to where Julian had stopped clearing away the remains of their lunch to watch the exchange.

'Please Mr Mayakovsky, there's no need to be vulgar.'

'I'm a theatre director; vulgarity is my stock-in-trade.'

'Not in the Porchester Theatre, Dublin, it isn't.'

'Well, that's what you hired me for. My reputation is well known.'

He crossed to Julian and put his arm around his shoulder as if to demonstrate his relationship with the ordinary Irish. 'Every dog in the street knows what I am like. Ask this waitering boy.'

The Porchester Theatre woman raised her eyebrows towards Julian but kept her mouth shut. Her green knitted skirt reached almost to the floor, and a slight twitch from Julian's shoulder suggested it was the skirt he was watching.

'Tell the nice lady,' the director said.

'Is it more drinks?' Julian asked, and he smiled for the committee woman.

'Tell the woman what you know about me.'

'Sure I never heard of you,' Julian said. 'Maybe you should

go back to England or Russia, and let the committee run their theatre any way they like.'

'But they invited me.'

'Maybe they bit off more than they bargained for.' Julian stepped aside and Mikhail's arm flopped away from his shoulder.

'My contract has six months to run.'

'Your appointment was not a unanimous decision,' the committee woman said.

'There's a surprise,' the oldest of the women actors muttered.

'We're leaving now.' Mikhail waved his arms at his cast. 'We have a rehearsal. And this debate is spoiling the mood.' The actors rose as Mikhail blustered towards the woman to brush her out of his way. But she extended her left hand to his chest and indicated with her right that everyone should sit down again. Mikhail's eyes followed the Claddagh ring glinting as she took control; the heart turned away from the world to indicate it was not available.

'What's the single most important issue in Ireland today?' She was addressing the four women around the circular table.

None of them wanted to play; they deferred to Mikhail.

'How should I know?' He turned to Julian.

'It's a fair question,' Julian smirked, 'for a man who prides himself on knowing the Irish intimately.'

'I can see it's a trap,' he said to the woman. 'But have it your way... Mass unemployment. The cream of your youth emigrating. The state of the arts. The national debt.'

The woman shook her head.

'And gay rights,' Mikhail said, looking her up and down as if she might need gay rights.

'Abortion,' the woman said. 'Abortion.'

'Not easy enough?' he asked. 'An end to forcing women to

go to Birmingham? A play about issuing travel vouchers from doctors' surgeries?'

The woman dropped her chin towards her chest in a kind of surrender to despair. Her long hair slipped over her shoulders in baby steps as she shook her denial from side to side, the shiny black stark against the cream of her Aran sweater. Mikhail could not see her face, but her eyes must have been open because her ringed hand dropped to a speck of fluff on her skirt and brushed it off.

'The committee has decided to postpone the opening of *A Song for All Saints*, at least until after the Pro-Life Referendum in September.' Her left hand touched the golden baby-feet brooch pinned above her chest as she spoke. 'We have received scripts for two plays that are relevant to Irish life today. They deal with current issues. You will begin rehearsals immediately, or resign. We open in two weeks.' She turned to face the door and the hem of her skirt took a full second to catch up. She nodded at Julian as she passed.

'My mother knitted herself a skirt just like yours,' Julian said, 'but when she tried it on, the weight of the wool dragged it down to the floor; she had to unravel loads of rows before she could walk without tripping.' He smiled at each of the actors as they left but ignored Mikhail Mayakovsky.

Summer of Unrequited Love

THE ERRANT CHAMBERMAID... ATTENDS TO HER NOVENA

Jul '52

Josie had completed only two of her nine First Friday Novenas when a familiar forty-a-day voice convinced her that the Sacred Heart was answering her prayers. She'd put her trust in Him and now she was being rewarded.

'My name is MacNamara. Mrs MacNamara.'

Josie watched from the stairs as Mamie Cadden signed the hotel register and then turned away from reception with a sweep of her fur coat, allowing her high extended hand to release the pen back onto the counter.

Why did Nurse Cadden want to stay at the hotel when she lived only a few streets away? Had the woman who'd shamed Josie on the doorstep the other day done as she'd threatened and run her out of the house?

'I need the room for two days. I'm going out to dinner in ten minutes. Send up a jug of washing water. Where is the boy to carry my bags?' Her booming tone was as dismissive as ever.

Twenty years later, wearing a different uniform, and with

her puppy fat gone, especially from her face, Josie would not be recognised by Nurse Cadden. The Sacred Heart was giving her one chance, she had to do it right. She would wait until Nurse Cadden was settled, or maybe until the morning when Josie went into the room to make up the bed. *Please Nurse Cadden, I need your help. For old times' sake. Your former assistant. The girl who testified to detectives that her employer only treated women for dandruff and chilblains.*

But here she was, sweeping up the stairs towards her without waiting for a response from the girl looking after the desk while Mrs Burns was out, and sending Josie into the nearest bedroom trying to look busy with important hotel business. Nurse Cadden would make demands on idle staff just to assert her authority. Thankfully the room was empty, and she stood behind the closed door with her heart banging like the punch bag thing at the fairground that men pounded to prove their power.

'Thank you, Sacred Heart,' she whispered to the crucifix over the bed, 'and you too St Theresa.' The Little Flower was often in her thoughts when she was doing her devotions. 'I will speak to her in the morning.'

There was a danger that when the manageress returned she'd recognise Nurse Cadden, and even though the hotel was empty with all the deputies being back in their constituencies for the summer recess, Mrs Burns would cancel the booking and demand she leave, instantly. Which made the situation urgent. But Josie's heart and breathing would not allow her to open the door, never mind form the words she'd need. And a helpless Josie would get Nurse Cadden's horsey laugh, followed by a reminder that having seen all those women at the house in Rathmines, Josie should have been more careful. Not to mention the question of the money.

Go back to the kitchen, girl, she'd say, and exhale her smoke into her face. She'd sweep Josie away as easily as she'd extinguish her cigarette or open doors without touching them. Josie would have to become like the woman in red gloves, breezing into Nurse Cadden's room, standing proudly; to remind her of her perjury, demand she sort out her little problem. That's all it would take, and then the two of them could have a cup of tea and reminisce about the old days.

Dolly Considine's Hotel

JULIAN DRESSES UP AND GOES CYCLING

June 1983

When he was eight and still called Paddy, rule number three in his spying instruction booklet – free with his weekly comic – was: 'Look out for unusual behaviour'. So when he noticed that Sylvia sometimes exchanged her tight-fitting skimpy clothes for flat shoes, loose slacks and a black jacket over a pale grey blouse, he wondered what kind of rendezvous she was leaving the hotel for.

'Julian,' Mrs McClean shouted as he made to follow Sylvia towards the stairs, inserting herself between him and his prey. 'Bring that coal up,' she said, and pointed to the Hannafins' filled bucket inside the back door. She was in her tennis outfit again and carrying a duffel bag, her racket protruding.

'Where's Brendan?' he asked. Humping coal upstairs was not a lounge boy's job.

'Do as you are told.'

The second rule of successful spying was 'Never let your prey out of your sight'. But Mrs Hannafin wanted to talk. 'The fire is for himself,' she said. 'I have to keep him warm. He's an old soldier. He deserves the best.' Part of Julian wanted to linger, to hear more, and explain to her what his mother meant when she accused him of playing the old soldier, but there was a spying rule about not being distracted, so he put the coal by the hearth and raced back downstairs. The Hannafins would get their story, in their own right, or as part of something fermenting in his head called 'The McClean Dynasty' about a corrupt political family. Either way, the fictional Hannafins would be freeloaders, paying for neither rent nor food, and even demanding regular buckets of coal. Two elderly codgers with a hold over Dolly that had something to do with the Civil War.

Rule number seven related to independent means of transport, which had been meaningless when he was eight. Now, it meant borrowing Brendan's bicycle, loosely chained up in the basement area outside the boys' bedroom window. And the rule that had most excited young Julian when he was Paddy had been 'Wear a disguise'.

An eight year old did not transform himself into a different person by drawing a mascara moustache under his nose or getting into his little cowboy outfit. Perhaps the spy instruction booklet was hinting that he should dress up as a girl, in a school gym slip, with white socks up to his knees, and a blond wig with pigtails down to his shoulders. But he hadn't had access to such props.

Although Julian hadn't yet met him, and therefore didn't recognise him, Mr Cathal McClean, looking like a lawyer in a slim pinstripe suit, was waiting for his taxi to the office when Julian leaned over the reception counter and grabbed the long white coat and pork pie hat abandoned by Mikhail Mayakovsky when the theatre woman announced the cancellation of his play. Mikhail's sweaty smell floated out of the fabric, and Julian imagined him bursting into the boys' bedroom naked beneath the coat, the pork pie hat balanced on his erection.

Julian held the hat with three fingers the way he'd seen men do and nodded at Mr McClean before he dropped it onto his head. It was large enough to slip down over his eyes if he didn't deliberately push it back. He tucked the coat-tail into the belt to stop the hem catching in the rusty bicycle chain, and spied Sylvia not having yet reached Kelly's Corner, time enough to cycle round the long way and be leaning against the chemist's shop door with the hat down over his face when she passed. Why would she imagine he was anything other than a man desperate for the pharmacy to open so his prescription could be filled? Nonetheless, he turned to the display of cough mixtures in the window, and held the bicycle ready to jump on if she came towards him. A pair of the spying spectacles advertised in his brother Christopher's American comics would have allowed him to see behind him. He'd experimented when he was eight by holding his mother's compact mirror to his temple and all he'd seen were stars from the strain of focusing on the reflection.

A police special branch car without identification marks wailed towards him, one small blue light flashing on the roof over the driver's head like a clown's hat. A bearded man grinned at him from the back of the car as it rounded the corner. What the fuck are you doing, the grinning lips mouthed beneath the wail, using your detective talents to follow innocent barmaids when you should be finding out what we're doing to your terrorist boyfriend?

He gripped the handlebars tightly to stop his fingers from lifting into a V sign.

'Release Malone, yiz bastards.'

The shock of his screech making him forget Sylvia until he

saw her running for the number 19 bus rounding the corner. He jumped on the bike and pedalled in circles on the wide footpath in front of the chemist. Torn between expressing his anger and the need to follow Sylvia. Round and round, with the coat bunched up to his tummy, until he remembered rule number ten. 'Real spies never give up'.

Summer of Unrequited Love

THE TESTIMONY AND PARANOIAS OF MIKHAIL MAYAKOVSKY #2

Jun '83

Vodka. The burning sensation of it is pushing back my eyeballs and squeezing my neck muscles, making me relish my closed-off breath and the dry nausea beating against me; it is my only love. Look at me, demanding the remove-me-from-consciousness embracingness of it; the fire-me-up loin-girdingness of it; my simultaneous transformation into bull and matador; my silver-trousered loins turned towards the double horns while simultaneously baring vertebrae four and five for the sword.

I have such ambition, such spectacles, pinned down, chained, clamped into the smallest spaces. My brain suppresses a million varicose feelings steam-pressuring to be free. Prodding the vein walls for the tiniest weakness, the gullible pinhole offering kindly relief, only to be taken advantage of by the ripping-open, pushing flow, the spurting deluge-drowning, the engulfing vortex of excitement and action and sex and world-changing life-enhancing up-your-arse penetration.

Yet also wanting nothing but to be the Denton Welch of day to day, pricking out my power in tapestry, stitching in a sheltered corner of my Kent cottage garden, listening to the songbirds in the trees above my head, and the wood pigeons beyond puffing themselves up and exaggerating their power, with no idea that in a month or two they will be silent, and I will still be here under my tree or wrapped in a blanket in the conservatory, adding to my tiny tapestry or darning socks when needlepoint becomes too intense and I need to grope about for a little light relief.

Dolly Considine's Hotel

JULIAN REMEMBERS THE SMELL OF CHOCOLATE THAT ENCIRCLED THE CADBURY GIRLS

June 1983

For fuck's sake, he'd practically lived on the 17A daily for two whole years. Monday to Friday afternoons arcing back and forth through Dublin's northern suburbs while his mother was at work and his brother Christopher was introducing girlfriends to his youthful jazz collection, the front door locked against his embarrassing baby brother.

And here was the sister bus or even the mother bus, the plain number 17, parked opposite the house Sylvia had just gone into using keys taken from her pocket. The same single-decker model, maybe even the same actual bus he'd sat on planning Christopher's murder. Did Sylvia have a flat in the house, or a cleaning job? He wanted her to be the paid companion to an ancient spinster endlessly recalling the days when she flirted with the crown princes of Europe.

He'd had no way of knowing when she was going to get off the number 19, so had stayed well behind as it approached each stop, then pedalled faster to nearly catch up when she didn't, watching out for the indicator light, and forced to let Mikhail's coat hang open to dry out the sweat leaking down his arms and sides.

The glass in the number 17 bus resting at its terminus allowed him to monitor Sylvia's house without anyone inside seeing him. The building behind him offered a noticeboard to justify a person wheeling their bicycle into the weed-infested forecourt for a closer view, perhaps to mull over the information displayed. Hardly surprising if a person noticed the house across the road had its curtains open, no nets, and a tidy front garden, at least from this side of the road. All honour to the rules in his spying textbook.

'If it's the parish centre you're looking for,' the bus driver said, 'then you've come to the right place.' He removed a cigarette from a box but didn't offer one to Julian. 'The opening times are displayed just there,' he continued, joining him and tapping his lighter against the notice board. 'Excellent services for young drug addicts.' Taking Julian back nearly ten years to when he'd known every driver on the 17A. His very own seat towards the back, one row in front of where the Cadbury's factory girls and women, smelling of chocolate, sat talking at the top of their voices, but not bothering the boy clutching his school bag to his stomach as if it held either secrets or a hot water bottle to keep him warm. The drivers were like serial part-time fathers who got so used to him they didn't even make him get off while they went for their cigarette or waited for the timetable-designated time to begin the arc back towards the other end of the route.

What did it mean that the terminus was opposite Sylvia's house? Nothing, he told himself as he dragged his finger through the bus dust to declare *I heart 17 bus*. He put his head through the open door to smell the life he'd lived on board plotting revenge on Christopher. He was sniffing the air for memories when the door to the house opposite opened and Sylvia emerged holding a child, a girl, by the hand.

'This is the bus stand, you can't get on here,' the driver said, unaware Julian was using the bus to hide, not to go somewhere. 'You'll have to cross the road,' he said, helpfully pointing at the stop on the opposite footpath, at the very place where Sylvia was standing. If either he or the bus moved, she would see him. Julian gave the man his best ten-year-old stepson smile; if the buses were related maybe the drivers were too. 'But seeing as I'm ready to go,' the man said, 'I suppose it would be okay. Save you risking the traffic.'

Julian pulled Mikhail's hat down further over his face and searched for the exact fare before sidling into the equivalent of his old seat and turning his face away from where Sylvia stood. He would go one stop, and then come back to collect Brendan's bicycle. Except that when the bus went around the roundabout and doubled back to the official first stop, Sylvia was waiting to board. He couldn't get off. Nothing for it except to hold his open journal up in front of his face as she paid her fare and ushered the child, definitely a girl, ahead of three older women struggling with shopping bags on wheels.

Fuck.

Summer of Unrequited Love

THE ERRANT CHAMBERMAID... TAKES MATTERS INTO HER OWN HANDS

Jul '52

'Do you know your dates?' was the first question Nurse would ask a woman. And she'd ask again after she'd examined her. From the hall outside the treatment room, Josie would sometimes hear her say, 'I'm afraid you're mistaken.' The very tone she'd used when she was confronted by the detectives, the image of that last day in Rathmines forever fixed in Josie's head: Nurse's folded defiant arms, the corner-of-the-mouth cigarette, the curling smoke inhaled through flared nostrils, the cigarette being removed before she tossed her head.

'I'd say you're fourteen weeks,' Nurse told the woman in the red gloves. For all her cockiness and her complaints about Josie, she'd betrayed her real self when she pretended to be less far gone than she was.

'Now this little fella,' Nurse said, 'would be no good for you. This is the candidate we want.' But Josie had heard the words from outside the door. She'd seen nothing.

'Just give me a douche,' the woman in red gloves had said,

'and put one of those in,' speaking as if she was in charge. The smell of Jeyes Fluid flooded out into the hall afterwards, and Nurse Cadden had sent her out for a large bottle when she came in to clean up the treatment room.

Now Josie was standing by the bed where Nurse Cadden would sleep when she came back from her dinner. Except maybe she wasn't coming. The suitcases on the bed contained no nightclothes, no outfit for the next day, no toiletries. Nothing but Nurse Cadden's equipment and her potions, all wrapped in green cloths and folded terry towels. She sat on the bed and felt the coolness of the brown rubber sheet against her hand; could it be the same one she'd cleaned blood off a hundred times? But as she unwrapped Nurse Cadden's terrible tools, the horror of her first excursion into the treatment room in Rathmines came banging back into her, reminding her they had wanted to invade her, and rip her sixteen-year-old insides the way her father cleaned out an old boiling fowl on its way to the broth pot. And yet the exposed array reassured her also, told her they would resolve her dilemma.

It all looked familiar; the hand pump, Nurse's boxes of sea tangles, the jars with names that Josie could not pronounce, the syringes and glass tubes with fat ends and thin ends, a thing for pulling out where no hand could fit. She'd learnt how each of them was to be cleaned and sterilised and put into its right place in the instrument drawers, but had never seen them used.

'I'm afraid you need more than a quick douche darling,' Nurse Cadden had said to a woman who was so far gone she couldn't button her coat. 'You've left it too late for my help.' Josie was not going to make that mistake. She couldn't be any more than two and a half months. She knew the date because 'it' had only started after Easter, and Easter had been in the middle of April.

She found three rubber pumps at the bottom of the suitcase,

the tubes tucked in beside them rolled up and held tight with elastic bands. Josie would need to be washed out, so what better than to pump disinfecting water to where it was needed? She sniffed at the red rubber for the memory of the Jeyes Fluid, thinking of the women the tubes had been inside since she'd last cleaned them.

'It's your thing,' her older sister had said to twelve-year-old Josie when they got home from school one afternoon. Two boys they'd passed had put their index finger to their chin and pulled the flesh over it, sneering at Josie's embarrassment. But except by the face cloth and her knickers, her vulva had never been touched, until Mr O'Brien had begun calling it her Madeleine, and had stroked and caressed it, until she convinced herself that her friend Maureen was right, she was entitled to her fun.

She experimented with sitting, and squatting, and lying down on the bed. She even tried bending over her knees like a runner getting ready for a race, but she needed both of her hands to steady herself, so bending over couldn't work. And when she thought she was right with two pillows under her bottom, and lying back with her head tilted forward by the bars in the bed frame, she realised that pulling her drawers down around her thighs was not enough, they would have to come off completely.

'You'll have to remove your underwear when you go in to see Nurse Cadden,' she'd often said to visitors to the Rathmines house. 'You know how to do that, don't you?' Getting every response from tears, to embarrassment, to a laugh from the tarts that'd be back at work that evening to pay for what they'd spent that afternoon.

Of course Josie got the order of things wrong, and had to get off the bed again to carry the washstand over from the window, hoping the sun had taken the bitter cold out of the jug of water or her stomach would cramp up and... but she refused to think about cramps. 'Hot water is for the mornings,' Mrs Burns would say if she went to the kitchen, 'not for seven o'clock in the evening. Unless perhaps you have a secret rendezvous you forgot to mention to Mrs Burns?' And then whether to pour the Jeyes Fluid and water into the basin, or make up the mixture in the jug and balance it in the basin? That would allow it to be higher, which she knew it needed to be. But then the tube kept slipping out of the jug. She wished her friend Maureen or her older sister was there to help. But she draped a green towel over the jug, and that kept the tube in place.

The nozzle attached to the rubber pump was small compared to Mr O'Brien's thingy, but it was different, and the business end was rigid, and she couldn't find any Vaseline in Nurse Cadden's case. Soap would give her a rash, an ongoing penance to remind her of what she'd done. Her soapy hands made the tube slippery, and once the rigid bit was inside her, the rubber buckled and pushing was useless. How far should it go in, and had she thought of everything? Should she have filled the pump with the water before she put the tube in, and if she didn't where would all the air go? She didn't want air inside her. It would be like having wind. Everything was connected.

Going in the second time was easier, but she had to wriggle it about to get it beyond something in the way. She didn't want to do herself an injury, but then she gave a sort of flick of her wrist and the whole tube almost disappeared, and although it was a relief, a frozen solid feeling entered her and promised to stay forever.

Her father used Jeyes Fluid when he was sorting out the young male calves. He and another labourer would stand over a young thing kicking against the ropes hobbling its legs, until one of them would hunker down with his penknife to cut at the calf's business so he didn't turn into a raging bull. And just before they released the rope, her father would throw a cup of Jeyes Fluid over the cut to stop it from going septic.

It wasn't just the cold water that made her shiver. It was the smell, and the pumping, and thinking about where it was going, and having to touch herself, as well as what would happen if she stopped. But please God it would soon be over.

How would she know when to stop? And when she was full, should she let the water soak her insides like a tea-stained dishcloth, or manoeuvre herself onto the chamber pot immediately? She pressed one of Nurse Cadden's green towels against herself to stop the water flooding out over the rubber sheet and onto the floor.

The whispering from the landing outside the door froze her hand in mid-squeeze; the hissing tone belonged to Mrs Burns, but the words were unclear. Pray Jesus she is not there to eject Nurse Cadden from the hotel, or worse that she knows Josie is inside the room.

A knock followed by 'Open this door. I wish to speak to you.'

'Are you in there?' Shouting, and more knocking.

Mrs Burns might be clutching her pass key, ready to let herself in. The rattle of the doorknob made Josie sit up ready to spring off the bed, and with the quick movement the nozzle twisted against her. There was no pain, more a sensation like doing something with her neck and knowing that she would wake up with a crick in the morning.

'I'm putting a note under this door,' Mrs Burns said. 'Please read it and abide by what it instructs.' The paper's appearance reassured her, but Josie didn't move again until Mrs Burns's voice began to fade as she made her way downstairs.

The other end of the tube had pulled but not fallen from the jug. She wanted to cry, and she wanted a hot bath, and she wanted to sleep. But she persevered with the pumping.

Her hand beginning to cramp from squeezing the red ball, but there seemed to be less resistance now, and she asked the Sacred Heart to confirm that that was a good sign.

Dolly Considine's Hotel

CHIEF OF DETECTIVES IRONSIDE LENDS A HAND

June 1983

Julian was staring out of the kitchen window, wondering what the bearded special branch man in the wailing car might have thought about the nutter in the long white coat and oversized hat screaming hysterically at him. Should he weave the incident into his story about Sylvia's day off, or his story of Josie's demise? He was so absorbed with his plotting that he didn't even know Mrs McClean was in the kitchen until she slapped a torn sheet of paper onto the draining board between him and the window. The scare was worthy of Brendan. Her broad-shouldered two-tone jacket and low-cut top loomed over him, aided by her extra-high heels.

'What is this, Julian?' Mrs McClean lifted her hand off the crumpled sheet. The writing was his, a page from his journal, the rest of it thankfully tucked out of sight inside his shirt. She stood back with her arms folded high over her bosom. He wondered if he could say *her eyes blazed with anger as they moved back and forth between the paper and his face like a shuttlecock in a badminton match.* A lame image maybe; unless he could help readers imagine it being a vicious contest...

The ~~McClean History~~ McClelland Dynasty

(How three Generations of a Political Family betrayed (for their personal gain) the idealists who died for Ireland)

He'd written the words on his first proper morning while Sylvia, and then Brendan, tried to stop him getting under the shower. He'd sat on the floor outside the bathroom, spunk-sticky and piss-smelly, and set down the title and subtitle, and waited for the words of the McClean family history (retitled the McClelland Dynasty) to appear on the page. He was a writer; he only had to poise his pen under his story's title for half a million words to spill out onto the paper; he demanded, he deserved, an unstoppable blockbuster. But while Sylvia showered, and then Brendan, smoking and grunting, wanked over the girly magazine he'd had rolled inside his towel, not one further word appeared on Julian's journal. So when the bathroom door opened and Brendan said no time for a shower now, pissy boy, Julian had known for sure he didn't care about Mrs McClean or Mr McClean or their son William as subjects, and sealed the conviction by ripping the page from his journal, scrunching the aborted history into a ball and dropping it onto Sylvia's make-up-stained cotton wool in the plastic wastebasket under the sink. If he wasn't being swept along, wasn't enthralled, wasn't forced, to surrender to his subject, if his subject did not threaten the torment of total control over his mind, then he had the wrong subject.

But now the page was back, and the woman whose story had not overwhelmed him wanted answers. 'It looks to me as if some journalist is doing a hatchet job on your family,' Julian said. 'What do you think?' He sniffed at the paper and held it up to the foggy light coming through the kitchen window, as if to check for invisible secrets. 'I saw a TV programme once; a detective lady rubs a pencil very lightly over the paper, which reveals the indentations of words written on previous pages, and gives clues to the writer's identity.' He moved his hand rapidly back and forth to illustrate. 'Would you like me to try?'

'You wrote those words, Julian. You left the page in the bathroom this morning. I demand to see the rest of your notes, now.'

What was she talking about? This morning? He wanted to tell her its history, ask where it had spent more than a week, but he mirrored her folded arms, and then lowered them to reassure the journal pressed against his stomach. Luckily the cold basement had encouraged him to wear Malone's chunky bulge-concealing jumper. He'd be in St Stephen's Green in a few minutes, ready to enjoy the sun and to record the deluge of words about Josie damming up in his head. But had he been hasty in rejecting Mrs McClean? She was gripping the table now as if her anger might overturn it, and send plates and trays and morning papers crashing onto the kitchen floor. Maybe she was more interesting than she looked, especially in today's outfit. He smiled at her to cover his examination of her angry face, and noted the white of her gripping fingers, and the indentation which remained on her bosom, marking where her fists had been. It would be details like this that could bring her to life on his pages. He moved towards her and extended his right hand. If they shook, he might get a hint of secrets she didn't want uncovered. Or at least get the feel of her skin and the strength of her grip. But she ignored his plea.

'Mrs McClean,' he said, 'your kindness in taking me off the streets, and giving me a start in the Dublin hotel trade, has not gone unnoticed by other members of staff. I believe it has caused jealousy. When I was shaving this morning, my razor fell into the wastebasket and it contained nothing except some make-up-soiled cotton wool.' He checked to see if he had convinced her. But her face was unmoved. 'So that paper,' and he began to tap it with his index finger the way he'd seen a dozen TV defence lawyers perform, 'was placed in the wastebasket after I finished shaving.'

The paced and sincere delivery and flashes of the tapping finger of chief of detectives Ironside were in his mind, then he was the wheelchair-bound prosecutor taking himself slowly across the kitchen to the washing machine where he gripped the lid, his back briefly towards the judge, before slowly pivoting round to stare into the face of Mrs McClean.

'I rest my case,' he whispered. 'But I will accept your judgement,' and he shook his head as if what she was suggesting was unbelievable. Then he turned back to lift the lid and remove the sheets Sylvia had told him to hang out to dry at the end of the spin cycle. Ordinary life would have to go on even as he mined it for inspiration and no matter what terrible things were befalling him personally.

Dolly Considine's Hotel

A VISIT TO THE THEATRE

June 1983

'Did you take Brendan's bicycle on Tuesday morning?' Mrs McClean shouted from halfway down the stairs as Julian was shutting the front door behind Mikhail and his actors after their lunch. He looked up at her and shook his head.

'Where would I be going?'

'Did you see or hear anyone taking it?' She was wearing her dark green coat, maybe she was going out, although his own mother sometimes forgot to take off hers until she was on her way to bed.

He shook his head again. 'Why would anyone bother? It's a crock.' By now she was face to face with him beside the little reception desk. She smelt of flowers and he was tempted to lean in and sniff some more. The afternoon was looking too wet for St Stephen's Green, but if she was off out, he would relax with his journal in the Porchester Lounge, setting down his account of the adventures he'd had following Sylvia.

'Brendan needs a bicycle to carry out his duties. I have

therefore decided that the staff will donate all their tips until there is enough money to replace it.' She reached for a small parcel sitting on the reception counter, pulled it towards herself and examined the markings and details for the addressee.

After driving through miles of boring suburbs, Sylvia and the little girl got off the bus beside a public park, allowing Julian to go and speak to the driver.

'You want to go back?' The driver looked perplexed. 'You just missed the eleven-thirty. You'll have half an hour's wait. If it's on time.'

He hoped the parish centre would make some use of Brendan's bike.

'This parcel is for the theatre next door,' Mrs McClean said. 'Kindly take it in to them and tell the Russian he needs to make other arrangements for his deliveries.'

After his father left home and his mother officially became a single parent, a charity had given them tickets to see the Christmas pantomime. He didn't imagine that the tiny arty Porchester would have the stalls and dress circle of the Gaiety Theatre, with seats for hundreds, but he wasn't expecting what he got. The Porchester Theatre could manage thirty-one patrons, not with real seats, just spaces on the three stepped plywood platforms stretching from wall to wall and a pile of thin cushions doled out one at a time for the audience to sit on. The actors were waving their arms and moving about in what looked like random patterns when he arrived, and, except for managing to avoid bumping into him as he crossed the space between the door and the seats, they ignored him. He draped Mikhail's long coat (the oily stain made when the hem caught in bicycle chain out of sight) over the lowest step, put the pork pie hat on top, climbed the shallow rake to where Mikhail was sitting, and placed the parcel on his lap.

'Mrs McC says you're to stop abusing the hotel's facilities,' Julian said as he lifted a script for something called *Catherine's Dilemma* off the cushion beside Mikhail and plonked himself down.

'Does that include you?' Mikhail smirked, and brushed the backs of his fingers along the emerging black roots of Julian's hair.

'You're supposed to be walking windmills. I want to see the wind,' Mikhail shouted at the actors; he stood up, keeping his knees bent to avoid the low ceiling and swayed and varied the motion of his arms as he made louder and softer blowing wind sounds through his lips.

'I'll pay you whatever Dolly McClean pays you to go around the pubs and restaurants distributing these flyers,' Mikhail said as he tore open the wrapper. 'The theatre committee have graciously consented to a "three-night only showcase" of *A Song for All Saints*, but they refuse to pay for publicity.'

'Maybe,' Julian said. Most of the light in the theatre was focused on the actors, but he took his journal from under his shirt to see if there was enough for him to write. His adventures following Sylvia needed to be recorded, but it was Josie he could feel echoing around the theatre space. He wanted to write about her attempt at an abortion and her dying.

'What's great about you is that you want nothing from me,' Mikhail said.

'Josie never asked me for anything,' Mr O'Brien told the priest in confession. Julian wrote the words and angled the paper to see if he'd be able to read them later.

'Other boys want me to bring them home, want me to give them presents, want me to marry them. You just want to fuck.'

Mikhail put the flyers on the floor and wriggled his hand inside Julian's belt to get hold of his cock. The actors stopped their circling and looked up into the darkness for more direction.

He needed to think about Josie's final moments before Mikhail distracted him. Whether she'd say sorry to the baby, or not, or curl into a foetal position for her final exit. And then there was Mr O'Brien. He had to protect these decisions from Mikhail's probing fingers. Did a writer's situation seep into his text? Would anyone reading about Josie's self-administrated abortion intuit that another man was holding his erection as he plotted?

'There was a drunken fumble in the linen cupboard one night,' Julian wrote on behalf of the haberdashery traveller, *'but truly, Father, I know how babies are made, and we didn't do that. And then I maintained a respectful distance until I could find another hotel and remove myself from the occasion of sin.'*

'Ideas, Kevin,' Mikhail shouted at the insipid boy actor. 'You actually love Catherine. You've been nursing a stiff cock for weeks, and now she is saying yes! Can't you imagine what that feels like?'

Kevin nodded, but without certainty.

'What does Kevin ask you for?' Julian said.

'He's straight, but he thought that if he threw himself at me, I'd get him work in London. But in England, they don't even want to sleep with him.'

The boy held out a tentative hand towards the woman playing Catherine but did not look comfortable.

'Be assertive, Kevin,' Mikhail shouted. 'Catherine wants you to kiss her, but even more, she wants you to take responsibility. She wants you to risk rejection. Surely to have this beautiful woman loving you is well worth the possible humiliation of

171

rejection? What's a little shame compared to a fabulous fuck? Huh?'

And he wrenched his hand out of Julian's pants and leapt each row down into the performance space.

'You're declaring your cock's intentions. Grab it,' and he reached for Kevin, who was not so insipid that he couldn't step backwards out of Mikhail's reach. The boy covered his crotch with both hands, and Mikhail slapped him on the face: the boy would have to suffer the slaps or let go shielding his cock.

'Say it Kevin: Look what I have for you Catherine. This is what you want. Take it, now.'

Mikhail turned and climbed back over the seats. Julian put a line through what he'd written. The haberdasher was of no interest. Josie was his character.

'Right,' Mikhail said. 'Keep your two hands on your cock for the rest of the scene, Kevin. And all the better if you can make it hard. You don't mind, do you Catherine? I certainly don't. This is a dull play. I want to see movement, danger, risk, life.' And he plunged his hand back into Julian's pants.

Summer of Unrequited Love

THE ERRANT CHAMBERMAID... TAKES A MRS CULLEN'S POWDER

Jul '52

When she had finished her treatment Nurse Cadden always gave a lady a Mrs Cullen's Powder to see her home, as well as enough of the folded papers to get her through the night. The card displaying the wraps hung on the back of the door in the treatment room. And Josie could tell how well Nurse had taken to a lady by how many of the card's nine retaining elastics needed refilling.

It was impossible for Josie to move without releasing the water distending her insides, so she held one of Nurse Cadden's green cloths against herself to stem the flow and struggled off the bed to squat over the chamber pot. Almost immediately the gushing sound told her she needed to empty it, but attempting to kneel forward brought on hot and cold feelings, and she felt her insides collapsing the way a sheet releases its tent of air as it sinks onto a bed. She managed to lift the jug and basin off the washstand, thinking she might be able to hunker over that instead, but her knees would not cooperate, so she emptied the contents into the basin instead and sat back on the chamber pot. She pulled towels off the bed, dried her legs as best she could, pushed the wet and bloodied ones away from her, and squatted back down. She didn't want to see what was coming out, so draped another towel over her thighs.

Were the stomach cramps telling her it was still inside her? Or that she needed a number two? She was in the wrong position for that, and her knees now refused to let her inch forward. Whatever came out would have to be managed. She lifted the towel covering the chamber pot; it was almost full again. She groped about in Nurse's suitcase, still up on the bed, and found the card of Mrs Cullen's Powders, resting herself before she could unfold the noisy paper. She leaned her head back to allow the contents to fall into her mouth and some powder fell onto her upper lip and made her sneeze, sloshing liquid from the chamber pot onto the bedside rug. The stains would have to be cleaned up or they would be reported to Mrs Burns. She scrunched the empty paper and dropped it to the floor, before reaching for another, and another, until her mouth tasted dry and the cold in her fingers began to make it difficult to open the papers without spilling most of the powder onto her nose and down her front. She would have to change her dress before she took the cup of hot milk up to Mrs Burns's sitting room to say goodnight.

She thought the water coming out of her should be the same dull colour it had been going in. But it was getting redder and redder until now it looked like pure blood, and thicker than she thought pure blood should be. Her cramps back and front, her painful squatting knees, the blood on the rug, and the certainty that she was doing a bad thing, were all becoming mixed up with forebodings about the return of Nurse Cadden. The furious fur-coated figure looming over her speechless at the sight of her old parlourmaid half naked, and her equipment and towels soiled and bloodied, before she dragged Josie to the door and threw her out.

Her arms and legs did not have the strength to push herself up onto the bed, so she tugged at the blankets until they fell around her, the corner of Nurse's suitcase digging into her shoulder as it slid down also. She had barely allowed herself to fall sideways onto the floor when her duties to Mrs Burns and the hotel reminded her that the breakfast things needed laying out in the dining room. No wonder she wanted to close her eyes and rest for a few minutes. And she was getting colder.

The amount of blood coming out was frightening her. Maybe if she pushed a pillow under her bottom, or even two pillows, that would lift her too high for it to come out. But her hips refused to lift, and her hand was unable to push the pillow under. She tried to fill the space between her thighs with absorbing cloths to catch the mess, hoping her strength would be back before the towels were completely soaked, and then she would try again with the pillow unless it was no longer needed.

Outside the door the rest of the hotel seemed quiet. Mrs Burns might have instructed someone else to make her hot milk, and as it was so late, perhaps Nurse Cadden would not be coming back. Maybe she'd never intended to, but only wanted the room as a safe haven for her equipment because she'd been tipped off about the police coming to search her home.

When her strength was back, she'd have to check the mattress for stains, and turn it if need be. That way Mrs Burns would never know. And then she would go upstairs to the maid's room and maybe sleep a little late in the morning, and not answer back if Mrs Burns shouted at her for being slow.

Whenever there was a shooting party crossing her father's field, young Josie had gone out to watch the birds rising up out of the undergrowth as the beaters advanced. She hated it when the line of guests, with their guns pointing, began to shoot. Most birds just fell to the ground as if a line had whipped them back to earth, their wings surrendering without a struggle. But sometimes a bird seemed to hover, her wings continuing to beat, but not effectively enough to propel her through the air. And Josie would say a prayer to St Theresa asking her to lift the bird into the cover of the tree just a few yards away. And she'd wonder if the bird was in pain or was puzzled that her wings were beating but she was not rising or going forward. Did she feel panic when she realised she would be joining the other birds already down? Could she see the dogs moving towards the spot where she would hit the earth?

Summer of Unrequited Love

CATHAL MCCLEAN MEETS HIS WIFE'S LOUNGE BOY FOR THE FIRST TIME

Jul '83

I recognised him as the strange-looking boy I'd seen wearing a funny hat and coat some mornings earlier when waiting for my taxi. Now his shirt had strands of grated cheddar stuck to it, although perhaps that was because the small round bar tray was not the best thing to carry my supper up two floors. But I said nothing, not even when I saw my sandwiches were soggy from tea slopping out of the teapot and that milk was pooling on one side of the tray as it listed on the crooked pile of papers I'd been going through since I came home. If he knocked, I didn't hear him, and only knew he was in the room when I found him stooped over me.

'Wake up, Mr McClean,' he said. 'It's your supper.'

Cigarette smoke drifted up from the bar below, and someone murdering 'Danny Boy' was vying with the television delivering the day's cattle prices. The singing might have been coming from the street, because I often hear my son William sneering at Sylvia's rule about it being a 'talking only' bar before dawn. I half-opened my eyes as he placed my supper components in a line along the edge of the table and drained the milk from the tray back into the jug.

'Now your sort are always helpful,' I said as I lifted my head and opened my eyes fully, 'so long as you think people are on your side. It's when you think you've been crossed that the fun starts.'

Dolly says he's a journalist spying on us. She always invents a profile for the boys she takes in so that I suspect nothing of their true circumstances. I seldom warm to them, even though my own arrival in Dublin in the fifties was not so different – although I was never on the run. But whatever else this one was, he looked like an angry Nancy who'll stay for a month and storm out in a fit of pique over some stupid remark no matter what trouble that gets him into with his handlers, whoever the current batch are.

'Woe betide the man, or woman, especially the woman,' I said, at a disadvantage slumped as I was on the couch, with him standing, almost to attention, just inches away from me, his arms by his sides, his head angled slightly, and his eyebrows raised in tolerant amusement. 'I've seen it so many times. A hand-picked team working swimmingly, gold-medal-Spitz swimmingly. And then some buffoon fails to manage a moment of pressure, or has a misplaced presumption of intimacy, and wham, you might as well abandon the entire shebang and start again.'

Dolly has the staff trained to have my supper on the coffee table just after the early evening news. Except recently I've been delayed on party business and coming home to a pot of cold tea and curled-up sandwiches, which made tonight's the first delivery of my supper that I've witnessed since she started complaining about this one's sly motives.

'Yous want to be team players,' I said, 'but it's not in your nature, and never will be.'

I let him mull over my pronouncement while I spread a bit of mustard on the shredded cheese. 'You show me a successful maverick, a man that eschews the team, and I will show you a bum boy.'

The hand holding the round tray moved as though it was going to wave it like a fan or skim it across the room like the young Americans I see in St Stephen's Green playing with what look like colourful flying saucers.

'Even more amusing is the number of times I have seen talented men who came up against the casual or careless or thoughtless remark of some innocent gombeen, making him flounce off in a sulk that everyone predicts will be the last anyone hears from him, only to find, lo and behold, the buckoo was only warming up. A couple or five years and what do you know? He's on the front page of *Newsweek* or *Time* and being hailed across the world as an overnight success.'

I posed the quarter-sandwich on my bottom lip as I murmured my grace before meals. My neck ached from looking up at him, so I dropped my head to concentrate on my supper. He could sneer down at me if he liked. Or he could take my speech as a prediction of his future. I had his measure.

When I looked up again, he was holding the tray in front of him – the yellow beak of the Guinness toucan facing me – like a shield, maybe to warn me off. He waited until I poured the tea before he flopped himself down on the couch beside me, with the tray back on the paper bundles, and Sylvia below in the bar expecting him; but he'd clearly decided she could wait.

'Did Mrs McClean know Josie Geoghan the chambermaid that died here in 1952?'

'A very interesting question. I would say it is likely, but she would have been very young, so I expect she doesn't remember her.' I knew there would be a follow-up enquiry but was surprised at the change of direction.

'What happens when someone gets arrested?' he asked.

'The thing to do is to avoid being arrested,' I said. 'Much better to stay out of the clutches of the authorities. Always one step ahead. If you've any doubts, ditch any incriminating papers, and go. Didn't your people teach you anything?' Which jumped him up off the couch and out the door. Whereas all I wanted was to let him know he could trust me. Even in my cups.

Summer of Unrequited Love

THE TINAHELY GOFER... LEAVES HOME

Sept '64

The enclosed back porch was a glass box with nothing to do except look after Brendan's mother's geraniums sitting in odd saucers and lined up like boy scouts in red berets on either side of the kitchen door. It smelt of Shep or dry sweet geranium, or, immediately after breakfast, of the fresh tealeaves his mother packed around the stalks. On sunny days Shep would lie on the bit of mat between the porch door and the kitchen door, moving only to keep out of the shade as the sun went from behind the shed to over the potato field on the village side of the house.

When he was younger Brendan just ended up there, his soldiers or his toy tractor on the mat beside Shep. And if he got too warm, he lay down with his arms and legs out, the way Shep's were, absorbing the heat. Sometimes he'd put a hand on Shep and get snarled at and bitten in return. He could have pulled his hand back quickly but was convinced that Shep knew he meant him no harm. They were pals. Porch pals. The kitchen window above them open for his mother to tell him to leave the dog alone or to close to keep out the sound of his singing.

The St Kevin's bus wasn't supposed to pick up passengers until it got to Glendalough, but the driver lived in Tinahely and brought the bus home every night. This particular morning, at the bottom of the lane, twelve-year-old Brendan Wright was clutching his little suitcase with his mother beside him when the bus arrived.

'The woman's name is Mrs McClean. Say it.' His mother was in wellingtons, she didn't mind the muddy grass verge. He was on the bottom step of the bus. Their faces at the same level. 'Do you hear me?' She made it sound like an adventure.

'Everyone knows the St Kevin's bus stop in Dublin,' the driver said. 'He'll be all right.' And he pulled Brendan backwards into the bus so he could close the door. Brendan was up on the front seat when Shep came running down from the house. His mother lifted her hand as if she was going to wave but Shep started barking and pawing at the door, and the wave turned to a swipe to shut him up.

The bus's jigging made the seat material itch the backs of his legs. He put his hands flat under them and listened to the driver whistling and looked out the window for things to see. When he heard barking again, he thought Shep had run after them, but this dog was brown and Shep was black and white. Mostly white. Loads more dogs chased and barked as they drove through the mountains, and though he wasn't fooled again, he did wonder if their barks would be relayed back to Shep.

None of his father's dogs were allowed into the house. They hung around the gate waiting to growl at walkers or nip at the ankles of cyclists on their way up over The Gap. In the evening at feeding time, or earlier in winter, the dogs stood inside the open shed looking out at the rain, like the unemployed men he saw in the village when he was cycling home from school.

The bus stopped for people in Glendalough, but there were plenty of empty seats so he was left alone with his suitcase on the seat beside him. He recognised the tune the driver began to whistle when he got to the main road, and Brendan began to hum but not loudly enough to be heard. He didn't know all the words to 'Thady Quill' and had once asked his mother what 'for finding men's murtin' meant, but she'd only looked at him as if he was stupid and never answered.

He'd never seen a woman in trousers, but there she was facing him when he stepped down off the bus, and her coat was open like she was sorry she'd worn it. He hoped this was Mrs McC. She had bright red lips and carried a chocolate handbag and matching umbrella. His mother wore headscarves, but this woman's head looked as if it had an upside-down steak and kidney pie tin on it. Red. Not big enough to keep her head dry. She smelt too. But it was nice when he got used to it. She took his hand as they walked from the bus stop. By himself, he might have felt like running, but she had a slow way of moving as if she was being inspected by the people who passed, and besides, he didn't know where they were going.

'How old are you?' she asked. He'd been told to say fourteen if anyone questioned him, but he forgot. 'Twelve,' he said. 'Or maybe I'm fourteen. I'm not sure.'

'You look small for fourteen.'

He was the biggest in the class. And he had muscles. 'I can carry things,' he said, 'easily.'

But she was puffing too much for more talk, and gripped his hand tightly as if she needed to, to stop him floating away, him being so small and light.

There were houses in and around Tinahely that had an upstairs. But every house in Dublin had at least three, they even had to walk up steps to get to the front door of her house. It would take a brave person to go all the way to the top, but once inside he was so distracted by the pictures of horses and dogs on the wall, a different one every two steps as he went up the stairs, that he forgot to remember, and was higher than the roof of the house at home before he even noticed.

She let go his hand while she took off her hat. She started with the long pins that went right into her head and held the first one in her mouth until she had the second one in her hand and then stuck them both back into the hat. She told him to put his suitcase down and then he followed her into a room whose ceiling was so high his brother would have to stand on his father's shoulders to paint it and where the vast windows reached so close to the floor that he was frightened to go near in case he fell out onto the street miles below.

She gave him a cup of milk and pointed at a long couch covered in newspapers and knitting, a pile of folded sheets and bolster cases at one end. 'Sit there now while I see if William is awake after his nap,' she said. It was ages before she came back carrying a small fair-haired child with her.

'Now Brendan,' she said, 'I want you to play with William until teatime.'

He didn't know how to play with a child, he only knew about dogs. One dog really, and that one didn't like to play. But he said nothing. Maybe they were similar, and the boy would bite him if he tried to cuddle him. He was sleepy-looking, his thumb in his mouth, his face red all down one side.

'William had a walk this morning. But tomorrow when you're settled you can take him over to the Green. He'll need plenty of fresh air if he's going to thrive and grow up to be like his daddy.'

Summer of Unrequited Love

NOTES FOR A STORY FOR PADDY THE PORTER
(1883–1956) #1

And then the little troublemaker was to be found behind the reception desk that had fallen into redundancy since Dolly Considine stopped taking guests, ignored by all unless Brendan needed to change a blown fuse or the bulb in the Sacred Heart lamp. Here's Julian foostering about under the piled-up bolster cases, filled with starched laundry folded by the troubled Magdalene girls and sentenced to linger out of sight in the hopeless hope that Dolly Considine would need them when she got the rest of her hotel back. More than a quarter-century of dust and God knows what sort of spiders, mice and their leavings had accumulated until Julian took to slipping his scurrilous writings in between the redundant signing-in books and transaction ledgers that sat on the shelf above the counter overhang. What he called his active journal tucked under his shirt, the spiral wire digging into his stomach, distracting him from his duties as counter wiper and ashtray emptier. The wiry irritation a reminder to set down his fabrications and sketch out the scandals he was inventing instead of forgetting his stirrings and becoming the lounge boy he was paid to be.

'*No bleeding on duty,*' he'd had Dolly Considine say in his journal, and then made her *kick him, Rosa Clebb–like* after she saw that the blood the spiral had released from under his skin had *stained his white shirt with his very non-blue blood.* Then the blaggard was encouraging the scribble-filled pages with kisses before he lifted them up onto the shelf, whispering to them as he pushed them, uninvited, between the hotel's records: 'Return to me with atmosphere, fade and curl your pages with shocking histories, be as vampires to your shelf companions.'

He was fingering the page for June and July in the 1952 guest register one afternoon when Brendan's whistle forced him to duck down below the level of the reception desk's half-door, the suddenness of the drop scattering dust that had begun to accumulate before he was born, and forcing him to push his face between two bulging bolsters to suffocate his breath, suppress the sneezes kicking against his squeezed nostrils, and take tiny in and out breaths until he heard the street door slam out Brendan's whistling.

It was when he lifted his head and wiped his streaming nose in a starched but dusty sheet that he found the little floor safe, as redundant as the reception desk itself since Madam sold off the accommodation areas to clear the hotel's debts. The key found nestling among the dried-up fountain pens and the perished Now Due, Overdue and Paid rubber stamps, the rusty keyring also bearing a tag giving details of the insurance company that would reward the finder. Whatever outrageous forgery he'd been planning for the historic 1952 register, it was abandoned for a new scheme. 'My little pretties,' he whispered as he touched each journal in turn, 'this place of refuge shall be your new home. Sleep, dream, ferment, and I will come back for you and make you famous.'

Summer of Unrequited Love

JULIAN PLAYS CUPID FOR JACK AND SYLVIA

Apr '77

Sylvia was holding out her hand for payment from a young Fianna Fáil hopeful in the Kickham Room. Jack was sitting up at the Porchester side of the bar waiting to be served.

'I have to be careful not to touch mine,' he said, their beginning marked out with ambiguity. Not that he was likely to forget the occasion, what with the feelings he'd brought into the hotel himself, but it was her red eyes and the gaps in her mascara that distracted him enough to let him know there was a new server behind the bar. He blinked at her for several seconds before he asked for the drink he'd been promising his own dammed-up tears since 1.15pm, when his day had turned very bad.

'I'm allergic,' he made himself say. 'If I get booze on my fingers and then… Red wine is the worst, followed by spirits. They go red as if I've been crying.' Maybe he was drawing attention to her tears. But he couldn't just ignore them. Better to share an advance explanation for any of his own if his second gin opened the floodgates.

Except for when she said her name and the price of his drink, it was Jack that did the rest of the talking. He was on his third gin when he said, 'Sylvia, will you marry me?' His bar stool wobbled, but he held onto the counter, crossed his left knee over his right, and tilted his head upwards, as if to say he had nothing to be ashamed of either. So why shouldn't they both live happily ever after in his house in Beaumont with her child? The three of them playing happy families.

'What have you got to lose?' Jack asked, not the most flattering marriage proposal ever.

'Mister.' She didn't even know him well enough to call him by his first name. 'Mister, I am not looking for a husband. I have a husband already.' She retreated to stand over the open floor-hatch and passed the last crate of empties down to Brendan (had he heard?) in the cellar below. He waited until she'd slammed the floor hatch closed before he replied.

'You're not the first recruit Mrs McClean has brought from the nuns' rescue centre for fallen women. She's had a new girl every year, for as long as I can remember. And when they complain about the long hours, the rude customers, or even the lousy money, she'll swear never to try and help those ungrateful girls again.'

Sylvia fussed about the counter with a cloth during the lecture. Even when he said, 'And then Mrs McClean relents, and in comes another tearful escapee grateful to be free of the nuns, starting the cycle all over again,' she only pursed her lips and rinsed out the cloth and dried her hands, her eyes concentrating on what she was doing.

'You think I could never love you?' he asked.

'I don't care if you love me or not,' she said. 'I already have a man to love.'

'Except he's not with you, is he?' It was a cruel way to put it, and maybe not a good tactic. Especially when he went on, 'You haven't seen the swine since you told him you were pregnant.'

'Yes I have,' she said. But she didn't deny his character.

Indulging in big angry gestures in the tiny space behind the bar in Curragh House results in glasses flying off the shelves and blood oozing from anything that gets in the way of the splinters. That first afternoon Sylvia settled for banging his fresh drink down on the counter, splashing it on herself as much as on him. All down her front.

'This is my only fucking dress,' she said, looking uncertain whether to remove the empty glass and mixer, or escalate her own reaction. 'I can't work looking like this.'

'Put the apron on,' he said, and pointed to a whiskey-branded thing hanging on its nail by the Powers ad. None of the girls liked the apron but it was there for a reason.

'You know you'll never see him again, whoever he is. He should have been with you these last few months. Has he even seen the baby?'

She sliced a lemon and put a finger in her mouth. Whether to stem blood flow or taste the juice, he couldn't tell.

'Married, I suppose?'

'I would never, never...' She waved the knife in his direction. 'This is none of your business. He will come for me.'

'Except the nuns wouldn't have let you out of the hostel unless you signed the papers.'

'What do you know?'

'You could have your baby back. The three of us in my nice house in Beaumont. Just promise to marry me, that's all.'

'That's all? What do you think I am? You think that because I might have made one mistake you can get away with improper suggestions? Treat me like a prostitute? Some animal you can have cheap sex with?'

'I'm sure you are a very attractive woman,' Jack said, 'but I will not be wanting sex, thank you.'

'And what will you be doing when I'm asleep beside you?'

'You'll have a room of your own. A lock on the door. Free to come and go as you like. The two of us running the house, and your little boy, or is it a girl, with all the love of his natural mother and a doting stepfather.'

He could see her searching his face for the catch.

'And if you meet someone, or if the father turns up, I won't stop you going. Otherwise, we can have a lovely friendly life together.'

'You know nothing about me. I suppose you make the same offer to every girl that's brought into the place.'

'I never needed to get married until today. It would be a favour for me as well as you.'

'I don't want any favours.'

'You want to keep your kid, don't you?'

They didn't speak to each other for half an hour after this exchange, although she replenished his glass when it was pushed towards her and deducted the cost from the coins sitting on the counter.

At half past eight Mr McClean stood at the door to the Porchester Lounge and looked in at the new girl behind the bar.

'That's what you'll have to put up with,' Jack said. 'Mr McClean creeping up the stairs in the middle of the night looking for a feel of your tits.'

That's when she slapped him for the first time. She might have shocked herself, because when she spoke again, she was gentle. Not apologetic, not regretful, just gentle, as if he was a naughty child, and she'd slapped him for his own good. He wanted to believe she was considering his offer.

'Have you made a girl a promise?' she asked just after eleven. 'And now you want to get out of it by marrying some innocent who knows nothing about you?'

'Say yes,' he said. 'Say you will marry me, and then I will give you all the details, and if you're not happy you can change your mind. We could be married in Kildare Street registry office next week and have a church wedding after that if you like.'

But she still said no.

Summer of Unrequited Love

CATHAL MCCLEAN SHARES HIS WORK DIFFICULTIES WITH JULIAN

Jul '83

'I'd been planning to spend the afternoon watching the workers on the Women's Right to Choose stall,' he said to me, 'but Sylvia went out and left me looking after Jack Norton, and two young men who spent the entire afternoon talking and drinking in the Porchester Lounge. My life is dominated by the whim of your wife's customers.'

The coffee-table stack of papers is topped by a device inappropriately delivered to my home. A metal affair with levers and springs and straps like some torture machine waiting for a victim to fall into its jaws. I continue with my dozing, waiting to see what he'll do with my supper tray.

'That horn blaring,' he said, 'is the taxi I called to take Mr Norton's young friends to the ferry terminal. I'd much rather be off to London with them than bringing you your supper, although the slightly older, slightly stockier of the two kept saying, "It just depresses me how fucked this country is," over and over during their five-hour session, five hours, in the Porchester Lounge. God he was boring.'

I gave him a snore-filled standoff until he said, 'Leap onto this, sleeping, drooling man,' and then there was a thud as he pushed the device to the floor, popping the eyes of my sprawled self open. Still, I managed to move my hands with ecclesiastical slowness from the cushions by my sides to conjoin beneath my pinstriped stomach.

'It's a turf cutter and squeezer,' I mumbled, as if I'd been asked. 'You strap one onto each foot. The inventor claims it takes the back pain out of cutting turf, and because the cutter's body weight is used to squeeze out the water, it could be a boon to fatties.'

'It has no place on the supper table. Did your mother teach you nothing?' he said, putting the tray down. I opened my eyes and pushed the contraption closer to him with my foot.

'When Sylvia got back, she had to tell the depressed one to keep his language down, several times, after which he'd whisper "totally fucked" a couple of times, only to tirade loudly again after his next sip of white wine. Jack Norton encouraged them to reel off the places they were going, a worldwide splurging of the redundancy money paid out when their double-glazing factory closed down.'

He arranged the quartered ham sandwiches on the plate and turned the cup right side up ready for my tea. 'It looks like a cross between a malevolent potato chipper and the ceiling-decorating stilts my father left behind when he ran off to England. Incidentally qualifying my abandoned mother for free turf, courtesy of the state.'

'The Irish people have been cutting, drying and storing turf the same way for thousands of years,' I said. 'The Auto-Turf-Cutter will drag the process into the twentieth century.' But he'd moved over to the window to look down at the horn-blowing taxi.

'My son William says all industry is un-Irish. Better to send enough of our people abroad to work and for them to remit money home to support the nation of poets rather than engage directly with such base activities.' I poised my fists to push myself upright and sent two cushions skidding towards the tea tray.

'Why are you helping him? Do you owe him a favour? Is he the son of a prominent politician? What's his hold over you?'

'This device is the logical development of the aspirations conjured up by our founding fathers when they liberated this country from the jackboot of foreign oppressors. Ideal for a cottage industry. I am bound to support its development.'

'Jack Norton is below on the street with an arm around each of those two young men. All I'd have to do is bang on the window and I'd be with them on the ferry. Jack would make sure they'd look after me and get me settled into London before they went on with their splurging.'

Providing British emigration officers don't have you on their watch list, I wanted to say, but thought better of it. 'And then, on the same day as the Auto-Turf-Cutter arrives, an English woman sends in a petition, signed by ten thousand of their woolly liberals, demanding that the Irish stop turf cutting. An end to the exploitation of the only natural resource we possess.'

'Eat your supper, Mr McClean,' Julian said and lifted the stray cushions off the floor.

'She even enclosed a draft government paper entitled "The Prohibition of Peat Export Act 1983", containing draft legislation to put a stop to the sale of Irish mulch to the flower growers of the world.'

'Only speak of mulchies, culchies and bog trotters if you're going to give me the real low down.'

'I want to share with you the dilemmas faced by an honest-brokering one-man think tank. And to ask for your sympathy when he is pulled contrary ways by powerful forces, not all of them benign.'

'Just tell me the story, Mr McClean. Was the virgin inventor sodomised on the bog while cutting turf with his uncle? Has he wasted his engineering education designing a machine that would recreate the experience? The new Irish fetish: the auto-self-sodomiser. That would be the factory to build. A new Irish export to rival the living sodomisers we've been exporting for hundreds of years.'

'That's the sort of dirty talk I expect from my son William and his friends. I had hoped you would be different.'

'Right,' Julian said and reached down for the tray. 'No supper for you. You can go to bed hungry.'

'Could you put a little mustard on the ham for me?' I said, loosening his fingers from around the tray. 'It is ham, isn't it? You cut them yourself, didn't you? Ah, sure you're a great lad altogether. Will you pour a drop more tea for me? My hand has a bit of a shake and I don't want to slop it all over the boss's papers.'

The standoff ended when he said, 'It wouldn't be my first time on the Dunleary ferry. My mother took me to see her brother Arthur. I don't remember anything about the journey except that she kept ruffling my hair and saying, "I should have cut that for you before we left; the boys in England will think you're a little girl."'

By the time Jack Norton's boys are on that ferry, Julian will be back in the Porchester Lounge serving my political masters with nightcaps after a day spent buggering up the country. The lad deserves better.

'I just don't think I'm getting the real story,' Julian said. 'And given that you think the world of me, I am entitled to it, no? Why are you holding out on me? Come clean McClean.'

Cheeky ruffian.

Summer of Unrequited Love

THE TINAHELY GOFER – BRENDAN ENTERS THE CELLAR

Sept '64

From the outside it looked like a room under the house, but when Brendan obeyed Mrs McClean and pulled back the huge greasy bolts to open the door he was confronted by a damp, foul-smelling world that was too dark for shadows and made him back out into her skirts and bosom. She pitched him forward into the smell of men's drink, and rotting things licked all over his face and into his nose and mouth the way the dog at home never did. He pressed back against her again like she was a pillow and above his head he saw her hand lifted as if she was going to smack down on him, and he closed his eyes and heard a click like a light coming on. The bulb swung shadows into high stacks of wooden crates leaning forwards as if waiting for her instruction to crush him into the rough ground.

Maybe being locked up would be okay for a while, although he didn't deserve it. It wasn't his fault William threw porridge on the carpet. But if he kept his eyes closed, and thought about

Shep, he could manage a day in there, so long as she didn't send him back to Wicklow.

Mrs McClean's next push had him reaching out for the nearest crates to stop himself from falling. Something sharp cut into his fingers and the stack threatened to fall on him. He tucked his hands into his underarms to keep them from touching anything again.

'Now get on with your duties before I send you home,' she said.

But he didn't understand which meaning to take from her words. He turned to see if her face would say, but she'd already stepped back outside, glancing at her red shoes to make sure she hadn't scuffed them before looking up and down the hall like the inspector did in his old school, checking for changes since his last inspection.

The wooden crates were filled with bottles. Full ones and empty ones. Right up to the ceiling, although there was no ceiling, just the bare beams holding up the floor upstairs. A forest of stout and ale bottles side by side waiting to be drunk. She must drink a lot. Her and Mr McC.

'Put the empties up on the footpath, and move the full bottles away from the wall,' she said, back again, holding his ear and leaning into him like he was an imbecile. He couldn't reach the top crate, never mind lift it down to move it. Even standing on two empty crates with his toes and legs and arms straining as hard as he could, all he did was make the bottles wag nervously from side to side like Shep's tail did whenever his mother tried to drive him from the porch so she could sweep the floor. He sat on two empty crates near the door and cried. He wanted to be with Shep, the pair of them lying together in the sun in the back porch, even if Shep never licked Brendan or let him cuddle him.

'What are you doing, Brendan?' she was shouting from the

kitchen. 'The delivery will be here at ten and I don't see even one empty crate up on the footpath. Have you forgotten where your suitcase is?' It was just inside the front door, packed and ready. She'd carried it down the stairs. Less than two days out of Wicklow and back in shame, covered in the porridge William had smeared on him instead of eating.

If he was in a cartoon he'd pull out a crate from the middle and for the split second the crates above were sitting in mid-air, he would turn, stack the crate in its new place and turn back to where the next crate would have reached the right height for him to pluck that one, and then the next, super-fast until he had moved them all to the new place, and not even one smashed to the ground. Except you never saw a cartoon character pushing things upwards to stack from the bottom. It would be easier to wish he was six feet tall and as strong as a man.

'Put the new stock behind the old stock.' Her voice was further away, and she sounded as if she was imitating someone else when she said, 'We must rotate the stock.'

If he didn't know what old stock was and what new stock was, or even what stock was, how could he move it? And if he managed to do everything right, she might still walk him to meet the afternoon bus back to Wicklow. Maybe if he turned off the light and hid among the towers of crates she would think he'd run away. Or maybe if he wished and wished and wished, William would throw himself to the floor and beg his mother to let Brendan come and play with him.

She'd have sent him home the day before except the last bus had gone by the time he got back from St Stephen's Green with William. The little brat had run around in circles as soon as he was out of the pushchair like a dog that'd been stung and was trying to bite the bee out of himself. But it was Brendan she slapped around the ears until they were numb. As if it was his fault that William's coat was torn and his knee bleeding.

He didn't cry when she hit him. And 'the girl' had taken him down to the kitchen. She'd wet a tea towel under the tap and handed it to him to cool his ears. Two flights of stairs back up to the sitting room, and no trouble balancing Mrs McC's dinner and something for William on the huge tray. He spilt nothing, and William ate everything. And when he brought the tray back, the girl put a chop out for him with mashed potatoes.

'Eat that,' she said, and he didn't even know her name.

But this morning Mrs McC didn't bother hitting him. She'd taken William away, holding him clear of her black blouse, to change him out of his porridge-covered clothes, and when she came back she was carrying Brendan's suitcase. It sat on the sitting room floor while she used the telephone and talked about 'the order'.

At least Mrs McC hadn't said anything about him crying while she was on the phone. It was the suitcase that made his tears drip onto the carpet. He kept his head down so she wouldn't see, and he didn't rub his eyes, and the tears disappeared into the carpet's swirls. He should have eaten the little bugger's porridge himself. That would have shown William. *Don't mess with Brendan from Tinahely. Nobody messes with Tinahely Brendan. Nobody.*

Instead he had to get down onto the carpet with a knife and scrape the porridge off before it dried. It was stupid having carpet on the floor anyway. They had lino in Wicklow. And he never cried there either.

Never.

But none of this was going to help him move the crates or stop her sending him home. He was fucked. He knew he wasn't supposed to use that word and he would now deserve everything he got, but he couldn't help himself. He was fucked,

fucked rightly. He had to accept it; he was going back to fucking Wicklow.

Summer of Unrequited Love

A STORY ABOUT CATHAL MCCLEAN'S NAME

May '26

'Given my God-granted rights and responsibilities as your father, I hereby name you Cathal Niall McClean,' the man said, leaning over the improvised cardboard cradle. He put his pointing finger in the baby's tiny fist. 'Your name is Cathal,' he whispered. 'You're a lovely boy Cathal. My lovely son.' And to seal his pronouncement, he wet his thumb in his mouth and signed a cross on the baby's forehead. 'Cathal it is.'

On the day Stanley Henry Nigel McClean's mother went into the nursing home in Birr for her confinement, his father was thinking about the inaugural conference of De Valera's anti-Treaty Fianna Fáil party in Dublin. The unreliable trains were the problem, but his elder sister heard of a spare seat in a car, told him it was meant to be and two days later sent a telegram to his hotel to announce that a forty-hour labour had resulted in a beautiful ten-pound son. And when he phoned her at the family seed business, she said, 'Ah sure so long as you're back to bring them home, Peggy will understand.'

But a week passed before he got away, and by then his wife had registered the child's name and was in possession of his birth certificate. 'Your pique is over now, Peggy. No harm done,' he said when he was home. 'We'll get the paper reissued. He will be Cathal Niall, after my poor murdered father.'

Her refusal resulted in him referring to the boy as 'son' in his wife's presence and 'Cathal' when she was absent. The town and the surrounding farmers took an amused or a rigid view about the rights and wrongs of it depending on where they stood on the privileges of a head of household, not to mention their thoughts about the recently attempted violent separation from Britain, or the suffering they'd endured when the liberators set about killing each other to determine which of them had the best plan for Ireland's future.

In Cathal's growing up years, a farmer who was big enough to take the value of his custom for granted might ask the boy his name, especially if either of his parents were presenting a statement of the farmer's account. But even a farmer with a more modest holding who saw the boy sitting up on the counter in his short pants and the hand-knit jumper that itched around his neck might say: And how old are you now, young man? Is it five or six you are? And Cathal would say: I was born on the same day as the Fin Fal party. I'm the same age as Fin Fal. Me and Fin Fal are like brothers.

The whole country could date the commencement of De Valera's party with the same certainty as they could recall 'the night of the big wind'. Even when he was old enough to pronounce the party name properly, the same farmers, getting ready for the planting season, would ask again, and smile and ruffle his hair when he answered, listening out for any response from the parents standing at the yard door watching the labourers counting out purchases.

'Now Peggy,' his father said on the afternoon of his sixth

birthday, 'it's time we gave Cathal his proper name.' The three of them were in the upstairs dining room overlooking the main street, the curtains drawn early to make the tiny flames more impressive, and the lingering smoke of the blown-out candles picked out by the shaft of sunlight coming in where the curtains didn't quite meet.

'So you can have him join the Irregulars and go about the country killing for Ireland?' his mother said.

'De Valera wants peace.'

'Oh, he's finished "wading through Irish blood", then? Is he planning to take the oath of allegiance?'

'Ah that's all in the past Peggy, and remember it wasn't the Irregulars that killed the boy's grandfather.'

The knife that cut their wedding cake, brought out only for celebrations, would need to be cleaned, put back in its box and returned to the sitting room sideboard.

'I've brought a son into the world, and I'll not have him murdered in his bed, or dragged from the same bed to lie in ambush for other men.' Red candle wax had dripped onto the white tablecloth. She would let it set hard before she picked it off.

'Do you think his sasanach, protestant, names will make him immune if it all flares up again?'

'His name is Stanley Henry Nigel.'

'I won't stand for it Peggy. I am your husband; I demand that you defer to me on this matter.' He gripped the massive dining table as if he was going to upend it.

The boy got down from his highchair without anyone demanding that he excuse himself, and left the angry silence, his face smeared with birthday cake chocolate. The hissing and glaring were unchanged when he returned with his father's old Luger. He wanted to lift it up over the table and to push the butt into his father's table-gripping hand, but the chocolate cream on his small fingers made it difficult to hold upright, and he was tired from missing his afternoon nap because of his birthday. There was nothing he could do to stop the gun from slipping away from him. The ear-searing noise reverberating inside the mahogany underworld as he followed the gun to the floor. Then he could hear nothing, not even them arguing. At least five minutes passed before anyone heard the wailing, his baby brother woken from his nap in the next room.

Summer of Unrequited Love

IF JULIAN CAN'T MARRY JACK OFF TO SYLVIA, HE'LL RECAST HIM AS HIS BOSWELL #1

'What's your job here?' Julian asks, his fingers flicking pages of the magazine stack he's sitting on. He's wearing one of those eye mask things that sleepless American wives wear in movies. And his wrists are tied behind his back with what looks like the cord from a silk dressing gown. I'm trying to make sense of what I'm seeing. I'm in my office, I'm entirely sober, I've been rereading my piece on the Dusseldorf Retail Equipment Show 83, when, without even a pantomime puff of smoke, he's facing me across my desk. Of course I'm surprised, and scared. A person can't just appear on a pile of magazines, like the mugs of tea I sometimes don't notice being dropped off by my assistant on his way back from the kitchen.

'I am the editor of *Gondola* magazine, the bible of the world of shop fittings in Ireland. You're sitting on the latest print run, on its way to be pulped actually, for legal reasons.'

'Yea, you're a journalist, you write to order,' he says as if what I do is a crime.

'I learnt my trade at RGDATA and *Checkout* magazine.'

'How would you like to write about me?'

I wasn't expecting that. 'Excuse me?'

'My Curragh House Hotel stories will be published in about six months, and after that I'll be churning out stuff regularly, interspaced with getting into scrapes, falling in and out of love, getting awards and a reputation. I'm inviting you to be in on the ground floor.'

'Wow,' I say when he's finished his little speech. I mean who wouldn't want to write (and read) about some silly teenager with delusions of becoming a literary celebrity in half a year? Should I ask him if he has a publisher, or if he's finished a single story yet? I just want him out of my office, or maybe not. There is something weirdly compulsive about him, like a rare steak browning in a very hot flame-licked pan. The bubbling, the hissing, the smell of burning butter and frying meat making your salivary glands flood your mouth with anticipation.

'Do I get to see samples of your own work before I say yes?'

'All in good time Jack, all in good time. You should start making notes straight away though. If you have a camera you could take a picture of me sitting on – what did you call the magazine? – *Gondola*? You could say *he floated into my life on a gondola, in fact on a stack of five hundred "Gondalas".* How about that?'

'I was planning on getting something to eat when you... er... appeared. Why don't we discuss your ideas over lunch?' He could interpret my segue any way he liked. His silk-cord-tied wrists sprang apart, as if miraculously, and he peeled the eye mask off with a stripper's flourish.

'Now that you're in,' he said, 'I want you to appreciate that this will be a professional relationship. I won't mind the overwhelming and helpless desire you have for me; in fact, because you will never refer to it directly, your lust will give your writing an exciting edge of frustration. But remember you will never eat any of the candy in this store.' He held up his hand as if I was going to contradict him. 'You will always harbour fantasies of me being drunk, and you getting lucky, or cling to delusions that if you tell me about your pathetically sad life story I will reward you with an occasional mercy fuck. Believe me when I say: never, never, never.'

I led the way across Kildare Street, grateful to be relieved of the sight of him for a few seconds. But he caught up and stood in front of me, facing me, a hand to my chest, stopping me outside the entrance to The Saddle Room.

'However, I also reserve the right to feed the world the excitement it needs. Even to the point of occasionally hinting that I am your fawning boyfriend,' he said, no doubt feeling my heartbeat through his fingers.

'And how will I describe our lunch today?' I asked. 'What are you wearing?' Allowing myself to find out what it might be like to play along with his fantasies.

'Say I'm wearing ripped jeans, bare flesh and red boxers flashing beacon-like as I walk. My white T-shirt is tight across my tits and my retro trainers and cheeky little baseball cap, lime green, complete the ensemble. If the manager doesn't want to serve us, I'll get you to slip him twenty quid, hold my cheek up for him to kiss, pat his bum with a squeal of delight, and say: No hiding us behind the parlour palms. I want to shock the clerics, the culchies and the Foxrock matrons. In the dining room I will hold your chair and tuck you in. And if the waiter tries to unfold your serviette (or do I mean napkin?), I will slap his wrist and say, that's my job.'

'And what will we eat?' I could get into this, after all I've just produced fifteen hundred words about visiting Dusseldorf 83 without even leaving the office.

'The most expensive food on the menu, and the best wine, and I'll watch you squirm over the cost.'

'And what about a spot of hiding under the table or behind the curtains, to eavesdrop on the other diners? Isn't that what you like, Julian?'

'You're getting a bit above yourself. Remember you're here to write about me, not tell me how to behave.'

'I'm sure I can learn to do that.'

'Just big me up Boswell. Big me up and enjoy the ride.'

'I need the toilet,' I said when we reached the bar, and I wondered if I should slip through to the lobby and leave him to it or come back and go with the gig.

Summer of Unrequited Love

THE TINAHELY GOFER... ENCOUNTERS PADDY THE PORTER

Sept '64

Brendan moved away from the stacks of crates in the hope that the empty bottles would get the idea and rush up onto the footpath, and the full ones would inch away from the wall to allow the new ones to slip in behind. He was starting to wave the stack forward when he saw the old man in a hidey-hole made out of crates and grey army blankets. The light didn't reach far into the nook, but the man was shaking with the bigness of his laugh.

'The cut of your face when she pushed you into the beer cellar,' the man said. 'I bet you thought you were a goner. Your little tear-stained face. What a sight.'

'I wasn't crying,' Brendan said. But then thought he should say something else. 'Do you live here?'

'No,' the man said. 'I'm Paddy the retired porter. And you must be Dolly Considine's apprentice porter.'

'You mean Mrs McClean?'

'That's her married name.'

'She's given me your job?'

'That's all right. I have another job. I sit here and guard against the intruders from the theatre next door. But I also need a young assistant. An apprentice to help me with my guarding.'

Paddy didn't look as old as Brendan's grandfather. But his clothes were like something he'd seen in *Mise Éire*, the film. The school had shown it for Easter, rebels hiding from the Black and Tans. Like when his father sang about the men of Wicklow ambushing the English soldiers in their barracks and then having to go on the run. Sleeping in barns and ditches and cellars.

'I wasn't crying,' Brendan said.

'Fair enough,' said the man. 'That's fair enough.' The light was too weak for him to see if the face believed him or not. 'I heard her ladyship issuing instructions. In my day the delivery man used to pass the empties up to his apprentice waiting on the footpath, and then arrange the new stock here in the cellar. Proper gentlemen, and grateful for the opportunity to demonstrate it. Not like the boyos today.'

'What am I going to do?' Brendan blurted. He held his arms rigidly against his sides so his clenched hands would not be able to rub his eyes and start them crying. 'She'll send me back to Wicklow. I want to stay here. It's not my fault her baby is wild.'

The man stood up from his crate chair and seemed to reach out for Brendan's head as if he was going to ruffle his hair. But Brendan felt nothing. 'When I was your age, I had to take most of the bottles out before I could lift a crate. It took me longer, but I got the job done. Her ladyship, not this one, but her mother's sister, used to laugh at me standing on an empty crate to reach the high stacks. She called me her little faggot.'

Then the man moved towards the cellar door and waved Brendan to come after him.

'I bet my old trolley is still here. You put an empty crate on it, fill it with empty bottles and then wheel it out into the front basement area, and then you do the whole thing in reverse up the steps to the street.'

'Are you a ghost?' Brendan asked.

'Ah sure you're in a hotel now. You get all sorts in a hotel.'

'This is a hotel? Really?' His father was barred from McGuiggan's Exclusive Hotel in Tinahely. And when his first cousin was home from America it was the only place for him to stay, and they wouldn't let his father into the bar to see him.

'It wasn't for exclusive hotels my brother gave his life,' his father said over and over when he came home, shouting, banging his open hand on the kitchen table and looking round for someone to agree with him, but later he subsided into mutterings, his hand rubbing circles on the tablecloth like a blind man feeling for grains of spilt sugar. Brendan had stood across the road from McGuiggan's after Mass on the following Sunday and cursed them for upsetting his father.

'I'm living in a hotel,' he said. 'Is it an exclusive hotel?'

'It's even better than that,' Paddy said. 'It's a private hotel. That's why you have to help me to keep the intruders out.' He held up his fists to ward them off. '*They shall not pass.*'

'*They shall not pass,*' Brendan repeated with a brave grin at Paddy. A private hotel no less. He could see Shep warming himself in the porch at home in Tinahely and wished he could tell him.

When William McClean was fourteen, he named Brendan the Tinahely Gofer although his mother forbade him from saying it in front of him. Even earlier he'd noticed that Brendan often walked with his head down. 'Are you looking for money?' William asked a million times before he was ten, which always lifted Brendan's head for a few minutes, until he forgot and it dropped back to its usual angle.

A couple of weeks after Brendan was sent to Dublin, his mother wrote to say that Shep had taken to worrying sheep and had been shot because no dog could survive long in Wicklow after that. She said in her letter that she missed Shep not being around the place, even though she'd never paid him any mind when he had been.

Brendan always went home for a week in the summer, and for the days after Christmas, back in time for New Year's Eve. Mrs McC needed him in the run-up to Christmas, and for New Year, otherwise he might have gone earlier and stayed longer. But no one ever remarked on it, either he was in Wicklow or he wasn't. The first thing he did when he arrived was check the back porch for Shep, in case his mother had been wrong about him being shot.

Sometimes his two older brothers came to Dublin for business, and his mother came up when she was having her tests, but they never called to the hotel. They hated Dublin, and got their jobs done quickly so they could be back in Wicklow before dark.

Summer of Unrequited Love

NOTES FOR A STORY FOR PADDY THE PORTER
(1883–1956) #2

He came bounding through the front door with his head swinging from side to side, his eyes darting up the staircase and on towards the ladies and the back stairs, sweeping staccato style over the prints in the foyer and the old reception desk, his entire body twisting to skim the spaces beyond the open doors of the Porchester Lounge and the Kickham Room. For all the world like one of JFK's secret service bodyguards checking the place out in sixty-three, when Dolly convinced her brother-in-law Giolla-Íosa that Curragh House would be the perfect stop for the cavalcade to refresh itself on the way to the Kennedy ancestral home. Except Julian's job was to collect dirty glasses and empty ashtrays, not manage security or dig up the past, or spend his spare time spying on Sylvia.

Still in role, as they say at the theatre next door, Julian is in the cellar passing the crates of porter up to Brendan straddling the open hatch in the bar floor above, and his eyes are attracted to a stretch of wall that was repaired after a bit of trouble, oh years ago. Two hundred years of annually applied whitewash protecting the callused bare brickwork, except on the small

214

newer infill; fewer than twenty layers to hide the lumpy bricks poking through like badly healed fractures. The glaring signal enough to make his eyes flicker to the spot again and again, until he is forced to investigate. Braille-fingering the texture for the different feels of the whitewash, like a Nazi hunting for Jews in secret rooms.

He's a dangerous sort of a blaggard because he doesn't have the wit to understand what he might be betraying. Like a crazed rat, gnawing at anything to put an end to the itch in its teeth.

'Why is this wall different from the others?'

'Hm?'

'Break it down. Now.'

Julian was handing up a crate of porter. 'Hey Brendan. Do you recognise this?' Then, in a parody of the Wicklow accent, said: 'They shall not pass,' and began shadow-boxing at the wall. 'They shall not pass.' The twenty-four bottles raining down around him, shattering at his feet and spraying his shoes and trousers with foaming stout.

My own fault that when Brendan needed an easy task to bolster him, I appointed the tiny mite as Protector of the Wall, with responsibility for keeping out intruding theatricals from next door. Little did I know that, instead of easing away along with the other roles of childhood, Brendan's appointment would still emerge after an evening's drinking. Nowadays, it's not porter-stealing actors the hotel has to fear, but its dangerous lounge boy.

Dolly Considine's Hotel

DOLLY GOES TO THE THEATRE; JACK NORTON OFFERS WORK

July 1983

Jack Norton was finishing his second drink as Mrs McClean led her Brown Thomas coffee-morning friends out of the Kickham Room and into the Porchester Lounge, all the better (no doubt) to move them on into the theatre next door for the opening performance of Mikhail Mayakovsky's production of *A Song for All Saints*. Mrs McClean was wearing her shiny brown fur coat although it was July and too warm for a coat of any kind. She held out her empty glass for Julian playing his obsequious manservant role. The ladies were doing their best to look sophisticated, and slightly bored, and, having been warned, were denying any anxiety about the avant garde nature of the production, or the ordeal of their heels coping with the irregular seating arrangements in the Porchester Theatre.

'Good evening, Dolly,' Jack said. 'Not your usual first-night guest list?'

'Good evening Mr Norton. I'm afraid our politicians are busy with referendum rallies. Just a few weeks to go.'

Jack smiled at the thought that the same deputies would be on time for the opening-night drinks party, and would pick up enough information to speak knowledgeably to reporters in the morning if *Morning Ireland* was discussing demands for the show to be taken off.

'I understand that Mr Mayakovsky can be controversial and has a reputation for getting into fisticuffs with the audience,' Jack said. But Dolly had turned back to her guests.

Mayakovsky had been in earlier, pawing at Julian and whispering that he should defy Mrs McClean's refusal to give him the evening off. 'You're my muse,' he'd hissed, over and over, even when Julian was away making coffees in the kitchen.

Jack held his glass out to Sylvia for a refill and left the money on the counter, hoping she'd include him in the free drinks being enjoyed by the theatregoers. He was impatient to share some good news and wanted them to leave.

'I hope I'm not delaying you,' Mrs Hannafin said, coming into the lounge also dressed to go out, down to a squirrel thing around her neck over a green and blue flowery dress. She took a pale sherry from Julian's tray and sipped before she spoke. 'Himself is not well,' she said. 'The rain this morning has affected the rheumatism in his good leg, so I won't join you.'

'You're dressed now,' Dolly said. 'You might as well.'

'I'll drop in on Mr Hannafin,' Julian said, holding his tray out for the surrender of two empty glasses.

'If you're sure?' Mrs Hannafin said. 'Except I have no handbag.'

'Come along,' Dolly said. 'Isn't it all paid for? The only waste is Mr Hannafin's ticket. What about you, Mr Norton? Will you have a last-minute change of heart?'

Dolly never referred to Jack by his first name, although she'd known him longer than any of the other regulars, all of whom, with the exception of serving government ministers, she addressed by their first name.

'I avoid the theatre unless I am notified in advance of the political messages we're to be force-fed,' Jack said. He grinned at Mrs Hannifin and enjoyed the thought of her having to ask Dolly's impatient-looking friends what was going on on stage.

'Won't opening nights be obligatory for you in your new position?' Dolly asked, hinting that she'd been consulted by the party before his appointment was approved.

How dare she? 'My freelancers will do all that,' he said, smiling, 'supported by my cub reporters,' and he took the opportunity to look Julian up and down, as if to judge his suitability as a cub.

Julian put the glass-filled tray on the counter when the lounge door closed behind the theatregoers, and retrieved a couple of empties from the high table by the window.

'Go and tell our war hero that his wife has gone out,' Sylvia said. 'Then fetch the sandwiches from the kitchen and the ice buckets for the interval champagne.'

'*Ruby, don't take your love to town,*' Julian sang, hopping round the room.

'The ingratitude of youth,' Jack said, glad of an opportunity to deny his lust.

'Doesn't Hannafin have a volunteer pension, and get to stay in bed all day when the rest of us have to work?' Sylvia said. 'More than adequate recompense for the couple of weeks he spent gallivanting around the country shooting at the English and scaring the life out of ordinary people.' The angry tap above the tiny sink splashed hot water onto her.

Jack engaged his heels with the cross rail on the bar stool and sat upright to announce: 'I'm to be the guest editor of the *Evening Press*'s magazine page, at least until a permanent appointment is made in the autumn.' He was clearly speaking to Julian pulling at the lounge door. 'I'm launching a new gossip feature. And a certain birdie tells me that you... er...' He didn't want to name whatever it was Julian did. 'I'd pay a guinea or two for a tasty titbit.'

'Nothing we hear or see in these rooms can be communicated to any outsider,' Julian said. 'Our first loyalty is to Mrs McClean.'

'And your second?'

'Don't encourage him,' Sylvia said. 'Isn't it bad enough that every time I turn my back, he sneaks off to his scribbling? Mrs McClean is tormented. The last thing we need is any of it getting into the papers.'

Knowing Dolly as he did, Jack expected that the combination of her own cunning and Brendan's muscles ensured she read every word Julian wrote; it would all be pretty innocent, or she'd have run him out weeks ago.

'You can phone in your copy,' Jack said. 'We'll have a dedicated hotline answering machine.'

'I don't do journalism,' Julian said. 'I write for art only. But Sylvia could do with the money.' And he continued on his way to the kitchen.

The lights would be down in the theatre and the women who'd taken off their heels to climb the high steps to their seats would be wondering whether it was worth putting them back on before the interval when no one could see their stocking feet in the dark. Mayakovsky would be in the dressing room waiting to lead the players on, checking the audience regularly to see if his little muse hadn't relented, and taken the seat, with his name on it, in the front row. He'd have a slug of vodka each time he checked, to help him with the pain, unless the theatre committee had already searched him and confiscated his hip flask.

Sylvia pulled open the drawer under the bar and swept Jack's drink money in off the counter where it had lain smiling up at her for nearly an hour.

Summer of Unrequited Love

MIKHAIL MAYAKOVSKY HAS AN EXPERIENCE, MAYBE?

Jul '83

Mikhail Mayakovsky wedged himself into a bucket chair in the Porchester Lounge, closed his eyes and held his glass at an angle so that anyone looking at him would imagine it had paused on its way back from his lips, which it had, in a way. He needed to shut down the evening. Someone was playing Erik Satie on the piano in the Kickham Room, melancholy, distant and hesitant, as if being composed as it was played. Had it been a concert he might have drifted off, but here in Dolly's with the smoke and the jostling and laughter of over-loud men and women working to convince each other how amusing they were, sleep would never come. Besides, his heart was still racing from the pills he'd taken to get him through the press preview of *A Song for All Saints* compounded by the coffee the chair of the theatre committee had poured down his gullet when they'd found him with his eyes shut in the front row an hour before curtain up, the smell and bitter taste of the liquid dribbling from his mouth ending his pre-performance meditation. He opened his eyes to the secretary holding a baby's pink plastic bib thing under his chin, the straps digging into his neck. Four other silhouetted committee heads were shaking at him.

'Wake up, Mr Mayakovsky. The journalists are here. You must wake up.' The secretary was rocking him, and the cup rattled against his teeth, spilling more of the coffee.

The stage-left lantern behind the silhouettes was blinding him. It should have been focused on the spot where Howard falls and takes Leroy in his arms, but instead was pointing at the seat where Mikhail had been asleep. The purple gel had been removed, and the lantern would have to cool before he could put it back, after which he would have to get Leroy and Howard to walk through the scene and speak their lines until the focus was right.

'Theatre managers' fucking panic,' he shouted at them. 'I've toiled for ten years to stage this play. Do you know that?'

They were not expected to answer. They'd been subjected to the details of his struggle before; he'd even included it in his original pitch to the Porchester's artistic sub-committee.

'Ten years of agonised planning and suffering,' he continued, 'and like Jesus riding on a donkey into town, you dress me in baby clothes and force-feed me coffee.' He tried to spit out the last of the bitter taste. 'And my setting is destroyed,' and he lurched upright, sending the coffee in the plastic well of the bib bouncing down his front and soaking into his flies. He sloughed the liquid sideways, debating whether to walk out and leave them to it or stay and be even more dissatisfied. The wetness of the coffee taking him back to the night he'd pissed himself, Jerry dead in the morgue and he asleep in a doorway in Marble Arch. Comforted while it was happening, but cold and regretful at dawn when he was woken by the gentle rhythmic kicking of his foot by a rubbish-truck driver wanting him to move so he could get at the bins. '*My old man's a dustman,*' he'd sung for the man, who didn't seem to speak any English.

'My lights. My lights,' he said, and picked the discarded gel off the floor. 'Where is your respect... ?' But there was no point. They were fearful he would not be awake enough to play Leroy, or to explain to the journalists what they'd witnessed on stage. Who in turn, if they bothered to review the play at all, would miss the point and drag in anecdotes about the Abbey in 1951 or the Focus in 1966.

'You're so fucking pathetic. Not even pathetic. Just boring. Why do I bother my head?'

And the committee members shifted about from foot to foot. They knew it was better not to argue with him, and they were right. Ten years of wishing would all be over in a few hours. Worthwhile or not, it would be over, along with the blur of the previous two months of casting and rehearsals and his anger at the foreshortened run. No wonder he was drunk. His total absorption was about to end. How would he get through the next two months, the next two weeks, days, or even the night?

And then he was being fucked – *there is a God!* – on the floor in the Porchester Lounge (or was that another night?) by the skinny urchin who imperialises over his girls every day during lunch. A sudden pause in the boy's pumping at the sight of the condom Mikhail produced from his shirt pocket. What is the life expectancy of a condom? Had he been carrying it around for nearly a year? Transferred it from jacket to shirt to jacket to shirt in some sort of torturing optimism that it would get used or despair that it never would? The streetlight outside provided only meagre illumination, but enough for the boy to see the gift being held in front of his eyes. The recoil not so much caused by the pocket-worn wrapper as by the realisation that

223

there was a witness to the menaces he was engaging in, that the object of the necrophiliac's desire was not only not dead, but was awake enough to demand that, if he was to be fucked, then the cock would be sheathed.

Mikhail's fresh-out-of-college debut productions had resulted in lots of starfuck moments, passions exploding at first-night parties or with closing night relief. But since Jerry, nothing. The drunken fumble in seventy-two that had led to ten years of something… whatever it was, it had at least passed the time. And when Jerry had left him for the crematorium, he was ten years older and ten years more of life had been served, followed by months of being too absorbed with grief to think about himself, even if it was all about himself.

He envied the people who got angry at his productions. Envied the spontaneous eruption of their butchering desires. The righteousness that allowed them to spit the fury into his face, the entitlement to pulverise him, spurred on by his laughter. How many theatre foyers' carpets had been stained with blood from that weakness in his left temple which opened with the least provocation, the theatre management calculating when the laughing director had generated enough publicity and it was time to rescue him from the angry punchers and snapping pressmen. The pain endured by Mikhail was nothing compared with the satisfying knowledge that he had facilitated suburbia in its transcendent moment; had briefly allowed middle-class theatregoers to be the ruffian street brawlers that he, Mikhail, could never be.

And then the adaptable creature was back at it, as if he'd taken Mikhail out to dinner and seduced him on the front steps of the hotel with an invitation to 'coffee', and was now taking his due reward rather than plundering uninvited when any guard he might have had was off duty.

Although that might have been another night. Perhaps after

the opening of *Catherine's Dilemma*. Whenever it was, he'd opened his eyes regularly to monitor the boy's face with its customary sneer, letting him know he wasn't particularly enjoying himself but was happy to keep going for the sake of having started.

Summer of Unrequited Love

IF JULIAN CAN'T MARRY JACK OFF TO SYLVIA, HE'LL RECAST HIM AS HIS BOSWELL #2

My brain wakes me at dawn to tell me exactly how I should commit Julian to paper. But by the time I am out of bed, finished with those essential little tasks, and have plonked myself down in front of the computer, I am as full of ideas as an empty carrier bag blowing around the beach at Dollymount Strand. At five-thirty in the morning when my hangover should be smothering all my impulses, the words appear with the confidence of the seconds ticking away on the bedside clock. But with a Bodum of coffee inside me and my fingers poised above the keyboard, my mind is blank, and the arrogant stream has dried up and disappeared for the day.

On Monday, while I was in the shower, I glimpsed him leaving the house and waited with him for the bus that would carry him away from Cabra. A few hours later there was a flash of him carrying a breakfast tray up the hotel stairs.

Today, at the end of a fruitless and frustrated day of starts and restarts, I have made up my mind to visit Cabra. I will walk the streets where he grew up. I will see the boxy little houses. I will look over a garden wall at the array of painted packing-case extensions tagged onto the backs of the houses like in the shantytown landscape of a South American city.

Pinks and pale blues predominate, his journal says, *but they all have badly cut tar-paper roofs.*

Am I making it up, or do I recall searching through old electoral registers for a family with two sons? A pointless exercise when both sons had left home before they were old enough to vote. But it should be possible to cut down on the number of houses. I already know his house number was uneven, which reduces it from 147 to 74 houses. I asked him once if he'd lived in an end house or in a terrace, and he wouldn't say. I know the house next door had climbing roses, but could they still be there?

Would going to Cabra be legitimate research, or obsessing? Knocking on a random door to ask the old lady if she knew of a family with two sons that ran away and left their poor mother to face old age alone, barely able to fend for herself, and dependent on the St Vincent de Paul for a hot meal in the middle of the day. You can see the woman looking at me suspiciously.

Now what was their name again? Trying to be helpful.

And I'd look into her eyes to see if maybe she could be his mother, and I'd have to say, *I don't know. The young man I knew had a 'nom de plume'.*

A what?

And I'd say, *Never mind, it's okay.*

There's no point in being angry with him. I should think myself privileged for knowing him, although I wish someone, somewhere, could feel privileged for knowing me. I know he used me, but it's well known the gifted are destined to foist their single-mindedness on their friends and lovers. If I'd complained, he would've said, we are free agents. Which of course is true, although just as completely, untrue.

I don't for an instant suppose he was a writer of such calibre that he will merit a published biography. But if I thought anyone was gathering notes for one, I'd begin a journal of my own; recollect conversations, create a retrospective file of our correspondence, possibly one sided. Prepare to gush to the graduate student from the tiny (or prestigious) American university about how lucky he is that I've kept copies. Something to balance Julian's warped description of our relationship as recorded in the stories.

God knows what I was doing the afternoon I went into Curragh House for a swift half before my pottery class and found him fluttering about like a parakeet looking for a perch. According to my office diary I was due to be at the Shop Fitters and Fitting exhibition at the Royal Dublin Society, but I have no recollection of it. I did produce a piece for the magazine, so I might have attended, although it's just as likely I cobbled something together from the pre-exhibition handouts. The freestanding reciprocally supported shelving unit doesn't change that much from year to year.

The description of how the day went for Julian, as contained in his journal, corresponds pretty accurately with how it is described in his story 'Getting Out'. Except there is no mention of his visit to the bus station gents' toilet. Which may date from an earlier or subsequent visit.

On Wednesday I woke up with the decision already made to visit Fassaugh Avenue immediately after breakfast, and I began a meditative game of Freecell on the computer to put me in the mood. I sat in front of the screen and flicked cards, until I was stuck, or out. Either way I started a new game again, and again, until eight hours had passed, and I could legitimately push back my chair and stroll angrily to the shops to buy something for my dinner; another day of avoiding Julian over, except for the fleeting shadow at the back of my brain popping a face in front of me when I was distracted that faded as I tried to verify whether it was him or someone else.

The phone was ringing when I got back from the corner shop with my bag of Italian ingredients. It was my mother wanting to talk.

'I didn't want to disturb you earlier because I knew you'd be working,' she said.

I rushed her off the phone with one-word answers and stomped into the kitchen to heat up the tomato sauce and boil the pasta. I tore the skin off my thumb grating the Parmesan. I could barely look at the meal after that, what with my stinging thumb and my anger with him for making me waste my day. Only the thought that I was cannibalising myself brought enough humour to the situation to allow me to eat.

Today was not much different. Except that Dolly McClean was intruding, wearing a nurse's outfit, complete with the flying wimples of my childhood, and insisting that I write about her, even though she has very little to do with the story. But I listened as a plan was made to use her as a way to approach Julian. An oblique segue to enable me to look without looking, to remember without remembering. And yet maybe my real fear is not that I will be overwhelmed with feeling if I settle down to reconstruct our time together, but rather that I will barely remember his fucking face. Leaving me shaking with the sadness of forgetting.

And his skin? What about his skin? When we were together, I convinced myself that the DNA in my finger had been rewritten to include memory cells. The very tips filled with exploding bubbles from the stored sensation of touching his skin. All I had to do was visualise, not even imagine, just think, not even think, do nothing, just be. Even when he was gone, the sensation memory was so alive in my fingers that they could never not feel the feel of him.

And that was just the part I could gibber about to my friends. The part that was polite enough, never mind capable of being hinted at with inadequate words. And yet now, this morning, he is absent. Not just not here in reality, but not here at all. Not in my fingertips, or any part of my skin; he is barely in my memory. It is as if I have never known him. Why the fuck am I wasting my life trying to tell his story?

Dolly Considine's Hotel

THE HOTEL TRIES TO ABSORB JULIAN INTO ITS VERY ESSENCE

July 1983

'Where are you going with those?' Mrs McClean demanded, almost leaping out of the kitchen as he was trying to sneak past with Malone's books under his arm. Her delivery was paced, but her tone suggested consequences for the wrong answer. She reached for *The Heat of the Day* and smiled at the faces of the couple looking into each other's eyes on the cover. Her sudden checking-up appearances had become a feature since she'd been given the page from his journal. 'I wouldn't have imagined these appealing to the likes of you,' she said.

The darkness through the grubby window was beginning to lift by the time the last drinkers had gone and he'd stumbled into the basement bedroom. Brendan was snoring in one bed, and in the other a stickman constructed from Malone's books had been arranged face down under the blanket. If Julian's version of Mr McClean saw it, he would advise treating the book-made-man like a threat, a warning. Too subtle for

Brendan. Sylvia maybe? Or William McClean? Malone
himself? He was too tired to care and swept them onto the floor
so he could sleep. But after breakfast he knew he had to get rid
of them.

'A friend of mine owned them, but he's finished with
reading,' Julian said, smiling at Mrs McClean. 'Now they're on
their way to Oxfam.' Flicking pages had turned up no buttery
smudges, no favourite bookmark, not even the fresh-laundry
smell of Malone's clothes or the leathery smell of his bag.

'Put them in the Kickham Room,' she said, her blue
fingernails scratching at the figures on the cover as he replaced
the book. 'In the book cabinet. It should be open.' Her eyes
scanned the stack, perhaps for signs of his journal hidden in its
midst.

The need to be rid of them raced him up the stairs so
quickly that within one breath his nose was almost touching
the door's reeded glass, the gloomy light inside making him
pause. He'd been planning to abandon the books on twelve
random park benches in St Stephen's Green, watching to see
who picked them up and hoping they would maybe inspire
stories of twelve separate fates in the future.

'You brought me speckled and brown from Ennis,' a
northern Irish voice, strong and rich, from inside the room.
'But a lift is a lift, not ownership.'

The lines repeated, and then again, the emphasis shifting
from the first 'lift' to the second. And then to 'ownership', as if
the meaning were being experimented with.

The woman was in one of the bucket chairs, her pleated
brown skirt covering her knees, her dark coat enclosing the
back of the chair right to the floor. Her left hand was pressing a
book face down against the carpet, her spread fingers keeping
it pressed like it was a bird that would fly away if she didn't
restrain it. Her hair was bundled up at the back of her head, a

small hole at the centre of the tight knot like an open mouth that would speak if it were allowed. She lifted and turned her head to look at him. The black streaks of tears on her cheeks visible even in the gloom. Maybe she was wearing too much mascara.

'What is it?' she whispered.

'Sylvia said I would be okay till five.'

'Have they telephoned for me?'

The pause between each of her utterances was not quite long enough for him to reply.

'Mrs McClean wants me to—' he began.

'Can I not be left alone? This has to go out on Sunday,' she said, raising the book and allowing it to flap at him. 'They're waiting for me in the TV Club.' Her voice was husky and syrupy and northern Irish. Familiar, too. From the sound alone he could have taken her for a man, but everything else said woman. Nora Barnacle waiting for James Joyce to take her away must have looked like this. Someone on the radio, because her face was unknown to him? If she kept talking her name might come. But she turned away and slumped back into the chair.

'I have to fill the library,' he said, trying to sound as if he was on official hotel business. His head held up to stride manfully except the lounge carpet was misbehaving. The matted, normally supportive pile had turned oily, slushy, as if it would suck him down like the quicksand his mother had warned him about, that lurked in the waters off the beach at Dollymount.

If you find yourself in quicksand, his mother had said, the worst thing you can do is struggle. He had to spread his weight. Push his feet wide apart, perhaps gamble everything on a dive to the floor to lie there spreadeagled, his surface area resisting without struggle until the sucking powers gave up. All the sooner maybe, if he could banish the gloom. Sweep open the curtains, and flood the room with clean, purifying, rescuing light. The books could help, laid out like stepping stones. Safe islands for him to walk on.

'What are you doing?' The sound of the books being skimmed to the floor elbowed the woman out of the bucket chair.

'The curtains,' he said. 'The curtains.'

'No light,' she said.

'I want—'

'No light.'

'Just until the floor—'

'No light,' she repeated. She advanced on him in two steps and grabbed his extended arm. Her feet were not sinking.

'The carpet... not like Curley's Hole?'

'What are you talking...' she began and stopped. 'Sylvia. Sylvia,' she called.

And as if by magic Sylvia was beside him, grabbing his other arm; maybe they would walk him back to solid ground. Except they did not move. Only stood and stared, not at him but at each other. A connection tuned to allow information – some encrypted story – to flow, or confirm, between them. Two women sighing at the stupidity of a man or all men. Only a moment and then Sylvia began to pull his arm towards the door.

'The books,' he said. It seemed safe to reach down now that the carpet's determination to suck out his life force was suspended.

'The books, the books, I have to...'

The woman said, 'Shush,' and stooped for one. She read the title and held it to her forehead, in some sort of greeting. 'What are you doing with these?' she asked.

'They're not books,' he said. 'Open them and they become birds, they will flap their wings and fly to other worlds.'

234

'Where did you get them?' The woman flicked the pages under her nose and sniffed. 'Why did you bring them to me? Did someone give them to you?' She was shaking him.

He gestured his restrained hands towards the glass-fronted cabinet in the alcove to the left of the Kickham's half of the bar.

'Please take him away, Sylvia, and I will look after these,' the woman said. She balanced the first book between her elbow and left breast and stooped over to pile the others on top.

'Sorry, Miss Cunningham,' Sylvia said, and pushed him out in front of her.

'Who is she?' he asked when they were in the hall.

'Don't do that again,' Sylvia said, and began to climb the stairs.

He watched the woman's reeded movements through the glass as she held each book close to her forehead, maybe to sniff or whisper a promise, before it joined the stack snuggling against her breast. The tower tilting in her lap as she sat back in the chair and leaned down to retrieve her own book from the floor.

You brought me speckled and brown from Ennis…

But a lift is a lift, not ownership…

He whispered the words to himself as he descended to the basement. He tried to imitate her slow, sensual delivery. The meaning not in the words but linked to some eternal question. No doubt to do with men and women. Her delivery making it sound at least as important as life and death. But he felt alone and empty without the books, he should not have abandoned them. They'd been entrusted to him for safe keeping. They were Malone's. They meant something, and she knew it.

Summer of Unrequited Love

NOTES FOR A STORY FOR PADDY THE PORTER (1883–1956) #3

You don't organise a refuge for boys on the run without lackeys, and runners, and embedded monitors; weren't they bound to know sooner or later that there was a cuckoo in the nest? And then the young fool wouldn't keep his head down, but acted like he had rights, and that those rights extended to exposing any secrets he could sniff out, like a French pig snouting out truffles.

I took Brendan under my wing when Dolly Considine first brought him to the hotel, and I was right to do so. But if Julian wanted help from an older man, it wasn't going to be me. All that cockiness. Hardly a word to say for himself; but the jutting-out chin, the sneer, the elbows just so, all screamed loud and clear that he had a million things to say, if he could be bothered. And when he did speak, wasn't it only to distract from what was going on behind his weasel eyes, his scheming brain working out what you were worth to him, how he could use you, what he could blame you for? Any fool could tell, he either had ten generations of smart Dubliners behind him, or his people hadn't yet finished scraping the country mud off

236

their shoes, and, in his shame, he was determined to be more Dublin than the Dubliners themselves. The runt of the litter, Brendan called him, suggesting he should have been drowned at birth.

Dolly Considine's views were very clear from the way she began to circle him, at a distance, always facing him, even in the bars, where her size and the obstructing furniture left little room for intricate moves. That heroine has opened her home to a football team of scared little mites, their troubled heads filled with the burnings and killings in their hometowns or the sacrifices expected of them when they returned to their families. Brittle buggers, liable to fly off the handle if they thought they were being misunderstood, but brave, nevertheless. Not exactly employed, but expected to help out, away from public view; in the kitchen, helping Brendan, a little decoration, a suitable recompense for a warm bed and Sylvia's cooking.

But you've taken me up a blind alley. Julian is the boy we're talking about, sweeping into the place like a coiled-up spring. God only knows what he could have wanted, pretending to be on the run from up north when he didn't even have the accent. Looking for shelter in a place that had never employed a Dubliner in all the sixty-three years of my experience.

Dolly Considine should have run him out, the way she's run out hundreds of drunks, him not knowing he was out until he found himself on his arse in Hatch Street, his coat flying after him, if he was lucky, and then only after Brendan had checked the pockets for what he called 'a fine, for the effrontery caused to Mrs McClean'.

The McClean brothers can look after themselves, and that Jack Norton too. It's Dolly Considine I worry about, and the reputation of her poor dead father. And Sylvia – as Mrs Burns, the old rip of a manageress used to say, 'fresh from the nuns in Sean MacDermott Street, one of the girls grieving for their babies given up for adoption, but much cheaper, and grateful for a chance to earn a reference before moving on.' How dare he drag all that into the open?

It's a terrible thing to think of the men and women that died at the hands of the English so this little weasel would be free to twist the truth of our aspirations into his self-serving lies. It's to the innocent I'll give my sympathy, not to that little runt. A nasty piece of work that will deserve the trouble that's bound to find him, as sure as eggs is eggs.

Dolly Considine's Hotel

JULIAN HEARS WORRYING NEWS FROM THE RADIO

July 1983

As the blaring music was not country and western, Sylvia and Brendan must have lost control of the radio. But it was the loudness Julian tried to close his ears against, not Gloria Gaynor, in the hope that Josie might be lurking on the first-floor landing with something to say. It was Sunday. The hotel's bars were closed until evening. Julian was free to walk in St Stephen's Green and go through the draft of his story about Dolly's father, Terence Considine. Josie would have known him. Unless his own mother, who'd been lurking somewhere behind him since he woke up, insisted he write about her pregnancy with his brother Christopher. She hadn't featured in a story since 'My Mammy was Throwing Petrol Bombs'. Josie would know nothing about his mother, and maybe she wouldn't whisper about Terence Considine's fall from favour either, as it had occurred after her death. But the basement-kitchen radio had gone to the news, the volume enough to drown out anything Josie might have had for him.

'Gardaí report that the middle-aged woman was a volunteer at the Women's Right to Choose stall, which incidentally has been located outside the GPO since the previous government announced plans to hold an abortion referendum. "The woman appeared distracted," a witness said, and "upset following an altercation with two visibly pregnant women visiting the rival Pro-Life stall" – who reportedly took exception to something the dead woman said. Although Gardaí have not named her, witnesses told reporters that she was from North Dublin, in her forties, and had two sons working in England.'

William McClean was buttering his way through a rack of toast when Julian entered the kitchen. The Sunday newspapers were spread like a fan of adoring accolades, but between sweeps of the knife over the toast, he was watching Sylvia in her attempts to keep the stuffing inside the lamb she was rolling for the McCleans' Sunday lunch. Another man would have held the bloody edges for her while she tied it up, but no doubt a laughing account of his slumming Sunday morning sojourn with the staff, delivered while savouring the lunch upstairs with his parents, would provide more satisfaction than actually helping her.

'What do you think of that, Julian?' William picked up and waved the *Sunday Press* at him. '*Abortionist chased to her death by pregnant mob. Pro-Lifers commandeer bus to run down Choosers.*'

Julian began loading the breakfast dishes into the steeping sink. The *Sunday Press* didn't do sensational headlines.

'It's here in the paper,' William said, and reached behind him to lower the radio. 'Is this the kind of country you want to inherit?' Julian gushed the water into the sink to drown out his voice, but William persisted. 'According to a passer-by, "The woman in the white fur coat spoke with a 'common' accent and spat at the dead woman." I mean abortion is a terrible thing, but she didn't deserve that. Now did she?'

Julian's mother always looked after the stall on a Saturday. The young woman's name was Kate, his mother liked her. Suppose his mother was dead? What would he do?

'Can you imagine, Sylvia, the pair of them all roly-poly, clutching their invitations to the birthing suite at the Rotunda, stopping at the GPO to drive this unfortunate liberationist to her death under the wheels of a double decker? Their final act of rebellion before they surrender to the shackles of motherhood.'

Sylvia had removed some of the stuffing and was managing to keep the roll of lamb sufficiently closed to get it tied up before pushing more stuffing in from the open end.

'It doesn't say what number bus it was, but as she was unlucky maybe it was the thirteen. Would you include that kind of detail in your stories, Julian? Does the number thirteen even go up O'Connell Street?'

'Shut up, you twit,' Julian said. He snatched the newspaper out of William's hands and began to shred the sheets and scrunch the strips before throwing them back onto the table.

'Mr McClean hasn't read that,' Sylvia said. 'You'll have to go out for another.'

'Sylvia, don't be hard on Julian.' William pushed back his chair and lurched to his feet. He was still drunk enough to need the table to support himself until he got his arm around Julian's shoulder. 'In the words of the poet, our unfortunate lounge boy didn't get his hole last night. Or more correctly, I suppose, in Julian's case, nobody got his hole.' William shook Julian's shoulder in appreciation of his cleverness. 'I was discussing his case with a friend last night, and he remarked how unfair it was that the Sunday papers don't have personal ads for boys like Julian. Sheep-shagging farmers can meet their imperfect partners, but bumboys have to languish unsatisfied. It's not fair.'

If he listened to every bulletin, he'd eventually find out

the dead woman's name. Better to be certain before he went charging home in an emotional panic; and if his mother was dead, what would be the point? He was already too late.

'I propose we set up a stall for Julian at the GPO and invite passers-by to sign a petition. Once this referendum business is over, there'll be campaigning stalls going a-begging. We'll need piccies of your bum-bum, Julian, to decorate the wall and to give away. Nothing vulgar now. Although with the Pro-Lifers currently displaying aborted foetuses in jars, and enhanced colour photographs of dismembered babies scattered round the floors of murder clinics, who could possibly object to some tasteful pictures of Julian's skinny little tush? Am I right, Sylvia?'

But Sylvia was now absorbed with getting the rickety oven door open without burning herself. She balanced the roasting tin on top of the washed cups arranged by Julian on the draining board. A small piece of the stuffing fell out onto the roasting tin and left a sneering-mouth-shaped hole in the rolled-up meat. This third generation of the McClean dynasty will be eating more than his share of me soon, the lamb seemed to whisper. Do you think he cares if your mother is dead or not, so long as the innocent gullibility vote for him?

Julian looked to see if Sylvia had heard the lamb's speech, but the scorching oven door had touched her bare forearm, and she pushed the two boys aside to run cold water over the emerging red mark.

William levered himself along the table to the radio and restored the volume to join in the chorus of 'Going Back to My Roots'.

If Mammy is dead there's nothing I can do, Julian told the tap Sylvia had left running, and turned it off so tightly his hand hurt where the crosshead dug in. I'll honour her life and mark her passing with a story. She'll have to manage with

Christopher and my father back from England. I'm not going home.

Summer of Unrequited Love

COMPILING WILLIAM MCCLEAN'S ELEMENTS FOR THE THREE GENERATION DYNASTY

The girl could easily be one of the punks William's father claimed were living in St Stephen's Green. His real father that is, his mother's husband, the man he's always thought of as his father. Except that Julian, bold as brass, while he'd been larking around in the kitchen that very morning, in front of Sylvia and Brendan had said, 'He's not your father, you know.'

Everything about the punk girl screamed tragic, from the black of her chain and badge-covered jacket to her tiny tartan skirt over fishnet stockings right to her pierced head topped with brittle spiked hair. He hated to agree with his father, but she did look repulsive. Not much of a mother either, throwing the bread to the ducks herself instead of letting the kid in the pushchair poised over the edge of the pond do it. Which might have shut up his bawling and stopped the buggy rocking closer to the water.

If his father was right, she and her boyfriend were living by spit-roasting ducks in the bushes, a flagon of cider keeping cool in the pond, the fat making a hissing sound as it dripped onto the embers, the smoke drifting towards the full moon, the locked park gates no bar to the indulgence of their perversion.

'Cathal McClean is not your father,' Julian had announced, not even bothering to sugar-coat it with doubt. Mother was right: he was a thug. Why would anyone believe him? Except that Sylvia – did everyone have doubts? – didn't contradict him. Not convincingly anyway; something different about the way she argued instead of threatening to slap his face, her usual way of ending his cheek.

Usual? What usual could there be? He'd been with them a month. Barely a month, and already he's acting like he has a right to speak his mind, never mind the right to make up stories about William's family, and now William's legitimacy.

'Aren't you getting above yourself for a kitchen porter?' William had said, although his mother had checked him before for speaking like that to the staff. Wait till she hears the latest; the thug will be out the door and maybe sleeping in St Stephen's Green himself, trapping ducks with the rough-sleeping punks for his own sustenance. 'And if you're so smart then, and my father is not my father, who is? Answer me that.' William had expected Julian to play for time, and maybe hint at an affair with one of the drinkers from the bar.

The buggy's front wheels were now in the water, a couple more thrashes and the punk woman's kid would be joining the ducks in the pond.

'The Taoiseach of course.'

'Garret? Garret Fitzgerald?' William laughed; his mother would never sleep with anyone from Fine Gael. 'Garret the Good? No fucking way.'

'Not him, the real Taoiseach. Our Giolla-Íosa is not just the nation's father-in-waiting.'

'My uncle? You've never even met him.'

'Well your mother has. Check out if they were together... I estimate New Year's Eve, 1961.'

Uncle Giolla-Íosa hadn't been to lunch since May. He'd invited William to accompany him to thank Sylvia and Brendan personally for the wonderful meal. Five punts each and cinema tickets for the matinée performance if they left quickly, which they did.

'Your mother says you want to drop out of university,' Uncle Giolla-Íosa had said as he watched William searching the kitchen cupboards for the makings of after-lunch coffee to bring back upstairs.

His uncle had leaned against the kitchen table in the same spot from where Julian had made his announcement, sipping the beer he'd taken from the Kickham Room on the way down. He'd already offered William the other bottle, in mock conspiracy against his parents upstairs in the family room, which of course he'd refused.

'It's exactly like school, except in school the teachers cared about me.'

Uncle Giolla-Íosa had always been at his late grandmother's house in Offaly whenever his parents took him on a visit. His mother, father and uncle had grown up together, hung out together, joined the Fianna Fáil party together. What else had they done? It was disgusting enough to make him want to kill him.

'I wish I'd gone, you know,' Giolla-Íosa said as William arranged the cups on the tray. 'Although I'd have tried for Earlsfort Terrace, it looks better on the CV, to the electorate that is. But your father was set on Trinity.'

'Fat lot of harm it's done you,' William said, which was the nearest he could get to saying, maybe Daddy wouldn't be a drunk if you'd been with him.

'If I'd played hurling for the county, I'd have two terms as leader under my belt by now, but in future years it'll be the boyos with the top degrees who make the grade,' he said.

'Daddy doesn't care if I stay at Trinity or not.'

'I assure you, William, your father cares deeply about your education. I know he does not want you to drop out.'

His uncle's words took on a different meaning after Julian's pronouncement, the prick.

Julian was running out of steam. Maybe he'd set up an interesting situation with William, but where was the story going? If truth be told, he was bored with William. He had all the pocket money he wanted, his university fees were paid for, a guaranteed job when he qualified, and a dynasty to inherit. But none of it made him interesting. He'd also have to find out if Cathal had gone to college or not, and if so whether it was to Trinity.

Blame wasn't the right word, but some of Julian's lack of steam was down to Paddy the Porter. Paddy had started him off with the McClean history, but more than a week had passed since Julian last felt the slightest chill on the stairs. The beer cellar, the boys' bedroom, the kitchen, even the doorways in the dank basement hallway leading to the front and back yards had all warmed up in a kind of conspiracy. Or did ghosts hibernate in summer?

He needed Paddy to rant about William's arrogance, his boorishness, his easy acceptance of privilege and his secret perverse desires for punk girls. If Paddy came back, he might get a description of the afternoon William was conceived, hear a whisper of what Mrs McClean thought when she knew she was pregnant and find out if Cathal McClean knew he was raising his brother's child.

Lovely Paddy had helped him with Dolly's father's story and

had helped to start William's. Paddy had slept in ditches and in cowsheds when he was on the run during the Civil War. He'd trapped ducks and eaten wild berries. And William wanted a taste of what that had been like. But the coward needed to be close enough to the hotel to come home when the rain and the cold became too much, even with the punk woman thrown in, her bondage trousers, her rough jackets and chains, her green- and pink-dyed hair, and... Julian didn't know what had to come next. He had to be patient with Paddy, listen out for him, agree to any terms, and then the sweet man would tell him the rest of William's story.

Summer of Unrequited Love

NOTE TO SELF:

I am officially bored finding out what Sylvia does on her day off, Julian wrote in his journal. *She collects a little girl in Rialto and takes her (on the number 17 bus) to the park in Terenure to play. Any details about the child are unimportant for my story. I have everything I need. End of detecting. Over and out.*

And while I am on the subject: I hereby abandon my plans for letting Jack Norton be my Boswell or invent a fake sexual relationship with me for his own fantasies. His story will require a separate endeavour and might have to wait until I am older and understand people better.

The McClean/McClelland Dynasty story is bubbling away nicely.

Dolly Considine's Hotel

JULIAN TAKES A TAXI TO TERENURE

July 1983

The taxi had three stickers in support of the Pro-Life Amendment in the window and a small luminous statue of the Virgin Mary stuck to the dashboard.

'I've never had a Curragh House employee in my car,' the driver said. 'Only the family and punters.'

'Where would we be without the punters?'

The man turned his head to get a better look at Julian.

'Have you been there long? I don't remember you pouring any politicians into the back of my cab at two o'clock in the morning.'

'I look different after midnight,' Julian said. 'I'm taller, my head is squarer, my nose is big and bulbous, and I wear very thick glasses.'

'You're joking me, aren't you,' the man said and slapped his knee.

Maybe he should have sat in the back seat. Still, the driver could be a source of information.

'A man like you must have picked up some amazing fares from the hotel over the years.'

'I've seen them all,' the man said, his face showing the struggle to remember someone that would impress Julian. 'The ministers, the party spokesmen, and the mistresses. I could tell tales, but like a priest and the seal of confession, a taxi driver is bound by obligations.'

'Mistresses is where I would draw the line,' Julian said. 'You have to earn a living and everything, but ferrying mistresses?'

'Oh, I get called to take her home when it's not convenient, or to go round to her place first thing in the morning to take the pair of them into town. Many a morning I'm obliged to drop her off at Brown Thomas before taking him to the train station to go back to his constituency and his wife.'

'Ah, that's not right,' Julian said, 'not right at all. Still so long as they pay their fare and don't actually fornicate in the car, what more can you ask?'

'I suppose,' the man said. 'But it's shocking to hear... *I have a big vote on Wednesday; I'll taxi round to yours after that.* Elected representatives shouldn't be flaunting that kind of thing.'

'And what if she has to go over to Birmingham for a quick fix? I mean, with all these Pro-Life stickers,' Julian said, pointing at the windscreen, 'would you tell her to take the bus to the airport?'

'I'm beginning to think you're a cheeky young man,' the driver said. 'And if you were a son of mine...' The man paused as if to imagine the scenario.

'What would you do to me, Daddy?'

'I'd box your fucking ears, you cheeky thug.'

'Boxing my ears would be okay,' Julian said. 'It would set me on the path of righteousness. I only ask that you be even-handed with me.'

He'd been washing the breakfast dishes when Mrs McClean

gave him a folder and instructed him to get into the taxi waiting outside. 'Mr McClean is at a meeting, expecting these papers. The taxi-man knows the address. Hurry now,' and she clapped her hands again, the way he'd noted previously. He flicked through the folder to let any secrets jump up at him. State secrets or party secrets, he didn't care.

'Are you Fianna Fáil or what?' Julian asked the man. 'A friend of Charlie's? Or a follower of Garrett?'

'Mind your own business,' the man said, pulling out in front of a car caught in the inside lane. But the number 14A bus coming towards them made no concessions and he had to swerve back in.

Temper temper, Julian wanted to say. But the 14A was on its way to the Phoenix Park and would pass through Cabra, near enough to his home to deliver a message. Tell Johnner he's a wanker, he whispered to the bus. And I hope he's having a lousy summer. And tell me ma, I'm glad she wasn't run over, and I'm sorry for the woman who was. The bus gave no hint of carrying echoes of his mother having sat upstairs or cursing him for not getting in touch since he'd run away, supposedly to England.

Then he said, 'It's just that Mr McClean is at a highly confidential party meeting in Terenure and I'm delivering these papers.' He tapped his open hand on the folder. 'There's a memo to Charlie telling him how he can win the next election, and another on phone tapping marked "Attention of Head of Service Only". All very hush hush. But vitally important if you want Charlie back at the helm, or if you think Garrett should be allowed to go on grinding the country into poverty. Do you know what I mean?'

At this hour his mother should have been on the bus that took her to work, but according to the radio a big crowd was expected at the funeral of the woman who'd been run over, including all the volunteers from the stall. She'd have left Christopher's breakfast on the kitchen table because he'd have been out late with his mates the night before. She might take this very 14A home later, picking it up at the stop in Phibsborough after getting a chop in Quinnsworth and a bag of potatoes to make chips for her first born.

'VAT on children's clothes, the Pro-Life Amendment wording, Dr Paisley, the H-Blocks dirty protests, it's all here. Are you sure you don't want a look?'

'I'll tell you what I want. I want you out of my fucking cab.'

'My fare is paid. If word gets back to Mrs McClean that you mistreated me, it might not bode well for your future prospects.'

They stopped to allow a funeral cortège to turn into a church on the left, and the driver blessed himself. On their right a light-skinned man with an afro came out of the public toilet rubbing his fingers against his lips; he looked at the tips and ran his other thumb across them.

'Are you upset because I haven't mentioned Labour, or Sinn Féin Workers' Party? Are you hoping to hold the balance of power in the next election? Well, it's still all here. How would Charlie know if you knew his little strategies? Hm? Hm?'

The man turned the radio volume up and distorted 'Every Breath You Take' as the car stopped at the traffic lights. He revved and changed in and out of gear until he could go. But once they were around the corner he stopped again.

'Here,' he shouted, and handed Julian a piece of paper. 'That's the address. It's the first turn on the left just past the *Sunday World*. Now fuck off.' He reached over and pushed open the door, and with the other hand released Julian's seat belt.

Julian held the door as he stood on the roadway.

'Thanks for the lift, Daddy; I'll tell Mammy you were asking for her.' He left the door open and walked the way the man had pointed, pausing outside the gates of the *Sunday World* to have a quick look at the previous Sunday's glass-protected front page. All the folder actually contained was multiple copies of something entitled 'New Strategies for Party Funding' and subtitled '(in a year with two general elections and a constitutional referendum)'. Julian would morph them into something much more exciting or find the love letter Cathal had been writing the last time he opened the folder.

He would deliver the papers pronto and find a quiet place to spend quality time with his journal. The taxi driver would definitely get a mention, although he might have to give him wild hair or a missing little finger.

Dolly Considine's Hotel

FOR ONE NIGHT ONLY: JULIAN'S FINGER IS A STAR

July 1983

'Sit,' Mikhail said and pushed Julian down onto a cushion in the front row of the theatre beside an old-fashioned tape deck. 'You press here every time you hear the word "abortion".' Mikhail released the pause button and 'Every baby a wanted baby' exploded from speakers concealed beneath the raked seating.

'Press down immediately and release it the next time you hear "abortion",' Mikhail said, and 'All terminations are murder' boomed out.

'Etcetera,' he said and lifted the deck onto Julian's lap. A tangle of red and black wires pulled out from under the seats.

'Can I have a script?' Julian asked.

'It's on a loop: "abortion", press to release, press to pause. Easy?'

'Why can't I have a script?'

'Because I want you to listen. I thought you were good at that.'

'I am the stand-in assistant stage manager, and if the ASM was here she would have a script.' He pushed the deck back on the cushion and stood up.

'Just do what you're told.'

'For God's sake Max, stop playing games,' said the actor called Imelda, the one who reminded Julian of his mother. She clenched her fists and hissed as ably as Mikhail.

'I have asked my ASM to do a job and he is refusing to obey me.'

The theatre is the size of the hotel's beer cellar, the boys' bedroom and the kitchen all knocked together. The audience come directly from the footpath down the steps into the basement area. The door opens into the performance space, the crumbling brickwork smelling of cold damp and cigarette ends, the three rows of seats rising up the back wall.

'A theatre needs somebody to be in charge,' Mikhail said, 'and in this one it is me.' He looked around as if for support. 'And my authority is being challenged by the ungrateful youth that I have so generously drawn under my sheltering wings.'

The ticket seller is a grumpy man in an Aran sweater wearing a bus conductor's bag to hold tickets and money. It hangs from his neck instead of the low-slung hip arrangement of the last bus conductor he remembered, before the buses went one-man. From his crooked arm hangs a long black umbrella, in case he has to order latecomers to stand outside in the rain until a suitable moment arises in the play for them to cross the performance space and take their seats.

He shook his head at Julian.

Imelda's character required a nun's outfit. Everything black except for the white bib-thing biting into her neck just under her chin. 'Sweetie,' she said as she reached for Julian's right hand, selected his index finger, and looked as if she was going to sniff or address it. 'For one night only,' she said, looking directly into his eyes, 'we need this finger to press this button and release the anguished cries of Mother Ireland. We do not have a tech box, so you'll be out of sight under the audience. The audience must believe her screams are coming from the tormented depths of hell.' She smiled and brushed the backs of his fingers against her cheek, as if promising heaven would be his reward. 'Are you with me?'

'If Sister Dymphna had been like you, Josie would still be alive and planning a birthday surprise for her soon to be thirty-year-old son,' Julian said.

'He won't get another stage management job in this city,' Mikhail said, 'or in any city where I have influence.'

'You will be alone with the tape deck in the dark,' Imelda said, 'under the audience, looking up at their bums and feet. A light would reveal your secreted presence.'

He'd tell Mikhail to go fuck himself, except he hadn't known about being in the void beneath the audience. Close enough to hear their anticipating chatter: their silhouetted shoes playing footsie with strangers or fidgeting with anger at the propaganda playing out in front of them.

'For you,' he said, and revolved his index finger in her soft palm as if communicating a secret sign. 'But could I please have a script?' He smiled at Mikhail. 'I promise not to read it, but if I can clutch it to my chest, I will feel part of the theatrical family. All the better to press that button, and make my own small contribution to the performance, and your directorial reputation.'

'Don't fall asleep, and watch out for spiders,' Imelda said, and began to make her way to where a very pregnant-looking teenage actor was staring out from the tiny dressing room.

Mikhail lifted a hatch and exposed the space under the seats. He reached for the back of Julian's collar, and using both hands twisted him down onto the bare seat, then turned him into the dark mouth and pushed.

'This is not over, you little prick,' Mikhail said.

Julian did not resist as he was tumbled in. He banged his head when he tried to stand up. He said nothing, even when the tape deck was pushed almost into his face, the wires confusing his fingers.

The ticket seller waved the first two members of the audience towards their seats and wiped his nose in the cuff of his Aran jumper before Mikhail dropped the hatch back into place, sealing Julian into his darkened underworld.

Dolly Considine's Hotel

JULIAN FINDS AN ENVELOPE AND RECEIVES AN UNUSUAL REQUEST

July 1983

'I'm here for the interview,' Julian told the man who opened the door. He put on his biggest smile and held out his right hand, clutching Cathal's papers to his breast with his free arm, one corner of the folder resting on his hip the way he'd seen the schoolgirls in Coláiste Éanna clutch their slim folio holders as they walked home or waited for a bus.

The man was no older than Julian, just better dressed, his suit new, the shirt and matching pink tie looking exactly as they would have done in the presentation box in the shirt shop. He began to extend his hand to take Julian's, but then diverted it to the inside door latch.

What would his mother say if she saw him handing over a bunch of Fianna Fáil papers to this lackey instead of giving them to a campaigning group or a journalist of her choice while she was attending the funeral of the woman who'd died asserting the rights of women to decide whether to stay pregnant or not?

'What interview? With whom? There's nothing arranged. Who sent you?'

Julian waved his free arm over his shoulder, back towards the junction with the main road.

'This is the right house, isn't it? Am I late? It's less than an hour since the instruction came from HQ. I've been sent by the very top,' and he patted the folder.

'Are you from the *Sunday World*?' The man scanned the cars on the road as if checking for watching cameras, or backup.

'I have the dossier,' Julian said. 'I was told to discuss it only with the boss. Those are my instructions.'

'Just fuck off,' the man said, and, grabbing the folder, pushed Julian out of the porch and closed the door, not noticing in his fluster the envelope that slid out of the papers onto the front step.

'I'd never vote for you,' Julian shouted through the letterbox, as he picked up the envelope to tuck inside his journal. 'And a hundred quid says you have a tiny dick.'

He was walking back to where the taxi man had thrown him out of the cab when he made up his mind to go and see his mother. He would confess to her how he had delivered the papers, take whatever criticism came, and offer her the envelope and its contents.

'Hey Mama Hey,

You're just a 14A away,' he sang.

But as he reached the main road, he recognised he was near the park where Sylvia had taken the little girl the previous Thursday when he'd been trapped on the 17 bus. He could divert himself to the park now and build up a picture of the two of them playing or walking. He might even work in the Fianna Fáil lackey, perhaps have him eat his packed lunch on the same bench frequented by Sylvia. His mother would have to wait.

Descriptions of the summer flowers, the rain shelter, the tree-packed view, the suburban tiled roofs beyond, all flowed into his journal as if the story had been waiting for him to come to this very bench, half his arse sticking through its broken slats. He was describing the girl's hair when a voice said, 'What are you writing, mister?'

Did all little girls look alike, or could this be her again? He'd left Sylvia at the hotel, but he lifted the journal to his face before looking around. No one nearby except several teenagers on bicycles and a couple of lady pensioners. He'd called her Trudy in the story. Her name didn't matter but he saw that he would have to adjust his description of her hair; it was more blond, and longer, than he remembered.

'I'm writing a story about a little girl who meets her mammy every week in the park,' Julian said. Why should he lie?

'Are there any ghosts in it?' she asked.

'Do you think I should put one in?'

'Of course.'

'But which ghost?'

'What do you mean?'

'Do you know a ghost that would like to be in my story?'

'Don't be silly,' the little girl said. 'Ghosts don't want to be in anyone's story. You just have to put one in. Just make one up. They don't exist anyway.'

'Well, what about a name for the ghost?'

'Sharon,' she said. And then someone else was shouting it.

'Sharon. Sharon, come back here. Now.' He had to turn right around to see the woman on the grass behind him. Two boys were kicking a ball nearby, older-looking than Sharon, black. The woman was dressed like a student, with beads in her hair and loose tie-dyed clothes.

'Stop bothering that man.'

Sharon sat up on the bench beside him. 'Would you like to be my daddy?'

'What would I have to do?'

'Nothing. Just be him. All my friends have a daddy. But I don't. Even Patrick and Seamus have a daddy, except he lives abroad.' She pronounced 'abroad' as if she didn't know what it meant, and she pointed at where the two boys were watching, not kicking the ball.

'Well, so long as I don't have to do anything, I will be your daddy,' he said.

'Okay,' she said, and jumped down from the bench to run back towards the woman and the little boys. 'I have a daddy. I have a daddy.'

He could hear Sylvia banging things in the kitchen because he was gallivanting in the suburbs instead of cutting and buttering bread. *We have twelve booked for lunch. The sandwiches won't make themselves.* He'd have to tell her the taxi man drove off and he had to walk back because he didn't have the bus fare.

He put his pen in his pocket and closed the journal. He would change the colour of Trudy's hair when he was on the bus. He nodded his head as he passed the woman. The ball had gone into a bush and the boys were pushing each other as they went towards it. The woman was picking at a fingernail. Only the little girl was paying him any attention, smiling, and looking satisfied.

He'd just missed a bus so had time to examine the envelope. It was empty. Just a phone number on the outside in pencil, which he phoned from the box by the bus stop.

'Portlaoise,' a male voice said.

'The prison?' Julian asked.

'What can I do for you?' the man asked.

'Are you holding a man called Malone?' But instantly realising it was a stupid question, he hung up.

Summer of Unrequited Love

THE TESTIMONY AND PARANOIAS OF MIKHAIL MAYAKOVSKY #3

Jul '83

When I am old, I will live in a home for old people. My juices will be dried up, my brain will be stultified and resting. I will be happy waiting for God to take me. Now I wait for the armed agents abseiling down the outside of every building I live in or visit; they will come crashing through the shattering glass firing shots into the air and at my legs to take me down. They know nothing about me, have confused me with somebody else, unless unbeknown to myself I am the arch terrorist, the threat to international security they suspect. Waiting for me to make the fatal slip and copper-fasten their certainty. Otherwise how to explain why they hold back – unless it is because I am part of something bigger, just a cog in a world-threatening machine, and they are waiting to bag the entire gang, root and branch, guaranteeing the destruction of the web of betrayal. Their patience guided by the sure knowledge they are making the odds better for themselves. But whatever they believe about me, it's also personal – my class betrayal, my failure to live up to expectations.

I have a hope though, and it is this: that when the drugs and disorientation have made me reveal everything I know, there will be peace; I hope to be conscious enough to enjoy that peace, for a little while, with whatever of my mind remains.

In the meanwhile, I read about the world, I study the groups and the trends, I delve into their aims and objectives, and their methods for achieving them. In that way, I am hopeful that I will know enough to convince my tormentors that I know much more. That I have untapped reserves of knowledge, which, with a little encouragement, a little kindness, they will be able to extract from me.

I am hopeful that with this strategy I can play for time and develop a relationship with my captors, face to face. Make them keep me alive. Although when they find out I know nothing important, never knew anything important, they might just finish me off, bang.

Or by myself, having held on for so long, I will turn instantly old, and my drying juices will dispatch me directly to the home for the God-waiting.

Summer of Unrequited Love

CATHAL MCCLEAN IS MADE TO SHARE A VERSION OF HIS HISTORY

Jul '83

'I'm sure my father put them onto me, because they called me Cathal from the very start, when my mother's people knew me as Nigel. They said there was a sleeping cadre and I should join it. Our job would be keep ourselves primed, ready at a moment's notice to go into action. In the meantime, I was to take up the civil service commission offer and forget about university. Barely a week in Dublin, looking forward to being a student at Trinity, but I was told, no more education. Ireland needs civil servants, loyal civil servants, not college boys.

'The revolution will kick off again shortly, was the message, one final push and Ireland will be shot of England once and for all. I said I didn't like the violent language, that enough people had died for Ireland. I wanted to live for her. My contact shook my hand and said, "Yes, yes, that's exactly what we want. Men of your calibre will be essential in implementing the new order: prime minister Atlee has surrendered India; he's not going to hold out for six tiny counties in Ireland. De Valera was too soft with Churchill. He missed his opportunity, and now, with Churchill gone, it's time to get tough. The English will be out by Christmas fifty-one, and the whole island will be one republic."'

'Should I call it a cadre of calibre?' Julian interrupted me. 'Will I say the old guard thought going to Trinity would provide The Cadre with no calliper?'

'Are you listening to me, or just trying to be smart?'

'I'm looking for news,' he said. 'Today's news. You're a man of power, you move in the corridors of power, every day, and your brother is known as the real Taoiseach. But you talk about ancient history, except it's history that never happened; I want substance, but everything you tell me is shite. And not even thick, rich shite, but scuttery, watery shite.'

'What would you like to know about...' and I swear he looked around at our cluttered little private sitting room as if it would help him with the questions to ask. He lingered over the framed certificate I got for my part-time studies in Public Administration, then at the family photos on the sideboard, before moving to the trinkets in the display cabinet. He'd be interrogating the couch I was sitting on next. Asking the saggy cushions and stained armrests to help him. 'Don't your own handlers run classes for you?' I muttered. But thankfully he was too absorbed to hear me. It would be dangerous to acknowledge he was anything other than a lounge boy. 'Are you expecting Dolly's few bits and pieces to prompt you with the correct question, turn you into an instant political correspondent, a pundit who has dedicated his life to his subject?' Maybe Dolly had started sheltering a different type of boy. They tar and feather drug dealers now in Belfast, or knee cap them. Is that what he's getting away from?

'Tell me something I don't know.'

'I never drink at home.' With an afternoon of Jameson inside me, maybe I wanted to be provocative.

'I don't give a damn,' he said with the intonation of Clark Gable.

'No. I suppose not. Still, I promised Dolly that if they took me into central office I would only drink in Buswells or at party conference, and I've kept my word. Here I am, living above a candy shop, and yet I never touch a single sweet.'

'And what about the Taoiseach? Both the actual and the man William calls the Real Taoiseach. Are they partial to a sweetie or two?'

'Am I to understand that details of government or opposition policies are unimportant to you? That what you want from me is gossip, accompanied by just enough background to make your inventions plausible?'

The way he began loading my tea things onto the tray suggested he didn't want to be understood.

'My ex-friend Johnner says we live in a banana republic; that must mean secrets.'

'Shed loads of them,' I said. 'Do a tour of Leinster House, sit in the visitors' gallery, spend an hour with the press corps in the bar at Buswells, and you'll be let into enough secrets to inspire a hundred thinly disguised true-to-life dramas. Read the newspapers, political magazines like *Magill*, that's my advice.'

'Will it tell me how often the Taoiseach gets a ride?' He spat out the words as he pulled the tray up. My teacup rolled off its saucer onto the carpet. 'Or who he's doing it with at the moment? One or many? Actresses or journalists? Do they openly speak about the Real Taoiseach fucking his sister-in-law?'

'The *Phoenix* might, but I don't think that's any question to ask the husband of the woman being referred to. Mrs McClean is a good woman. A good wife and mother. A faithful companion, and a loyal party member.'

'And you expect me to write about that? To make an irresistible story out of your lip service; to construct a titillating narrative from your platitudes? I want muck. I want to be sickened yet stimulated by your revulsion,' his waving arms and hysterical tone reminding me of the dominatrix in a cheesy porn movie that did the rounds of the government secretariats when a man from the censorship board was on secondment. I was tempted to tell the boy to get another tune.

'Where is your disappointment?' he said. 'I want to feel it. I want to see the impotent rage caused by the betrayal of your idealism, the waste of the young lives sacrificed in the interests of letting De Valera and his hoodlums indulge their sad limited vision and corrupt Ireland's ambitions. Show it to me. I am depending on you. You can't let me down.'

And then I was alone in the sitting room, with the door left open, and me grasping the couch arm to help my breath return. And then the music for the television news came on, and the reader smiled and said, 'Good evening,' as if it was another ordinary day.

Dolly Considine's Hotel

JULIAN TRIES TO MAKE A PHONE CALL,
SEVERAL TIMES

July 1983

When Julian and Johnner were at school in Coláiste Éanna, they made contingency plans for the inevitable *what if* situations they would encounter during the years before they were free of their parents' control. It was their favourite game, played mostly while walking to school to distract them from undone homework, and resumed on the way home to distract themselves from thinking about gangs from the saints' estate punishing the rest of the world because they were trapped between the railway lines.

What to do if more bombs went off in Dublin was a regular topic.

The stories to tell an intrusive press about growing up in Cabra when Johnner had a number one record in the charts became very important when he began playing the drums.

So did the agreed circumstances in which the life-support

machine would be switched off, after they'd read *One Flew Over the Cuckoo's Nest*, being too young to see the film.

How we will make contact, when our families forbid us to see each other, or take us to a strange city or country without allowing time for goodbyes? Julian inspired this last scenario out of fear that his father was going to forcibly remove him to London, and that his mother was planning preventative action by taking him into hiding in America.

It had been easy to agree the contact method. But they'd agonised over a predictable arrangement that wouldn't enslave the one in Dublin, or endlessly frustrate the one trapped abroad. After three weeks of arguing Julian promised to be at the phone box outside the shopping centre in Phibsborough at seven (Irish time) every evening for a month. Johnner readily agreed to the time but set the days as the twenty-fifth of every month for a year. Johnner was born on the twenty-fifth. They sealed the agreement by taking turns to ring from the phone inside the shopping centre while the other waited by the box on the street.

For the six nights before 25 July all these years later, Julian's dream landscape was dotted with broken phones or scrambled babbling over crossed lines. On the day itself he watched the payphone by the reception desk to see if people making calls got through. At five minutes to seven, the call-box number was engaged. He cursed whoever was speaking, excluding Johnner, who might be in the call box holding the receiver to his ear and moving his lips to keep any queue at bay until seven o'clock when he would hang up to receive Julian's call. And bang on seven he had an answer after only two rings.

'Is that you, Johnner?' Julian shouted.

'This is the phone box in front of Quinnsworth in Phibsborough,' a woman's voice told him.

'Is there a queue outside? Anyone waiting?' he asked.

'Only two fellas,' she said. 'They look like they're waiting for their girlfriends to turn up.'

'Could you describe them?' he asked.

'Are you a pervert?' And the woman hung up before he could shake his head. No one else answered by the time Sylvia pressed the money-back button at a quarter past and told him to make his private calls in his own time.

There was no point in ringing the house because Johnner's mother kept the cordless in her apron pocket. And the sound of Johnner banging on his drums would drown out the ringing if she was out. But it wasn't the first summer that Johnner's father had put his son to work in his office. And it was his habit to buy the factory-floor lads a first drink after work on a Friday as a way of soothing any grievances caused by his shouting at them during the week. Bygones be bygones for the weekend, was how Johnner reported his father's motto.

Four days later, when he was supposed to be in the kitchen making coffee for a television executive, the barman in McSwiggans answered 'Hello?' almost immediately. A shout of 'four Guinness' and the rattle of bottles brought the smoky bar down the line to the phone box across the street from Curragh House.

He had to shout Johnner's name three times to be understood, but in a minute Julian's friend of more than twelve years was saying, 'Who is this?' And the voice, even surrounded by the shouting and raucous pub noises, released something in Julian's neck, making him want to melt to the floor. He clutched the phone bookshelf and tried to wedge his head into the corner. The Perspex sheet covering the user instructions felt cool against his cheek.

'Johnner, it's me.'

'Where are you? I can't hear you.'

'I'm stuck. What should I do?'

'Stuck where?' Johnner's voice clearer as the door was closed against the pub noise, the receiver wire no doubt stretched out into the hall.

'Just stuck.' He didn't want to start by saying he was in Dublin.

'What, like your glue bag won't come off your face?'

'Not like that.'

'What about two dogs fucking? Ask someone to throw a bucket of water over you.'

'I am just so…' How could he say he was stuck without ambition, stuck without Johnner, stuck with Mikhail, stuck in Dublin? 'There are all manner of forces pressing down on me. I am stuck in this God-awful hotel… What's to become of me?'

'What are you on about? You stupid fuck.'

'I am s-c-t-u-k, I am s-t-u-k-c, I am s-k-u-t-c, I am s-u-t-c-k, I am u-t-s-c-k, I am u-t-c-k-s, I am k-c-u-t-s,' he shouted. The letters-out-of-order game they had played together for eight years. He pressed his forehead hard into the corner and waited for Johnner to remember old times and join in. 'No matter which way you look at it, it is the same: What am I to do?'

The silence broken by laughter and shouting, briefly louder before dying back. He would try a different approach, surely Johnner would remember The Trading Descriptions Game.

'I am cornered.'

'Mesmerised.'

'Concrete shod in a river.'

'Jailed.'

'Jailed' producing a pause which could mean the end of the line or the beginning of a new branch.

'I am Sing Sing-ed.'

'I am Kilmainham-ed.'

'Mountjoy-ed.'

'Portlaoise-d.'

Back in Johnner's parents' living room, I am Central Mental Asylum for the Criminally Insane-d would have seen them rolling around the floor with hysterical teenage giggling.

'This isn't the summer you promised me,' Julian said.

'Yeah well, that's life.'

'You have my money. I need it to get away.'

'Your brother's money. How would you feel coming home after years of slaving away in a foreign country to find your prize jazz collection gone?'

'Selling his records was your idea.'

'Well, you should have listened to your conscience.'

'I've always listened to you.'

'Your problem is being too easily led.'

A smack in the mouth from a Finglas gurrier would have shocked him less. He did not need any more of this crap.

'Look Johnner, I need the money now.'

'I went around to your house with me da and gave it all to Christopher while he was home.'

Christopher? *Christopher?* They'd always called him 'Bully'.

The anticipation of broken receivers, full coin boxes, interrupted and terminated calls always made stepping into a phone box a signal to Julian to have his violence ready, and as he listened to Johnner he began to want to smash the receiver against the coin box again and again until he could no longer hear the bastard. Except then he wouldn't be able to tell him about Malone, receive his understanding, ask for his help. The pressed-hard plastic receiver was flattening the folds of his ear. The capped brass screw digging into his forehead. How come it was Malone that got arrested, but Julian that was trapped?

Help me Johnner. I can't be in love.

A tapping on the Perspex door warned him it was about to

be opened and there was only the crackle of static coming from the phone; the pub noises were gone.

'Your lips weren't moving,' the woman said. 'Are you finished? I must catch my son before he goes out. I can't babysit on Saturday. I've got an opportunity.'

She shook her head and stood sideways-on so he could slip out. She reached up to take the receiver from him and he sniffed his mother's hand cream as he released it. On the footpath outside the box and without the hard plastic pressed against his ear, the pain asserted itself. It began to fade as he mounted the steps to the hotel's front door.

Dolly Considine's Hotel

THE FROWNS OF FORTUNE STRIKE JULIAN'S MORNING PLANS

Sat 30th July 1983, 09:00

The dress suit William had worn to the fashion show organised by the Wolfe Tone branch of Ógra Fianna Fáil to raise funds for the Pro-Life Amendment campaign was creased and stained, and his bow tie was tied tightly around his lower arm like a lover's token. He was drinking coffee from the mug Sylvia had been using to warm her hands after loading bags of ice cubes into the freezer when Julian had gone upstairs to collect the McCleans' breakfast trays. William put the mug down and grabbed the returning Julian from behind, whooshed him off his feet, began to la-la-la 'The Blue Danube', and waltzed him back to front round the kitchen table like a full-sized rag doll. Julian was squeezed so tightly his feet only touched the ground when William's shoulder brushed against the high-level grill and made the bacon crisping under the blue flames splutter out a stardust of burning fat.

'Sylvia,' William said, sounding breathless, 'don't you think Julian and me make a lovely couple?'

She'd been staring at the crossword in *The Irish Times* since she'd finished loading up the breakfast trays, although she didn't have a pen to fill in the boxes because Julian had taken it when she was making her coffee to write *pishogues* on his palm as a reminder for later when he could be alone with his journal. The pen had been in his shirt pocket since.

'And what about his little tush, Sylvia?' he asked, twirling Julian round and pushing him into her face. 'I mean to say, ain't it the prettiest little thing?' Spinning him away in time for Julian to see the fork she'd lunged at where his bum had been.

'What do you call a man with more than one hole in his arse?' William asked.

Julian wanted to think about his morning; a minimum of two hours writing on the Green, then across to the Shelbourne to meet Mikhail. 'I might have some news of your friend,' Mikhail had said the night before as he and the theatre committee went off to have dinner. 'See you before twelve.'

'Called Ron,' William said. 'Geddit? Cauldron.' Laughing so much he had to lean on Julian to stop himself from falling over.

'I think they're always called Anders,' Julian said.

William's laughter faded as he removed his arm from around Julian and stretched for the edge of the table. 'Tell him Sylvia. Tell him what the straining water thing is called. It's a cauldron, innit? Tell the fucking oik.'

'It's nine o'clock in the morning, William. You've been partying since three o'clock yesterday afternoon,' Sylvia said without looking up from the crossword.

The tomato ketchup stain on William's jacket was shaped like a question mark, and his shirt was spotted as if a mouthful of red wine had exploded with laughter. His eyes were bright and darting, from whatever he'd been drinking or snorting.

'I hear your mother on the stairs,' Sylvia said. 'It'll be *why don't you go to bed darling?* and *please stop pestering the staff darling* before you can say Charlie Haughey.'

But William was not ready to surrender. 'But does our little louche lounge lad have even one hole in his arse?' And he pushed a finger into Julian's trousers where he imagined an anus might be.

'Why don't we find out?' Julian said. 'Let's get it out in the open for once and for all.' He raised his arms so William could unbuckle his trousers. 'Would you like me to bend over or will you go down for a look?' Julian's waistband was open, and William's fingers were tugging at the zip when Sylvia grabbed his hand.

'Upstairs now,' she said. 'Beddy-byes for tiredy boy.' He released Julian and offered the finger to Sylvia.

'Here smell that, and tell me if there is or isn't a hole. Brendan tells me you take it up the bum, and that you like it rough. Is that true Julian? I'm quite broad-minded you know, and after some of the things I saw at the Trinity ball this year, I am officially unshockable.'

'You sad fuck,' Julian said as he buckled himself up. 'At least Brendan knows what he doesn't like.' Brendan himself didn't look that certain.

'William, I can hear your mother coming,' Sylvia said.

'Not recently you haven't,' he said. 'In fact, I think the last time my mother had an orgasm was the night I was born.'

'Try not to be vulgar, darling,' Mrs McClean said as she entered the kitchen. 'Perhaps you should get some sleep.'

'Yes,' Julian said, 'you must be fagged out from all your partying.'

'Did you hear that, Mummy? You've hired a little comedian. The faggot says I might be fagged out.'

'Sylvia,' Mrs McClean said, handing her a sheet of paper, 'there will be seven for Sunday lunch. The menu will be rack of lamb, roast potatoes, marrowfat peas. You can roast a chicken for the Hannafins and staff. Send Julian up to O'Toole's immediately so we get the very best of the lamb. Brendan can help him with the vegetable shopping. Make sure you have enough rosemary.'

'Of course, Mrs McClean,' Sylvia said. She looked at the piece of paper and reached into Julian's shirt pocket for her pen.

'Saturday is my morning off,' Julian said.

'When the next Taoiseach pays us the honour of having Sunday lunch at our hotel, Julian, I expect my staff to do everything to ensure the event is a success. Do I make myself clear?' Mrs McClean turned and linked her arm through her son's and walked him towards the kitchen door. 'Come along, darling, your uncle Giolla-Íosa will want to see you looking your best tomorrow.'

Going shopping would delay his journal plans. But at least there'd be the chance to study Brendan out of his natural habitat. The baboon insisting on carrying all the bags to prove how strong he is, and Julian will *ooh* at his manliness, hint at the things other people say about him, and encourage him to talk back about them. It could be a good morning. And at half-eleven he'll insist on dropping in on Johnson's Court church for Saturday confession while Brendan guards the vegetables and has a cigarette on the footpath outside. Eventually he'll realise Julian has slipped out the other door. But if he learns something about Malone from Mikhail, then a clip around the ear might be worth it.

Sylvia handed him the shopping paper, and two five punt notes.

'It says *collect lamb from O'Toole's in Terenure*,' Julian said. 'That's miles away. It'll take me all day. Why can't I go to the usual butcher?'

'She orders the meat from O'Toole's when Giolla-Íosa is coming,' she said. 'It's from the family farm in Offaly.'

'Well then Brendan can go by himself.'

'Brendan is getting the potatoes from Camden Street. Take the bus from around the corner, up and back in an hour. Then the two of you will get the rest of the weekly shop, as well as Mr McC's suits from the dry cleaners, flowers from Grafton Street, and Mrs McC's new dress, which is ready for collection from BTs.' She even clapped her hands.

'I can't do all that,' Julian said. He had to see Mikhail; if there was news about Malone, then nothing was going to prevent him getting it.

'And when Giolla-Íosa comes down to the kitchen tomorrow to thank us personally for such a beautifully prepared meal, and to offer you a job in the kitchens at Leinster House, what then? We're all getting jobs when the next government comes in, aren't we Brendan?' And she giggled. It was the first time Julian had witnessed her allowing her bitter sneer to be hijacked.

'Oh, jobs for the boys,' Brendan said, 'for me and you Sylv, but not for runty faggots.' He pulled the pan out from under the grill and began to eat the bacon abandoned by William when his mother dragged him away. It was dried to a crisp and he ate the meat straight off the wire tray. Two rashers in his mouth and another hanging poised to go in.

'I'll need money for the bus then,' Julian said and folded the note and the punts into his pocket while Sylvia searched her purse for loose change.

'No jobs for runty faggots Sylv,' Brendan repeated and laughed as if it was a shared secret, spraying Julian with half-chewed bacon. The feel of Brendan's spittle on his face telling him to take the two fivers and disappear for the day. But Terenure itself was calling him back, he'd been before, with

Cathal's papers, and in the park where the little girl Sharon had asked him to be her daddy. He had to go, even if that meant he couldn't help Brendan, and would have to let the rack of lamb sit on the hotel-room floor and bear witness while he fucked Mikhail.

He might have to pretend that Mikhail was William, powerful William, leader in waiting of the Fianna Fáil party William, future Taoiseach William, and therefore deserving of a good rogering for the terrible things he and the dynasty had done and would do to the country.

Dolly Considine's Hotel

WILLIAM THREATENS TO SERVE A WRIT OF HABEAS CORPUS

Sat 30th July 1983, 11:45

Julian was back on the bus with the Sunday meat's coldness pushing into his thighs when he decided that the older McClelland generations should appear incorruptible, even if the dynasty had collective responsibility for spawning their wheeler-dealer baby. His fictionalised version of William McClean is of a fast talker who only has to sneer at any of the girls working for the McClelland family to get himself a blow job in the laundry, the back kitchen or the administrative office attached to the dynasty's sprawling mansion in the heart of Dublin's embassy district, but he would let William's grandfather ooze warmth, friendliness and dedication to the ideals of the country's founding fathers, while allowing that the McClellands' constant smiling and the odd high-profile favour might have distracted attention from their real aspirations. It would be hard to credibly claim that William poisoned his family retrospectively, but his toxic influence could bring the entire edifice down on their heads. Perhaps it was in the nature of dynasties to be corrupt.

'Oops,' Julian said when he saw Mrs McClean shaking her fist at him from her sitting room window. Wasn't he here, fresh off the bus with the rack of lamb, dry-aged for fourteen days according to the butcher? What more could she want?

The inspiration for Cathal McClelland, revolutionary turned malleable civil servant, shook his head as he passed Julian on the hotel steps, his lips pressed together tightly to prevent held-back words from spilling out. But would three generations of the same family, holding seats in the Dáil at the same time, also be stretching credibility? Was that even a possibility, when it was barely sixty years since the foundation of the state?

It was the absence of a welcoming rattle from the Porchester Lounge door that gave the loudest warning that something was up. 'Fuck 'em,' Julian swore, and put the lamb on the narrow reception counter and his journal on top. 'Nothing will stop me being at Mikhail's hotel by twelve.'

His journal's front cover was stained from hiding under the meat bag out of sight of the boisterous Spanish students on the bus's upper deck heading into Grafton Street for an afternoon of shop-girl intimidation. He liked the idea of his notes for stories, plays and even poems being stained with the blood of the lamb, although he had yet to be properly inspired poetry-wise.

'Brendan, Brendan,' Mrs McClean was shouting on her way down the stairs. Maybe her angry face was nothing to do with Julian, she might have lost her tennis match, but he half-ducked inside the old reception counter, hoping to hide his journal, just in case, the little safe key out of his pocket and poised for insertion when she slapped her hand down hard on the bag of lamb and as he began to back out again, bounced him into the piled-up laundry bags. But even with his nose and eyes clasped shut against the risen dust, he managed to slip his journal to the furthest reach under the redundant bedlinen.

'You have no business inside this counter,' she said.

He allowed the sneezes to render him unable to speak, until he said, 'Mrs McClean... I... had a prayer answered by the Sacred Heart, and I promised to touch his feet when I got back from the butcher's.'

'Don't lie,' she said. 'You have betrayed the trust I placed in you. I demand your notebooks.' She grasped the counter flap with the hand not resting on the slapped lamb.

'Mrs McClean, I...'

'Now Julian,' she shouted. 'I know the books are in the safe. Open it.'

Every word he'd written since he'd started in the hotel was in there. Malone in the bus station, sketches for Mrs McClean and Cathal. He couldn't let her see them. The journal he'd just pushed under the laundry was nearly full. Josie, Sylvia, and since the trip to the butcher's, his restarted political dynasty story. Three generations of powerful men heading for destruction. The paterfamilias weeping, not with shame, but with grief.

'I don't have the key to the safe, Mrs McClean,' he said, moving his fingers to wriggle the thing up his sleeve.

'Open it now, Julian, or I will call the Guards. Final warning.'

'Please Mrs McClean, what have I done?'

He'd hoped for secrets the afternoon he'd found the safe. Had imagined a child finding a long-lost diary in the back of a forgotten drawer. His hand shaking as he turned the handle and pulled the door. But all he'd found was a bundle of laundry receipts from the 1960s and a recipe for chocolate truffles, cut from a newspaper.

'Brendan,' she shouted again. 'Brendan.' She pulled the half-door closed and the counter flap down to block Julian's exit, and went to lean over the stairwell above the basement.

'Brendan! Come up here this instant.'

Julian could just about reach the public phone from inside the reception desk. He took the receiver and dialled 999. 'The Gardaí,' he said to the operator and handed the receiver to Mrs McClean. 'She's connecting you.'

'You're in enough trouble,' she said, and hung up. 'Just open the safe. I demand to see these notebooks of yours.'

'I have no notebook.' He put on his most incredulous look and held out both hands to her, palms upwards.

'I rang O'Toole the butcher and he said you were writing while he was preparing and wrapping the meat.' A standoff while she waited for him to answer.

'A letter to my parents, posted in Terenure.'

In school he'd hated history, but he'd need to know more if his story was to be convincing. Independence from the British had happened in the twenties; that was a fact. Followed by the Civil War when some people didn't like the treaty. But elections couldn't happen during a war, could they? It would have been years before the McClelland dynasty got its first government minister. Mrs Hannafin wouldn't mind telling him.

'Ah Brendan, there you are.'

Brendan looked as if he'd been asleep. The fucker hadn't started the shopping. Julian had to be at Mikhail's hotel by noon, but if it came to it, what was more important, his journals or information about Malone? He didn't care at all about being sacked, although he didn't want a hiding from Brendan.

'Yes, Mrs McC?' Brendan asked.

'Open the old guest safe inside the reception desk,' she said and lifted the counter flap to allow him in.

'Where's the key, Mrs McC?'

'He has it,' she said, pointing to Julian. She grabbed him by the collar and dragged him out, the way he'd seen her grab the drunks she escorted off the premises when they'd became too loud or demanded a drink on credit. 'Search him,' she said.

'Is there a fire?' Mrs Hannafin was on the stairs. And just behind her William McClean. 'I heard shouting,' Mrs Hannafin said. 'I thought there might be a fire. Should I get himself out of bed? He's not feeling too well, so I don't want him disturbed unless it's an emergency.'

'No fire, Mrs Hannafin. Just a little industrial relations problem.'

'My poor late father was pals with James Larkin,' she said. 'He knew all about industrial relations.'

'Why is Brendan fiddling in Julian's trousers, Mama?' William was still wearing the evening suit trousers but had removed the ketchup-stained jacket. 'What am I witnessing? I am a student of the law, you know.'

'Nothing to concern yourself with. Brendan has it all in hand.'

'Why Mother, you know not of what you speak,' her son said.

'Brendan, have you found the key?'

'It's probably in his underwear, Mama. Brendan says he's a woolly woofter. I say Brendan, you know he's enjoying your manly hands fumbling about his person. What has he done, Mama, for you to cause him such carnal pleasure?'

'Trinity has turned your mouth foul, darling,' she said. 'Please go away now and mind your own business.'

'But with his arms above his head, and his crestfallen face, he looks like St Sebastian tied to the stake, waiting to be shot full of arrows.' Julian had raised his hands high out of reach of Brendan, which allowed the key to slide inside his shirtsleeve, the lost-key tag thankfully catching between his t-shirt and the hair of his underarm. If he didn't move, Brendan might not find it.

'It is a peculiar thing to be doing to the young lad,' Mrs Hannafin said, 'when he makes such lovely scrambled eggs. Not too soft. Even himself has remarked on them. Has he been very wicked?'

'The safe key has disappeared, Mrs Hannafin, and I am eliminating Julian from my enquiries.'

'Oh dear, is something missing?'

'I am not aware that anything else is missing, Mrs Hannafin.'

'Then technically Mama, no crime has been committed. You must release the prisoner. I shall seek a writ of habeas corpus.'

'I can't find it, missus,' Brendan announced. Although he continued to feel about Julian's torso.

'He must have hidden it,' Mrs McClean said.

'Or he never had it in the first place.' William was trying to ease himself between his mother and Julian. 'What is your evidence, Mama? I will be his advocate.'

'Darling, please go to bed. You're tired from your... your party. You need to sleep. Just leave this to me.'

'But Mama, I have taken an oath. My life's work is to defend the indefensible. Even this miserable specimen of humanity deserves to be adequately represented.'

'Where is the key, Julian?'

'I'm sure it'll turn up, Mrs McClean.' He dropped his arms, and it slid back towards his wrist.

'My mother was a great believer in St Anthony,' Mrs Hannafin said, jostling in behind William for a better look.

'As soon as I'm free,' Julian said to her, 'I'll be up to collect your breakfast tray.' He smiled at Mrs McClean, and Brendan continued feeling from the shoulder down towards his wrist. Stopping short of touching his bare skin.

'And to think I entrusted you with state papers for my husband's meeting. For your sake I hope they were delivered safely.'

'Will I search the bedroom, Mrs McClean?' Brendan asked.

'Didn't I hear him fiddling with the safe and I coming down the stairs not two minutes ago? It's here, sniggering at us.' And moved as if she was going to touch him herself, and then changed her mind, her fist opening and closing as if whispering to the bag of meat how she felt.

'Is my client free to go?' William asked, yawning as he spoke. 'I have a distressed Romanian family to see in my chambers. Come along Mama. Release him. You have no case.'

'This sleeven is making up lies to sell to the newspapers and to nourish our enemies. It's your future he'll destroy, darling.'

'Is he an informer?' Mrs Hannafin asked. 'We shot them in the Troubles. It was the only way. But those times were different. We're all friends now.'

'Would you like me to call a locksmith?' Julian asked. 'I'm sure that shop on Dawson Street could send someone round.'

'There you go, Mama. My client wants to be helpful. Release him now or charge him.'

'You are not allowed inside the reception desk,' Mrs McClean said. 'If I see you in there, I will call the Gardaí and have you charged with breaking and entering. Do I make myself clear?'

Julian looked to William for guidance on the acceptability of this proposal.

'Yes, yes, yes,' he said. 'Agreed. Although it has to be said, Mama, that he might need to enter the desk area in the legitimate execution of his duties. Could we agree that if he can show just cause, or if he receives a direct instruction from Sylvia or indeed from yourself, then such circumstances will neutralise the effect of the breach?'

'The reception desk is redundant. No one has any reason to go in there, ever. In fact, Brendan will nail the door shut. Brendan, fetch your tools. You will never see your notebooks again. Nail it up Brendan. Keep this little spy away from his papers.'

'Agreed,' William said again, and took Julian by the arm to move him away.

'This is not over. Put that lamb in the fridge and get on with the shopping. And I hope Mr Hannafin will not be disturbed when the hammering starts,' she said, looking at the other woman.

'Congratulations,' William whispered as he began to steer Julian away from his mother. 'You'd never have gotten away with that if I'd been searching you. I'd have stripped you down to your underwear. But I don't care about your grubby little diary. I might even help you get it back if you promise not to upset Mama so much. She really should get rid of you.'

You're not elected yet, he'd make the grandfather tell his grandson in the story. *And if I have to die in the attempt, I will make sure you never are.*

'Did I have breakfast?' William asked. 'This excitement has made me hungry. Bring me porridge, and bacon on toast,' he said, turning back to watch his mother point out to Brendan where to hammer in the nails.

'What about the Sacred Heart lamp, missus?' Brendan asked. 'How will we know the bulb is blown if we can't see it?'

'Don't forget the fuse-box Mama,' William announced, 'and the electric meters. The meter reader will need access.'

There would be no nailing up of his journal now, although he liked the idea of a future builder's apprentice finding the key and releasing the stories to the world.

'William is wrong about his mother,' Julian told the meat as he made room in the fridge. 'She doesn't want to get rid of me. Deep inside she knows she is not being betrayed or slandered, but immortalised.' Only Essence of McClean will go into the stories. He will capture their family auras and motives, their unique versions of universal human truths. And when the world reads his completed work they will accept as coincidence the shared external facts of the McClelland family and the McClean family in exactly the same way that all whiskey starts as barley and water. They will see that it was Julian's distilling mind that boiled and fermented the raw observations and gave back a rounded story to the world, matured, mellowed and complex.

'It's my calling,' he hissed in at the lamb as he closed the fridge door. I was inspired, he will tell the *London Review of Books*, by the way the politicians strutted into the bar, demanding drink and telling stories about the men in their own and the other political parties. Maybe he should change the point of view to that of a young, naive teenager from Cabra who ingratiates himself into the political elite, turning himself into a circulating sex toy, unwittingly trusted, even loved, by the wily wheeler-dealers.

Mikhail was waiting for him in his room at the Shelbourne Hotel. The innocent boy child enticed by the old man promising information about Malone. Did Mikhail worry about corrupting Julian, or was he happy to use Julian's youthful naivety to bolster his own flagging idealism? Maybe he should let Mikhail stew for an hour, or he should even stay away. Except knowing Malone's fate was important. Malone and himself had started their journeys side by side in the bus station. They'd woven each other into their futures. He'd been a stranger then, but now, and it didn't make sense, he knew Malone better than he knew anyone. It was as if they had grown up together, like twins or at least like best friends. The two of them sitting together was like no other five minutes of his life, and instantly available by closing his eyes, taking the same length of time to relive, second by second, as it had taken in reality. He was certain that Malone would come back for him. It was ordained. He was being tested, he had to listen and learn and be patient. Mikhail would know something.

Dolly Considine's Hotel

THE TESTIMONY AND PARANOIAS OF MIKHAIL MAYAKOVSKY #4

Sat 30th July 1983, 13:30

'My duties to the Sunday roast,' Julian said, 'and my irresistible loyalty to Mrs McClean delayed me.' His face had on his coiled, sneering, abused look, which I find so attractive and so intimidating, qualities aggravated by the black roots pushing out blond hair. Within seconds he was darting looks about my room in the Shelbourne, ferreting for clues lurking in the deep-pile carpet, tucked behind the disarrayed, half-opened curtains or taking refuge beneath the unmade bed. Searching not for empirically discernible clues alone, but for any remaining half-lives and echoes of clues laid down over the lifetime of the room.

He moved to the window to stare out over St Stephen's Green without moving the curtains. 'Was it from here that British soldiers raked machine-gun fire into our patriots in the park in 1916?'

'Probably,' I said. I'd been writing stage directions for a new London project when reception rang to say my guest had finally arrived. He arranged his arms and squinted one eye over his imaginary rifle and shuddered from the recoil.

'I can smell that someone else has been here,' he said.

'Yes, a young man I have not seen for more than twenty years.' I stood up and my white hotel bathrobe fell open. He turned away from the window and came to stand in front of me, ignoring the revealing gown and looking up into my eyes directly.

'Has the young man changed? If so, describe him as he is now and was then.'

'He remains a slim black teenager. He remains naked, except for the towel enclosing his slim waist, and forever running back and forth along the hallway between the communal showers and my room in the West Side YMCA in New York, clutching his balled-up pair of knickers. He will pause outside my door, but only if he can get inside without being seen.'

'And he was here, in this room, today? Is he here now?' I followed his gaze to the bed, the sheet I sleep under clearly demonstrating the bed's emptiness. Then he sought out other nooks where a boy could hide.

'He never stays long. I was not expecting him, overlaid as he has been by other young men who have engaged with me since.'

'More memorable? More present? More lingering? What transpired?'

'I stood at the foot of the bed and he pressed himself against me briefly. I held him securely with my left arm and allowed my right hand to slide freely down his back to his hard teenage buttocks, the merest hint that a finger might brush lightly between or even part them being enough to send him exploding all over my stomach.'

'Paradoxically leaving you high and dry?'

'I turned to get him a tissue, and he grabbed his towel and fled the room.'

'Like a tiny prey that sees his would-be killer briefly distracted?'

'The rooms at the Y in Manhattan are not much bigger than the size of a single bed. A little circulation space, a table for writing, and a bedside locker.'

There was a pause before he put his hand to my naked stomach and circled a finger around the rim of my navel.

'Is there any record of his visit other than the dried film of cum that ran down your leg, and the tissue he didn't wait for soaked with a substantial part of his discharge?'

'He left a pair of grey silk briefs, labelled "Made in Italy".'

'Which you still have?'

'Which I bring with me everywhere, seeking out suitable candidates to slip into them.'

'And you can produce for inspection now?'

'I was in need of decluttering some years ago and my cleaner found them in my underwear drawer. "And these," she said, holding the elastic wide between the thumb and little finger of her right hand. "I think it is many years since you have been inside these. No?" And she dropped them on the pile she'd selected for the charity shop.'

'A Polish lady? With very large hands? What else did she throw out?' He moved right in and pressed against me. I looked down at his tight hair and army surplus shoulder pads and wondered if he was not warm and sweaty in all those clothes.

'Mostly shoes and trousers.' I stooped my head and whispered into his left ear. 'And five double-breasted jackets (never worn) which I bought one afternoon on the King's Road to impress a young reporter and forgot to send back.'

He stepped away, reached for the flaps of my gown and the belt, and tied me gently back to decency.

'Did you give Cinderella a name? Mr YMCA? Mr Silk Knickers? Mr Tiny Hard Buttocks? Mr Sensitive Anus?' Speaking to me but returning his interest to the room. What price the update on his precious Malone now? If he suddenly remembers would I feel fury rise in me like an overflowing toilet cistern?

Would I bollocks. I was already imperially annexing the feelings tunnelling into me from his sneering questions, ideas emerging as to how I could use them in my new London project.

He peered at my astrakhan draped like a soft empty shell over the dark wooden chair, my shower towels heaped like snowy Alps on the scarlet bed throw, yesterday's turkey-gravy-and red-wine-stained shirt waiting on the pale carpet, the abandoned toothbrush on the bedside table with paste sinking into the bristles.

'Does he always leave you high and dry?'

'That is our destiny,' I said and bristled his hair with patronising glee. Then I stood by the window and watched until he crossed the road into St Stephen's Green and disappeared beneath the foliage.

Dolly Considine's Hotel

JULIAN'S JOURNAL MOVES INTO TEMPORARY
ACCOMMODATION

Sat 30th July 1983, 19:00

Julian had heard Bláithín Cunningham rehearsing her poetry readings in the Kickham Room several times since he'd found her in the dark that first Thursday when she'd cried out for Sylvia to rescue her. But today she was in the Porchester Lounge and Sylvia was on a break. She didn't respond to his 'Good evening, Miss Cunningham' or even acknowledge him until she was sitting with her book open, and only then to confirm that she would have 'my usual'. He had to ask her what that was. She was wearing her Nora Barnacle coat with its almost black lapels, a posy of dried pink flowers attached on the left.

'I've heard you reading poems on the radio,' he said, placing her drink on the table, but she didn't look up.

When he finished cleaning up after the last of the Saturday afternoon crowd, he stood behind the bar with his notebook. *She doesn't like the way the young barman is watching her*, he wrote. *She tries to ignore him, but his hands are below the counter where she cannot see them, and it makes her feel vulnerable. He gives her the creeps. She wishes Sylvia would rescue her, although she daren't look towards the door in case she alerts him to her fears.* Julian stuffed his journal under his shirt and took his damp cloth outside the counter when at half past six Jack Norton sat up at the bar, just as Sylvia returned.

'Do you remember the books I gave you to put into the Kickham Room library?' he whispered as he wiped Miss Cunningham's table. 'They're gone! It's as if they were never there.' And still she ignored him. He may even have stepped over her handbag, but if he did, he didn't notice.

An hour later the jumped-up thing in the suit who'd opened the hall door and snatched Mr McClean's papers out of his hand at the house in Terenure beckoned Sylvia out to the hall. He was wearing the same suit but a different fresh-from-the-box shirt and tie. She directed him up to the McCleans' sitting room. Half an hour later she told Julian Mrs McClean wanted him.

'I'm serving,' he said.

'Now,' Sylvia said.

It was a summons not a request, and her tone contained more than one warning. He daren't bring his journal with him, down his trousers or not. The worn green leather handbag on the floor just inside the bar, snuggled in with a variety of others entrusted to Sylvia for safe keeping, was slightly open and seemed to be offering sanctuary. The transfer so fast he didn't feel the spiral wire scratch his stomach until the sting emerged halfway up the stairs. He'd be back to retrieve his journal in a few minutes, with or without a job, the handbag owners still parading between the lounges waiting for the signal to send them onwards to the wine bars in Leeson Street or home for an early night. By which time, he would either be safe, or sorry.

Dolly Considine's Hotel

JULIAN SEES A FAMILIAR FACE ON THE TV

Sat 30th July 1983, 20:00

The TV's jumpy lines made it look like a recording. A brass band marching off the stage, winding their way through the auditorium as they played. The camera panned over the applauding audience, lingering on a young woman with light-coloured hair smiling at her male companion. The very image of Malone. Except it could never be Malone; this man had a cheesy smile and short hair, and Julian's Malone had neither of those things. Whoever he was, he stared straight to camera, giving a thumbs-up, and then he winked, at all of Ireland.

'You may sit there,' Mrs McClean said to Julian, pointing to a kitchen chair at right angles to where Mr McC was snoring, his pale blue cardigan crumpled from his sliding down the couch. Opposite him sat the jumped-up thing from the house in Terenure, and beyond, on the extreme end of her couch, Mrs McClean, her back to the arm rest, all the better to have a panoramic view of the three of them. Her knees were touching, and her hands were cupped into each other on her lap as if matters were all settled; but her eyes and mouth seemed to be taking turns at moving, as if discussing politely between themselves. She was wearing a loose-fitting black dress he hadn't seen before, the mother-of-pearl buttons done up to her neck.

'This is Mr Taylor,' Mrs McClean said. 'He is a solicitor. He has something to say to you regarding your employment at Curragh House.'

'How old are you?' the man asked.

'I'm eighteen, Mr Taylor.'

'Goo-o-o-d.' The man flicked at his bundle of pages but was looking at Mrs McClean. She nodded.

The tray with the plate holding the remains of the fried rasher and egg he'd brought up for Mr McC's supper was waiting for any small encouragement to slide off the piled-up folders on the coffee table. Could it have been Malone on the TV? If so, did they know it was him? Were they telling him something, about Malone? Was the thumbs-up a signal, a call to action?

A drip of egg yolk was solidifying on a page leaking from a pink folder, and Julian imagined a day when Mr Taylor had become a snooty government minister and was refusing to touch the eggy paper. If Mrs McClean was not so paranoid Julian could have noted this authentic detail while it was fresh. Instead his journal was taking refuge inside some woman's faded green handbag and he was facing a distracting drama which would guarantee that the words he eventually set down would lack his youthful spontaneity and his unique accuracy.

'The Curragh House Hotel prides itself on being a discreet haven for those politicians entitled to a break from the responsibilities and pressures of running the country,' Mr Taylor said. 'You have been observed making entries in a notebook, and when challenged you have refused to let your employer read what you have written.'

He watched to see if the rolling credits would include the recording date and reassure him one way or another, but the tape ended and ejected itself, making the screen go to snow. The hiss shutting out Mr Taylor's Mid-Atlantic accent until at a further nod from Mrs McClean he turned it off.

'My client is concerned that you may be breaching her family's confidentiality, as well as that of her customers. My advice has been that as you have failed to heed the warnings she's issued she should dismiss you. You have no security of employment, not least because the post itself is casual and seasonal, but also because you have been in the position for only a matter of weeks – approaching five, I believe?'

He looked down at the front page of his papers and scanned before beginning again.

'My client designated late June, early July as a trial period, during which time you were to provide references from –' and he looked down at his notes again – 'a cocktail lounge in Jersey called The Blue Lagoon?'

Julian's eyebrows raised themselves as if in surprise.

'This you have failed to do, and without any explanation or request for an extension. Therefore I have advised Mrs McClean that she is free of all obligation to you.' He paused again and looked at Mrs McClean for instruction.

If Malone was able to go on TV with girlfriends and swan about showing off his face and smiling at the country, then what was the point in Julian hanging around? He was being sucked into situations that allowed people like Mikhail Mayakovsky to take advantage of him with promises of help and information that never materialised.

Fuck Malone, fuck Mikhail. He was going home. His brother would be back busking round Europe. Time to ring

Johnner and tell him they were going camping; a music festival with rain, and mud, and beer.

Fuck 'em all.

And yet when Mrs McClean nodded, he smiled at the solicitor.

'My client has, however, developed a fondness for you, and is reluctant to dismiss you at a time when alternative employment and accommodation will be difficult for you to obtain. In view of this, I have suggested that you enter into an agreement promising to respect the confidentiality of the McClean family and the customers of Curragh House. Doing so will be a condition of your continued employment.'

Julian recognised the smell of the man's aftershave but couldn't name it. He leaned a little closer and felt it push up his buoyancy, suddenly aware of being like one of those round bottomed dolls that can't be knocked over.

'Where's the pen?' Julian asked.

'Perhaps you should read the document first?'

'I recently lost contact with someone who is very dear to me and I occasionally make a note to help me plead my case for reconciliation. I find that being in Curragh House provides opportunities for quiet contemplation, but my writing is very personal.' He restrained himself from confessing to return Mrs McClean's fondness, but looked at her, and hoped the tightness in his throat was showing in his eyes.

'I shall summarise,' Mr Taylor said. 'The document requires you to confirm that you are not working for any journalistic medium. This includes newspapers, radio, and TV. In addition, you will have to confirm that you have no affiliation to any political party or investigative agency, that your actions are not inspired by any political or ideological conviction and/or financial incentive. Can you do that?'

Mr McClean muttered in his sleep, his head lifting to shake

with a loud snore. He was horrified by what he was hearing and was telling Julian not to sign away his soul; his left foot jumped beneath the coffee table and his dinner tray slid onto the floor revealing two Woolworths notebooks underneath it. They could be Julian's.

'I better pick up the tray,' Julian said, starting to rise. How did they have his journals? Had Mrs McClean read her father's story? Was this a trap to make him grab them and run? Or were they telling him he could hide nothing for long?

'Leave it,' Mrs McClean said, and he sat down.

'I should point out that by way of encouragement, Mrs McClean has agreed to set up a joint savings account with you. Under this arrangement twenty percent of your wages will be deducted and lodged weekly, along with a similar amount, pound for pound, donated by Curragh House.'

He paused, and Julian imagined the smile was supposed to let him know what a lucky boy he was.

'Should you leave your employment voluntarily, and providing my client is satisfied that her confidentiality has been protected, you will be paid all the accumulated money in the account. If she is not satisfied you will get nothing.'

He'd never see the money, but he didn't care. He had to stay, even if the man on the TV was Malone, because he'd become part of the hotel, taken his place among the stories, joined the lingering characters. He smiled at each of them, leaned forward to sign, and repeated his earlier response. 'Where's the pen?' Being closer to the two notebooks, he could see they were new and unused.

Mr McClean's face, miming the events playing out in his dreaming head, was enough to keep Julian on the couch, but Mrs McClean stood up before the ink was dry and gave her grimacing smile.

'Kindly pick up that tray and bring it to the kitchen,' was all she said.

Three of Mikhail's actors were pushing into the Porchester Lounge in front of him to return drinks bottles emptied during the evening's show. He went straight to the flap in the bar counter and waited for Sylvia's attention to turn elsewhere so he could retrieve his journal. Except the green handbag was gone, and so too was Bláithín Cunningham.

'Fuck fuck fuck fuck fuck,' he spat, which caused him to get a smack across the ear from Sylvia and a sympathetic leer from Jack Norton.

'Get out from behind my bar and take their orders.' She pointed at Mikhail's women surrounding their usual table near the window.

'Mr M not with you?' he asked them as he pushed a finger into each of the empties; the rattle of them clashing together vibrated slightly in his hand.

'Do you miss him?' said the one who wore leg warmers during the day, and she nudged the older woman who sometimes protected him from their teasing.

'I thought that if the performance had gone well, I could congratulate him on his success.' Or spit in the fucker's drink for dragging him to the Shelbourne for nothing except getting his fingers bent backwards by Brendan as punishment for giving him the slip while he waited outside the church in Johnson's Court.

'And if we played to an empty theatre?'

He said nothing. What would Miss Cunningham do when she found his journal?

'Could you possibly offer him some, say, consolation?'

'The barman's role, miss,' he smiled. 'Mr M likes his vodka.'

'But not when he's looking for consolation.'

'He's at a party in Bartley Dunnes this evening,' leg warmers said. 'Do you know Bartley Dunnes?'

'Only by reputation, miss,' he smiled.

'We'll be sure to let him know you enquired after him.'

Miss Cunningham would be puzzled, would wonder where it had come from, and might think she'd picked it up by mistake.

'Enqueered after him,' the third woman said, and rattled the wooden bracelets going halfway up each arm. The three women giggled loudly and in key.

'Perhaps you don't want a drink?' he said.

Had she stopped off for a pint of milk on her way home and found the stowaway when she was paying? *This journal belongs to Julian Ryder.* She would read his name inside the front cover, as he'd inscribed every jotter since his first, using his then name, aged four and a half, with his mother's help. What would she do when she saw his notes for the McClelland political dynasty, or when she found his description of her blowing the politician in his Mercedes? Jesus H.

'Ah, he's in love,' a woman in a low-cut red dress said. 'I asked for two bottles of lager darling,' and she pinched his cheek as if he were a child.

'That's the second mistake you've made, fool,' Sylvia said. She was dressed like a country and western singer, with high white boots and a blouse with a line of frills hanging across her front which she swung at Jack whenever she turned to talk to him.

It was just after midnight when Julian heard her say, 'What's she doing back?' and he knew Miss Cunningham had found his journal. Four men were standing around the table she'd sat at earlier, their thighs pressed against the edge as if to keep their crotches separated. She sat into one of the bucket chairs being ignored by them.

'Good evening Miss… Can I get you something?' He smiled his best smile and tried to bow without looking too stupid.

'It seems you already know what I need.'

'But otherwise you're really interesting,' he blurted.

'A tonic water, please, and ice.' Her voice was loaded with her Edna O'Brien smoky sexiness, but there was a locked-up muscle thing going on with her face that made him see her striding through the Wicklow Hills, beating back the heather and gorse with a blackthorn stick, for no other reason than that it dared to brush against her billowing skirts.

'Coming right up,' he said. The green leather handbag was on her lap, but if the journal was inside it was not visible.

'I suppose she's been jilted by lover boy.' Sylvia pursed her lips at Jack. 'He'll be in a wine bar in Leeson Street lining up some new dolly bird, instead of being with—'

'Say no more,' Jack interrupted. 'On the other hand… maybe the wife is getting a look-in this weekend.'

As there was no obvious place to put her drink, Julian handed it to her. 'Will there be anything else?' One of the men surrounding the nearby table gripped his shirt and tugged him away.

'Can you get us some refills here?' His voice was loaded with American insistence and drowned out whatever Bláithín had replied.

'You look like a jack-off circle,' he said to the man holding his sleeve, ready for a punch. 'I've seen a picture in a magazine.'

'If you get us our drinks, we might let you join us,' he replied and pushed Julian towards the bar.

'Well?' Miss Cunningham said when he'd finished with the Americans.

'I didn't hear what you said.'

'I asked what time you finish.'

'Mrs McC will come down in about an hour and start taking people's glasses… Maybe one? Although if a gang of regulars came in…' He pressed the edge of the tray to his lips to stop himself from babbling.

'One-thirty at the corner of Hatch Street and Harcourt Street,' she said, and handed the tonic back to him. She stared so directly at him that he looked away. If it was the movies, he'd insult the American jack-off circle and start a fight, and in the distraction search her bag. But the journal might not be there, and besides it was too late. She'd already left.

The glass was warmer where her fingers had touched it, a pale lipstick mark near the rim. He sniffed for perfume cling. But all smells were overwhelmed by the Americans, experimenting with French cigarettes. She wanted to negotiate. Something in return, and if he didn't deliver, she'd go to Mrs McClean. But he had to have his journal back. It had ideas, the flashes, the first impressions, the snagging pricks that stopped him in his tracks as he went about his day. Trying to recreate any of them would produce second-hand crap; vague recollections of how he thought he might have felt, and faded versions of ideas he might have had.

I want my raw, dirty pictures. She's not keeping it. No fucking way. His open palm struck his temple.

'What did you say?' Sylvia was holding the ice tongs up to his face.

Jack was laughing. 'Oh Sylvia,' he said. 'Leave him alone. He was talking to himself.'

'Do it Sylvia. Take my fucking eyes out. See if I care.'

She stamped on his foot. 'Watch your tongue inside this bar. You are not a customer.'

'Sylvia, the bar is closing.' It was Mrs McClean. How long had she been watching? They were down to Jack and two stragglers. One of them humming to himself, and the other dozing and ready to tip forward out of his chair onto Mrs McClean.

He would do whatever Miss Cunningham asked; even sleep with her if she wanted. A life experience. Fodder for his stories. His Maggie May moment.

'Julian, this is not a doss-house. Kindly escort him from the premises.' She'd do it herself but for the young solicitor being with her. What had they been talking about for the last three hours? The knot of his tie looked way too small and tight for the early hours of a Sunday morning. What would he say if he knew Miss Cunningham was nearby reading a description of Mrs McC achieving orgasm by lifting drunks off the floor and woman-handling them out onto the street?

'Yes, Mrs McClean,' Julian said and shook the man's shoulder.

'Goodnight,' he nodded at the solicitor clutching his briefcase.

'Behave yourself now,' the man said.

'Will I be getting a copy of the agreement?' Julian winked at him. But a grunt from the sleepy drunk allowed Mr Taylor to pretend he hadn't heard.

Dolly Considine's Hotel

IS THIS A DATE OR A TRAP?

Sun 31st July 1983, 01:30

He positioned himself on the corner of Hatch Street and Harcourt Street, just across from the Television Club, remembering that besides being a dance hall, it was where Miss Cunningham made her radio recordings. Back in his Cabra bedroom, a poster named a band his brother Christopher had been in – a support act for The Sands – when they played the TV Club. That alone kept him out of the place. But after the fire in the Stardust, his mother begged him to stay away from clubs altogether, and he'd promised without any difficulty. The crowd emerging onto the rainy street looked more like showband-following culchies than the gobbing punks he'd heard being talked about in the hotel. A night for Brendan, he thought, picturing him wedged between two pillars with a pint in his hand, leering at any girls he thought might be looking in his direction. But not Miss Cunningham... She'd prefer... what? Secret wine bars, intimate little venues that the people crossing the road towards him would know nothing about.

Sylvia and Jack spoke openly about Miss Cunningham's relationship with her politician Sylvester, but, in his descriptions of them, Julian had changed the colour of her hair and his political party. That might be enough to stop her recognising herself, although he had used their real names. *In for a penny, in for a pound...* he clapped, and rubbed his hands together like a farmer, watching a Garda cross to seven people trying to squeeze into the back of a Cortina with its engine revving in the middle of the road.

And then a sports car pulled up at his feet.

'Hey,' Miss Cunningham said. 'Hop in.' Then she said, 'You look surprised at my TR7,' and touched his arm. 'Oh, you're wet.'

'Well, it's...' He didn't know which statement to respond to. Yes, he was wet. And yes the sports car was a surprise: fine, he'd adjust his picture of her. On the other hand, the music was traditional Irish, slow and wailing, sounding alien beneath the guttural engine, and if she'd wanted to impress him by roaring away from the TV Club, then the queueing taxis and the excited and heedless drunks making their way across the road forced her to weave slowly to avoid any collisions. She turned into a laneway, crossed a main road, and soon they were away from any streets he recognised.

Where were they going? To her brother's house to meet a baseball bat? To Sylvester's for something even worse? Another solicitor? Would there be negotiation or just action?

'Miss Cunning—'

'You may call me Bláithín.'

'Bláithín.'

'Well?'

'Is the heater working? The rain has soaked into my clothes.' She fiddled with the controls and warm air blew into his face. 'Why did you give me your notebook? At least I assume it was you, and not Sylvia playing a stupid prank.' If there was anything particular about her voice it was in her pronunciation of 'stupid'. It made her sound American. New York American. Mafia New York.

'Did I get anything right?' The car stopped and his head banged into the windscreen. There was no obstacle, it was a warning. 'The brakes work.'

'Perhaps you should put your seat belt on.'

The roads got wider and the car went faster. They were definitely heading out of town. If she dumped him in a field, how would he get back to Curragh House? The evening hadn't brought enough in tips for a taxi, if taxis came this far out.

'Are we just driving around?'

She didn't answer.

Fine, he would sit back and enjoy the ride, writing in his journal was hardly a capital offence. He could say it was all gossip he'd heard from William McClean. Except of course his 'Inception Statement', written on the inside cover of every new journal to remind himself of his dedication to youth, and truth, and beauty, might undermine his claim.

'This is grand,' he said, rubbing his hands together again. 'It takes hours for all the chatter and buzz to quieten in your head after a shift in the bar. You get all worked up being surrounded by punters demanding a good time. A drive is just what I need. It'll make me relax. Help me sleep. You must feel the same after a performance.'

'Don't babble,' she said. A grievous tone in her voice.

Sometimes Johnner would come around to the house while Julian was having his breakfast, and Julian would tell him about the dream he'd had or sketch out an idea for a story. And then without warning, Johnner would empty salt into his cornflakes. As if anyone had been stopping Johnner from

310

talking. As if salting Julian's food was the only way for Johnner to say whatever he'd come around to say.

'Don't babble,' the alien life form said as it pressed the hyperspace button and the sickening thrust made everything go dark. The menace in its voice together with the hyperspace forces were reshaping every atom in his body. Luckily his thoughts were still strobing to the thought recorder strapped to the back of his neck.

Except he didn't have a thought recorder, she had his journal, secreted somewhere about the car. He could allow his hand to search casually under his seat and maybe hers, but even if he found it, it would be too dark to write. Better to close his eyes, and stack things into some sort of memorable order, in the hope of recall kicking in if he ever got to hold pen and paper again.

'How old are you?' He wasn't even thinking about her. No woman likes that question.

'Thirty-seven.'

'Really?'

Thirty-seven-year-old vamp Patricia Bryson roared her prancing sports car out of the roundabout like a lion leaping onto its prey.

That was so corny. He needed subtlety. Something about the number or depth of her crow's feet, or some childhood revelation to link her to a particular time. Women driving sports cars had probably been done to death by those writers he avoided in the library. When a man bought a sports car, it was to compensate for his small penis, but why would a woman do it? Penis envy maybe? Is she a lesbian? The darkness allowed only a grey profile. Was this a lesbian profile? Sylvia didn't like her. Did Bláithín leer over Sylvia the way Jack drooled over him?

'Do you fancy Sylvia?'

'Mind your own business.'

That was a yes then. Gosh. Poor Sylvia. Still, women were better at handling that sort of thing.

'Gosh.'

The darkness outside was total, so they must be beyond the city. Where the fuck was she taking him?

'You can turn the heat down now if you like,' he said. 'And what about the music? Shouldn't it be late night jazz? A sexy, smoky woman's voice? Alone with a double bass?'

She pushed a cassette into the player. The same traditional, but slower, lamenting lost lives, wailing love. Fuck it, he was too young to lament.

'Can I look at your collection?'

She said nothing so he groped up a handful of tapes. But there wasn't enough light to read anything. He closed his eyes and wondered if he should just sleep. Even if he jumped out of the car he'd have to shelter in a barn or under a tree until daylight allowed him to find help. Assuming the locals weren't already alerted to his presence and ready to hunt him down.

'It's not Deliverance, you know,' thirty-seven-year-old vamp Patricia Bryson gushed lustily.

'But am I not being Kidnapped?' he asked.

He would have to find out what *Kidnapped* was about before he included that image in anything for publication. Otherwise PhD students in American universities would struggle endlessly to understand the reference.

'Have you read any Robbie Louis Stevenson?' he asked.

'Robert Louis Stevenson. Stories for boys,' she said.

'What do you read? Just poetry?'

'You mean besides diaries that I find stuffed into my handbag?'

'It's a writer's journal.'

'Whatever it is, it does not belong where I found it.'

'When you give it back, I will say: Naughty journal. Stay out of Bláithín's handbag.'

'If you see it again. If you survive this night.'

'You're scaring me now.'

'The strangest people listen to me on the radio. People who think I am speaking to them, one on one. Solitary, isolated… Men, who for whatever reason are, or think they are, utterly alone. A good sprinkling of psychopaths. Long Kesh prison is filled with men who think I am Cathleen Ni Houlihán reincarnated, the very personification of Ireland, any one of them would rip your head off at the least hint that you were besmirching my image and with less thought than I would put into opening a bag of frozen peas.'

Thankfully they're in jail then, he wanted to say, but no one stayed in jail forever. Still, organising a strangulation at that hour of the night might be short notice even for one of her psychopaths.

'Being inspired by the people I meet is hardly a capital offence.'

'We'll see. Can you set a fire?'

'Arson? Will it save my life?' The brush of something along his jawline poised him for someone concealed behind his seat, until he convinced himself it had been her fingers.

'Silly,' she said. 'A turf fire. With paper and firewood. Were you a boy scout? Or are still a boy scout?'

'Yeah. No trouble. So long as you have matches.' He told himself he was not scared and wriggled his feet the way Malone had done in the bus station. Although they hadn't helped him.

Summer of Unrequited Love

THE TINAHELY GOFER: GET YOUR COAT, YOU'VE PULLED

Brendan knew he'd seen her in the Television Club, in the Crystal Ballroom, even in the NBU in Parnell Square, and she was a sure thing.

Tonight, he's been watching her for over an hour. But he'll wait until the right moment before he sidles over and puts his arm around her. Whether it'll be around her waist or her shoulders would depend, but he wants it to be her waist.

How'ya? he'll say. He's been repeating the greeting over and over since he saw her coming out of the ladies' toilet just after midnight. She'd pushed away some drunk and then disappeared into the dance floor crowd. She'll have others thinking about riding her, so he'll have to get the tone right, as well as the words.

'How'ya?' He notices himself giving a little shake of his shoulders as he whispers the words. It could be a shock if he said nothing at all; if the first she was aware of him was an arm around her, maybe already squeezing her close to him. But he is no stranger, hasn't he seen her loads of times; sometimes with

314

her friend, dancing if they like the band, or leaning against a pole talking if they want to ignore the men.

Brendan might give her one dance, but she'll get the message as soon as she feels his arm around her, and the little pinch he'll give her; and before he knows how he got there, he'll be riding her in her bedsit in Dorset Street, or Rathmines, or wherever she lives.

He is experimenting with how it might feel to use his left arm to squeeze her when he finds Seanie McGurk nodding and blinking very close to his face and blathering about how glad he is that the band is terrible, because bad bands make the girls more willing. Then he shuts up, as if he's only been talking to distract Brendan from looking at something.

Seanie was the first Derry boy given shelter by Mrs McClean. That was more than five years ago, well before the hunger strikes, at least the ones where the men died. He looks older now and has a limp that wasn't there before. Brendan wonders why he isn't saying sorry for the day he disappeared without a word. Or, thanks for the great nights out, or will you ever forget the all-night chats we had about Ireland and girls?

'I'll get you another drink,' Seanie says. 'By rights it should be your round, seeing as I bought the first, but for old times' sake.' McGurk's arm is now around Brendan's shoulder, and he begins to drag him away from the pillar where he's been keeping a lookout for the young one he has his eye on.

I'm not just standing here you know, he wants to say, but a drink would be okay too. And all the guff about it being his round – if McGurk wasn't such a vicious thug, Brendan would smack him, but not before he has the drink safely inside. Sylvia, and Julian, the little cunt, get loads of free drinks, but it's Brendan who does the hard work. He doesn't even get any tips. A poxy drink from McGurk, after the way he's treated him, is the very least he deserves.

'Would you like a drop in that?' McGurk says, producing a Baby Power and holding the open bottle over Brendan's Smithwick's. Watering good whiskey, but Brendan nods and widens his eyes to show it makes him happy. He doesn't want to smile because he's smiled at men before in this place and found himself having to give them a kick in the bollocks later. He's pretty sure McGurk isn't queer, but he barely puts any whiskey in his own glass, and Brendan has to take a sip of his pint to make room for the rest of the Powers.

Then he says, 'What time is it?' And shakes his watch, as if it's stopped, before grabbing at Brendan's arm. 'Look at that; almost two o'clock. I've been here nearly three hours and the only person I've spoken to is you. What kind of a carry on is that?'

Brendan pulls his arm back. If it's nearly two then he has to find that young one or there'll be no ride. He begins to check the hair and dresses of women moving towards the cloakroom in case she's already going for her coat. Then he scans the dancers and nearby wallflowers, but what with her being such a small thing, and the moving crowds holding up their glasses so as not to spill their drink, it's no surprise he can't see her.

'Has Mrs McC found the Pope's periscope yet?' McGurk asks, referring to a thing he set up in the cellar so Brendan could watch what was going on in the Porchester Lounge. He nudges his elbow against Brendan and gives a dirty laugh.

'I haven't seen it for ages,' Brendan says. 'I think it got squashed under a stack of crates, by mistake.' They're never supposed to talk about this, especially in public. He should go and stand near the cloakroom. Let McGurk babble away to himself, Brendan doesn't owe him anything. That man burnt his bridges when he disappeared without saying goodbye.

'I hear you have a new boy in the bar,' McGurk says. 'Watch

out for him. He's not supposed to be there. His name isn't even Julian.'

Brendan is interested, but he also wants a ride, and she'll be giving up on him if he doesn't make his move soon.

'I've put two German magazines in the usual place for you. And if you keep an eye on this Julian for me, I'll fix you up with that wee girl I saw you eyeing up. And plenty of others when you get bored. Hm?' He squeezes Brendan's shoulder again to help him understand it's a promise.

His shirt is scrunched up where McGurk's fingers have dug into his biceps. He doesn't need McGurk to fix him up with young ones. It's all arranged. He can already feel himself riding her; all the more exciting because he's done it by himself. And he's found out that Julian is not Julian. He looks around at the cloakroom crowd, ready to say I have to go to the jax, but when he turns to speak, McGurk is gone.

The fucker, Brendan thinks, but not for long. He holds his drink in one hand and uses the other to keep people from bumping against his glass as he shoulders through the crowd. His fingers are twitching like they're already gripped onto her titties, and he has to take deep breaths to not kick anyone.

If he meets McGurk another night, he'll say, I went looking for you. Everywhere. And then this young one started making a show of me with her kissing and pawing me in front of people. I had to let her drag me away. You know how it is.

Dolly Considine's Hotel

A CITY BOY IN DEEPEST DARKEST COUNTRYLAND

Sun 31st July 1983, 03:30

It was one of those low whitewashed cottages that feature in lithographs of famine-starved families being evicted in their night clothes, with armed bailiffs and evil landlords' agents holding lighted torches to the thatch and using battering rams suspended on chains from giant tripods to demolish walls and prevent reoccupation. The land behind the house rose steeply towards a flat-looking hill in the distance and fell away in front at a gentle slope before rising to another easy hill. But he would not see that until it was daylight.

She needs to know she's doing her portrait no favours, was what he'd been thinking, when the length of the day behind him, the low seat, the darkness, the music, the motion of the car, and the occasional gleam from the rings on the fingers gripping the steering wheel all colluded with the heat, and lulled him to sleep. And when he awoke dry-eyed and lost, twisty roads and hedges were being picked out by the headlights, until there was a bumpy bit and the car was stopped at a funny angle, the headlights that had been controlling his eyes were off, and the noises from the driver's seat suggested Bláithín was getting ready for action. He could see nothing, but his fingers were still gripping the door handle he'd felt out ages ago in case she turned wild and he needed to exit: a flick of the lever, a tumble into the open using the momentum to roll clear, followed by a scramble to his feet, and running.

'Right,' Bláithín said, 'let's do it.' Which sounded like a cliché from an action film, and not the meandering French-countryside misty ciné she should belong in. Her line would be changed for the transcript to more apt, more memorable words.

There was birdsong, but the darkness and the slippy embankment tipped him over, his reaching hands revolted by the squelchy yuckiness that broke his fall. This was the country.

'It's a bit treacherous there,' Bláithín said and shone a torch so he could stand up. She threaded shopping bags onto his squeamish fingers.

'I'm always afraid bats will have taken over while I'm in Dublin,' she said, pushing open the hall door and directing the torch at the rafters rising above them. She swept from end to end along the underside of both pitches. 'That seems to be okay,' and she stepped further in.

'Okay' sounded so wrong from her mouth. But a country cottage was a very appropriate setting. He stood inside the door while she moved about bringing new areas out of the gloom with lit candles. The room was square and whitewashed, bits of rug on the floor, one door to the right, and maybe another at the back. A small window on his left, bookshelves – mismatching in widths and heights – lined the walls. The three huge armchairs facing each other looked too exhausted to argue over which of them was ready for the rubbish tip. The place smelt of damp, of old turf smoke, and of the clay that clings to potatoes. The smells and the cobwebs glinting in her torchlight held him by the door.

'Why don't you turn on the lights?' He wasn't impressed by candles.

'Close the door, Julian. No one's going to bite you. The stuff for the fire is all there.'

If Bláithín's psycho fans were going to murder him, they'd have seen the car lights snaking through the countryside; one of them would be holding a knife to his throat by now. He didn't recognise the newspaper he tore to roll into balls for the fire. It was too dark to read the fine print, but the headlines took him out of the cottage.

'*Noisy meeting in Cootehill.*'

'"*Co-op is ours," say farmers.*'

'*Pro-abortion women heckled.*'

Other news that was not news.

The sticks were dry and brittle, and he soon had a wisp of smoke streaming through the sods of turf he'd stacked to the edges and on top. When he blew into the gaps there were noisy flames.

The fire helped him to concentrate on what he'd already seen, and not to be distracted by Bláithín packing tins onto shelves. He needed to acknowledge the details and stack them inside his head. A descriptive record only, the urge to make interpretations to be resisted. The untidy mantelpiece, the pile of newspapers, the overflowing ashtrays, the roll-up tobacco pack and papers on the coffee table, the hairy hairbrush and matching lipstick compact. Much too easy to say these things proved she was untidy or lazy or had her mind on higher things.

Only if he saw the unexpected, was surprised at, say, an arrangement or juxtaposition of everyday things, would he suggest it encapsulated her to such an extent that, looking back, as an old man, at his youthful description in his journal, he would instantly recall the moment, the situation, even the feeling, if there had been one. He'd written nothing since early evening behind the bar, watching Bláithín. It had only been seven or eight hours, but his fingers were twitching as if they'd never hold a pen again.

He turned to watch her bend her knees and pivot her head as she poked a knife under the eye-level grill. The harsh blue flame illumining little except itself, but painting her face grey when she leaned in to inspect whatever she was toasting. Was he witnessing a routine domestic action that signified nothing? Or would this be the image that would stay with him for the rest of his life? He had to resist casual descriptions. An action, or the manner of its execution, or the resonance of a detail with another time would have to express a unique facet of Bláithín's character or it would not find its way into his journal. The alternative was to allow the prejudices he already had to enslave her, twisting her actions into taking on meanings that had nothing to do with her. And that would be a betrayal of everything he believed in.

She stooped to let her elbow push the ashtray and tobacco away from the edge of the small table and made room for the bottle of wine, two glasses, salt and pepper, pack of butter, bunch of cutlery and plate of toast.

This was not a woman to make two trips to the kitchen when her task could be managed in one, demanded to go into his journal.

The wine was already open, so his bar skills were not needed. The middle armchairs had room enough for two of her and she tucked her feet under her long skirt as she sat back.

'Pour us a glass there,' she said. 'And help yourself.'

Her voice was unique. But what had a voice to do with character? She could be a murderer, a republican, a saint, could be anything or nothing, and still have the same voice. Nor would it be the fact of her being a sexual athlete, a loyalist or a performer that would make her interesting.

There were the childish little mouse nibbles she gave her toast, suggesting she'd been eating like this since her mother and she first sat down after a shopping trip to town, perhaps in this same armchair, and ate their treat with melted butter dripping down their fingers. And what about the thoughtful way she sipped her drink? As if listening for what it had to say, a message from the vineyard or the grape pickers. What could she hear?

He smiled at her. 'This is very cosy.'

His mother watched programmes apparently set in tiny rural cottages filled with people sharing their culture with the viewers of television land. A message from the real Irish. Musicians and dancers ready to demonstrate the simple pleasures. The camera panning over a storyteller with his elbow on the mantelpiece, lighting his clay pipe from a glowing sod of turf. The air thick with tobacco smoke and lively with chatter. Porter and snuff going the rounds, a pot of spuds boiling away on the hearth.

'We should be drinking buttermilk,' he said.

She looked at him. Her eyebrows rose.

'But the wine is nice too,' he said.

'Spanish,' she said. 'For hope.'

He'd never heard that before. Perhaps it showed on his face.

'James Clarence Mangan, "My Dark Rosaleen"! You must have done it in school?'

He nodded so she would stop.

'Good luck then,' he said. His uncles never touched a drop without uttering the words and lifting their glass.

'Tell us a story Mr Storyteller,' she said as she topped up her drink. 'A tale from the town. Let me hear the cry of

322

the dispossessed, the city's wail of longing. A tale filled with the regret of separation from your true roots. A vignette to illustrate the soullessness of the urban existence.'

In the bookies in Phibsborough once, putting a bet on for Johnner's mother, he'd watched a man's lips moving as he whispered the names of the horses. Maybe they'd hear themselves being called and tell him which one had been chosen to win. Why had this come into his head?

'I want to hear you read,' she said. 'I want to hear your voice, the Dublin voice. Hear it from the source, not the paid performers and gigolos that make their money filling us with romantic nonsense about Dublin in the rare auld times.' She was on her feet then, pulling at papers on the table, inspecting and rejecting, before stretching to the nearest bookcase and pulling out a slim volume.

Why didn't she give him his journal and ask him to read out the bit he wrote about her? It would be embarrassing for them both, but he would avoid looking at her so she could squirm privately. It would be only fair.

'Here,' she said, 'stand up.' She handed him the open booklet and picked up a candle to stand beside him to illuminate the words.

'This will have to do,' she said.

'This? Is it a poem?'

'Don't think about it. Just read.'

There were dry crumbs around his teeth, but he swilled wine and swallowed.

'*Surely the beach at Portmarnock was no stranger*
to the sight of a four-year-old doing a number one?
He could have squatted between two parked cars.
Perhaps a Morris Minor and a Ford Prefect
shining side by side with Sunday polish,

applied after Mass while the mammies made the sandwiches.'

She grabbed the paper out of his hand and threw herself back into her armchair. 'That's enough. I can hear your terrible loss. Your anguished cry to be united with your people. Dublin is such a soul-destroying place. How have you ever survived?'

He smiled, but she was not looking at him, just hugging her knees to herself, her eyes closed.

'Ah sure, isn't Dublin surrounded by the countryside? Except for the bit facing the sea, of course.'

'But it's not the same. Julian, you poor boy, come and sit by me.' She patted the area beside her in the armchair, her eyes open again.

'Ah sure I'm grand here,' he said and turned his legs so they were draped over the arm of the chair, all the better to watch her lips moving as she spoke, still able to soften his focus and be mesmerised with her sounds alone, or search for the connection between the rich smoky honey of her voice and the frumpy reality. On the radio she took turns to be an Amazonian, a Valkyrie, Grainne Mhaol, or Cathleen Ni Houlihan, just as she liked. How could he ever reconcile what she projected with the wispy woman in front of him?

She stood up and crossed to the door that opened off the room.

'Let a bit of heat in,' she said as she pushed the door inwards. And when she sat back down, she had a joint in her hand. 'Sean makes these for me,' she said as if he should know Sean.

'While employed by the national broadcaster?'

'He's freelance.'

If she was only opening the one door, then it looked as if she was expecting him to sleep in the same bed. Would it be like the sleepovers he'd had at Johnner's, pyjamas, and heads to toes? Or was this a seduction? He looked again but could see no images of how they would be. How bad could it get? Grist to the mill and all that. She'd probably be wild after the wine, and angry about what he'd written and feel the need to prove him wrong.

She held the joint out towards him. 'Guests first,' she said, after she'd taken several tokes.

It was mild and pepperminty, and he knew it would put him to sleep if he was greedy.

'It's good stuff,' she said.

Outside the window was lighter now. But there was no cock crowing. They always had cockcrow in the pictures. He was in the fucking country, he wanted cockcrow.

'You're so self-contained,' she said. 'Is that what city life does?'

'Ah I'm just a bit shy.' He'd said this before, and it seemed to help in lots of situations.

'I won't be able to shut you up when I get to know you. Is that it?'

He didn't want to remind her that he was more of a writing-down man. He took another toke of the joint and leaned towards her. She didn't move, so he stood up and reached it to her. Still she didn't move, only puckered her lips for him to insert it. This would be the moment when her intentions became clear, her hand reaching to stroke his leg, or to wrap fingers around his as he inserted the joint, distracting him while he concentrated on not letting the burning thing fall into her lap. He stood waiting, but she sucked in the smoke and closed her eyes, as if he was not there. He sat back down.

The wine was sour after the grass on his tongue, though the taste woke him up a little. But if she was quiet for too long, he would fall asleep.

'You're a little prick, you know, for writing about me like that. Private notebook or no, it's not gentlemanly. It was a surprise, I must say. I thought you had better manners. And putting it into my bag where I would find it was very hurtful. Frankly if that's your seduction technique then it's a mighty queer one.'

He allowed his right hand to twitch, like a film loop of a hand reaching to poise a pen over paper, again and again. She held her head up like a pecking bird looking around her. Then she drew smoke in and held it while she stared at him, exhaling as she stood up.

'I don't see how you can have the nerve to sit here in my house as brazen as anything and not have the decency to avert your eyes, never mind offer a sincere apology. It's not how things are done.' She made a bit of noise in the kitchen area and then the door to the presumed bedroom slammed closed. He turned to confirm, and it opened again.

'Don't drink all that wine please,' she said, 'and don't forget to bank the fire up.'

What was she on about? The bottle was empty. She'd had most of it. And his sad little fire was more smoke than flame.

'The wine was gone. She'd had the most of it.' He whispered the words to fix them in his head. It would be a springboard line for his journal. He leaned into the low table to search for blank paper she wouldn't miss; even his own mother kept scraps for shopping lists. His pen already in his hand, twisting like a divining rod tuned to blank paper.

Under a leaning bookcase he found an old calendar for a butcher in Cootehill, twelve small pages that would take the observations insisting on being recorded. And when he'd finished, he'd stuff it into his pocket and push the two big armchairs together for sleep. Hanging from the back of the front door were more coats than a tramp would get through in a lifetime; he would not be cold, even if the fire died down, but that was hours away yet.

The wine was gone. She'd had the most of it, he wrote and

looked to the words to tell him if he should work in reverse through the evening or leap straight back to the moment when he found her green handbag missing from behind the bar.

What was she so angry about anyway? Any woman should feel privileged to be in his journal. The character she will inspire will have sex and love, talent, money and fame. And even if the original is a pale ghost in comparison with the larger than life heroine she will inspire, Bláithín is interesting enough to make Julian notice her. Strong enough to support a fictional version, flawed enough to provide authenticity.

Nature, her own choices, and happenstance, have worked together to make her the complex woman she is today. She should be proud of their handiwork, warts and all. What greater honour can there be than to have a life turned into art?

Whoever was knocking was not looking for Julian. It was probably Sylvia, after Brendan. His job to go for the Sunday papers, not Julian's. Let him answer the door. Julian was not getting out of bed.

'I was at first Mass,' he heard a man's voice say. 'And I thought, that's my obligation out of the way for another week, what about a little indulgence?' The voice more matter of fact than self-satisfied; not realising, perhaps not caring, that he might be challenging the gods to strike him down.

'I brought orange juice and croissants. I know you never have anything fresh in this house.'

'Well come in so.' Bláithín's voice. 'The programme will be on shortly.'

'A poem is it?' he said. And if Bláithín replied, it was by smiling or nodding her head or squeezing his hand.

What was she doing in the boys' bedroom? And who was the man? Julian's eyes fully opened before he remembered he was not in Curragh House but in the deepest countryside. Was this a psycho fan come to dispatch him while he slept in the pushed together armchairs? At least he'd kept his clothes on. So when he arose from under the sleep-giving overcoats, and knelt up all the better to defend himself, he was surprised to see a regular from Curragh House.

'But you're entertaining already,' the man said. 'A bit early for that, or is it leftovers from last evening? A young whippersnapper. Well, Blath I never thought you had it in you. Ya girl ya.'

'Now Sylvester. Come in if you're coming. Are those croissants warm or will they need the oven?'

'Take them, girl. There's only enough for two. I get too many second-fiddle opportunities in the House.' He handed the bag to Bláithín as Julian pushed the armchairs apart and stood up. He could do with some food. Let the man leave the stuff and fuck off.

'How ya?' Julian said.

Bláithín had the man by the arm. She was dragging him into the house.

'I can't abide sloppy seconds you know, Bláithín. Not my style at all at all. Do you know?'

'Come in and meet the young troublemaker from Curragh House. A writer, no less, that could be the ruination of us all if we don't watch our step. Best stay on his right side if you don't want a rough profile.'

'Why would you give him the time of day Blath? That sort are always trouble.' The man spoke as if Julian wasn't close enough to see the sheen on his newly shaved face, and smell the fresh croissants.

'A moment of madness Sly. But we're all intact.'

'I don't know what the neighbours will think, girl. A thing like that doesn't escape their attention.'

'And if they see him leaving with you, and being dropped at the bus stop in the village, won't they think he's a friend of yours? The company of a respected TD, what more could anyone ask for?'

'It was you I was thinking of. He can fend for himself.'

They were flirting now, the croissants somehow passed to Julian and the two of them waltzing into the bedroom. The door closed and Julian suddenly possessive. How dare he just waltz in, without so much as a by-your-leave, and straight into the bedroom with his host? Forcing whatever notions he'd entertained about Bláithín's intentions to be adjusted by the evidence. Well, he was off the hook. He could do what he liked now. He could have the run of the croissants while they were up to whatever it was that geriatrics got up to. Water into the kettle and onto the cooker. A glass filled with orange juice. The cupboards searched for coffee or anything else that would qualify as breakfast food.

He rubbed his hands together as he ran through the opening lines for his journal's morning entry. He checked his back pocket for the out-of-date calendar, filled up as far as July. June to January available before he ran out of space. But with any luck he'd have his journal back before that happened, or a new one purchased in the first shop he passed on his way back to Dublin.

He was biting into the first croissant, buttered and covered with jam, when he noticed Bláithín's car keys. He swallowed a mouthful of juice, put the other croissant into his jacket pocket, and gently opened the hall door. Bláithín's car was at the bottom of the slope, another bigger one behind. He found his journal in the boot, it wasn't even locked.

'You fucking boy ya,' he whispered. 'Welcome home baby,' and he kissed the cardboard cover. It was cold and damp and smelt of smoke. 'We'll soon have you right as rain,' he said as he stuffed the book beneath his shirt. He didn't dare go back to the cottage, but unlocked the driver's door and put the keys in the ignition. She might think she left them there herself.

Guided by the church spire pushing above the trees, he took twenty minutes to reach a small village. He asked in the only shop about bus times.

'The next one now will not be till twelve,' the woman said. 'But a young fella like you will have no trouble getting a lift if you continue to the main road.'

'You mean hitch?' he asked. She nodded as if she'd said more than she should. A radio played in the background.

'Is that *Sunday Miscellany*?' he asked, recognising the presenter's voice.

'We never miss it. One of the stars, Bláithín Cunningham, lives just out the road. She's from further north originally, but such a lovely voice. And once the programme is over, she'll be in for her paper, as ordinary as anything. You could stand there browsing through the magazines and catch a glimpse if you like. Especially if you buy something yourself.'

'And what time is Mass?' he smiled.

'Just starting now,' she said. 'My husband is over at the church manning the paper stall.'

'Well I might as well get Mass and wait for the twelve o'clock bus. Thank you.' He touched his forehead as if he was wearing a hat and left the shop. Once outside he ran to where he imagined the main road was, and right enough the very first car stopped to pick him up.

'I'm only going as far as Navan,' the man said. 'Will that be okay?'

Julian rubbed his hands together and smiled to show his appreciation. 'Just mighty,' he said. 'Just mighty.'

Less than half a day in the country and most of it spent

asleep, but already he was sounding like he'd lived there all his life. He had to get back to civilisation as quickly as possible.

'Tell me this,' the man said. 'You are not from these parts, and I can see you're a broth of a boy, so what is it that has you hitching a lift to Dublin at this hour of the morning without a proper coat or even a bag to carry your toothbrush?'

'What do you imagine it might be?' Julian asked, noting that the man had a full head of very white hair and freckles all over the backs of his hands.

'When I was your age, I would have been fleeing from one bed, or rushing to another. Rejection and seduction are the poles of life.'

Had he been rejected? The ancient politician brought into the boudoir, and the stripling driven out onto the open road by his pride? 'I'm getting married tomorrow,' he said. 'I was at my stag party in town last night and the boys drove me up here and left me trussed up like a chicken in a shop doorway. The kindly proprietors saw me struggling to find comfort, took pity on me, and gave me a bed.'

'And what about breakfast? Didn't they offer you any breakfast?'

'They were fasting from midnight and didn't plan to eat until they came back from Mass. They asked if I minded waiting, and I told them I didn't, but had to pick up my wedding suit by twelve noon.'

'I hope you and your bride will be very happy,' the man said as Julian got out of the car in Navan. 'And may all of your children be brought up in the faith.'

Julian smiled and thanked him for the lift. His tips from the previous evening were enough to pay for his bus fare, and a pint of milk to go with his second croissant. He settled himself into a seat near the back of the bus and took his journal from under his shirt. It was warm and dry now, but the smell of smoke was just as strong. He flicked the pages and found several had been burnt out. His first job would be to describe Bláithín leaning back against her car holding the book so the offending pages could be isolated for burning.

His one regret was that he hadn't asked her to read his favourite poem. It would have been a moment to be recalled and relived at will. The mysterious poem read by the sexy–voiced woman. But he had to balance his regret against the possibility that she mightn't like Emily Dickinson, or worse, might have read poem number 712 in a dismissive or even repulsive way. At least now he could imagine her reading it exactly as he wanted, and make her read other poems, any way he liked, as often as he liked.

Summer of Unrequited Love

Bláithín Cunningham raised her poetry book to shield her eyes from the afternoon sun as she emerged from the darkness of the Curragh House Hotel to walk to the TV Club studio for her recording. Today she felt driven to the shady side and almost collided with the sign for the Eye and Ear Hospital reminding her to keep hers open.

Watch and breathe, darling. Breathe. Distracted by the memory of the interfering lounge boy having his hand held by Mikhail Mayakovsky as she'd passed the Porchester Lounge on her way out. There wouldn't be much comfort from a wee urban whippet of a boy with cold claw-like paws, she'd thought. Not that Mikhail Mayakovsky would mind. Flattering and stroking staff would be sport to him, and part of the whippet's job to let the customer have his way. None of her business.

The first time Bláithín had crossed Harcourt Street to the Television Club, she'd wanted to be a Dubliner. But the poetry had dragged her back to Cavan, thankfully, and now she only visited to tape her weekly radio slot. If she got it right first time,

333

she would be home before tea; a brisk walk to the hill above the cottage, as far as Maher's Field, for a reassuring look across the land towards Cootehill, and then back to her hearth and her buttermilk soda bread browning in its three-legged pot, the smouldering turf sods melting to ash as she walked. Then a bath later in the turf-warmed water to wash away the image of the whippet boy clawing at her for attention.

'My little man was asking for you.' Sylvester's car almost knocked her over, and banished the smell of fresh bread and turf smoke. 'Eyes and ears, Bláithín darling.'

'What are you doing here?' She knew what was coming and although normally she didn't mind, the lanes around Cavan were a lot more private.

'I was in the House listening to Garret the Good lecture us about social responsibility when my little man reminded me that it was Thursday, and that Bláithín Cunningham would be in the recording studio.'

Had it been Sylvester McManus TD holding the lounge boy's hand, that would have been a surprise. But Sylvester didn't do hand holding. At least not in front of Bláithín.

'Jump in,' he said, already leaning over to push open the Merc's passenger door, his hand beckoning her, then patting the seat.

Easier to imagine those fingers gripping the plaintiff hand of a constituent in his surgery, the woman's face flooded with tears at the difficulty of getting planning permission for her son's new bungalow. If, that is, Sylvester held surgeries, and didn't just make them up to get out of awkward situations.

'Just once around the Green,' he said, 'slowly.' He raised his eyebrows and patted his stomach as if it was he that would be doing the eating. Like a teenager when it came to fellatio, just the hint being enough to make him wet.

Sean, the recording director, will smell Sylvester off her

and criticise her delivery. The last time he'd demanded instant attention, in the women's toilet at Curragh House, Sean had gone to eleven takes before he let her go, making it two in the morning by the time she got back to Cavan.

'Maybe we could go up to the Park later?' She sat in but kept the door open with her foot. 'There's been a power cut all day, and Sean will be frantic if I don't appear now.'

The trees in the Park would provide a little discretion; she was entitled, she had her own public persona to look after. And it would be her that Sylvester's wife, and God knows how many children, would hate if the papers got hold of a photo.

'I could ask Sean to do the take straight away and we could go to the Park about four-thirty.'

'My little man...' he said, as if she were denying a plaintiff his justice. 'I have to be back for a phone call, replies to enquiries submitted at my surgery yesterday.' She'd heard all his surgery-calling stories before: *Bláithín, darling, the surgery was overrun*, when he was late. *Ah Bláithín darling, you know Wednesdays are surgery nights*, when he didn't want to see her.

'Six o'clock.' She revised her offer.

'Ah sure I have a vote tonight. A big vote. I'm expected to speak at six. My name is down. I can't disappoint them. I was hoping you could help me concentrate my thoughts.' He started the car. It was settled. 'Think of it as a favour to the country. You know how anxious I get.'

'Irish people care about the favour, not the favour maker,' she'd often heard him say. 'It'll be on my gravestone: "Remember the favour not the favour-wright".'

'I'll have you back in ten minutes,' he said as he pulled out. 'Once around St Stephen's Green will be enough,' pushing his seat back so her head would not bang against the steering wheel. 'And try not to dribble on my trousers. They already think badly enough of us culchies in Leinster House. I don't want them thinking I forget to shake my little man when I take a leak.' He smiled at her above the sound of 'Bat Out of Hell' from the stereo. 'Go on now. No need to be shy. You know you love it.'

Dolly Considine's Hotel

JULIAN RETURNS TO THE SCENE OF THE CRIME

Sun 31st July 1983, 13:30

Even if Julian didn't believe in signs, synchronicity had to be respected. Here he was stepping off the bus from Navan, back in Busárus where it had all begun, with the taste of the milk that had washed down Sylvester's croissant still sour in his mouth, when who did he see getting out of his loving parents' car? Only Peter Sweeney. The clingy, needy Mr Collins, who barely a month ago had begged Julian to come with him to London. All Julian would have to do would be to say hello and the invitation would be renewed, if not by Peter then by his loving parents. It was likely that Bláithín had already phoned Mrs McC to tell her about finding his wicked journal and him breaking into her car to retrieve it. The gods were giving him another chance and this time he would be braver, would put his arm around Peter's shoulders and say why not? I'm ready to spread my wings. Let's go. Nothing to rehearse, just smile and let Peter do the work.

He stood behind one of the large supporting pillars to

regulate his excited breathing, pushing thoughts about his journals and Malone's clothes back to where they could not interfere. It was really going to happen. Peter was kissing his mother and shaking hands with his father. His backpack bulging with clean clothes and the favourite foods his parents knew were unavailable in England. Already beginning to walk in Julian's direction, and then wow, fuck, stooping under the weight of his own backpack, Johnner was shaking hands with Peter's parents and punching Peter's arm, and the pair of them together were beginning to walk towards Julian. Barely time to bundle himself into a mob moving towards an announced departure bay for Cork before slipping sideways along the side of the bus and getting shouted at by the inspector for endangering himself near reversing vehicles.

Out on the street he swore that he would never abandon his journals again. It was time to rescue all his notes and ideas from their hiding places, say goodbye to Curragh House and go home, but his determination was threatened when he rounded the corner into Hatch Street and was dazzled by the sun glinting off the windscreen of Bláithín's car parked just beyond the hotel. Maybe he'd walk round the block until the car had gone. He was barely in front of the hotel's granite steps when the driver's door opened and Bláithín rose out of the car, like a genie from a lamp, her full-length white dress plain like a nun's, but not at all nun-like when topped by her wild red hair. She stepped onto the footpath and leaned against the passenger door just as he'd imagined she'd done when she burnt the pages from his journal. She folded her arms and looked at him, her sunglasses dazzling, like a model in a TV ad. He came as close as he dared, ready to sidestep, and she, using her bum, levered herself up off the car to lean forward and kiss him on the cheek; the same lips that only a few hours earlier had done whatever they did to Sylvester the politician in the cottage bedroom or maybe even on the pulled-together armchairs where Julian himself had spent the night.

'I'm taking you for coffee,' she said. 'We will stroll through St Stephen's Green and find a café in Grafton Street. Will Bewley's be open? I rarely find myself in Dublin on Sundays.' She took his hand, as if he was a child and she was afraid he would run out onto the road and be run over, or maybe to make it easier to push him under a passing bus, if she was so minded.

'Now,' she said, 'we are not going to speak of things heavy, but stroll gently like *les amoureux*. The sun is shining, the day is young, and we don't have a care in the world except a desire not to shock the populace with the intensity of our passion,' and she swung their arms as they entered the Green. They were not alone. Bands of youth, Spanish tourists and an exhausted-looking woman pushing a double buggy all glanced at the skinny teenager and the middle-aged woman in white with the mad red hair, hand in hand like two actors getting into character for their next scene.

And that was it. They had coffee in South Anne Street and then she walked him back to the car. She leaned against the door and let go his hand. She lingered longest over his shoes and his face as she looked him up and down. 'Sylvester was quite jealous of you, you know,' she said. 'Intrigued, and jealous, I would say, but he doesn't reveal very much.' She smiled. 'He's not a man to be crossed or to forgive easily. He asked me to promise I would not see you again.'

'Yeah, probably a good idea,' Julian said. Whatever was going on was in her head anyway.

'Sylvester and I go back a long way,' she said, folding her arms, signalling perhaps a bottom line, a decision reached, or the end of the truce they'd indulged in for the last hour.

Her fictional incarnation would get a different response,

but Julian gave his nodding serious half-smile. This was her breaking-up scene, or never-starting scene?

'I told him I'd stand by my darling.'

Which of them was her darling?

'I hope you understand.'

'Me too,' he said. She kissed him, almost on his lips, sank into the car and revved the engine like a boy racer as she turned the corner into Leeson Street.

Maybe he didn't need to understand. Just watch and record. That was his job.

Summer of Unrequited Love

DOLLY'S FATHER'S ABSENCE FROM THE WEDDING PHOTO SAYS IT ALL

Aug '83

'I've always told William he can sleep with whom he likes but if he gets a girl pregnant, he will have to marry her.' I was watching Julian's face and not the sugar I was spooning towards the cup of tea he'd just put down in front of me. I gave the tea a half-stir and leaned back on the couch. 'What?'

He ignored me in my haze but looked around our sitting room as if imagining the scene, and said, 'Was William caught in flagrante delicto? Was he sitting or standing when you made this head-of-the-house announcement? Was he slouching against the window watching the girls on the street, or moving towards the door to escape your onslaught? Did the pair of you stand nose to nose shouting father and son into each other's faces?'

'None of that matters.'

'Suppose he got two women pregnant at the same time, or even three? What then, Mr McC? Would polygamy become

Fianna Fáil party policy? Would there be a white paper? A constitutional amendment? What?'

William never answers me back like this. Is that because I'm his father? If Dolly were here she'd remind this bucko that his place is collecting dirty glasses below in the bar or attending to kitchen duties, as required. Still he cuts the ham just right, leaving the fat on – though probably out of malice; best I don't tell him it's how I like it. He's moving about the room like an interrogator, peering into the glass case, leaning on the sideboard, brushing his finger along the edge of the framed pictures of Dolly, myself, and William in his pram.

'This room is full of secrets,' Julian said. 'A hundred years of goings-on. They echo all around us if only we had the ears to listen; the very sideboard loaded with witness statements waiting for a willing dictation taker.' Then he picked up a family shot of our wedding, looking from the photo to my face and back again as if to follow some invisible thread between it and me. 'I assume that's Mrs McClean's father,' he said, 'wedged between the church pillar and the woman that looks the way Mrs McC does now.' He turned the frame towards me and used his nail to tap against the glass. 'Quite handsome, wasn't he?'

This is the way party workers try to get me going, telling me things that aren't true when they think I've had a few. Wasn't the wedding delayed until well after Dolly and her mother were out of mourning? I nodded with my 'considering' face on and waited for his next move. He held a seashell to his ear, all rolling eyes and lifted brows, as if it was revealing tales of William's naughty scouting trips.

'Is that a nice cup of tea, Mr McC?' he asked when I ignored his shenanigans. 'Would you like a slice of cake tomorrow? Are you partial to cake?' Then he settled himself on the scattered papers on the couch beside me. Wriggled his bottom and smirked, with me imagining the boss sniffing at his briefing documents in the morning after getting a whiff of something unusual.

'I'm working on those,' I said. 'A fine how do you do if I hand them crumpled to the...' My haze delayed my indignation, at my own, and his, trespass into familiarity. I had to assert myself. Tell him it wasn't right for a lounge boy to exceed himself, here on the couch beside me.

'The trouble with all your drunken stories,' he said, 'is that they don't have a beginning, a middle, or an end. You just ramble on and on, spewing out disjointed images with no plot.' And he squeezed my leg just above the knee the way schoolboys do to make each other's nerves jump. 'But, to be fair to you, the things you say do come back later to explode like moon dust crystals, little images which surprise with their familiarity, and which anyone with a modicum of talent could flesh out into full-blown stories. Do you know what I'm saying?'

Then it was up with his two feet onto the coffee table, his shoes resting on more papers to the left of the tea tray, as if his little speech had earned him the right. His eyes and fingers twitching as if my sandwich was now his.

'Still, it does seem a bit harsh,' I said, taking a sip of tea, ready to smack him if he went for my supper. 'I mean, to force a girl to leave everything to the hand of God when she could have a choice. What? Religion trumping science you'd call it, I suppose. William would, the bloody atheist. But whatever you call it, why should a gang of old men in nightdresses in Rome, who by rights will never be faced with the dilemma, or a gang of dried-up old biddies here in mother Ireland, have their views enshrined, not just into law, but into the very fabric of the stuff that underpins our laws? *This woman must have her baby, whatever the consequences.*'

But instead of answering, the bucko swung around onto his

right elbow and stared straight up into my eyes. 'If a person gets arrested by the Guards, how would you find out what's happened to him? Don't they have to charge or release within a few days?'

I lifted one side of the bread and dabbed on more mustard. The familiar rainbow bloom reassured me that I had the ham I liked, and that, for all his cheek, there was nothing he could do if I clicked my fingers and told Dolly to put him out on the street, pronto. Nothing. Not a single thing. I might say it to her too.

'Pregnancy is a serious business. Life threatening. And any bucko who can't deal with the consequences should keep his little man in his trousers. Do you hear what I'm saying? What?'

Which was the precise moment I realised what I have always known; William is not my son. Not my biological son. Something about this ruffian stretched out beside me and pouting as though he was posing for a malicious birthday card made me think about the barbarians at the gate; that the owner of the simpering eyes I was looking into was going to bring the whole edifice down around us.

'My God, Dolly, what have you done?' I muttered as the mustard burnt the base of some nasal tube in the middle of my head.

'If I give you his name, could you find out if they've released him, or charged him? And if he's still being held, whether he can have visitors?'

'Write his name down and we'll see,' I said. Him not moving but continuing to stare at me, making my eyelids too heavy to keep open even with effort. He couldn't have been hypnotising me, because I wasn't looking back. And besides, hypnotism needs words or some relaxing rhythmic movement. Maybe he was speaking so softly I didn't know I could hear him. I let my eyes close, all the better to listen. Total silence, but shutting out the scene was nice, nicer still when I concentrated on the nothing I could hear. No sound in the room, nor even coming up from the bar below. I recollected one of the regular tunes and hummed it, silently so he wouldn't hear. Eventually there was a movement on the couch beside me, and the sound of him opening the door opened my eyes. The tray was balanced on his left hand while the other stroked his hair.

'Is that what happened to you, Cathal? Your little man slipped out when you weren't looking, and wham, you were married before you could say to Dolly, do you fancy a ride or what?'

'My brother says the boss's wording for the Pro-Life Amendment will make the unborn lot think they're getting everything they want,' I said, 'but if it goes to court, the judges will tell them they've made a mistake. But by then it will be too late, and the boss will have another five years.' I couldn't see what he was doing with his face, but there were gestures.

On another night, the anticipation of the TV news would have sent me dozing again. But with the door closed behind him, I suddenly felt refreshed. I rolled my tongue around my mouth to recall if I'd eaten all my sandwiches or had downed a second cup of tea. I looked to the place where the tray had been on the coffee table to find the answer. But it was the absent document I noticed. The contract Giolla-Íosa's young solicitor had drawn up between Dolly and Julian. I'd been reading the preamble earlier, about an employer's right to confidentiality, and now it was gone. Its place taken by the wedding photo from the sideboard now looking up at me from the coffee table. Noticing, for the first time, a gap where Dolly's father would have been, had he still been alive. Yet I distinctly remember the photographer telling us to move closer or we wouldn't all fit in.

I shook my head at Dolly's smiling face, recalling the static given off when I touched her dress, and promised myself to tell her nothing about the missing contract, or the antics of her lounge boy. He's a good lad really, my 1958 face said, and probably only took the papers to have a copy made. It'll be back tomorrow. You'll see.

I was putting the photograph back on the sideboard when I saw the envelope. A familiar-looking telephone number in my own handwriting, and in a different hand: '*Free Malone. Free the Busárus One*'.

Dolly Considine's Hotel

THE TESTIMONY AND PARANOIAS OF MIKHAIL MAYAKOVSKY #5

August 1983

'Receptive' is such a loaded word for a gay man, don't you think? There are days when you just don't feel like taking it up the back bottom. A little cuddle, a little conversation, a little light banter, a little bitchiness, even a spot of dinner. But no, that fucker is not happy unless he has me down on all fours or on my back begging him to bang me, like I'd die if I didn't get it. Well, he can fuck off. I am an artist. I need love, admiration, companionship and stimulation. Stimulation.

If it was only about sex, I'd have rent boys lined up and be done with it. I don't have a problem about paying for sex. Paying would never challenge my ego. The time will never come when I think I am too old or too ugly for sex. I will always deserve sex.

He hates it when I sing that Human League song about the waitress and the cocktail bar. It shatters his concentration. Sometimes, if he has his eyes open, I only have to curl my lip and sing 'Don't You Want Me' for his rhythm to be destroyed.

But at least he notices it's me in the bed, or on the desk, or bending over the toilet cistern, my head banging into the down pipe with every thrust. That it's Mikhail Mayakovsky's anus interacting with his cock. He is not with some former lover or future lover, or alone with a porn mag wanking to beat the band. He's got the famous director with his legs in the air, his calves resting on his shoulders, his sphincter gripping tightly.

The little rutter loves to push into my prostrate. It's not unpleasant, but neither is it any great shakes. And just because I'm a bottom tonight, he shouldn't forget who's in charge here, who can put him back where he found him.

Summer of Unrequited Love

DOLLY'S FATHER AT HIS SISTER-IN-LAW'S HOTEL

Mar '44

The mac was clean but much too big for him, likewise his trousers, pulled up high with braces, and, although his collar looked about the right size for his slim neck, the shirt itself was made for a bigger man. His cap shouted docker, but when asked at the bar, he said he was working in the margarine factory in Liverpool. He reminded Terence Considine TD of the sailor he'd witnessed being brought ashore after his ship was torpedoed off the west coast of Ireland in the early years of The Emergency. The dry clothes – obviously intended for a smaller man – given to him by the fisherman who'd rescued him made him look like a variety show fall guy, but they didn't disguise his gratitude at being alive.

The manageress, Mrs Burns, was not at all pleased to see this boy in hand-me-downs mixing with the besuited politicians in the hotel bar, but the two Americans who'd swept him in, an arm each crossing over his shoulders, were regulars and big spenders, and she would not risk upsetting them. They announced that they'd met him in a bar in Abbey Street, but the look of him and his small canvas holdall suggested he'd been hanging round the toilets on the Quays, filling in time before setting out to Dún Laoghaire for the mailboat. 'He's our new mascot,' the Americans announced, 'a little Dublin leprechaun.'

The hotel bar was well used to American soldiers. Some people even liked them for reasons other than the drinks they bought. But Dubliners who'd voluntarily signed up to defend the British cause were not always welcome. They stood out from the crowd in their ill-fitting mufti, exchanged at Holyhead to comply with the 'no military uniforms' policy of neutral Ireland. This one was about half the size of the smaller American. A gurrier, more at home in O'Connell Street touting for dubious enterprises or operating con tricks on unsuspecting country people. He had no business being in Terence Considine's sister-in-law's hotel. None.

Maybe the boy was a little drunk when the two Americans swept him into the hotel, but he didn't object when they put their arms around him and squeezed him in bear hugs as if they were reuniting after half a generation of being apart or had survived some great ordeal together. They ruffled his short hair, and even removed a fleck of cigarette ash that had apparently landed on his eyelashes. 'Doesn't he have the cutest lashes?' the fatter one said, turning the boy's face around to the lamp to get a better look.

'You better not have the pox,' were the boy's second words to Terence Considine, who replied, 'And if I had, wouldn't it be good enough for a dirty boy who'd taken the king's shilling?' He was a typical Dubliner. Skinny, porcelain white except for his neck and hands, in need of a wash, but oh such a well-shaped and proud bottom. A boy bred for buggery.

The deterioration in Paddy the porter's rheumatism

coincided with The Emergency, as if it was Fascism itself inflaming his joints, and worsening his relationship with the manageress, Mrs Burns, although not much love had ever been lost between them. Her face often displayed the pleasure it gave her to instruct him to carry a guest's luggage up two or three flights, while his silent pride hid any sign that the task was more troublesome than lifting a slice of bread. Nor did he show the slightest rebellion if Terence Considine asked him to run a little errand, and later, when he knocked on the TD's door to deliver a report on the request, he was always happy to sit awhile and relate his stories of outwitting the Black and Tans during the War of Independence. It was true that he became uncomfortable if the subject strayed into talk about pro- or anti-Treaty friends being obliged to kill each other, but by that time in the evening Paddy had nursed his one small Powers and it was time to rinse the glass with a drop of water to ensure none of the precious whiskey was lost, and apologise for keeping the TD from his bed.

An unspoken arrangement between the two of them, worth ten shillings to Paddy, meant that if he noticed the TD eyeing up a likely lad in the bar and then setting off for the gents, the next thing would be Paddy hurrying down to the drinks cellar for a bottle of whiskey or a few more stouts. And coming out he'd forget to lock the door, which meant that if in the meantime an assignation had been organised, it could be completed in the cellar, witnessed only by the crates of beer and empty bottles rather than by punters coming into the lavatory to make room for a few more bottles back in the bar.

In earlier times, a door in the cellar's thick party wall had provided access between the hotel and the Porchester Theatre next door, which had allowed a variation on the arrangement with Paddy. But this had ended when Mrs Burns insisted the theatre brick their side up after a famous Joxer Daly was found drinking his way through a crate of the hotel's beer instead of being on stage tormenting Juno. The badly laid bricks and snots of mortar were a reminder of the actors that had come through in former days, but also hinted that a good shoulder would topple the barrier and allow free access once again, unless perhaps the theatre side was blocked with dead stage props and baskets of period costumes awaiting another turn in the limelight.

The cellar was a dark and dangerous place with rough edges and sharp corners. Of particular peril were the metal bands used to reinforce the beer crates that awaited the unsuspecting loose coat or trouser turn-up. A boy often had to be warned to take care, or be commiserated with when he'd forgotten. But otherwise, the system worked; the security of the door being locked from the inside meant the encounter would not be disturbed, and, with the noise from the bar directly overhead, a yelp or two of delight would go unnoticed.

Later, Paddy would treat the sight of the likely lad returning to the bar as the signal to remember he'd left the cellar unlocked, and in a few moments he would be found in the doorway checking for his keys. If the encounter had been helped with a bottle or two of stout, the price would be added to the ten shillings, so the bar tally would be kept right. And for all the strangeness of this particular porterly service that Paddy provided, his accompanying patter about the weather or the shortages due to The Emergency were exactly what would have gone with the provision of any other service for a needy hotel guest. As if it was the most natural thing in the world for a gentleman to emerge from the beer cellar with a look of smugness and satisfaction or, occasionally, of disappointment on his face.

'Your American friends are a loud pair,' Terence Considine said as he stepped up to the bank of grotto-like urinals shoulder to shoulder with the mac-wearing youth, his well-developed peripheral vision immediately stymied by the generous coat's interference with any easy attempt at gratuitous spying, forcing him to commit to an unambiguous trespass for a better angle.

'Ten shillings,' were the boy's first words. Such brevity and directness were unusual, but instantly exciting also.

'What do I get for that?' the TD asked, and the curtains were drawn back slightly to allow him a better view. 'Looks more like seven and six to me,' he said, but the slam of the main toilet door prevented any reply. Perhaps it was one of the Americans entering to make sure their mascot was not bringing good luck to someone else. The TD moved to the sink, ran the tap, and, while the new arrival concentrated on unbuttoning himself, gave signals to the lad to follow him.

Mrs Burns's impatience and sense of her position made her useless when it came to carrying out the little repairs residents often required. And as for getting their suitcases open when the locks were stuck or the keys mislaid, she should have been grateful to Paddy-of-the-magic-touch for whom locks seemed to wait only for the caress of his fingers to open and release the clothes swaddled inside. Less publicly known was the timely and sensitive way in which Paddy had hand-delivered the anonymous letter to the Taoiseach detailing the nefarious goings-on of one of his favourite ministers, which played no small part in convincing the party machine to support Terence Considine's nomination for the North Riding ticket in 1938.

He's been here before, Terence Considine thought when the boy entered the cellar in front of him, appearing to need no warnings about metal straps or sharp edges, and when he turned around and opened his mac it was to show that he had not tidied himself away but had followed him from the gents with everything just as it had been seen at the urinal. Only this time the goods were fully visible, and, with braces released, his loose trousers were falling to his shoes. A mercenary boy, or an unsure boy, can often change his mind once he has his money, so the TD's habit was to sort out that end of things first, even if it resulted in an immediate departure, with or without a refund. *Cast your bread upon the waters* was his favourite motto.

Terence Considine lifted the mac high over the boy's shoulders, allowed his own trousers to drop to his ankles, and even loosened his tie and stowed his collar stud in a pocket so it did not fall out and get lost in the stark shadows between the cellar's stacked crates.

He was ready for his imminent explosion when perhaps he was distracted by the sight of himself as he disappeared and reappeared from between the shadowy china-white buttocks floating in the dimness of the cellar. He turned the boy slightly to get more benefit from the single light bulb, all the better to appreciate his form, but caused the tower of crates supporting the boy to wobble, and his further thrust brought the stack above down on them both. A tumbling crate hit Terence on the side of the head, and, as he sank into unconsciousness, he was cursing the bottles and crates for depriving him of his reward and the waste of his ten shillings.

'What am I supposed to do now?' Mrs Burns shouted one evening when Paddy dropped a crate of stout just short of the bar where Terence Considine was sitting. For all her meanness and insensitivity she had a way of complaining that often led to help being provided without ever having to be asked for, at least directly.

'He can't lift anything,' she said, and then, as if to respond to her own attack, 'He's over seventy, for God's sake,' her tone changing to one of excuse rather than accusation, and petering out while she busied herself, as if to deny she had spoken at all.

'Doesn't he have a pension?' the TD asked.

'I'm sorry, senator. I didn't mean to speak. Paddy is a proud man and would never take a penny he hasn't earned.' Mrs Burns insisted on addressing the brother-in-law of the hotel's owner as 'senator' even though she knew very well he had only been a senator for two years while waiting for a suitable seat in the lower house to come vacant. He gave up correcting her when his wife suggested that senator sounded much more prestigious than deputy. Paddy did the same, but the TD never bothered to correct him.

'You mean his social welfare stamps were never properly administered?'

'While he has been here, Paddy has been treated as a member of the family. With all the benefits that brings.'

Terence Considine's way of tilting his head and nodding as he raised his eyebrows betrayed his urge to call the speaker a liar.

'What about the volunteers' pension?' he asked, wondering if Paddy stayed on at the hotel to spite Mrs Burns or if he had his own secret vice that was absorbing his on-the-side takings instead of funding his retirement. 'Mind you, he'd have to prove he saw active service to qualify.'

'Really senator, I'm sorry I spoke,' she said. 'You're here for a quiet drink after a long day in the Dáil. The last thing you want is to hear about my woes.'

'You mean his stories are just stories, that he was never a volunteer?'

'Rebellion is a young man's game. He would have been forty in 1920,' Mrs Burns said. 'Far too old to be gallivanting round the country, sleeping in ditches and depending on the scraps of food given out at back doors to survive. Still, it's not for me to say. A pension would help, but I can't keep him here in the hotel if he can't work.'

'Family member or not?' Terence smiled.

'You will appreciate that I'm not the owner. There's only so much latitude allowed to a manageress.' Which neatly put it back on him, married as he was to the sister of the owner – especially, if his wife was to be believed, as their daughter Dolly would inherit on her aunt's death. But Paddy would be unlikely to hold on till then, even out of badness.

Terence Considine heard banging, interrupting Elgar's *Enigma Variations* playing softly behind him as he delivered his 1939 speech to the Dáil in favour of Ireland remaining neutral and seeking an accommodation with Hitler. The elected representatives from all parties were squeezed up onto the back benches to allow the orchestra room to play. The music was an unsuitable accompaniment and a distraction from the arguments being made, and Fine Gael members opposite were signalling for him to shut up and respect the music. But De Valera was leaning forward slightly to give the impression he was listening, his eyes focused on the mid-air, his face as stern as ever.

'Senator, senator,' the voice of Paddy was calling.

There was no reason to answer. Firstly, he was a TD; no one listens to senators. The senate was just a sop to the Americans to make them think Ireland had adopted their system of government, and a slap in the face for the English that the country hadn't adopted theirs. Secondly, he was making the speech of his life. Only the Ceann Comhairle and his banging gavel could legally silence a permitted speaker. But the knocking persisted.

He awoke to the pain of a numbing weight digging into both his legs and sides, and the sight of himself trouserless and half-covering the cold arse of his likely lad. He freed himself from under the fallen crates and tried to stand, but his left leg refused to bear his weight. His limp shout of 'Okay Paddy' stopped the knocking.

'Wake up,' he said tugging the hem of the mac. 'Wake up, it's—' Natural daylight didn't get into the cellar, but the single bulb was enough to show his watch had stopped at twenty to one, the blood all down one side of the mac, and the broken bottles glistening all around.

'Jesus Mary and Joseph.'

Which brought him to his feet, aches and pains or no, and he pulled his trousers up, checking for bloodstains as his fingers fumbled with the buttons.

'Jesus Mary and Joseph.'

He had the bolts back and the door open to Paddy before he thought about whether that was a good idea or not. It was the same impulse that ruled him out for ministerial office in the reshuffle a few days after the famous 1939 speech. Lucky not to have been deselected in 1942. 'Your trouble Terence,' De Valera said to him later, 'is that you have not learnt to anticipate consequences before you speak. A politician has responsibilities. Always remember that.'

There are many, many Paddy Dunnes in the country, and several Paddy Dunnes fought in the War of Independence. Mercifully most of them were too young to be ready to claim a pension. The civil servant who researched for a possible application wrote: '*The most likely Paddy Dunne of "sufficient years" died in suspicious circumstances in an ambush in Co Cork during the War of Independence. The report carried out at the time by Southern Command states that none of the ambushed British soldiers appeared to have fired a shot, yet one of the volunteers was killed. The report concluded that as all the volunteers' guns had been discharged, including the victim's, it was impossible to say for certain what had happened.*'

The most symmetrical explanation forming in Terence Considine's head was that Paddy had participated in the killing of one of his own side, and had later assumed the dead man's name to remind himself of the terrible thing he'd participated in. Small wonder he hadn't applied for a pension.

As he opened the cellar door, he remembered the boy's nakedness and moved back to cover him as best he could. Paddy followed, and lifted a couple of crates before he sat down and began to rock back and forth, his face in his hands, crying silently. The sight of stoical old Paddy's tears was almost as shocking as the realisation that the boy was dead. Terence had to take charge. He was an elected representative, a leader of men; didn't that give him the authority to tell Paddy that sobbing like a schoolboy nursing his wounds after twenty of the best would provide no help at all?

Deputy Considine told the civil servant that he knew enough about the incidents and locations referred to in the stories to confirm that Paddy Dunne was not dead. He wrote a full reply and sat with him as he read out the final sentence: '*I conclude that in the confusion of the times, the names of the victim and one of the survivors were confused.*'

The civil servant smiled but said nothing. Terence watched his face: too chunky for me, he thought, with his red cheeks and ruddy good looks. Still, on a dark night, after several bottles of stout, you never know.

He left Paddy in the cellar and went to the gents' toilet to wash his face and hands. It was just beginning to get bright outside. In a couple of hours his career would be over, and he would be in custody.

Back in the cellar Paddy was on his feet, struggling to push empty crates away from the area around the boy.

'I've said an act of contrition into his ear, senator,' he said. 'He should be all right. Do you know his name?' He got a shaken head in reply.

How could he ask God to forgive the boy his sins and take him into heaven if He didn't know his name? What would Terence do on Sundays when the Mass reached the page of his prayer book where the bracketed (N—) showed where to insert the name of a departed loved one and speed their journey through purgatory? This poor tyke's anonymity might send him to hell.

'Give me a hand here,' Paddy said.

The TD wasn't sure he should allow himself to be ordered about but did his best to comply. 'Those fucking straps,' he swore, and pointed to a crate of beers upended and with a dangerous strap at an acute angle.

'It looks to me as if he bled to death,' Paddy said. 'Nobody's fault, it couldn't be helped. You were unconscious.'

Was he telling or asking? Terence nodded, his chin tucked in a little, unable to make eye contact with Paddy, who wasn't looking at him anyway.

'Stack the empties over there, and then the full ones here. I can't lift them, you see,' Paddy said. 'It's the rheumatism; even dragging is hard.'

Terence Considine began the formal War of Independence pension application for Paddy within a few weeks. But Paddy only submitted the forms after Mrs Burns agreed that he could sign the money over to her and continue to live in the hotel. She would also allow him to go on doing any little guest jobs he could manage for pocket money.

'The department requires more than just pub boasting in order to spend taxpayers' money, deputy,' the ruddy-faced civil servant smiled as he was handed the written statement taken from Paddy. It had complete details of the actions, the dates, the comrades and the casualties. Some facts (that had come to the TD's attention) seen in other claims were added for emphasis.

Terence Considine, knitting his fingers together, smiled back at him and raised his eyebrows sufficiently to warn him that his own future could be at stake if the pension application was rejected. The outcome was that '*on further investigation it became obvious that there could have been a mix–up over the names. The unit that had carried out the attack in which a man called Paddy Dunne was alleged to have died suffered heavy casualties the following week, and the investigation was therefore never fully concluded.*'

'*Claims under the Military Service Pensions Act can require the corroboration of fellow volunteers where identity is in doubt,*' he said in the letter of confirmation, '*but as most of Paddy Dunne's old comrades were killed, the testimony of the sponsoring Dáil deputy has been given more weight than usual.*'

A politician with two hundred acres who wears a shirt and tie every day will always be accused of being a gentleman farmer. There's no worse accusation, especially when it comes from the boyos in your own party looking to gain a bit of an advantage. When Paddy asked Terence Considine if he could lay bricks, he wanted to say that he'd spent his life farming the land the best way he knew, and that had always meant paying the labourers to do the manual work. The whole enterprise would grind to a halt if the labourers did the accounts while he spent his time building walls, fixing fences or mucking out cow stalls. And when it came to bricklaying, he'd never even held a trowel in his hand, but he'd ordered them when they were needed, and paid for them, and abused labourers when they mislaid or broke them.

Paddy already had the bricks, and although The Emergency had caused a great shortage of cement, he managed to buy a bag at the right price. His tone was impatient when it came to giving instructions about 'buttering' the mortar onto the bricks and laying them level and straight. Terrence's hands shaking and his fingers seizing up as he absorbed the facts of constructing a clandestine tomb within the thick wall shared with the theatre next door. A layer of bricks to shelter his daughter Dolly from the secret within when she eventually inherited the hotel from her aunt, hopefully forever unaware that her father had turned the hotel into a mausoleum dedicated to the nameless likely lad turning to dust inside.

Paddy insisted all clothes needed to go, but the rosary beads round his neck could stay. 'You'll need lime. Bags and bags of lime,' he said, as Terence lifted the dead boy over the first few rows of bricks and into the recess, Paddy then holding onto the slumped body as best he could while the other carried on laying, so he would be hidden even if he were to stand up and try to peer over the top.

'Paddy, there's a war on,' he said. 'There's no lime to be had. The farmers are crying out for it.'

'Quicklime, senator. The remains will have to be covered in it if the smell is to be kept down, at least to a level that will not be noticed what with the smoke above and the damp down here. In a warmer place the dregs of stout left in the bottom of the bottles would start to ferment, and disguise the smell, but here in the cellar it's often too cold. You'll need the lime.'

He understood then why he'd been told to stop the bricks short of the ceiling. This was the gap to feed in the fresh lime. A job Paddy promised to continue with, so long as he remained at the hotel.

'You never have to come in here again, senator,' he said, probably without irony. 'Once the mortar is dry, I will whitewash the wall and no one need ever know the secret inside.'

And, God forgive him, Terence Considine in his mind saw the quicklime eating away at those proud china-white buttocks and thought: At least I prevented those loud Americans from having him.

Dolly Considine's Hotel

JULIAN RETURNS TO CAVAN

August 1983

'Speckled and brown,
from Baile an tSagart
you transported me.
But a lift is a lift
not a summons to indenture,
not a transfer of ownership.'

Julian spoke the words slowly but without trying to imitate her accent. Bláithín's smile encouraged him. He was back in her house in Cavan, she sitting on one arm of the pulled-together armchairs where he'd slept and looking down at him over the coffee mug pressed to her lips.

'That's the poem I was rehearsing for *Sunday Miscellany* in July when you barged into the Kickham Room, all officious and ham-fisted.'

The glass door had vibrated with the sound as he'd listened

among the hunting prints in the hall outside, his right ear filled with her unstoppable whispering voice. The lines repeated enough for him to learn it off.

'What's it about?' was the nearest he could get to asking her why he was back in Cavan, why he'd obeyed her instruction to be at the corner of Harcourt Street after closing time, again. He looked at the isolated spots of butter on the toast he was about to eat instead of twisting his neck to look up at her face.

'Ach it's about a hen. A silly wee hen who jumps up onto a cart and hitches a ride out of the townland of Baile an tSagart thinking she'll find a better life in the metropolis of Spiddal.'

He himself had been in a stranger's car, a lift hitched to Navan, when the show was broadcast. Had she and Sylvester finished in the bedroom before her reading started? Had the missing croissants spoilt it for them?

'Poultry doesn't hitch lifts from strange men,' he said.

'You don't know Connemara hens,' she laughed.

'I think it's about the relationships between men and women.' It would be surprising if she didn't see that. 'The writer is a man, isn't he? Is it Paul Durcan? Do you know him?'

'Yes. I mean no. Yes, a man, no not Durcan.'

She wasn't ready to admit it was about men and women. But she was giving him breakfast in bed; why was he niggling her?

'The Irish poets wrote about their working lives and the living landscape that surrounded them,' she said, and leaned towards the coffee table for her own toast.

His journal was out of sight. She might ask to see what he'd written after she'd gone to bed. Nothing about her, so he might read to her while she drove him to Navan to catch the bus back to Dublin.

'Their animals dominated their lives. Livestock demanded, needed, far more attention than their womenfolk ever got.'

'I liked the way you read it,' he said, and leaned his head right

364

back to stare up at the underside of the roof, and listened to something scratching in the thatch. His Adam's apple bobbed up and down as if his mouth was flooded with saliva.

'It's a lighthearted poem about a silly hen switching allegiance from the country to the town. She'd have moved on again if another cart had come her way.' She touched his arm.

'*My children, not your breakfast* is lighthearted?'

'I only read the poems, Julian,' she said. 'I don't analyse them.'

She picked up the tray of breakfast things and headed for the kitchen sink. 'You're seeing the world from the chicken's point of view.'

'It's the way you read it. You were standing in for her, representing her.'

'No darling, the poem is the poet's story. It's his response to her hopping up onto his cart that's interesting.'

Was that an actor's darling or a lover's darling or a patronising mother's darling?

'But you made me see differently out of each eye, Bláithín. I tried to eat by pecking. I wanted to rescue her and stand guard over her eggs until they hatched, to puff myself up with pride when she clucked about the farmyard with her brood behind her.'

'You stupid boy. The poet was feeding and housing and protecting her from foxes. The least she owed him was her few miserable eggs.'

He whipped the blanket off himself and pushed the armchairs apart before putting his feet onto the stone floor. He faced her in his borrowed plaid shorts. A semi-naked porcelain-white statue with black roots pushing out blond hair, and clenched fists.

'What about a woman's right to choose?' Forcing out a smile as he repeated his mother's slogan.

'And most of all, the silly hen was the only bird living with the poet. It was a house without a cock,' she said as she moved to the bedroom door, her hand on the latch.

If he'd been another man, he'd have lifted that latch and spent the night, not on the armchairs but inside with her.

'And no cock means no little chicks. By eating her eggs, the poet gave her purpose. That's the point. Her eggs would have rotted in the nest where she laid them. Omelettes lent her life meaning.' She slammed the door after herself and he closed his eyes against the draught and the shock.

The hotel was a hundred miles away in Dublin. And yet he could hear Josie whispering, 'Tell her, if she's still in love with the poet, she should go to him and demand he returns her love.'

Summer of Unrequited Love

BLÁITHÍN RECALLS THE POET WHO DISTRACTED HER TEENAGE SUMMER (JUL '56) IN CONNEMARA

It was me you told not to get covered in Snowcem. Me who helped whitewash Peg's house when I should have been at my Irish classes with the other city girls. I don't deserve to be ignored or treated like some non-poetic low life. We have history. If I hadn't been there, your book jackets wouldn't say:

'*The living embodiment of Irish poetry.*'

'*The poetic recorder of the vanished life of the Connemara boatmen.*'

'*The final link to Galway's long–lost crois-wearing currach rowers.*'

Of course, it was you who wrote the poems, I watched you doing it. But you can't deny I was a part of the scene, part of you. More of a part, for that summer, than the handsome boatmen who bob up and down on the waves of your watery poems, and whom you only ever saw from the safety of the quayside.

We Snowcemmed Peg's house together in the afternoons,

when you were finished watching from the end of the harbour wall as the creels were being raised, emptied and re-baited, or at the beach at Trá na Mná as the upturned above-high-watermark-bound boats hid the carriers' felt-hatted heads and shoulders. We sneezed together when the grey dust you poured into the bucket billowed up into our faces. Hand over hand we held the stick to mix the slurry with the water drawn from the well down by the Summer College where my absence was marked in the register. Side by side we slobbered distemper onto the uneven walls of Peg's house. The whitewash brush bigger than your two hands, the clumps of fibres tied with string like giant meaty fingers.

And when you balanced on the ladder of tied-together birch to do the outside of Peg's upstairs bedroom, it was I who handed you up the chipped white-enamelled bucket to hang on a piece of wire twisted into an S. It was me that wedged my young form against the bottom of the bendy elevator while you clung to the top rung. Me who stopped the greenstick ends from sliding away from the gable and prevented you from crashing onto the treacherously rough shingle and moss-covered stones.

Where is your 'Homage to Snowcem'? Your 'Ballad of the Whitewashers'? Or even 'Bláithín's Stinging Eye'?

You can't paint me out of your history or recast me as a crois-wearing currach-rowing pampootied-lobster-potter, or the hitch-hiking hen from Connemara in your follow-up collection. I gave meaning to your poetic fucking life. You are famous now, loved now, alive now, because when you needed to be up a ladder, I was there to keep you steady. I deserve an entire collection: *To the Ladder–Wedging Cailín.*

Put that in the broken old dúidín I gave you the day I left, and smoke it till all your travelling chickens come home to roost.

Summer of Unrequited Love

IS THIS WHAT SYLVIA DOES ON HER AFTERNOONS OFF?

How does a weaselly, hopeless Dubliner like Julian manage to possess the entitlement of a first-born scion out of a thousand acres in County Meath? How does a dead-end lounge boy strut about like a final-year vet student with a family promise of his uncle's county-wide practice immediately upon graduation? An undernourished, stunted urchin appear out of nowhere, with his lifeless bleached hair, and big himself up as if he is a full-sized man with a natural blond headful suited to being whipped backwards or draped over one eye depending on what signals are needed?

Julian sneers at me, but I see the way he sniffs the air in front of every woman in the hotel and stares her down like he's man enough to back her into a corner with all the assurance of a Protestant landowner's son backing a trainee cook into the potato-sack corner of the big-house kitchen, and she only on her second day in the place and fresh out of the council estate in Navan and not sure what effect she's having on him. Me wondering whether the poor unfortunate has ever been up close to an innocent Catholic girl from the town, or whether it's fair to be driving him wild with her innocence and playful laugh unless she'd misunderstood completely when he said she smelt like freshly baked bread and he would die if he couldn't break off huge floury chunks to fill his mouth again and again till he choked with delight.

To bump into anyone else would have been preferable. But Julian, with his bottled-up secrets and a lifetime of brooding over his imagined sufferings, would be very quick to notice if I was not my usual self. And yet, if I have a mind to, why shouldn't I walk up the Rathmines Road on my afternoon off?

I never stare at Baby Greg, but today I'll be extra careful to show no more than a natural interest in the sight of a schoolboy crossing the road towards the mother waiting for him, even if she's not his mother. A touching scene that only a hard-hearted old bitch would not notice and smile wryly about at another passer-by who might also notice, which is the most I ever do.

He has rugby on Wednesdays but being Thursday and threatening rain he'll be out that gate at a quarter to four and straight across the road to where the Snatcher One is impatient in the car. The thing I hate most is that in a city full of schools they send him to a place that spews out little Protestant-like-clones in mini military uniforms, laying a patent claim to generations of exclusiveness and struts of entitlement while all the while pretending a people-embedded-tradition of simple Irish Catholicism. A far cry from the nuns that schooled me, however bad they were, or the brothers I'd have gone to, had I been a boy.

When I first found Baby Greg's school, I used to like waiting in the vestibule of Mary Immaculate Refuge of Sinners. The pictures of good works on the missions, the notices to read about charities and pilgrimages, the religious magazines and their honesty boxes made me feel calm. But for weeks it's been nothing but hectoring Pro-Life stuff, which is not the mood I want from a church. Mary Immaculate will have to do without my few pence, at least until the vote is over. When I'm early now, I confine myself to standing on the far side of the road and being awed by the towering Roman columns. Although the church's green dome now looks like the knuckle-dustered fist of God bursting through the roof.

The green cupola of the K-Cs' summerhouse that Gregory called the Cupolus Viridis is tiny in comparison, but draws just as much attention to itself. Sylvia, Mrs K-C would address me. I wonder if you'd mind laying out tea for four in the summerhouse.

Well I did mind. It wasn't my job, actually. Why couldn't she ask her lazy son, 'home for the summer hols'? The truth was she didn't want me in the main house when she was in the garden in case he got up to no good with me. She knew well enough what was going on.

Still, I enjoyed walking across the lawn as though it was a proper posh house with royalty and film stars awaiting my arrival with refreshments at the summerhouse, where I would curtsy, and maybe smile if spoken to.

Mrs K-C only bothered with outside afternoon tea on very warm days. The sun shining on the little green roof, the bees mighty interested in the multi-coloured flowers trailing down from the hanging baskets even if I didn't know what they were called. My mother has a small fuchsia, but the K-Cs' version was buxom enough for him to hide behind without being seen from either the big house or the summerhouse, and from where he could slide out to make me nearly spill the tea things with me stepping gingerly on the soft turf, with no proper path, at least not by the direct route across the lawn, and kiss me there behind the fuchsia, saying my lips were the colour of the fuchsia flowers leaving me not sure if I liked that or not.

'Mrs K-C doesn't approve of lipstick during working hours,' I said.

'Well, let me lick it off then,' deliberately confusing me into not knowing if I was or was not wearing lipstick even though I knew I wasn't, because at that time I didn't, and then reaching down to kiss me, his head bobbing about like a boxer's, as if the taste of me would depend on where his lips landed. His hair brushing over my cheeks and half-shutting my eyes before he closed in.

'I'm going to see a flat,' Julian's voice. 'You better come along and tell me if it's okay.' As if he had the right to ask, or to presume I wasn't busy, although I was. Saying it all before I could turn to see who was speaking, even if I already recognised the Dublin twang. It stands out among the country accents we hear in the hotel, which is ridiculous considering we're right in the centre of the city.

'You're moving out?'

'I mightn't like the accommodation,' he says.

'The landlord mightn't like you,' I say.

'Everyone likes me.'

'You've a lot to learn. Does Mrs McC know?'

'It's none of her business. I'll only stay there when I feel like it.'

The words slap into my face. 'What kind of... ?'

But it's almost a quarter to, so I turn, dodge between two cyclists and a car, and cross the road. Let him follow if he likes.

'It'll be a bedsit I suppose. Where is it?' I say when he catches up, not because I want to know but to distract him from watching me watching the pedestrian crossing up ahead, with the boys streaming towards it from the school.

I adjust my walk so I'll be the right distance from the Volvo when the green man lights up. I need to let myself be slowed from making progress by the hordes of escaping pupils surrounding me, without looking like an awe-struck culchie staring at the rich schoolboys crossing the road like it's the lawn at Buckingham Palace and they on their way to meet the queen.

It takes a count of fifty-seven from the church gate to the corner, walking normally; and the lights take twenty-five from the time the button is pressed. It might be okay to be seen passing the Volvo now and again, but when I'm here every Tuesday and Thursday she might notice me, even if it's a free country and I'm entitled to walk anywhere I like. Let her look, and she'll get the scowls I have squashed behind my smile.

'Richmond Hill,' Julian says. 'Do you know where it is?'

'Up along here,' I say, pointing. Forty-eight... forty-nine...

Sometimes she parks the Volvo in Richmond Hill if the main road is busy. I know the names of all the side turns from the fire station down to the canal. Fifty-two... fifty-three...

Baby Greg is carrying something, a tube, no, a rolled-up sheet of paper. A boy pushes past and bends the tube, and my hand goes up to my mouth because I want to straighten it out and check the rude boy and tell Baby Greg it will be all right.

When we get home, I'll run the hot iron over it and smooth out the creases, I'd say, or *Why don't you unroll it and let me see what you've painted?*

Fifty-six... fifty-seven...

Julian is looking at the street nameplate and one hand reaches out to drag me around the corner, but I've crossed to where the Volvo is, the lights have changed; my little boy is stepping onto the footpath just as I reach the Rathmines Inn. Fifty-nine...

I forget about Julian as Baby Greg comes around to the passenger side. He is so close I can smell the stuffy classroom clinging to him. He needs a haircut, and there are splashes of red and blue paint on the fingers clutching the rolled-up paper.

'Hi,' is all he ever says to her and climbs in. He looks so tiny on that big seat, and I keep walking, even though I know Julian will be fermenting his hurt if I don't turn around. I stop and try to look bewildered, my head turning left and right. Greg has a small cut over his left eye, the blood crusted and dry. I hate that fucking rugby. I'd find him a gentler sport if he lived with me. The accelerating car almost drowns out Julian's voice.

'Where are you going?'

'Sorry,' I say. 'I was in a daze. Did you say Richmond Villas?'

'Richmond Hill. You walked right past.'

I let him lead me back and around the corner.

By now Baby Greg is getting the painting caught in the seat belt as he tries to show her; I'd have insisted on inspecting it before we drove off. I'd point out the good parts and ask where he'd like to hang it. But all she thinks about is her tidy house, telling him it has to go in his bedroom.

'Here we are.' Julian tries to point my head towards a stretch of houses opposite the bicycle shop, which earns him one of my scowls. I walk ahead, past the open dustbins to steps up to the front door. An empty fish fingers box staring at me accuses the Snatcher One of not cooking proper meals for Baby Greg. He never complains. He has to serve his time and come back to me when he's old enough to decide for himself, or earlier if his father stands up to his mother, has the adoption revoked, and demands the family be together in County Meath.

The landlord is a right little gurrier, his arms are folded, his shirtsleeves are rolled up. He looks at me as if I can see inside his mind and he tries to confuse me by thinking things he isn't thinking. A red-faced thing with a gritted little mouth and hair wild as if some old woman had tossed it for devilment.

'I have two singles,' he says, 'one at the back upstairs, and one at the front. But I've promised the back one to a girl who is coming to see it on Friday. You can have a look anyway, but I can't let you have it.' He says all this to me without opening his mouth, and stares into my face like he is expecting me to lambast him.

'This is me sister,' Julian says, sounding like a country person himself, with the accent he's adopted. 'She has to like the room or me mammy won't let me move in.' The man nods as if he's heard such a story before but says nothing.

The first room is in the basement and looks out at the bins and the car park with the fish finger boxes. 'This one is nineteen,' the man says from the hall because there's barely room for one person inside. I think about Baby Greg living there and know that the peeling paper above the window and the smell from the bins would never let me agree to it.

'Well, sis,' Julian says.

'Grand for you.' I push past him into the hall. The landlord will notice we have different accents. Let them sort it out.

The other room overlooks a field of cut grass surrounded by the backs of houses. A couple of tall white wooden things, the size of barn doors on wheels, have a familiar look about them. They must be for something. This room is bigger, and up two steps has an alcove with a cooker and a press. A big old fridge stands beside the bed, as if the man doesn't know the difference between a bedroom and a kitchen.

'She prefers this one,' Julian says to the man. 'I can tell from her face.'

'I've told you now it's promised. And it's twenty-three.'

'I'll take it. I can let you have the deposit today and come back with the rent on Friday. Is there a rent book?'

He's got no right. No right to waltz in like it's his for the taking. And not a care for that poor young one when she comes on Friday, and finds her promised home occupied by a stranger.

'Mammy will sleep easy in her bed knowing I'm in a nice room, won't she sis?'

I look at the barn doors on wheels out on the grass and think, Baby Greg will know what they're for.

'Have a good look round and take in the details so you can describe it to Mammy and not have her worrying about me.'

I leave them to it. I might just walk to the house in Darty and catch a glimpse of him playing alone in the garden before his bath and his evening meal. But instead I turn towards the canal. I have to be back at the hotel for five. I've promised myself I won't go near the house on school days.

'You're no laugh, so you're not,' Julian says when he catches up. 'I had to tell him you're a schoolteacher and you were planning to spend your summer break in a cave in Greece, but you're giving it up to nurse our dying mammy.'

He tries to link my arm and dance me along, but I push him away. Baby Greg's school will close on Friday for two months. It is my broken heart I will be nursing for the summer. Afternoons spent walking casually through Darty, trying to look invisible while the empty and quiet garden drags me back again and again to peer through the tight bushes and work out whether they've taken him abroad for a month or he's just out for the day.

Julian skips ahead sideways, kicking one foot against the other like a madman. Gregory senior will spend the summer looking after the cats and dogs in his mother's brother's veterinary practice. Maybe he's hoping she'll die so he can marry me. But it wouldn't hurt him to find out about our child, or for her to know she has a grandson. Baby Greg is growing up under another name and calling someone else Daddy.

Summer of Unrequited Love

A JADED WILLIAM MCCLEAN INDULGES HIS DESIRES

Aug '83

William had been in St Stephen's Green all afternoon with his mother's photograph album and two flagons of cider, examining the photos for any hint that his uncle had slept with her. And by the end of the first bottle, he'd convinced himself that it gave him an advantage; some people had no doting father, whereas he had two, both making sure he got on in the world. Fucking bingo. But if Uncle Giolla-Íosa had come waltzing across the humped bridge that minute he'd have confronted him and told him exactly what he needed to do to make up for the years when his status was a dirty secret. Except it was the gardener he knew as Goggles that was on the bridge, ringing the bell to clear the park of people, trying to make his walking stick look threatening, and peering through his thick lenses for malingerers not hurrying to the remaining open gate.

Slipping through the dark bushes, William tried to impose his mother's dalliance on Grandma McClean's house in County

Offaly, but it refused to work. A hotel in the heart of the constituency did no better, because of the porters nodding familiarly with Uncle Giolla-Íosa's well-known face. Much more likely to have been his mother's coffee mornings in the Hibernian Hotel, making it easy for Giolla-Íosa to slip out of Leinster House, and into his mother, in a room overlooking Dawson Street. He even managed to put himself into the hotel wardrobe to watch his totally fussy, fawning uncle banging his overweight, sexless mother. Did they still avail themselves of his father's dozing in front of the TV when William was away with his student friends or at some Ógra Fianna Fáil event?

He took another swig of cider and peered down from Cowboy Hill at the last few stragglers being herded out of the park gate. It wouldn't be completely dark for two hours; enough time for him to set up his trap, gather wood for the fire, construct the spit, and lay out the two knives he'd taken from the hotel kitchen. In County Offaly no one would bat an eyelid at duck hunting, and if his grandparents were still alive he could be thundering after foxes or hares on horseback any time he liked. Instead he was confined to trapping ducks with a fishing net in the public park. His father had called it 'urban hunting' when he'd read about bones and the remains of a fire being found in St Stephen's Green. William had been outraged at the idea of hippies or unwashed punks killing the city's wildlife. They're the people's ducks, his father had said, they're entitled. And William had called him a socialist.

The cheeky chappie chose himself when he freely walked towards the trap, his head already titling towards the wing that should have sheltered it for the night. Closer, closer, that's it, and a flick of William's wrist and his grandfather's long-handled pike net was trapping it, the strings he'd attached pulled tight, and then straight into the water with the squawking thing, his mates joining in with the noise but not coming to the rescue. But by then the struggle was under water and except for some gurgling and churning all was silent; William's heart was racing and a jump in his penis made him hope he wasn't a pervert.

The noise of the blood thumping through his ears was drowning out the disturbed-water noises and would easily do the same for any intrusion by wardens racing towards him with flashlights and blowing whistles. He had to force his head away from the bubbling water to look around him. But his eyes moved like the blood in his ears, darting hot, but taking nothing in, not even that he was slipping towards the water himself, shortly to end up with the drowning duck, wet and cold, his adventure needing to be called off.

He held the net pressed against the bottom of the pond until the rest of the flock quietened, and beyond that, until the churning stopped. Then he sat back on his heels and congratulated himself on avoiding the shame of having to slink home like a Roman soldier bending beneath the Samnite yoke of defeat he'd read about in his Latin history.

Julian was repulsed by the ickiness of William's story. It did not have the mock-heroic tone that was present in Paddy's telling, and yet, unless it was that Paddy had found a more futuristic form of communication, this latest venture was coming from Julian's own imagination. William's lips brushing against his ear to whisper: Is it spoilt William's perverse feelings that're upsetting you, or the fact that all this stuff lives inside your head?

Back up on Cowboy Hill Mr Duck was quiet inside the pike net, but to be certain, William twisted the head round and round until the flopping neck proved it would not recover.

But the heat from the warm thing was taking the cold from his wet hands and he flung it to the ground like a heroine fooled into holding something revolting. He rallied himself by remembering how his mother managed the goose, sent up from Offaly in a cardboard box every Christmas. Brendan's job was to kill it with a meat cleaver and hang it in the backyard after it was plucked, the blood dripping into a dish and lapped up by the stray cats that came over the back wall from the girls' school on Earlsfort Terrace. His mother did everything else.

How will you be able to cut the fucking thing open, and stick your hand up its arse, if you're this squeamish?

He dried his hands in his jeans, and held a lighted match to the paper beneath the sticks laid out in a lattice pattern and set into a dug-out hole to keep the flames from being seen from the bottom of the hill.

His fingers cramped after a few minutes of plucking. And skin was coming away with the feathers until by experiment he learnt to pluck from the head downward. The underside responded better, and the soft feathers around the legs, although none of it was easy. The head had to come off and the wings as well. But it was dark, and not easy to see where the feathers were going or if the moisture on his hands was water or blood or something else leaking out from inside the bird.

He wedged the tail against a tree and pushed the knife he'd taken from the kitchen into where he thought was right if he was to clean it out. But he released something slimy and the smell was disgusting, and the contents of his own stomach retched into the air. William was not just revolted, but getting cold as well, and the smouldering sticks were producing more smoke than heat. Smoke that was lingering under the tree canopy and sinking down the hill. Without a proper fire he couldn't roast the thing or stay warm. But it was the torchlight coming from the direction of the bridge, and the barking, that convinced him it was time to go, and sent the remains of the duck arcing back to the pond, the torchlight then skimming the pond's surface when the splash sent the other birds squawking into the air.

At least he had proved he could catch a duck and kill it. But plucking, cleaning and preparing it for cooking took time and equipment. If he was camping in the country with a gang of students, he could show them how it was done. A lark to release tension when their exams were finished. He would embellish the story for the lads. The premature end brought on by the speeding lights and barking dogs coming towards him… also the surprise on the face of the couple walking arm in arm on the footpath opposite the College of Surgeons when he dropped onto the footpath in front of them, his bravura while he reached through the railings to swing his bag over just as the Alsatians reached it, the smell of warm barbecued duck filling the night air, and most importantly the feral punk girl in the bondage clothes who lived on the island in the middle of the pond who'd fellated him while he pushed his fingers through the diamonds of her fishnets, stopping briefly to beg him to dig his grease-stained nails into her thighs.

Summer of Unrequited Love

JULIAN EMBROILS CATHAL MCCLEAN IN HIS CONSPIRACY THEORIES

Aug '83

'Now would a boy like you see the distinction between the "equal right to life of the mother" and the "equal right of the mother's life"?' Cathal asked as Julian arrived with his supper tray. 'Does the first wording assign the right to the woman herself? And the second wording, ignore the person, assign the right to the life force within her? Would a future court understand the dilemma? That in order to logically recognise the equal right of the life force within the foetus (which is not a person), the mother would have to be understood in the same terms. She must be downgraded to the same status as the fertilised egg and be seen as distinct from her own life force. As if the rights should accrue to life itself, and not to the person. What?'

Cathal's eyes were closed as he spoke and his fingers were resting apart on his stomach, and he hoped he didn't look self-satisfied.

'It's all too late now with the referendum wording set in

law. But my finest work was the fifty-page report I prepared last year explaining the legal and moral distinctions in minute detail.'

'You're talking shite,' Julian said. The papers on the coffee table had been tidied into less dangerous-looking towers, but Mr McClean was his usual rambling drunken self.

'You rebuff me in my attempts to be your friend. Why is that?' Cathal opened his eyes.

Earlier in the afternoon Julian had brought sandwiches into the theatre and witnessed Mikhail rehearsing a scene between a boy and his brother's pregnant girlfriend. 'Why do you hate me,' the boy in the play had said, 'when I've always treated you so well?'

He had only witnessed a short out-of-context exchange before having to go back to the hotel to resume his duties, but Julian now replied to Cathal, with the words and intonation of the pregnant woman in the play, 'You promised to look after me, no matter how your brother behaved.' He pointed his finger and looked ready to throw the teapot in exactly the way the woman, apparently overwhelmed by the behaviour of the uncle of her unborn child, had thrown back the flowers he'd given her.

Cathal suspended his chewing and they stared in silence into each other's faces. 'Maybe I'm inclined to ramble,' he said eventually, sighing, and blinking at his supper. Did the boy mean Giolla-Íosa had reported him to his handlers? No, he'd have been removed by now if he had. 'I enjoy our little discussions, but I'd prefer you didn't pour scorn on me.'

'Then give me the insider's report from the corridors of Ireland's debating chambers; the gossip, the political intrigue, the backstabbing—' Julian had more to say, perhaps he had a real question, but Cathal interrupted him.

'I go to the office, I work ideas up into credible policies for the party to adopt or reject, I have a drink in Buswells, and then I come home. That's my life.'

'Or you refuse to see what's going on around you. You think it's safer to keep your eyes and ears closed, rather than allow your attention to bear witness.'

'You imagine the corridors of Leinster House, swarming with petition-clutching men being kicked out of the way by powerful ministers, and obsequious civil servants fingering pens and daggers in case a signature or a dispatch is required. What?'

'Shite, shite, shite. That's what this is, man. You're holding out on me. How can I respect you when you do that?'

Cathal placed a forkful of egg into his mouth and pushed some buttered toast in after it. The boy was sounding hysterical; why didn't he just ask about his friend Malone? He moved to the window as if the outburst might have triggered a cavalry charge up Hatch Street. But Cathal saying, 'My wife thinks she's helping those boys when she offers them respite from the mean streets of Derry,' had Julian back at the couch leaning over him.

'They've released Malone?' Julian grabbed Cathal's hand. Cathal waited until it was released and safely back on his stomach before he continued.

'There are reports of a group of young people visiting banks and post offices all over the country and lodging small sums of money into accounts managed by various groups supporting the Pro-Life Amendment Campaign and The Society for the Protection of the Unborn Child. It looks likely he is with them.'

If he thought this was more shite, Julian was surprised at the question that jumped out of his mouth. 'Why not make one big lodgement?'

Cathal looked pleased with himself. 'Thousands of small

donations will prove there is massive grass roots support for the amendment. The people are demanding the constitution be amended to protect the unborn.'

'But where would Malone get money? He's just ordinary.' Julian didn't want him to be rich, but comfortable would be okay.

'Contributions from Catholic American and Irish-American organisations. Some of it may be republican money, bank robbery money. A calumny of a suggestion, that in return for a percentage, the proceeds are laundered through the amendment campaigning accounts.'

'A thing like that couldn't happen. The papers would find out and expose it,' Julian laughed. But he wanted it to be true, and to run off and join this mysterious band of money lodgers.

'The people behind the enterprise are well able to manage the press,' Cathal said, shaking his head.

'Can I see him?' He could pack Malone's bag and be out the door in ten minutes, tops.

'I doubt it. Most likely they never know where they'll be from one day to the next. Their bagman is likely to pick them up from a safe house in the morning and drive them around. I'd say your friend won't be back in circulation until after the referendum.'

'But at least he's not...' Julian didn't know what Malone was not. Not in jail... ? Not dead... ? Was it okay to launder bank robbery money?

'I mean it's not as if he's conspiring to overthrow the state.'

'Depends on your point of view, I suppose,' Cathal said.

'He might not know where the money comes from.'

Cathal's tea couldn't have been hot, but he blew on it anyway, and said nothing.

My mammy told me I was not to be robbing banks. He could

hear Malone justify himself. Not sure whether to be pleased or sorry.

'And what about the books? The Mills and Boon lovey-dovey stuff?'

'If there was any significance in them, I'd have picked up half a dozen different explanations in my enquiries. But the grapevine is silent. I suggest they're just books. Your friend has a taste for ladies' romances.'

Julian backed out onto the landing, accepting that Cathal was passing on what he'd been told. But it was lies, at least about the books. The books meant something. Maybe the rest was true, but he'd have to listen out for his mother's response before he knew what to believe. She'd be organising final anti-amendment rallies, or a painting session for last-ditch banners, or fundraising for the hopeless 'No' campaign.

'Are you still sorry he was lifted?' he whispered, 'now you know he's working for the "Yes" lot?' Would her 'when they came for me' poem turn to ashes in her mouth?

He'd have to be brave and ask Bláithín outright what she knew about the books. Sniffing, or whatever she'd done, as she picked each one off the floor, could easily mean she knew why Malone had them hidden in his bag. Especially when, the day after he'd given them to Mrs Hannafin to read, but really for safe keeping, he'd found a man sniffing other books in the library.

Inside the living room, Cathal was wondering if there was anything he could say or do to save Julian, without betraying confidences that were not his, or not his alone.

Dolly Considine's Hotel

WHY HAS MALONE NOT COME FOR HIS CLOTHES, AND HIM?

August 1983

Please take care of my bag. My mammy packed it herself. She'll be very cross if you don't, and you wouldn't like my mammy when she's cross. In the first few weeks he only had to close his eyes to hear Malone's instruction. But by mid-August, Malone's voice, his expression, his swagger, his imagined form beneath his clothes, had become as vague as milky-pale cardboard daffodils remembered in tranquillity.

The trousers Julian was wearing, the underwear and socks no longer smelt of Malone, and the pristine unworn T-shirts that he'd elevated to represent Malone's torso-hugging purity, and which he'd promised to lovingly protect, had been dropped into a dustbin on Merrion Row after Brendan's boots had left them soiled like under-age brides bound to old men.

Even his attempts to refresh his memories with the notes in his journal failed to restore the vibrancy they'd first had. The descriptions were all there, but nothing could give them the

387

trembling anticipations that had filled those first few weeks. He felt betrayed. He'd been betrayed. He'd only stayed at the hotel to honour Malone, and if Malone ever had any intention of coming back for him, he'd have done so by now, or sent a message to say sorry.

'Maybe Malone's instruction was addressed to the policeman, not to you at all,' the bag itself suggested. 'After all, he was being arrested, he could have been confused about which bag was his. You should have owned up. Instead he's cursing you for the clothes that don't fit, and the books he doesn't have.'

'Fuck off,' he shouted and kicked at the soft brown leather. And kicked again, circling it, rotating and distorting it, a scuffing sound as the air inside was exhaled with each kick; the handles flailing, as Malone's own arms might have done, to protect himself from the policemen kicking him when he 'fell over' in the station.

'I never want to see you again, I hate you.'

Half of his summer wasted taking his place, when his recollection of Malone in the bus station had faded to a sort of washed-out-grey memory. As significant as a firm denim-clad thigh he might have seen taking the sun in St Stephen's Green and been allowed to be a bit-player in a mid-week wank fantasy before being filed away to be forgotten, not ever coming close to being the love of his life.

'Fuck you.'

Dolly Considine's Hotel

JULIAN DEBATES WHETHER HE IS EXPECTED TO SLEEP WITH BLÁITHÍN

August 1983

If I have to sleep with Bláithín it probably won't be unpleasant, but why would I expect to? was what Julian had written in his journal that Sunday afternoon after she'd revved away from the hotel like a boy racer. *It's obvious she has intentions, but more likely they are to do with having no children of her own and wanting to use her contacts in radio to help me as a writer.*

The ashtrays were all empty, every table top was wiped, and Sylvia was looking after Jack and Mikhail, beside each other at the bar. Julian had nothing to do except contemplate his life.

'He should have a label attached to his coat like Paddington Bear,' Jack said as Mikhail tucked into a plate of ham sandwiches with one hand and after every second bite extended the other hand for her to refill his glass.

Julian did not instinctively fancy women but had gone along with the attentions of a few. The blonde when he was thirteen, the Caribbean woman when he was in his third year of secondary school, and the friend of his mother's the previous Christmas. Whereas all men were attractive, at least in theory. That said, when they were competing for him at the dog pond or in the dunes at Dollymount, it was always the younger, or the slimmer, or the taller, or the more handsome, whose attentions he gave in to. And if it was a tie, he allowed himself to wonder if the man was a northsider, or a southsider, and that usually decided the matter. Doing his homework on a bench in the Phoenix Park, or working on his tan in Dollymount, Julian would have been generous to allow Mikhail to linger long enough, even for a quick eyeful. He'd told better-looking men to fuck off after the millisecond it took him to assess their lack of worthy qualities. And yet, mid-week, Mikhail continued to drag him up to room eleven for his dues, demanding first they pay their respects to Josie.

He supposed Bláithín was hooked on his writing, and waiting to see how he would fictionalise her life. Or might even be in awe of his raw urban youth. But bedding him wouldn't be important. And yet, by late August, he found himself being taken back to Cavan after the bars closed early on Sunday mornings, and with a late breakfast inside him, to the bus stop for the afternoon bus back to Dublin.

At least when Bláithín's sports car zoomed up to him across from the TV Club, she was sober. And he was free to talk or sleep all the way to Cavan, and then enjoy the bottle of red wine, white cheese and apple slices, followed by showering off the smells and stains of the hotel, and bed.

When she rolled him around under or over her, he tried to fix the details so he could recollect and transcribe them later. The way she arched her back, the curl of her lips when she thrust down on him, the Gothic shape of her fingers like two matching cathedrals towering over the high altars of his nipples. But later, alone with his journal, he could remember nothing of the feelings, beyond an elusive echo. The essential quality of fucking Bláithín refused to be released into his journal. And yet when he described how he imagined her behind the microphone in the recording studio, he allowed her to stretch back towards the memory of being in bed with her boy lover. Allowed the feeling of riding his cock to imbue her delivery with a quality that gave his back a nails-on-blackboard shiver whenever he heard her broadcast.

She never touched his back, only ever reached as far as his shoulders when they were rolling about, or balanced on his chest with the tips of her fingers when she was above him, expecting merely that he allow her full rein.

He noted in his journal how her friends smirked at the changes in her delivery and asked after the cause, which she denied. But he imagined it was only a matter of time before her literary friends would insist on meeting her mystery man, which would trigger new stories, and in a few years, his first novel.

Summer of Unrequited Love

THE TESTIMONY AND PARANOIAS OF MIKHAIL MAYAKOVSKY #6

Aug '83

My ten-year-old Fiat 124 Special T flies me from danger. My music and my sheepskin seat-cover swaddle me, cocoon me, and keep me safe. My sanctuary will be with me even unto the end, when together we find a place, a dock or a cliff perhaps, a handbrake-turn close to the edge for added excitement. So we start sideways on, flipping out into the void, over and over in a final dizzying approach. I even practise when I can, learn to make allowances for grass, wet or dry; cobbles, concrete, tar. Control is what I want, until it's time to surrender to the power inside my car and me. The compressed, champing-at-release power, the volcanic strength squeezed into one tiny balloon of brain and bone and skin and controlled not by massive external forces but by my sheer will, destined for the day when, briefly distracted, or exhausted, I turn my attention back to find nothing; and I will be no more, and everywhere will be the ash of the old world, smelling of sulphur, and cordite, and high semen, with just enough time for me to realise I am dead.

But for now, I confine myself, with the theatre, and sex, and drinking. I dedicate my life to giving you an intense experience. Be it in my bed, my theatre, or the bar where I am overlording.

The interrogation lights are blinding, the colours, the heat, and the smell; my touch, intensified, as if LSD heightened. I am happy when I take you to the edge of the abyss, when I make you piss yourself. One day I may need to let you see me sniff the poppers under my nose, bite the orange in my mouth, and feel the noose tighten around my neck, while my orgasm overwhelms me, forcing me to release my grip on the edges of my ripped-open stomach, and let my guts spill out onto the bedroom's shag-pile carpet.

Silly boy.

Dolly Considine's Hotel

BLÁTHÍN SHOWS JULIAN THE CAVAN COUNTRYSIDE

August 1983

It wasn't wild countryside, it was farmland, with cows here and there, deeply rutted tractor paths through fields with nothing growing, only grass, a stack of massive moon-buggy-wheel-like things on one side, and bushes and leftover branches all tangled up with ivy and barbed wire and rusty bed-ends on the others.

'It's called a hedgerow,' Bláthín explained. She took his hand to steady herself while she stepped over a fallen-over tree oozing black liquid like an unburied corpse. 'Oh what mushrooms,' and she pointed to deformed white shapes squeezed out of the dead tree. She brushed her fingers along a pale pink thing shaped like a repulsive cock.

'We could fry them up with a little butter,' she said, 'but we might be poisoned. Will we risk it? A lover's pact.'

Was she teasing or testing? Up till now she'd only required him to let her bounce up and down on his cock, which gave him the opportunity to take in the details of her face, and her arms and her moans, even if his journal couldn't capture the way her eyes screwed up and then relaxed a bit as she slowed and looked down at him, perhaps to check he was still there. Which made him screw up his own eyes, and adopt a faraway look, so she'd know he was enjoying himself; and what was not to enjoy, having her pussy slide up and down on him?

'Look at the nest,' she said, and pointed at a bush trying to climb out of a muddy trench. He could see no nest, although there was screeching.

'Listen to the babies,' she said. 'All eager to grow up and set up families of their own.' Something dive-bombed towards him and he ducked, catching his cheek on a prickly bramble.

'You're disturbing the mother,' she said, plucking at his sleeve. 'Leave her alone.' And she pulled him away as if he was poking a stick at a sleeping lioness. 'You can't come down here and trample anywhere you like. You have to respect the established order.' She swung her walking stick as if to defend the place from his intrusions. 'It's not Henry Street on Christmas Eve. We need rules to keep our way of life protected.'

'From the marauding foreigner,' he muttered. 'Pillaging and raping all around him.'

'I thought you were in the boy scouts,' she said. 'Don't all city children have aunts and uncles in the country?'

He sidestepped a bottomless muddy pool, the edge squelching up the sides of his cracked white safety boots. 'I could see the mountains from the upstairs back window,' he said. 'Is it all like this?'

After a vigorous bouncing session the previous week, he'd said, 'Do you do this with your TD?'

She'd laughed. 'Would you be jealous?'

'No, I just wondered, that's all.'

'You mean for your notebook?'

'Now Bláithín, you know I don't write about you any more, since you said not to.' She didn't believe him, but he had to keep saying it, and be careful not to leave his Bláithín journal anywhere she might find it.

'My TD, as you call him, likes only the one thing,' she said.

He didn't ask what that was, which gave him creative freedom. 'The man who only liked one thing.' He could have fun with that. But mostly he used Sylvester and her together as a way of slowing himself down when Bláithín was getting so carried away that he needed to stop himself from coming. The one time he'd let go… never to be forgotten.

'What have you done?'

'How do you mean?' he'd asked, dizzy with the intensity of it.

'You little fucker,' she said. 'How dare you? In my house, in my bed.' And she slapped his face, pulled him out, and got off him.

Ever since, he'd encouraged his mind to drift; but if she looked down, she saw a perfectly absorbed cock boy beneath her, a pained look displayed now and again, to remind her that he couldn't hold back forever. Only when her fingers became like the landing gear of two alien spacecraft hovering over his chest, and her nails descended to secure themselves, did he know she was about to finish, and he could listen to his own orgasm and perhaps give her a couple of little jiggles to confirm he was there. Not enough to suggest he was taking charge, but a gentle whoosh to edge her into her yelping and squirming and final collapse onto his chest, her elbows folded beneath her, her nails still anchored around his nipples.

'Did you hear a car in the night?' she asked as they turned back towards the house.

A tractor on the far side of the field was doing something that made a mist come out of a long extended arm. 'A car?'

'I'm sure I heard a car.'

'You mean like, one car?'

'That's all it takes.'

He didn't know what she meant.

'This is not O'Connell Street. Here a car stands out, especially after dark or parked up by the top field.'

'It could have been your TD friend, looking for a little consolation.'

She ignored him and began to climb the hill rising from her house.

It was Thursday. He should have been making breakfast for the Hannafins or waiting for Mr McClean's driver to beep the horn outside the hotel. Questions were being asked about his absence as Bláithín Cunningham strode ahead without him.

'Will I come with you?' he shouted as she began to run. What was so special about the 'top field' as she called it? His boots slipped on the steep wet grass when he began to follow.

'Oh Jesus fuck,' she shouted. 'Oh Jesus fuck.' He slowed down, not sure she'd want him to see whatever was upsetting her. She was pointing at the ground.

'It's a hole,' he said. The removed earth surrounded the small coffin-shaped opening, but not deep enough for a proper grave. Had it been a final resting place or a hidden secret? His breath hurt but he managed to say: 'Someone dug it.'

'Yes, but where is the… the… the—'

'The what?' Whoever did the digging had left footprints. 'Evidence,' he said. 'We can make a cast with plaster of Paris.'

But she began to stamp and sweep the mud back to where it had been removed from, as if the hole, and not its missing contents, was the important issue.

'I knew I heard noises,' she said.

The running and the new breath made him reckless. 'Was this all you had? Or are there more stashes?' And he looked around for a hint as to what country people buried in their fields. Were they like squirrels preparing for the winter?

'What do you know about this?' She grabbed his T-shirt, twisted it under his chin and shook him. 'Who are you?'

'Bláithín,' he said. 'What are you doing?' Words too cheesy to report accurately in his journal, so he repeated her name: 'Bláithín?'

'Who sent you here? Was it your job to keep me in bed while they did their dirty work?'

She was scaring him, partly because she seemed determined to shake some answer out of him, but also because he might have to resist her.

'Or did you get up in the night and help them? Where did they get through the fence? Show me.'

And she began to drag him towards the road.

'I should never have trusted you. A fucking Dubliner. Am I naive or what?' She let go his arm and turned back to the house.

Was he to follow or to wait to be asked? He kicked earth into the hole, and the blades of grass reappeared but there wouldn't be enough clay to fill it. And why would anyone care? It wasn't like it was a lawn. A fresh scar would stand out for a few days and then blend into the bumps, and hollows, and outright holes. Nature covering over the evidence.

Back at the house, the door was locked against him, and when she didn't open up to his knocking, he continued on down to the road. He'd ring the hotel from the shop opposite the church and tell them he'd witnessed a traffic accident and would be delayed while he gave a statement to the Gardaí. Once breakfast was over, no one would care. He'd hitch at leisure and be back in time to stock up the bar for the evening and serve the teas. Luckily the journal he'd left in Bláithín's house was new, so he didn't mind abandoning it. It contained nothing about her, but he'd have to buy another and a pen for the journey.

He listened out for the voice of Josie as he walked towards the village so she could tell him what had been buried in the hole. 'Was it guns for the IRA?' he whispered to get her going. 'Or a dead baby?' But if Josie was listening, she was keeping whatever she knew to herself.

Summer of Unrequited Love

BLÁITHÍN LETS RIP

Aug '83

'I look at you sometimes, and think you'd be as happy holding my hand as sleeping with me. You're so fucking passive.' Bláithín was off again, but he was absorbed with his notebook, speculating about motives, poking about in someone else's thoughts, looking for an action to squeeze into a metaphor and stand in for an unfortunate soul's entire existence. Debating whether to turn the hole in Bláithín's upper field from a hiding place for maturing poteen into the grave of a stillborn child or an arms dump for the local republicans.

'I don't always object to being used. Being used can be about need, without admissions of liability, the way mothers are treated by teenage sons locking themselves in their bedrooms but continuing to take the food and the money and the bed and the laundry for granted. At least they've got earlier, happier, memories to carry them through.'

There was no point in saying any of this to him. Even a simple raised-eyebrow level of enquiry produces that blank uncomprehending shake of his Spartan head. There's not even a *what are you on about Blath?* The ubiquitous snowy TV newsreader, speaking an unknown language in an action-movie background while the hero fights to save the world, would get more respect and understanding. She hated his bloody notebook.

'With your cool hands-off grin, your bemused look, your denial of wanting anything… and yet, so help me God, I don't know how or why, but you want *it* okay, and somehow more of it than anyone I've ever been this close to.'

She knows where she stands with Sylvester. The Fianna Fáil women milling around the party's watering holes, ready to be of service, are his for the taking. But he sticks with the tasty, far-out, eccentric little morsel that she is. For eight years he's sought her out for his blowjob, and when he's had it, he's grateful. When he leaves her he's released, energised and vibrant. 'But you want, you take, secretly, seamlessly, with no permission or acknowledgement, and, God bless you, maybe you don't even know what you're doing. And when you're gone, so is my energy; not with the collapse that follows sexual exhaustion, nor with the grief of parting; but with the emptiness of someone who's had her skeleton removed…

'I am a blancmange breaking the laws about surface tension.

'I am an empty used condom with your drippings trickling out.

'I beg you, you little fucker, tell me; why are you doing this to me? What do you want?'

Dolly Considine's Hotel

JULIAN REALISES HE KNOWS ALMOST NO IRISH HISTORY

August 1983

The central theme of Julian's three-generation political story required Dolly's and Cathal's parents to be on opposing sides during the Civil War. But the only thing he knew about the Civil War was that it started after some of the fighters in the independence war signed a treaty with the English. He also knew that the fighting was between the 'pro-Treaty' and the 'anti-Treaty' forces. Result: Julian had just spent the longest time in his entire life with a pen in his hand, without a word appearing on paper. Not a single word in fifteen minutes of sitting by the duck pond in St Stephen's Green.

Something in his recollection of school history suggested that when the Civil War was over, it was the anti-Treaty government that implemented the Treaty while at the same time steadfastly remaining anti-Treaty and refusing to forgive the people on the pro-Treaty side.

'That's just thick,' Julian said, and dug his pen into the page, as if it was the pen and paper that were responsible for his ignorance.

But they got him to his feet and lifted his head to swear up through the trees at the window in the Shelbourne Hotel from where he'd stood and surveyed the park when he'd visited Mikhail, back in July. His own stare was lingering behind the glass, winking sympathetically. 'Maybe it's not your ignorance of history but St Stephen's Green itself that prevents you from writing,' whispered the winking shadow. 'You're a city boy. Born to the streets. You need traffic and people, not ducks and bluebell-filled glades.' And he was propelled towards the Famine Memorial gate.

When Julian had left Curragh House an hour earlier, Cathal McClean had been complaining about his taxi and muttering about going back to bed. Yet, there he was, not in bed, not in a taxi, but threading through four teenagers who were inappropriately dodging in and out between the skeletal figures of the green bronze memorial. He had reached the pedestrian lights across from the Shelbourne Hotel, joining several raincoated tourists and a man with a briefcase, by the time Julian had almost caught up. Something about Mr Briefcase looked familiar, and suggested he was talking to Cathal. Could he be the man he'd found sniffing books in the Kickham Room library?

'Is this all you have?' he'd asked Julian. 'I was told you had an Elizabeth Bowen collection, but I can't see a single work of hers.'

The tourists were halfway across, and looking from map to street to see which way to go, before Cathal and Mr Briefcase stepped side by side off the footpath, and once across they seemed to hesitate before wheeling back to back and heading in opposite directions, like duellists taking the requisite steps apart before spinning back to pull triggers. Julian was certain they'd have been on opposite sides in the Civil War, had they been born then.

The tourists were blocking the footpath as Julian crossed just in front of a bus, and he had to walk quickly to get around the corner in time to see Mr Briefcase's dance-like trip up the steps into a small office building. The porter looked up from his newspaper as Julian held the glass door for a woman with a basket filled with sandwiches and shouted when he followed her towards the lift.

'You can't go in there, sir,' the porter said, pulling at the cuffs of his uniform jacket.

'This woman is.'

'She has legitimate business here. What is yours?'

'I am here to see Malone.'

'Which company does he work for?'

'He's a colleague of the man with the briefcase who came in a second ago.'

'I don't recall who that was.'

'Tall, in a suit, moving like Fred Astaire, like a man anticipating good news.'

'We get a lot of that here.'

'But Malone would stand out. He's young and wears a dark suit with a school tie, and a has a north of Ireland accent.'

'They seldom speak to me, once I know their faces.'

'I could rush the stairs and you wouldn't be able to stop me.'

'Ah now, for that eventuality my lad, there are contingency plans. I may look ineffective, but there are unobtrusive forces to be reckoned with. My advice to you would be this: go to the public call box back on the Green and telephone the various companies and government departments that occupy this building and ask for your friend by name.'

Should he trigger the unobtrusive forces? Or hang around

until Mr Briefcase came out? Or come back tomorrow with a basket of sandwiches and pretend to be delivering?

'I can't say fairer than that, now can I?'

Julian looked at the man as if for the first time, and beyond him at a board listing the occupants of the building, gold letters announcing unfamiliar-sounding government offices, and beneath them accountancy firms and what sounded like charities.

'That's the place,' Julian said. 'Malone works for Books for Prisoners.' It was all falling into place. It couldn't be a coincidence. Malone was up there now, discussing the whereabouts of his books with Mr Briefcase.

'Sorry son, that organisation moved out months ago,' the man said. 'I believe much of the donated material was considered inappropriate for the client group.' The man rose from his seat and placed his two hands flat on the counter between them. His hair looked deliberately short like a man disguising baldness, except he had an even growth of blackness over his entire head.

Did Paddy the Porter look like this? 'Don't you have a cap to wear when you're on duty?' Julian asked.

'Yes,' the man said, 'I do. However, I am only obliged to wear it if I am given prior notice, or if I see a government minister arriving for a meeting. Unlikely today with them enjoying the summer recess. The union negotiated this on my behalf, as I find a cap has militaristic overtones. I can let you have a list of telephone numbers for the present tenants if you want to telephone them.'

'Why are you helping me?'

'It might be no help at all. The men you are looking for might work elsewhere or nowhere. What do I know? My job is to do my job. I nod at the people going in and out to acknowledge their passage. If help is required, I try to provide it, hopefully at no great expense to myself.'

'Is your name Paddy?'

'Isn't that the given name for half the men in Ireland?'

'But how many are called Paddy Dunne? Are you a ghost? Did you used to work in the Curragh House Hotel in Hatch Street?'

'Now sir, would you like that list of companies or not?' He held a photocopied sheet out to Julian and allowed it to hover just above the desk. The nearest edge flickering gently, the way a fly fisher might dangle a lure over brown water in a slow-flowing stretch of river, calm after escaping from the mountains.

He should ask Mrs Hannafin about the Civil War.

'It was where Mr H lost his leg,' she'd say. 'Of course I know about it.' He would also take back Malone's books. They were going into the Kickham Room library to fulfil their destiny, whatever it was. Julian had no right to protect them from their fate.

'Then we'll see what happens,' he said to the man as he took the sheet of phone numbers. He tried to wink at him, but it came out more like a tic.

Summer of Unrequited Love

PARABELLUM FROM THE PLURABELLE – A STORY FOR PADDY

'The Liffey was a working river in the 1920s: stevedores and sailors, watermen and lightermen, sifters and dredgers. A steady stream of barges and boats, the water clogged with punts and boons, moorings and wharfs, ropes to trip over, and poles topped with vicious hooks for pulling bales.' The most reliable place to hear Paddy the Porter was between the stacks of crates in the beer cellar, right at the back, directly below the trapdoor used by Brendan and Julian to pass crates of full bottles up to the bar and receive empties back.

'There were five of us, and we made our way along the underground part of the river Poddle to where it drains into the Liffey. We were waiting for the tide to go out so we could get upriver to where O'Malley and his garrison were under siege in the Four Courts. We'd been fighting the English together, on the same side, only a few weeks earlier. But now the provisional government were using General Pugh's guns, British guns, to fight against our former comrades. They were betraying everything the men who died in the War of Independence stood for. And for what?

'We could smell the Four Courts fire long before we reached the outlet, the boom from the guns making the long narrow culvert buck like a lashing whip as shell after shell fell onto the seat of so-called English justice in Ireland, packed to the rafters as it was with the records of every man, woman and child in the country. Maybe it wasn't the best place for the anti-Treaty boys to stage their last stand. But it was the Free Staters that burnt all that history and used their English guns to do it.'

Julian was half-kneeling on the cold ground, half-sitting on a sharp-edged beer crate, writing the speech word for word, afraid to adjust his position in case he tore his trousers or caused Paddy to stop talking.

'Long before Ernie O'Malley gave the orders to surrender, the lads with me accepted there was nothing we could do, and they headed back up the Poddle. But I made my way under the wharfs that ran along the river wall, until I was opposite the Four Courts, and under cover of a cloud of smoke blown down from the fire, I climbed onto a tied-up barge. My pals would have been safely home by the time the proud stragglers began to emerge in formation, with their hands up, the water separating me from that awful sight framed by the smoke and tragic flames of the burning buildings and the records inside.

'When the wind blew upriver, I had a perfect view of O'Malley's top half, above the river wall, as he removed the gun from his holster and flung it out over the water; his lips moving with a shouted farewell. I couldn't hear the words, but in my heart, I know he said: The goddess shall have you.'

'Johnner got a gun just like this, one Christmas,' Julian whispered. 'It fired proper caps that smelt of gunpowder. He waved it about like he was "The Chap" in a movie.'

'It's a Parabellum.'

'Is that Latin?' Julian remembered something from school although he'd never done Latin.

'It means for war.'

'Not best war? As in paramount?'

'What would you know about war? A pampered spoilt thing like you.' A gurgle as if Paddy was forcing his gullet closed to prevent himself from losing his temper.

Julian had been in the boys' bedroom, reading aloud the list of company names given to him by the porter in the Kildare Street office, when he heard Brendan coming down the basement area steps. His fingers found the gun when he pushed the paper under his pillow. He knew that sending someone a bullet was a warning, but why would anyone put a gun under his pillow? Unless he was being set up, and would be caught with it, or Jesus, he was being given a mission, thinking he was really like Malone.

The noises from Brendan's banging in the kitchen signalled he was making a sandwich, which gave Julian time to grab the gun, push it under his shirt and get into the beer cellar.

'Ernie O'Malley was always known as a grand shot, and when it came to tossing his gun, it was as if he knew where it was going. It hit the water barely two feet from where I was, out of sight under the barge's tarpaulin. If I'd been out in the open, I could have jumped up and stopped it getting wet, but I'd have been seen.

'He'd thrown it for me: if the river goddess said no, and she did say no, I was to have it. I marked the spot in my head by lining up three points, and when the surrender was taken and they all went marching off to Kilmainham jail, and with the smoke from the burning Four Courts lingering over the water, I left my shoes on the barge and waded to where the river goddess held it for me. I was perished with the cold in the filthy Liffey, but I hardly noticed.

'I'm not saying I found it immediately, but eventually my bare toes engaged with the shape, and within no time it was pushed inside my belt, and I was taking a roundabout route back to the hotel. I was in bed for a week with the flu I caught, waiting outside the basement door for the cook to go to bed so I could slip into the kitchen for cloths to dry it and apply goose fat to stop it from rusting.'

'Are you saying that this is a famous gun?' Julian had never heard of Ernie O'Malley, but after finding the thing under his pillow he'd known he had to find somewhere to hide it. That was when Paddy started telling the story.

'That gun spent the War of Independence and the Civil War with the OC of the Second Southern division of the IRA. It is as much a symbol of Ireland's freedom as any of the paraphernalia they have above in the museum. It needs to take its place in the display cabinets. You should bring it to the curators and hand it over. Tell them the history.'

'It might have one more job to do,' Julian said. Anything could happen once he started ringing those telephone numbers to find Malone. He might need to be prepared.

'The Liffey water will have ruined the bullets. O'Malley was a hard man to kill off, but his gun will never fire again in anger.'

'Actually, Parabellum refers to the bullets it takes,' Bláithín wrote in the margin that evening when she came into the Kickham Room after her recording session. 'How about "Parabellum for the Plurabelle" as a title? And top marks for imaginative use of the facts as they are known about O'Malley. Every time I read your writing, I hear a voice tinged with Dubliner guilt. You will never be free of it until you connect with your heritage and embrace the past. But that doesn't mean you have to push yourself into a starring role in the story. Rather you should represent the subject, in this case the gun and its association with getting the British out of Ireland.

That's enough, and the telling will help to cleanse you, and facilitate your integration.'

Bláithín thought he'd made it all up, that there was no gun. But the proof was buried under a crate of Carling just below them in the beer cellar, tangible, brutal, heavy, the goose fat smothered onto it sixty years earlier dried up and hard.

'Why are you asking me to bring it to the museum?' he'd said as he dug the burial hole. 'Why not Brendan? He's your favourite.' But there was no answer from Paddy. Had telling the gun's story allowed his restless soul some peace, or was he cross with Julian for making plans to wave it in the face of anyone who didn't give him answers about Malone?

Summer of Unrequited Love

DANGER IN THE BOWELS BENEATH THE CORRIDORS OF POWER

Termination #1A

Aug '83

Outside on the street, the day had turned wet and miserable, but it was roasting in the dry, sulphur-smelling boiler room; the ancient pipes wrapped in cracked white bandages, criss-crossing inches above his head, were filled with roaring water threatening to scald him if he came too near, and making him cower closer to the coal-dust-covered floor.

In the movies, when a hero has a list of numbers to phone, he never gets a result from the first attempt. If he ever gets lucky, it's after loads of failures. But there he was expecting disappointment, when the man said: 'Yes, yes we know all about Malone. He hoped you'd have enough ingenuity to find him, so congratulations. Just come along over. He'll be here after lunch.'

The man waited for Julian to say, 'Coming right up, immediately.' But he was too excited to speak.

Four of Julian's journals flew past him, pages flapping, as he was pushed, and tripped onto the boiler room floor, with time only to stretch his arms down to break his fall. John Wayne would have rolled as he fell and got two or three shots off before he hit the dirt, whereas before the door had even slammed shut Julian was kissing coal dust, and ash and grit were caressing his teeth as first one bolt and then the second slid closed.

The fluorescents blinked off as he stood up, leaving one dull emergency bulb like an insect watching from between the criss-crossed lines of bandaged pipes, but allowing the red glow of burning coal inside the boiler's glass panel to draw attention to itself.

At half past eleven he'd been in the phone box at the top of Kildare Street with a pile of change, and the list of phone numbers given to him by the porter in Mr Briefcase's offices; and a few minutes later he was locked up with an infernal boiler and no sign of the man he'd come to see.

'Now what about the books in Malone's bag?' the man on the other end of the phone said, after a long pause. 'Have you kept them safely? Kindly bring them with you.'

Hopefully Mrs Hannafin still had them, but Julian said nothing.

'Malone is due to travel over to Galway in an hour, for the weekend, and I can happily say that he would like you to go with him, all expenses paid, if you can spare the time. Do you know Leinster House? Government Buildings? Please be at the porter's lodge in fifteen minutes, from where you will be directed. Goodbye now.'

Upstairs, or wherever the debating chamber was, the government and opposition deputies were haranguing each other about the Pro-Lifers and the Pro-Choicers. Was Giolla-Íosa in there? Or Bláithín's Sylvester? Was one of them allowing his concentration to waver between the debate and the anticipation of the news that Julian was safely in custody? Except they weren't, if the porter in Kildare Street was right; they were all on their summer holidays.

But what was Malone's part? He was from Derry, a proper republican, he could have nothing to do with him being locked up in the bowels of the establishment. Unless it was connected to the books... or maybe Malone had just been the courier, responsible only for delivery. But how did his journals end up here on the floor? He held the nearest of them under the dull bulb, and recognised it as one he'd hidden in the theatre the previous afternoon. Mikhail might have seen him. Had he handed them over? But, no matter what, by the time that porter gave him the list of phone numbers, his captors already knew about everything he'd written.

And what about the rest of his journals? Had these four been singled out; more guilty, or less guilty, than the rest? Perhaps he was being offered the opportunity to burn them. Except they didn't need him for that. Or was it his voluntary cooperation they wanted, which, if granted, would magically make the door open?

He hugged the four journals to his chest, and kicked the lever holding the boiler's flame door so it swung open, releasing a new, quieter, more insistent whispering from below the roar of the flames and the gushing, knocking water in the pipes. The sounds becoming more insistent, as if someone was turning a tap on full: *Malone is on his way Malone is on his way Malone is on his way.*

Could his captors, whoever they were, see him, or be listening from the next room? He knelt on the floor and put his two hands together in prayer. 'Dear Holy God, please help me. I seem to have upset someone, although I never meant any offence. Please let them know I am sorry and am willing to make reparation.'

He listened and inched closer to his prison door; nothing. But if he didn't know who he'd upset, how could he convince them it was all a mistake? He opened the first journal and ran his finger through the fan of paper to pick out one page, and from it one sentence, perhaps just one word, to fix into his head. But when he looked back his flame-enraged eyes refused to work in the dull light, and something blurred the place where his finger had landed.

'If you don't want to forget, don't burn the fucking books,' he shouted and tore a clump of pages from the first journal before scrunching them into a ball and pushing them onto the coals. Followed by another and another until the heat of the open furnace made the pain of his tightening, burning skin unbearable. He used the coal shovel to scoop up the remaining journals and dropped them onto the undiscriminating coals and slammed the boiler door closed.

'Julian's journals RIP,' he whispered. 'Go little papers, go little words, sacrifice yourselves in heating water to wash the hands of the crooked politicians fucking up the country.' He lifted his head to where he imagined the debating chamber to be and shouted: 'I fucking hate yiz.'

Bláithín, Mikhail, Sylvia, Brendan, the McCleans, all knew about the journals. Any one of them could have done the Judas on him. Well fuck 'em. He would start again, far away, free of them. He'd miss Sylvia's daughter with the name that didn't suit her. She'd walked to where he'd been sitting in the park and asked him to be her daddy. The rest of them could fuck off. Even if he wrote about his time at the hotel and included details of their shallow lives, their help would be inadvertent, would be in spite of them, not thanks to them.

His kidnappers would come to see him soon, and when they came, he'd have Ernie O'Malley's gun at the ready and would point it at them and saunter out with a cheeky grin on his face.

'Fuck the begrudgers,' he shouted, and waved the gun, but then pushed it back under his jumper in case there were eyes watching him out of the dull pink gloom.

Summer of Unrequited Love

A USEFUL LIFE, IN SPITE OF HIMSELF

Termination #1B

Aug '83

The man slid open the door's viewing slot. The kid was on the floor with his back to him, his legs folded elegantly to one side, his body twisted and leaning into the bench pulled out from its rightful place near the wall to the right of the boiler. His arms spread garland-like on the rough surface, his head resting on his right biceps as if he were listening for something the timber might have to say. His form curled around a focal point within the arm-made circle, the nib of his pen perhaps, or a line of cocaine crystals (the little fucker), or a tear-wet finger tracing among the scratched initials and messages left by former occupants allowed to pause here to consider their options.

The pose put the man back on the floor in front of the fire at his granny's, his head resting on her knees, the flickering TV viewed sideways on; sitting upright only to ask her for an acid drop or a chocolate satin, or because he heard his father's key in the front door.

'You're too old to sit like that,' his father would say. 'Sit up straight like a growing man.'

'Where are these famous notebooks?' the man shouted through the viewing slot. 'Put them where I can see them. Now.' A room packed with bags of coal, water tanks, the various ancillary pumps and equipment used by current and redundant plant. A million places to hide a few small notebooks.

'Are you sitting on them? Are they stuffed up your jumper, or down your pants, the sharp edges of the spiral facing upwards so as not to snag on your little penis?'

The kid didn't move. He might have been trying to compose himself before turning to face the man, or inconceivably, was adding a final note, with no intention of stopping until he was ready.

The man had been shouted at for not removing the notebooks when the kid was brought in, but that hadn't been in his instructions. And if the kid didn't volunteer them, he'd have to slide back the bolts, whip open the door and take them, with any reluctance resulting in smacks, although generally the man deplored violence. *Violence indicates failure* was his motto. But for some characters, it was all they knew; logic, negotiation, or pointing out the fragility of their kneecaps was a waste of time. What they begged for was enough violence to get them over the hump of reluctance to comply with the wishes of a stronger will.

Maybe the fucker was already dead, carbon monoxide from the open boiler ensuring he was out of his misery, and rigor mortis keeping him in his compliant shape. A model for a modern *pietà*, if we can find a Mary.

'Well, good riddance.' He'd tell upstairs that the kid had

burnt the notebooks. They wouldn't be rushing to claim responsibility for the dead body. He'd need a little insurance himself; a little perusal, in the bliss of solitude, as the poem says, after he got the body off government property. A good use for the extravagant tunnel built to facilitate the smuggling of politicians off the premises, well below the feet of murderous protesters. A touch of irony could be added by transposing him in his present pose onto a bench behind the Rutland Fountain in the bishop's park, the Garda authorities struggling to put together a coherent explanation. 'I told him he'd come to a bad end,' a former lover will tell a journalist following up the Merrion Square mystery body story. 'He had no ambition, and my devotion seemed to discourage him from bettering himself or engaging with the world,' she will say.

'Perhaps his death could be a lesson to the youth of Ireland?' the reporter might ask.

'I am writing his story, and plan to share it with the world.'

'Do you have a title yet? I could mention it in my report.'

'It will be called "A Useful Life, in Spite of Himself".'

Summer of Unrequited Love

A TRAGEDY OF SHAKESPEARIAN PROPORTIONS

Termination #2A

Aug '83

Pulling the trigger would reveal the bullets as duds; his best chance was to wave the gun around a bit and point it at whoever entered the boiler room, their surprise giving him enough time to slip around his taken-aback jailer and escape, remembering to pull the door after him, and delay to lock it. So when he heard noises outside, and before the first bolt was fully back, his hand was on his waistband, and though he fumbled a bit, the gun was in his hand and his finger on the trigger by the time the door swung open, ready for his one chance.

And then it was like in the pictures; one, two, three, in a row, bullets coming out by themselves. His trigger finger taking on a life of its own, the infamous kick not stopping the squeeze, again, and then again, despite his shock and him stumbling backwards. Understanding at last his mother as she had heaved petrol bombs at the British Embassy, towering over the crowd, clutching the hair of the man beneath her as she bucked and heaved the burning messages over the heads of the protesters. The same giddying elation was lifting him out of his body, only to die back instantly and return him shaking and spent to the sooty boiler-room floor.

The intruder wasn't Giolla-Íosa or Sylvester, or one of the special branch men from the bus station, or even the little man in the Kildare Street office who'd given him the list of phone numbers. Was this Malone? A modern take on Romeo and Juliet? The foolish gun making him misshape the face into that of a stranger so he could live with what he had just done. Wasn't Malone younger than this, taller than this, slimmer than this?

Initially the man's fingers gripped the door, but then they began to slip downward, his face not yet showing fear at being shot at, but anger that it was Julian, the light from outside enough to see his lips moving to shape words to curse him: 'You little prick.'

The goose fat applied by Paddy the Porter sixty years earlier had been hard and cracked, but with a bottle of cooking oil from the kitchen Julian had softened and cleaned it off, the trickiness of the long barrel overcome when he fashioned a couple of tampons, kept in a bag in the ladies, into nifty cleaning pads, the string perfect for pulling the wad through and getting the last of the caked grease from the barrel's inside surface. A skewer that had secured a rolled-up belly of pork helped when enthusiasm made him pull too vigorously.

'What would Mrs McC say if she saw me using her tampons?' he'd said to the cellar corner where Paddy the Porter normally lurked. But the silence that started when Julian threatened to use the gun to frighten anyone who got in his way was continuing. What would Paddy say now, if he saw the results?

At first even Julian thought the soundless talk was because he'd been deafened by the noise from the gun, but there was a gurgling hiss, timed to the movement of the man's mouth, the noise not matching the familiar shapes being taken by his lips.

'You cunt,' the man was clearly mouthing when he should have been thinking about his dying act of contrition. 'You cunt.' Struggling to increase the volume to get himself heard. The effort helping to make him sink to his knees and let go the door.

'You need to cover the hole to stop air getting between the lung and the ribcage' – his school's first-aid instructor's words coming back to him – 'otherwise the victim will not be able to breathe,' followed by stories about passers-by pressing credit cards firmly onto wounds. But Julian didn't even have a bank account, and Johnner's mother had cut up the Big Adventure Bank Account card to stop them getting their money. If he'd had it, he might have saved the man. But one way or another, if she hadn't cut up the fucking card, none of this would have happened. It was all her fault. Hers and Johnner's.

'Now what am I supposed to do?'

He stared at the dull pink glowing eye of the boiler as if it would answer him.

Summer of Unrequited Love

THE HORROR OF WHAT HE'S DONE DAWNS ON JULIAN

Termination #2B

Aug '83

Julian's eyes wouldn't allow the dead man's face to match the Malone profile he'd retained since the brief glimpse of it ten weeks earlier. But he needed to know if it was or wasn't him, so he forced himself down to search the pockets for clues, avoiding skin contact until he was sure. He found a meat sandwich in the man's jacket side-pocket and began to unwrap it before resting the contents on the man's shoulder and folding the paper around the guilty gun. Then he stuffed the gun into his own pocket and simultaneously reached for the sandwich to stuff into his mouth, eating as if he'd never eaten before. A new taste in meat, perhaps the haslet his mother was always promising to buy from the butcher's in Dorset Street.

'I heard the shots,' a voice said, and another man was leaning over him before he could even think about reaching for the gun. The man's cap was pulled down almost to his nose, but surely it was the porter from Kildare St, the one who'd given him the numbers to phone. He lifted Julian up and guided him away towards the rough wooden bench.

'Sit there now, sir,' he said. 'You've had a nasty shock.'

'I killed Malone,' Julian said, and began to unwrap the gun again, as if to let it see the awful thing it had done, perhaps encourage it to take the bullets back.

'It is unfortunate, considering your affection for him,' the man said, reaching for the gun. Julian was surprised how much lighter he felt without it. Were movie guns like movie luggage, even the wimpiest-looking character able to swing a full suitcase up onto a bed, or in and out of a car boot. But now guns. Not just heavier than he imagined, but more deadly too. Hundreds of bullets whizzed all over the place in movies and yet the hero and the baddie survived until nearly the last scene, whereas a few silly unaimed shots from a real live gun resulted in a man being dead. And noisier too. Not just the gun noisier, but death, the man rasping, trying unsuccessfully to shout, sounding like a half-blown-up balloon falling to the floor in a breathless 'phfffffff' instead of flying around the ceiling in a full-throated hiss. And taking so long, bleeding and dying, all that moving, on and on, and his staring eyes and his mouth continuing to insist he should be able to scream and to draw in air, until he gave up that part and just thrashed about until he was still.

An occasional twitch as the man from Kildare Street knelt over the body and began whispering into the man's ear. Too low for Julian to hear. That was another thing they didn't show in the movies, characters with ears hurting from gunfire noise. And it was staying with him, cracking in his ears again and again. Continuing to reverberate around the boiler-room pipes and overlaid with echoes of the rasping and hissing of the dying man.

'Come along,' the Kildare Street man said, 'we have to get you out of here.' He guided Julian around the body and the patches of blood leaking onto the coal-dust-gritty floor, out into the corridor and on towards the steps leading up to street level. Then the man reached over Julian's head and pulled his jacket upwards, sending his arms sideways like penguin flippers, before pulling it down over his face. He placed Julian's fingers on the lapels and drew them together.

'Cameras,' was all the man whispered, his own cap preventing his identity from being recorded, and then led him outside.

'I have to say goodbye,' Julian said, and the man pulled him again.

'No talking,' he whispered. 'The taxi is waiting. You will be given enough money to get to London. Ask no questions. Do not delay. This is your only chance.'

'I won't leave without saying goodbye. I owe Malone that. It can't end like this. It just can't.' He turned to push his way back into the building, and the man put his hand over his mouth to shut him up. His fingers smelt of cigarettes and even a little of the smoke from the gun, turning it into the smell of sex, and he was ashamed for mixing sex with death, but he couldn't help himself. The firmness of the fingers against his cheek, the palm of the hand pressed against his lips. He'd killed Malone, but he'd never touched him. He would not leave until he did that. He would touch his cheek, brush the backs of his fingers against his skin, say sorry, and goodbye.

But then the man's smell changed, a chemical smell that filled Julian's face, and he felt his legs crumple beneath him, and the man's arms encircled him, maybe so he didn't hurt himself when he fell.

'No no no,' he whispered. 'Not like this. Not like this.'

Dolly Considine's Hotel

A PARA IN HER BED

28th August 1983

He'd satisfied her, stilled her yelps and squeals, and then for almost an hour had sat on the edge of the bed listening to her breathing. He couldn't tell whether the sheepskin rug was cold or was damp under his feet. Country dark was total to a city boy, but at the heart of it, Bláithín's arms and legs were open like she was waiting for him to go again. The bed was warm, but not the place to masturbate. He needed space, and to avoid the chance of her turning over or waking up.

He felt his way through the dark, past the front room armchairs, to the window facing down the hill, the cold of the flags rising through him. But his cock warmed everything as it responded to his hand and gave its promise. Some early Sundays have a moon, but tonight it is invisible rain. He shivers when he's come, and wonders if the banked-up open fire might be a better place to spunk over the next time. If there is a next time.

'Dubliners have no ambition,' Bláithín said in the morning before she turned over to say hi or remind herself who else was in her bed.

'Have you studied every one of us?'

'I know well enough what you are. And it doesn't include any ambition.'

'Except to fuck you again.'

'That's not ambition.'

He'd already told her he was twenty-one and had left school five years earlier. So he couldn't suddenly remember that, in a week, he might be going back for his final year.

'I blame your parents. It's obvious they have no ambition either.'

'There's a call box up the road from the house, I could telephone it, and get a neighbour to pass on your concerns. Should I mention wanting to fuck you again?'

'Only if it shocks them out of their lethargy.'

Actually he didn't care if he slept with her again or not. His orgasm in the dark by the window in her front room had been better than anything she'd inspired. But he wanted the package deal: being swept up by her sports car after the hotel closed on Saturday night, and waking up in alien country on Sunday morning. It wasn't quite Bertie Wooster, or the famed British country house weekends. But it was a start. There would be big houses in Cavan that were crying out for a tasty morsel from Dublin, and she'd parade him around when she was a bit surer of him.

'I wanted to be a lance corporal when I joined the army,' he said.

'We don't have lance corporals in this country.'

'Not the Irish army; the Tommies, the backbone of the British empire.'

Her leap from the bed was spectacular. Backwards, the bedclothes preceding her as if she'd been jet propelled away from him.

She was wearing a nightdress. Flannel-looking, from her neck to the floor. Covered in tiny flowers. Like in the films, when the lovers are revealed to be wearing underwear; where had it come from?

'I have a fucking Para in my bed. Get out.'

'I only stayed a month, Bláithín. I left when I realised I might have to go to Derry or someplace.'

'You don't just leave the army. Once they get their hands on you, that's it, until your contract is up. And even then…'

'Well I did leave. Came home on furlough and didn't go back.'

He swung his feet onto the rug and held his arms out to her, but she stayed where she was. He rubbed his hair to look bemused. What was the fuss about? She grabbed her coat from the back of the door, which at the very least meant the outside toilet.

'I didn't even finish basic training,' he shouted when he heard her filling the kettle in the kitchen. He tried to give her a hug when he caught up, but she pushed him away.

'You're still in the British army. Do you have any idea what that means?'

'Is this about the national question?'

'There are places not twenty miles from here where you would be executed on the spot.'

'I was only in the catering corps. I was young and foolish, Bláithín. And under the influence of an older boy.' Half the lads in Cabra were supposed to have been in the British army at one time or another. It was what they did. Still, he'd probably done his weekend cottage aspirations no favours making that one up. 'Nobody knew I joined,' he said. 'Not even me ma; she still thinks I was picking onions. And I used a false name, and gave my address as the house of the other chap. That was two years ago. If anyone knew it was me, they'd have found me by now. You wouldn't shop me, would you?'

'And why not? Aren't your buddies killing our boys day and night, and enjoying the sport?'

'Oh indeed, Bláithín. But it was economic necessity that drove me to it.'

'Never, ever, say that,' she said and banged the frying pan down onto the cooker. 'Killing for money is not a job.'

'And once I realised that, I quit. The training was great. All that physical stuff.' He thought of throwing himself to the stone floor and demonstrating a few push-ups. But that might backfire. 'I was in great condition. Muscles everywhere.' He flexed his arm and pushed out his chest. 'And the money, although it's not great during training, Mammy really appreciated the help. But I gave it all up rather than participate in the murder machine. Even though I was only making soup. I hope you believe me Bláithín. I would rather die than kill a fellow human being.'

The corners of his eyes stung with the depth of the emotion. He sat on the edge of the kitchen table and bent his head over his hands.

'We'll say no more about it,' she said. 'But it's time you got going. I have things to do.'

It could turn into a Brendan Behan play: a message onto the grapevine, and the next time he was in Cavan he would be kidnapped and murdered. Or later, if they ended badly and she wanted revenge.

'You know you can be arrested and court-martialled if you set foot in Britain?'

'Or in the occupied territories?' he said, introducing a tinge of Ian Paisley to his accent, although that was not how the man would refer to the north of Ireland. 'Ulster!'

'Oh the smartness of the Dubliner.'

'I'll have to take the risk,' he said, 'because I never want to go back. I hated – ' he was going to say Aldershot, but thought better of it, and said – 'the place.'

Dolly Considine's Hotel

SYLVIA CONFOUNDS EXPECTATIONS; WILLIAM PLANS A PARTY

3rd September 1983

William's slouched-over-the-table body, his chair pushed back to its furthest reach, seemed to be taking a break from the usual Saturday morning performance for the kitchen staff. Julian was forced to hold his stack of returning breakfast trays high over the exposed bull neck to squeeze around him, but William, whipping his arms, head and body upright into the leaned-back chair, narrowly avoided contact with Julian and his tray of dishes.

William said, 'Let's have a referendum victory party.'

'What victory is that?' Sylvia, behind the Saturday editions on the opposite side of the table, asked. 'Is it the year of successfully distracting us from the criminal-mess-politicians-have-made-of-the-country victory, or the successful-hijacking-of-confused-moral-thinking-for-political-ends victory?'

Julian had woken up knowing he needed decisions. Malone was never coming back. He had to start by going home,

432

thinking about school, forcing an ending onto his *Summer of Unrequited Love*. He'd already started writing a choice of terminations, but he was not happy with any of them. But hearing Sylvia asserting views like this was distracting him. Was she reading from the newspaper?

'Oh Sylvia,' William said, 'women will always be free to visit other countries…'

'So, it's the now–children–let's–talk–about–giving–tadpoles–the–same–rights–as–women–instead–of–doing–something–about–emigration–and–jobs–and–drugs victory?' She was not reading.

'It's a national debate, Syl. The Irish nation wants to establish its moral stance in the face of declining standards in the rest of the world. On Thursday the people of Ireland will speak, and we will adjust the constitution to enforce their preference. That's democracy.'

Sylvia pushed back her own chair and stood up, and when she spoke it was in a kind of whispered hiss. 'This charade won't stop women getting abortions, it will just encourage them to make bad decisions, and increase their shame. And the outcome won't make a whit of difference to you William McClean. A: you can't get pregnant; B: Mammy will cough up the cost of a little trip to Birmingham for any young one you put up the duff.'

'Sylvia, wash your mouth out. At CUS we learnt that it's not about winning or losing but taking part.'

'And will the Catholic University School be happy if the amendment is rejected? Although like you, perhaps they just pay lip service to being so called Pro-Life.'

'Julian, do you think Sylvia is a tad cynical?'

Julian put the trays down in front of Brendan waiting by the drainer and began to scrape marmalade drips from the front of his trousers.

But Sylvia wasn't finished. 'Your generation was supposed to be different from the Civil War politicians, and you are; you're even more hypocritical.'

'Never mind that Syl, don't you think Julian is looking particularly green this morning? As if he's on the rag, or dare I even think it, does he need a quick trip to Birmingham himself? Do you Julian? Do you? Have you taken it up the bumhole at the wrong time of the month? You can trust us; we'll protect your guilty secret. Won't we Syl?'

The scraping knife was pushing the marmalade further into the fabric; he'd need a wet cloth. But why was he concerned with his appearance? Sitting in St Stephen's Green with his notebook, the stain would be covered, unless he's anticipating Bláithín Cunningham stumbling into him on his bench by the duck pond, him deep in concentration, utterly surprised to see her.

'The referendum party will be for both sides and for none,' William said. 'The Pro-Lifers will be in the Kickham Room, the abortionists in the Porchester Lounge, and the "don't cares" proportionately divided. Loyalties will be declared on arrival, and a coloured armband worn to designate membership: black for abortionists, green for Pro-Lifers, red for everyone else.'

Bláithín will want to see what he's been writing, and he will have to demur. A smile as he clasps the notebook to his chest and stands up to kiss her, clumsily.

'And your mother has already committed herself to this? The money, the extra staff, the five days in which to organise it? Have you even mentioned it?'

'Uncle Giolla-Íosa will plant the idea in her head, he's very good at that.'

'And who'll plant it in him, and dig in the fertiliser?' Brendan giggled, torn away from running his fingers around the breakfast plates to pick up the grease and brown sauce left by the Hannafins and the McCleans. Saturday always produced a crop of leftover bacon rinds.

'Very good question, top marks to the Tinahely Gofer,' William said, causing Brendan to shoulder Julian against the steeping sink with the joy of being praised.

'There will be appropriately named dishes: caul soup, terrine of early termination, abortion pie, roast unwanted baby with a menstrual red sauce, culminating with death in childbirth brûlée for dessert. What do you think, Sylvia?'

'I think you should save your humour for your Trinity friends.'

'Brendan will watch out for troublemakers, and you, Sylvia, will welcome all sides equally. But what about our little lounge boy?' William pushed himself up off his chair, moved to where he could look Julian up and down, rubbing his chin between his fingers and thumb as if wondering what to do with a leftover piece of jigsaw.

'I need to find a role for him,' he said, 'something provocative, a little theatre perhaps, to exploit his obvious charms. We'll need props. I'm sure the Porchester will have… things. You'll get your boyfriend to choreograph the entire evening. Won't you, darling?'

Mikhail had gone to London on business the week after the so-called anti-abortion plays opened. The waistband of Julian's trousers adjusting to not being stretched during rehearsals. It was unlikely he would be back.

'We will have make-up and costumes for the staff. Abortion doctors in the Pro-Lifers' party, and nuns serving cocktails in the Right to Choosers' room. It will be such fun. I need to start working on the invitation list straight away. Any suggestions will be appreciated.' And then the joy at his own ideas jumped him out of the door and returned the kitchen to the staff and their plans for their Saturday.

Bláthín would not be bumping into him in the Green; his tale about being in the British army had put an end to whatever it was they'd had. Maybe he'd write to her and tell her it was all made up.

When he was on his bench in St Stephen's Green, Julian wrote: *Sylvia has gone to Rialto to pick up her daughter, to take her to the park. It is seven and a half years since the pregnancy kit showed she was expecting little Sharon. If Gregory had offered her the money, she might have gone to Birmingham herself, but she would never have spontaneously wanted to destroy anything of his. She loves her daughter because she is his, and when his mother is dead, they will all be together in the big house in Meath.*

Dolly Considine's Hotel

JACK AND MIKHAIL CAUSE TROUBLE FOR DOLLY

6th September 1983

'This referendum party is typical of the irreverent mischief the students in Trinity College get up to,' Dolly told Sylvia, looking unsure whether to stress her pride in her wayward son or the horror of the chaos the party would bring. Either way she was distracted enough not to notice Mikhail Mayakovsky beside her, asleep in a bucket chair. 'God help me, I should have forbidden it, but he has to learn.'

Sylvia was leaning on the Kickham Room side of the bar and was not expected to answer. After all, what would she know about Trinity College or the need for a young political hopeful to manage his public profile? Although as a woman, she should understand the foolish ways of men.

'Please God the Right to Choose people will stay away.'

'Not this one,' Jack Norton whispered, not on his usual stool at the bar but at a table by the window in the Kickham Room. 'If only to see a demonstration of spoil-sporting Pro-Lifers at play.' His table was covered in the articles he was shortlisting for his final *Evening Press* magazine page, his thoughts disturbed intermittently by snores from the sleeping Mayakovsky, and then by Dolly, looking flushed, and wearing a corsage of tiny white flowers high on the shoulder of her as-usual black blouse. She'd come in to close the window and shut out the early September chill. His 'Good evening, Dolly' drowned out by the slam.

'What about the catering, Mrs McClean?' Sylvia asked.

'Julian will serve cocktail sausages and crisps,' Dolly replied.

Jack had also been disturbed by Julian ducking under the counter to go in and out of the bar instead of lifting the flap. At least his unflattering black trousers were easier to cope with than tight-fitting jeans might have been. An officious little thing with his damp-cloth flourishes on already clean table tops and sparkling ashtrays, and yet, so irresistible.

'William mentioned a special menu.'

'Sylvia, this is a small private hotel. Go to the Gresham if it's restaurant service you're after.'

'What about Curragh House's famous sandwiches,' Jack said, louder than his previous remark. 'With added salt so the punters drink more.'

'Mr Norton, I have enough on my plate without your unhelpful comments, thank you,' Dolly said, waving her finger at him.

'Why so serious Dollys McCleans?' Mayakovsky was awake. 'Always so serious.'

'Mr Mayakovsky, I'm glad you're awake. The arrangement we have with the Porchester Theatre is that the Kickham Room may, with permission, be used for dramatic rehearsals. We have no arrangement for sleeping.'

'Why so serious Dollys McCleans? Sleeping or rehearsing, it is all the same to the true artist.'

'Please heed what I am saying, Mr Mayakovsky.'

'Oh Dollys, call me Mikhail. And a vodka and ice please Sylvia. I go to visitors' bar.'

'We call it the Porchester Lounge, Mr Mayakovsky, because of our strong ties with the artistic establishment next door. Ties which I am sure you have no wish to damage.'

'I want to come to abortion party Dollys. I will decorate big cake with squealing babies for all miserable ladies to take home and turn into themselves.' And then the man was pulling his chair over to sit at Jack's table. 'I disgusted,' he said, 'these Right to Choosers, why they not come to party? They are sore losers, no?'

'We haven't had the result yet.' Jack did not like anything about Mikhail Mayakovsky, especially his phoney Italian-sounding Russian accent. And while his clothes were obviously expensive, the stains and smells, and the distressed look of him, suggested he'd been sleeping in abandoned public toilets for twenty years.

'Theatre committee make me direct two plays "suggested" because they represent dilemma faced by unmarried pregnant girls. Mummy marries daddy in first play, and baby adopted by loving family in second. Why neither makes abortion?'

Jack had allowed his free tickets to remain pinned behind the bar in the hope that Julian would notice the tragic waste, and offer to sit beside him in the dark theatre rather than let them go unused.

'Anti-amendment girls make protest outside theatre with placards saying *Porchester is Anti-Woman* and *Porchester is Anti-Choice*. But *In Dublin* magazine say: *Mayakovsky make choice so unbelievable, any sensible woman has abortion.* Committee accuse me of subverting text, and say they not pay. Nobody happy except me, because I do right thing.'

Sylvia brought his vodka to the table, and waited for the

inevitable request for a refill, but instead of swallowing it in one gulp he sniffed the glass.

'Every drink a wanted drink,' Jack said.

'I give up alcohol,' Mayakovsky said. 'No more drink. I am feel righteous.' He dipped his little finger in the liquid and sucked at it, looking from Jack to Sylvia and back as if he couldn't make up his mind which of them he wanted to impress, like a chimp looking for attention.

'Sylvia, you a woman, tell anti-amendment people: come to party. They owe me. They can show miserable lifers how to have good time. Or wreck hotel. Yes, maybe just fight and wreck hotel. No?'

'Mr Mayakovsky,' Dolly said from behind the bar, her arms stretched as if assessing whether the space was enough for additional servers. 'Please confine that sort of talk to the stage. This party will mark the end of a divisive and bitter constitutional campaign. But I'm sure the wishes of the Irish people will be clear.' She placed both her hands flat on the counter to steady herself, and pushed her shoulders back.

'I understand that Mrs Mitchell is to be the guest of honour,' Jack said, 'and that a presentation will be made on behalf of the countless unborn who will be saved as a result of her tenacious campaign.'

'I have not heard this, Mr Norton, and if it is true, I am sure it is not public knowledge.'

'She mother of Assumpta Mitchell, no?' Mayakovsky said. 'Assumpta was in play, beautiful-looking, even with clothes off, but she not like me when I say "Jesus". And when we rehearsing it was "Jesus", "Jesus", "Jesus" all the time.'

'Rumour has it that Fianna Fáil is hoping to harness some of Mrs Mitchell's tenacity, pure motive and low-key but steely-strong will for the general election,' Jack said.

'I know nothing about such things, Mr Norton,' Dolly said.

'Still, the party is bound to be a hoot if Ireland's number one mother and her eight surviving children turn up. Will Giolla-Íosa make the presentation?'

'Mr Norton, you really are losing the run of yourself.'

'In anti-abortion play Assumpta was delivered naked onto stage wearing nothing but blood-stain birth caul which she tear away while still in character of fumbling baby.'

'I'm almost sorry I missed that,' Jack said. 'Perhaps you could stage a reprise for the party? Mrs Mitchell may not have seen it.'

'There will be no shenanigans with births, or cauls, or anything else. Is that clear? This is a private party, Mr Norton. You may not get an invitation. Either of you. In fact, you should make other arrangements for the evening. It's not as if Dublin is short of drinking establishments.'

'Bravo Dollys,' Mayakovsky said. 'Such delivery,' and he stood up and bowed to his waist. His face was red when he straightened up and he clutched at the glass of vodka, neglected on the table since he'd declared he was off the drink. 'Bravo Dollys,' he repeated, although he did not bow again.

Jack said nothing. It was six o'clock, and as expected Julian had just passed on his way to the kitchen to collect the evening meal trays, the reeded glass in the door turning him into a jagged Zoetrope. Jack dragged air into his lungs, but it refused to release its oxygen. He checked the others' faces for signs that he was revealing his struggle. If he fainted would they help him? Almost worth a fall to the floor to hear what they had to say, but he nodded towards the bar instead, and held his glass out to Sylvia.

It would have been polite to offer Mayakovsky a drink, but lately there was an indulgence in the way Julian was treating the phoney Russian, with a compensating notch more contempt towards Jack. Mayakovsky was an artist, the world of commerce was obliged to keep him drunk without any expectation of repayment or reward. The artist's existence being recompense enough.

Mayakovsky moved closer and put his arm around Jack's shoulders. 'We are brothers in arms,' he said, and squeezed him. 'The banned-from-the-party men. We will make the headlines, no? Put it in your paper? The entertainment William ask me to make aborted. My friend, what are we to do?'

Julian pushed in the Kickham Room door in time to see Mayakovsky place his hairy face against Jack's and kiss him on the lips.

'We will take lesson from the choosing women and put protesting pickets on party. Yes Dollys McCleans. You cannot keep Mikhail Mayakovsky quiet when he wants to be noisy.'

'Excuse me, Mrs McClean,' Julian said, gesturing that her supper was on its way upstairs.

'You are barred from this establishment,' she said looking from the Russian to Jack. 'Kindly leave my hotel immediately or I shall call the Gardaí.'

Jack didn't believe he'd done anything to warrant this. He smiled to show her words had been addressed to the other man. How could he be barred when he was expected to let Julian torture him again the next day, and the day after that?

Mayakovsky smiled at her, and kissed Jack again. Something about being hugged by this offensive man was steadying his breathing, stilling his egg-shaking-in-a-carton self. He would survive the contempt on Julian's face. Not even a smile.

'I hate you, you little prick, why weren't you aborted?' Jack whispered and Mikhail, who could not have heard him, hugged him more closely.

Summer of Unrequited Love

WHO WOULD DIE IF THE HOTEL BURNT DOWN?

Termination #3A

Sept '83

The banging and her name being called made Sylvia half-rise from the bed thinking, it's not time to get up, it's still dark. But whoever was knocking hadn't waited for an answer, but was standing over her, and, as she tried to choose between kicking out with her feet and hiding under the blankets, began to tug at her nightdress. She felt for hands to push away, and listened for her screams, in case she was dreaming. Greg would never rough her up like this, nor Brendan either. Could it be Julian?

'Go back to bed,' she said, knowing this to be a reasonable response, but something told her it was William McClean. He'd never shown any interest in her. Was he drunk? He didn't have the right... And what would Greg say? And all that dirty talk in the kitchen... could it have been a cover for his nervous love for her?

'No way,' she said and kicked against him. She'd given in

to Greg too easily, and he was still with his mother in the big house in Meath while she skivvied in a shebeen to pay for his daughter's keep. 'Greg raped me,' she said. 'He will never help with his child, or love me, or take me home.'

William was now draping something over her head; a towel, a wet towel, water running down her back, and him almost lifting her towards the door.

'Is this a Trinity College thing?' she said, because his own head was wrapped in a towel too, like a sheikh in the desert, dragging her off to his Bedouin tent instead of them doing it there in her own bed. He wrapped her green weekday coat around her shoulders shouting in mumbles, 'Moke, moke,' like it was a secret student word, and repeating it until she heard it as 'smoke'.

'I've never smoked,' she said. He should know that by now. Even Greg had never offered her a cigarette. 'Never.'

He was pinning her arms, binding her inside the coat to stop her resistance, except she was trying to understand, not resist. Why did she have to leave her bed, if all he wanted was what men wanted?

'Let's stay here,' she said. On top of everything else there would be the shame of facing his mother in the morning, not knowing if she'd heard the grunts and bed noises from his room. Greg's mother had never said a word even when she was beginning to show, only organised a Dublin taxi to come and remove her to the nuns, her bags already in the boot so that she wondered if there had been troublesome girls before her.

And when he'd half-lifted, half-dragged her out onto the landing, her first thought wasn't that the hotel was on fire, but that only old wet turf from Roscommon would make all that smoke. It was playing hide and seek with the stairs and banister, making her cough, and William shouting, 'Keep the towel over your face,' his words muffled with him speaking through the towel over his. But finally she understood and took hold of William's hand. The softness of his fingers tender and giving, compared with her own, distracting her from feeling for the stair carpet with her bare feet, and yet in no time they were on the bathroom half-landing and noises were coming up to meet them from below.

Mr and Mrs Hannafins' voices: 'My crutches. I need my crutches,' from him, and his wife pleading that he let Dolly and Mr McClean help him down the stairs. Sylvia could see them because the smoke was clearer on the Hannafin side of the landing, curling out from all around room eleven's door to lick its way up the stairs, as if it was needed urgently in the attic.

Had Mr Mayakovsky used his key? It would all come out; she'd have to deny giving it to him.

'Sylvia,' Mrs McClean shouted. 'Thank God you're okay. Take Mr Hannafin's arm here, and then go down and wake Brendan and Julian. Hurry now.' And she passed Mr Hannafin's cradled arm over to Sylvia, like it was a heavy salami that needed slicing and turning into sandwiches for a reception after one of Mr McClean's party meetings.

'William, what can be burning in there? Are you sure we shouldn't take a look?'

'Mother, we did it in school, in the science lab. This much smoke means the fire is being starved of oxygen, but if you open that door the entire room will explode, and we'll be engulfed in a ball of flame. Let the fire brigade open it. They're the experts.' He was coughing between his words and tugging at Mr Hannafin the way he'd tugged at Sylvia in the bed, but Ireland's hero was refusing to let go the door jamb like a schoolboy on his first day.

'My medals,' he said. 'I'm not leaving without my medals. I gave my leg for this country. I'm not going to be shamed on the street with no sticks and no medals.' Mr H was well able to use Mrs Hannafin's shoulder to hop down the stairs, his free hand sliding along the banister. Sylvia had seen him do it, dozens of times.

'Where's Brendan?' Dolly said to Sylvia. 'He should be helping to move Mr H. The perfect opportunity for him to demonstrate his prowess. I swear he can have his cards for this.'

Cathal was looking sleepy in his beige dressing gown, waiting for Dolly to tell him what to do. But suddenly he wrenched Mr Hannafin's gripping fingers from the jamb, lifted the arm over his shoulder, and began to drag him down the stairs.

The noise of people banging on the front door came towards them, and the sound of breaking glass. Fire brigade bells in the background, and someone shouting, 'Fire, fire,' as if the occupants wouldn't already know, unless they were on the ground floor, or in the basement where maybe there wasn't even the smell of smoke yet.

Mrs McClean had her handbag wedged under her flowery-dressing-gowned right elbow, and one of Mr McClean's work suits trailed down the carpeted steps behind her, the hanger looped over two fingers.

That'll have to be pressed before Mr McC can wear it again, Sylvia thought, or maybe even dry-cleaned. It takes more than an airing to banish smoke that gets into the weave, he might even have to put up with whiffs, if it's the only suit that survives.

Summer of Unrequited Love

DOLLY VISITS THE CITY MORGUE

Termination #3B

Sept '83

'The first thing you should do,' the Garda sergeant said, 'is ensure that all your family, known guests and staff are accounted for. And then I will organise a car to take you to the morgue. It will be disturbing, as there will be damage to the remains, so you should ask a member of your staff to accompany you, perhaps someone who was working last night and might be aware of any unusual circumstances that pertained. I will be appealing for witnesses to come forward, but if the habits of the victim were known to you or your staff, then it might help in clearing the matter up quickly.'

As a child, when she accompanied her mother to the laying out of a dead neighbour, Dolly was usually put in the kitchen with the bereaved family. But sometimes the endless pawing by early mourners waiting for the wake to start drove her into the room where her mother was working, where she then sat quietly, fascinated that the empty thing being washed and dressed in burial clothes had been breathing, and farting, and shouting for God to take the pain away, only a few hours earlier.

The body from room eleven lay on a trolley in the morgue's main corridor covered in a blanket she recognised from the hotel and looking like it was queueing to be seen by the doctor but was letting her skip ahead into the examining room. An orderly wheeled it in behind them, and parked where the light was strongest. The sergeant peeled away just enough of a corner of the blanket to reveal a scorched and blackened head, hairless and shrivelled.

'Wouldn't it be funny,' Brendan said, standing well away, 'if you had to identify people by looking at feet instead faces?'

Dolly's reputation was for making instant decisions, for clicking her fingers at the questioner (all the more surprising for a large woman who otherwise moved slowly) before the question was even fully formed. Never one to say, can I sleep on it and tell you tomorrow, or I'd like to discuss it with my bank manager, or my confessor. Everything was either yes or no, and delivered disturbingly instantly for the askers of the question, who didn't know that Dolly McClean had narrowed down everything in life into the things that mattered and those that didn't. Which wasn't to say she was always right. She'd thought that marrying Cathal would matter. Oh, it gave William a father, which would help if her ambition for him to be Taoiseach by the time he was thirty-five was to be realised, but otherwise...

Consequently, when the Garda sergeant said she would have to come down to the city morgue to identify the body, she'd already made up her mind; it would be one of her regulars who'd sneaked up to room eleven and fallen asleep smoking. She would name the person, and that would be the end of it.

'A woman who worked in a shoe shop should know feet better than faces,' Brendan was babbling. She'd brought him along because Sylvia was so distressed that William was organising sedatives, and Julian had disappeared; hopefully it was the last she'd see of him. There might even be a way of linking him to the fire.

'I'm afraid I don't recognise him,' Dolly said.

None of the dead bodies from her childhood prepared her for the smell of burnt meat or having to put a hand to her mouth to still the nausea.

'I don't believe I've seen him before.' She did not invite Brendan to look or confirm her statement.

'Thank you,' the sergeant said. 'We'll just have to wait and see if anyone is reported missing.' The blanket corner was dropped back over the blackened head, and sent up a waft of smoke and charred skin. If they proved his identity, she'd claim to have been horrified with shock because of the disfigurement. *How could I have known it was my popular and well-respected lounge boy?*

Summer of Unrequited Love

EULOGY: BLÁITHÍN CUNNINGHAM

Termination #3C

Sept '83

Julian, with his thin whippet prick and skinny pale body, had tickled her insides. A winding urban invasion of the countryside, but not likely to change anything, the country and its ways well able to manage weekending Dublin suede-heads. Cavan had seen his like before, although it was the closest Bláithín Cunningham had let one come to her. She'd teased herself with proximity to his city ways, allowed him to distract her from her immutable place among the lakes, hills and woods of Cavan. Her anchorage broad enough to resist the challenge of more powerful men with powerful cocks and from powerful places, awed to be fucking a poet, or 'poetess' as Sylvester had referred to her in his early boasts, fearing that 'fucking a poet' might need a reassurance about her being a woman. But happy, once the facts were known, to explain to 'unreconstructed man' the leg-opening qualities of referring to a modern lady poet or actor in gender-neutral terms.

Sylvester's haunches were wide enough for two little whippets, but for all his power and connections, even if there was no question of fancying, he could no more have walked hand in hand with Julian down O'Connell Street than he could be seen in public with Bláithín.

'What do you think of my penis?' Julian asked her one Sunday morning while they were lying in bed listening to *Sunday Miscellany* on the transistor, minutes after she'd called him 'my little whippet.'

'If I come back as a dog,' he'd said, with Mozart playing in the background, 'I want to be a quality dog, from Dún Laoghaire or Killiney, well cared for by a big family. It will be okay for them to call me Julian, so long as I'm a luxury dog. Maybe a Labrador. But not a bare-necessity fucking whippet, always cold and shivering, and with a whippet penis to boot.'

'Long and thin goes too far in and doesn't suit the ladies,' Bláithín had said, and she wrapped her crimson shawl tightly around him and he pulled himself towards her for warmth. He could be respectful, and that was nice. 'When I'm engaged with your penis, I may think of it, although I am also too engaged with myself to think about anything at all. But I shall kill you if you write this in your journal. You know that, don't you?'

And then her skinny Dublin youth was no more.

Summer of Unrequited Love

CATHAL IS ASKED TO DO HIS DUTY

Termination #3D

Sept '83

Cathal went to a lot of funerals. Giolla-Íosa expected it. The party expected it. They provided a car and a driver, and never objected if he went to the reception afterwards and commiserated with a whiskey or two. But there were additional reasons to attend Julian's funeral. The McCleans had taken on a trainee barman, not knowing he was concealing his real identity and history from them, and the foolish employee had fallen asleep with a lighted cigarette and died in the ensuing fire. Cathal and Dolly's presence at the funeral would show that the McCleans were good employers who had nothing to hide and were happy to help the Gardaí in their efforts to uncover the boy's true identity and the circumstances of his death; and as a goodwill gesture to his family (wherever they were) they would arrange and pay for his funeral.

'We treated him like a member of the family, like a second

son,' Dolly told the first reporter who enquired, but changed tack after the follow-up question: 'Then how come his adoptive mother didn't recognise him on the slab in the morgue?'

The review committee set up to manage the Pro-Life Referendum was due to meet immediately after lunch, resulting in Cathal not being able to attend the small reception to be hosted by Dolly in the pub across from the cemetery. Instead he squeezed his wife's elbow just as the rosary started and stepped between graves to get back to the footpath, where Giolla-Íosa's driver and car were waiting for him. He saw but paid no attention to the purple-haired woman walking in the same direction. Did she know the driver would be taking a piss behind an archangel-protected shopkeeper's mausoleum when she pushed in after Cathal onto the back seat?

In the bar in Buswells, Cathal watched the Paddy-optic bubble fresh whiskey into its reservoir, and gripped the bar counter to steady himself while he waited for his first malt of the day. 'Don't bother dressing that up.' He winked at the barman. 'I'll have it as it is. And give us a chaser with a drop of red.'

He normally avoided being alone in Buswells because he was easy pickings for favour-seeking farmers or newspapermen sniffing out government scandals. But he was shaken after the funeral and needed something to steady his nerves before the review committee meeting, and perhaps a bit of fortification before he pushed through the dozens of seemingly ever-present protesters, with their placards and slogans, blocking the entrance to Government Buildings.

Giolla-Íosa would already know about the woman from his driver. But to avoid the charge of abandoning his unlocked vehicle, he might have put a different gloss on the occurrence. Cathal would have to be careful.

'You know that boy was murdered,' the woman had said as Cathal squeezed himself against the far passenger door. He clutched his briefcase as if it would shield him, but the only thing it contained was the minutes of the last review meeting, and his copy of *The Irish Times*.

'The Gardaí say he was smoking in bed.'

'He never smoked,' she said.

'He might not have been alone. But anyway, he shouldn't have been in the room. He was trespassing.'

'Or held against his will.'

'It is the human condition to look for conspiracies,' Cathal said. 'They are exciting, but rare. Please God the Gardaí will find the truth, but you better leave the car now or my driver will arrest you.'

'You're a good man, Cathal McClean,' the woman said. 'Read this. It's Julian's account of getting the job in your wife's hotel. Read it, and you will have questions.' Thankfully she got out then and stood watching while the driver sat in and started the engine. They were just pulling away when she grabbed the door handle and ran alongside as she opened it.

'Ask your wife how the boy died. Ask your wife,' she shouted. And the handle was wrenched away as the driver accelerated along the muddy graveyard path.

He was ready for his chaser, but he needed the gents first to ensure he could savour the pleasure properly. Raised voices were coming from the front door as he passed through the hall.

'I am entitled to be here.' A woman's voice, a Dubliner, a little rough, but not uneducated. 'It's my right to have a drink where I choose.'

The reply was muffled and he was tempted to ask the porter to repeat his response so he could consider it. Clearly the woman did not have a right to drink anywhere she chose, but it might be interesting to sit her down and explain the difference between rights and privileges in a liberal democracy.

'Tell the Guards,' she was shouting. 'What do they care? Didn't they see me coming over?' He guessed she wanted to use the toilet. A democracy might be obliged to allow protest, but was it obliged to provide toilet facilities for protesters? It was an interesting question. Cattle, horses, birds and insects were permitted to relieve themselves without a thought for anyone, even their own kind, but humans have developed mores, and set up sanctions to control random relief.

When he got back, Giolla-Íosa was drinking his chaser and reading the pages the woman had given him in the graveyard. 'Where did you get this?' he asked.

'I don't expect my briefcase to be rifled when I go for a leak,' Cathal said, and nodded at the barman for a fresh drink.

'Where did you get it?' Giolla-Íosa repeated.

'I think William might have left it on the coffee table at home, and it got mixed up with party papers.' He smiled at his brother. He never lied to GI and he fiddled with the coins for the barman to distract himself from feeling the danger.

'You won't mind if I hold onto it then. It gives an interesting insight into the mind of a young working-class Dubliner. Have you read it?'

Cathal shook his head for his second lie. 'I'd forgotten it was in my briefcase. Still, I should return it to William.'

But Giolla-Íosa folded it lengthways like a legal brief and slipped it into his inside jacket pocket.

When their mother was dying in St Luke's Cancer Hospital, she'd asked him to take care of Giolla-Íosa. 'Your younger brother is not like you,' she said. 'You're resourceful, you'll survive anything. But all Giolla-Íosa has is his charm and his good looks, and when they're gone, he'll be on skid row.'

Cathal had risen from the chair in the semi-private ward, and through the window watched a bird his mother called a willie wagtail bending forwards and backwards, its tail flitting up and down, as if laughing at him. Earlier he'd asked her if she wanted more pillows; it was disturbing to see her lying flat in the bed with her eyes closed, and the covers smoothed neatly around her as if she was already dead, only waiting to be transferred into her coffin. He put his hand over hers to reassure her that his brother was not as fey as she imagined. But her skin was dry and loose, her fingers nothing but covered bones; he said nothing.

It was a theme she returned to again and again as she slipped away.

'I worry about your brother.'

'Do you think Giolla-Íosa will be all right?'

'How will Giolla-Íosa manage when I'm gone?'

'I'll going to nip home for a minute, and then walk to my meeting,' Cathal had told the driver when they reached Leeson Street on the way back from the graveyard. He'd already made up his mind to be late for the referendum review committee meeting.

A neighbour across from the hotel had consoled them on the night of the fire. She'd insisted she could accommodate one person for a few weeks, and Cathal had gratefully accepted after Dolly announced she was moving into the Shelbourne with William. Sylvia had gone to her sister's, and though the boys' bedroom was littered with chunks of wet plaster from the collapsed ceiling, Brendan was probably still staying there. At least his presence would discourage looters from stripping out the banisters and fireplaces.

The board covering the front door's broken glass had attracted three one-line chalked messages:

'Murderers.'

'He was dead before the fire.'

'Justice for Julian.'

Cathal had no idea what he was looking for. He'd been in and out several times to collect clothes and papers. Today it felt colder, and the damp smoky smell was more offensive, perhaps just in comparison with the warm September afternoon going on outside. The collapsed ceilings, the peeling wallpaper, the wet stair carpet littered with bits of fallen plaster, made him want to be angry with someone.

'You foolish boy,' he said, once he was inside room eleven, 'and you too Josie; you were foolish in your time. Is it the very room that's cursed?' The blackened, burnt bed was still there, and a wet bundle of clothes swept up into the corner by the fireman's hose, among them the trousers and jacket he assumed belonged to Julian. Why had the Guards not removed everything for forensic examination? Especially the mattress, for clues as to the cause of the fire?

'That woman is well known in the graveyard,' Giolla-Íosa had said. 'No death is natural or accidental in her world. It can be very distressing for mourners.' He smiled at his older brother and left the bar.

Cathal knocked back the rest of his drink and struggled out of the chair. His back hurt and he hoped it wasn't the change of bed or an oncoming cold that was causing it. The two security men at the door nodded at him.

'Okay lads?' he said as he passed, and lifted his briefcase in a kind of wave; did he always do that? A young man who'd treated him differently, and for whom he'd had hopes of a sort, had died in his wife's hotel, and here he was gesturing with his briefcase as usual.

'All I have in here is my newspaper,' he said to the nearest Guard. 'And I keep it there, so I don't get ink on my fingers and shirt cuffs. We can put a man on the moon, but we can't make permanent ink for newspapers. It's a funny old world, as the boss says, although in his case he means, it's a funny old world when a gurrier like me can rise so high.'

The two security men nodded and rubbed their hands together and shuffled nearer to each other as he descended the steps. Nothing he could do would bring Julian back, and he would need all his dispassionate judgement if he was to get to the bottom of the mystery, if there was a mystery. Was the woman right? Had he unknowingly participated in a murder, or was this just an example of a weaker specimen of humanity allowing itself to be weeded out for the benefit of those left behind?

What a terrible thought.

Summer of Unrequited Love

EULOGY: MIKHAIL MAYAKOVSKY

Termination #3E

Sept '83

The hotel's gents are in the basement, down a bloody rickety staircase, with a slippery handrail, and covered in wobbly carpet that's difficult to negotiate after a voddie or two. One day I won't bother; I'll just sit on my tall stool in my long coat and let go, it won't be my fault, but their treacherous bloody stairs' fault. Better a moist carpet than a broken femur.

On that day though, I put off going well beyond the point where I thought another drink would dull the pain, and a kind of recklessness overtook me, and I actually looked forward to a fall on the stairs. The pinched-faced one with the pointy nose was coming up the stairs towards me with a tray of Irish coffees as I staggered out of the Kickham Room, closing the door on someone's impression of *Gymnopédies* on the piano. His trousers looked too big and not the style expected of a 1980s youth, but before I knew what, I had wet my ring finger, slipped my hand past the skin-side of his trouser band, nudged his underpants elastic out of the way, and slipped the moist digit into his little hole, right up to the first knuckle. I wanted to kiss him but that would have required leaning away from the supporting wall, which would have sent us both tumbling back down the stairs and infusing the Curragh House carpet with the smell of cream-gone-sour that would linger longer than my stale piss, had I opened my floodgates. I had to settle for a little squeeze between my outside thumb and my inside finger.

When poor Jerry died in London in eighty-one, I insisted on being present while the embalmer worked with assuredness and dispassion on the empty shell of my departed lover. I watched as he was turned this way and that to be shaved and have his shrunken butt stuffed with tampon-sized wads of cotton wool, the white-coated man so full of life as he applied lying rouge and lipstick and filled out the cheeks to how he thought people might remember them – a denying mask for Jerry's final public show. The embalmer paid no attention to me, even when I offered to show him the effect his work was having on my cock, my persistence persisting until I offered to roger him there and then before we lifted my unrecognisable Jerry into the coffin, ready for display.

But this one, this little lounge boy, whose hole my finger had worn like a brief wedding ring, must have been too badly burnt for a bit of rouge. Not even a public photograph to put into the newspapers to help any relations claim the body or recognise him and come to the funeral. The coffin closed to prevent us from seeing what the fire had done to him.

'When you're finished,' was all he'd said, rocking in unison with my wobbly self, to steady the tray.

'When I'm finished what?' I said.

'When your finger is finished with my hole, put it back into your mouth.' And it is to my shame now that, even in my drunken reckless state, and in spite of my readiness to entertain this urchin thing, it was my index finger I licked, and sucked, keeping the penetrating digit isolated until I knew a little more about the place where it had been. He smirked at me, and I knew it was not the end, and that my tongue would be replacing my finger soon enough.

'Those coffees will be cold,' I said, and pushed myself away from the wall, and indeed did slide down the stairs to the basement on my arse. But managed to hold my water till I made it to the gents.

Summer of Unrequited Love

EULOGY: PADDY THE PORTER

Termination #3F

Sept '83

History will rightly say he ruined madam's life, ended the McClean dynasty, and killed a much-loved institution. A better-raised boy would have surrendered to the school bully sitting on his chest; *let him have the bloody sweets, you foolish child*. His legacy will be the investment company next door getting the extended offices they've always wanted, and for half nothing. The McClean connections not strong enough to prevent the fire being labelled terrorism, and any insurance payout being woefully short of what will be needed to return the hotel to its former glory.

'China' is the word I'm looking for. Bandied about by madam's other upsetting customer, though that one managed to live twice as long in spite of his borstal boy adventures, renowned for putting his arm around the shoulders of a likely lad and regaling him, for better or worse: *We're Chinas we are. You and me.*

But never mind him. It was just the word 'China' I was thinking about, thrown about like it was a commonhood instead of being kept as something rare, to be saved not just for Sunday best, but maybe only used in retrospect, for a eulogy, death allowing an outing, the recognition of how much he'd been loved.

A right pair of heartbreakers, him and Julian, even mine in the right circumstances, but not the way he encouraged the advances of that hysterical theatrical, or the lovelorn Jack Norton. No, it would have been manly, comradely; the way men were in the Brotherhood during the independence war. Soldiers, as ready to die for each other as we were for the cause.

Well the little fucker is dead, but there was no cause. Worthy or not. No cause at all. Just him dead.

Summer of Unrequited Love

CATHAL MCCLEAN INVESTIGATES

Termination #3G

Sept '83

'He was a bad-mannered little prick,' Cathal McClean told the chief superintendent of the Gardaí with responsibility for Government Buildings security. 'But even a little prick has a right to life, at least once he's been born.' His aim when he spoke to the chief superintendent was to gather facts, and therefore he shared nothing with him except the inescapable fact that the boy was dead, and that although the body was found in the hotel bedroom, it didn't mean he'd died there.

Cathal wasn't like other party workers. They started with the given conclusion and cobbled together arguments to justify how they got there. They were the boyos with the agenda: to protect the party, or deliver for the boss, or seal the business deal, or satisfy some bloody farmer down in the bog who'd been promised a favour. Whereas he established, and listed out, the facts. Then turned them into topic headings and fleshed out each segment to build a full report. The conclusions flowed naturally from the facts. It might be naive, but at least with his way the party knew where it stood before it glossed the facts with politics.

The woman in the ministerial car at the funeral had said, 'Listen Cathal, you know more than you know you know.' She'd talked in riddles. But he liked riddles. Conclusions were easier to believe when they had to be dug out of the available information like diamonds from a hill of shit. They were acceptable because they were inevitable.

Giolla-Íosa had told him not to meddle, and that was another fact, connected or not. 'Leave it to the Gardaí,' he'd said in Buswells after he'd rifled through Cathal's briefcase and taken Julian's story.

'Except the Gardaí have closed their investigations,' Cathal told him the following day, after the chief superintendent had agreed to give him twenty minutes between meetings.

'Their report is completed,' Giolla-Iosa said, 'which will help Dolly with her compensation. If you go raising suspicions about a murky side to this business, the insurance company will shout terrorism.'

'A boy is dead,' Cathal said.

'And none of your interfering will bring him back.'

His brother and party workers didn't like it when Dolly called him an idealist, because they were all idealists, soldiers of destiny. Their grandparents, and their parents, uncles, brothers, sisters, cousins, and friends had died for the ideal of a free Ireland. But for Cathal, debate and policy were about squeezing the ideal into ideas. He was for locating the principles, distilling to essence, finding the pure nub of the matter; not only representing the subject, but being the subject, the subject made flesh. That was his role. And when he sat at party meetings, the wide boys trying to bully delegates into taking a particular stand, or to show what stunning orators they were, it was his job to steer the faithful back to the topic, and prevent its being hijacked for party political reasons or personal gain.

The chief superintendent was almost a family friend, and was as informal as ever when he joined him in the bar at Buswells. He tried to chat about the protesters outside Leinster House, and the upcoming Pro-Life Referendum, but Cathal reminded him about his twenty minutes.

'Good man yourself Cathal,' he said, 'diligent as ever.'

People never said things to his face, but he always had an idea of what they were thinking. Hardly an Ard Fheis in thirty years had gone by without someone calling him Falstaff when he was barely able to keep his eyes open after a weekend of feeding them ideas to turn into party policy. Not two years since the boss himself called him a buffoon, barely five feet from his drained carcass. A slap on the back over the cooked breakfast in the morning: 'Ah Jasus Cathal, you were in mighty form last night. The things you were coming out with. Mighty altogether. We'll make a chat show host out of you yet. You're hiding your light under a bushel in that poky office in Leinster House.' They measured their normality by his excesses. And then stole an idea he floated to demonstrate what they had to put up with from the loony side of the party, or to palm off as their own if it looked like a goer, or 'something the party might think about' if there was danger in it.

'Let me get this straight,' the chief superintendent said. 'The tragic death in your wife's hotel, which, to the detectives who investigated it, had all the appearance of the carelessness of a young drunk falling asleep with a lighted cigarette, you believe was murder. You further suggest that this killing was carried out by, or with the knowledge of, Fianna Fáil party officials on behalf of your brother, and/or your wife, for reasons of which you are not certain other than it had something to do with the Civil War – which, I need hardly remind you, occurred before you were born.'

Cathal had chosen Buswells as his investigation HQ, and red lemonade with a drop of bitters as his investigation beverage the better to read this policeman, and other subjects, more acutely.

'The lad was about to reveal a secret.'

'And you know the details of this secret?'

'I don't.'

'The lad had been at the hotel since the end of June; not even three months, but was threatening to put into the public domain a revelation of such magnitude that it drove someone to murder him rather than endanger the McClean dynasty. But you don't know what it was?'

'That's correct.'

The man stared at his whiskey for several seconds before he spoke again. 'As a friend and as a policeman, Cathal, I find it hard to believe that you, the most senior McClean alive, would not know about a sixty-year-old family secret if there was one. Nor that you wouldn't know who might have revealed this terrible information to your wife's hapless lounge boy.'

'The play is the thing,' Cathal said. 'The play is the thing to catch the conscience of the king.' The line had come into his head and was uttered before he could stop up his mouth. And it propelled the chief superintendent to his feet and across to the window overlooking Leinster House. Hamlet had staged a drama to trick his stepfather into revealing himself; but Cathal had no plans of that sort. Could he be using the word 'play' as it related to games? Except Cathal didn't play games. He was against games. And if he ever tried to play, the clever boyos in the party would be ahead of him by a mile; if he was good at anything, it was the truth. Neither was there any king, unless that was how he thought of his brother.

'Cathal, I've known you for many years, and although you can be prone to ramble a bit in drink, I acknowledge that when you're sober you're the most reasonable man that ever walked God's earth.' The chief superintendent smiled as he sat back down.

Cathal nodded.

'Tell me what it is you would like me to do,' the chief superintendent said.

Maybe the policeman understood the sense behind his words better than he did himself, and was going to take him seriously. His integrity and dedication to facts would come to the rescue. Giolla-Íosa only had to click his fingers and party lackeys got into a competitive huddle to work out what it could mean. Admittedly it had taken a bit more for Cathal to get there, but his concise sober mind and his reputation with this good honest policeman would cause something to happen. He might not be as brashly powerful as Giolla-Íosa but he had his own quiet power; he could get things done when he spoke to the right people.

'Investigate. Charge someone,' Cathal said. 'See justice is done.'

'I spoke to your brother yesterday. He says you're working too hard, that your mind is overwrought with this terrible business.'

'You spoke to Giolla-Íosa? Why?'

'When you said you wanted to see me, I rang him to—' He hesitated as if delicacy was required, something that he could not discuss, or that might involve telling Cathal some home truths. 'I had another matter to update him on, and I mentioned your proposed visit just in passing. I said what a privilege it will be to speak to two members of the McClean family within twenty-four hours.' He smiled again.

'Except my brother could be a suspect. And now you've notified him. Put him on his guard.'

The chief superintendent pushed himself up from the banquette again. 'Cathal, it's been good seeing you. I have the facts of the case. Giolla-Íosa didn't seem to me to be a man with anything to hide. In fact, he asked if for the sake of his sister-in-law and his nephew, I could look at the file and see if it contained anything untoward.'

'And?'

'Of course I agreed to speak to the investigating officer, and if there is the slightest whiff of cover up, or leads not followed up, I will see to it that steps are taken.'

'And you'll keep me informed?' Cathal stood up. Perhaps it was the best he could hope for.

'Well, now that your brother is taking an interest...' He seemed to expect Cathal to understand what he was saying.

'I may not be Giolla-Íosa McClean, but the assistant Garda commissioner is a regular visitor to Leinster House. Perhaps I should have asked him to...' He left his own sentence unfinished.

'Ah Jasus Cathal, you're terrible serious. I only meant that this does seem like an extended family matter. A sort of domestic affair, and the Gardaí are traditionally wary of such matters. We're not really equipped...' He put his arm around Cathal's shoulder, and leaned in as if to sniff the air for any sign of alcohol. 'Maybe you should take a few days off. Why not go down to the country seat until this blows over? I mean yourself and Dolly could have been killed in the fire, not to mention young William. His mother and Giolla-Íosa have such high hopes for him that it would have been a national as well as a family tragedy. That's a lot for any man to have to deal with, aside from the dead youth, and then to be discommoded by living in temporary accommodation while the Gardaí investigate and workmen put things to rights. It could be months before you get your home back. Small wonder you're upset.' He reached back down to the table for his glass and swirled the whiskey round and round before he tossed the lot into his mouth.

'I recently did a course on the psychology of interrogation. We were encouraged to be "intuitive", no less. A man like me, with forty years of smacking first and asking questions later, being asked to ignore the evidence and just be intuitive. Haven't I been intuitive all my working life?' He rubbed his finger round the inside of his whiskey glass and sucked the last drops. 'But just now it struck me that maybe you blame yourself for some of this. That if things had been different you would be living in a nice house in Blackrock, or Sandyford, where you would have known who was asleep in your home instead of being at the mercy of a drunk lighting his last cigarette and burning the lot of you.'

A man wouldn't last thirty days, never mind thirty years, in any political party without being able to smile and cover up what he's feeling inside. It was no surprise to Cathal that he shook hands with the chief superintendent and thanked him for his time, or that he waved his briefcase and nodded an acknowledgement to the doorman on their way out.

It was only when he was alone on Molesworth Street that he felt the scream rise. It started where he imagined the red lemonade and bitters was sitting in his stomach and rose in a convulsive rage through his abdomen, circling his chest and pummelling his heart so much on the way up that he had to put the back of his briefcase-clutching-hand to his mouth and grip his throat with the other in an effort to keep it all in. His eyes stung with the injustice, the misunderstoodness of it all.

Across the road, he transferred his grip to the slim neck of one of the baluster bottles forming the defensible space in front of Freemasons' Hall and told himself to breathe.

That copper had patronised him, insulted him, accused him of neglecting Dolly and William and putting their lives at risk. Cathal had never cared where they lived. It was Dolly who wouldn't hear of living anywhere else; she insisted the hotel would be where she brought up her son, and where she'd entertain the party faithful.

Cathal worked for the party, gave them ideas to help them win votes, but it was the ideas, not the votes or the loyalty that motivated him. Whereas Dolly loved Fianna Fáil itself, she thrived in the company of their elected and soon to be elected men and lived for the opportunity to debate the ideas they spouted, taking extra pleasure from knowing they might have come from Cathal and in turn been inspired by something she herself had observed. But it was the hotel that made it all possible.

A sign on the front of Freemasons' Hall told him there would be a book sale on Saturday. Why should he care? He didn't. He insisted he didn't, although he read the words through several times, as if it was a quotation from scripture displayed in front of a Protestant church and erected to help him in his hour of need. His hand hurt from the tightness of his grip on the baluster, but he left no impression on the stone bottle. His grip steadied him; he would breathe and move on, have a stroll around town, take a look at the shops avoiding the routes between the Shelbourne and Brown Thomas in case Dolly was meeting some of her ladies for lunch. She wasn't the enemy but he didn't want to see her. Maybe he'd never want to see her again.

Was that possible?

Something about that smug copper suggested that it wasn't

just them all being nearly burnt in the hotel fire that was Cathal's fault. There were other things too. Things to do with Dolly, and even William. He didn't know what he'd done, but the chief superintendent's sneer echoed other sneers, perhaps a lifetime of them, the unguarded smiles and shakes of the head that people exchanged when they thought he was drunk. And he may well have been drunk, but it was the chief superintendent's sneer that tapped into the accumulated repetitions and totted them all up. As if to say: Now you know the truth Cathal. That's the bottom line. Finally you have the tally. The total. The upshot. The conclusion. The end.

Was it to be the end? An end without words? His potential buried along with Julian, Giolla-Íosa's career in mortal danger and William's tainted before it had even begun? And what about he and Dolly? No explanation, no irreconcilable differences, just the two of them never bothering to live together again. The future filled with separate ways, the past adding up to... nothing. Some fucking ending that would be, whether he solved the mystery of Julian's death or not.

Maybe the chief superintendent was right and he should take some time off. Julian wouldn't suffer from a delay of a week or two, and he'd return to the investigation refreshed, ready to start again. His forensic mind available to analyse whatever was thrown at him, his meat cleaving brain eager to sear the waffle from the facts, and present the unadulterated truth on the serving plate, palatable or not.

Dolly Considine's Hotel

PARTY PREPARATIONS AND A SURPRISE
VISITOR

7th September 1983

'I don't care if it's short notice, the party is tomorrow, so it's tomorrow or never. Do you understand me?' William McClean was hissing into the public phone by the old reception desk. On the stairs above, Julian clutching his 'penultimate-ever stack of breakfast trays' slowed his descent to avoid a tumble. In the Porchester Lounge, Jack Norton was on his usual high stool, but facing outwards, watching a tape of Pro-Life campaigner Mrs Mitchell's referendum campaign highlights (TV and VCR generously sponsored by RTV Rentals) interspaced with clips of her overcrowded home life, surrounded by children and grandchildren. It was coming to the end of its loop. Julian wanted to speak to Jack, but Sylvia was leaning on the bar, watching Mrs Mitchell also. He would have to wait.

'Listen to me, I didn't have to approach your company, but my uncle Giolla-Íosa McClean mentioned your name,' William told the fifth potential supply company that morning, and Julian paused to wait for his promise of the free publicity that would flow from whoever-they-were catering/ entertainment/security Ltd sponsoring the referendum party, as well as the privilege of being invited to witness the presentation to the high-profile woman who would be crowned the voice of Ireland's unborn. He didn't mention Mrs Mitchell by name.

William hung up and leaned his head down onto the old reception counter, his loud Hawaiian shirt out of sync with his mood. Julian put his trays on top of William's clipboard, the note under the teapot evidence of Mrs McClean's agitation at her son's hissing phone calls and his earlier excited pacing of the Kickham Room with Mikhail Mayakovsky, who was still there, watching another TV set (generously sponsored by RTV Rentals) blaring out live reports about 'brisk attendance' at the polling stations and images of the smiling Taoiseach casting his vote.

'*May I remind you again, Julian,*' and he paused in his reading aloud to see if William would lift his head, '*one teabag per teapot, not three. Final warning. DMcC.*' William extended two fingers into a V and lifted his head to dial another number.

'Mr Norton, just a minute,' Julian said, abandoning his trays when he saw Jack heading for the front door. The man stopped and turned. William was watching, but that was not going to stop him. His summer in Curragh House was almost over; he needed something to show for his time. 'Can I speak to you?' Julian said and reached inside his shirt to pull out folded pages. 'A contribution for your column.' Jack began to open it, but Julian shook his head and looked back to William, who had put down the receiver and was coming towards them.

What he'd written would not be suitable for Jack's gossipy column, but he might know an investigative journalist to pass it on to. He had hoped his first completed piece would be a story about his time in the hotel, but in fact it was a detailed account of the secret MI5 sting operation involving Malone and his books. The plan had been to get the IRA to organise a mass breakout from Portlaoise Prison. A German anarchist had been recruited by MI5 to convince the IRA that he could coat books with a chemical that would release a knockout gas when it came into contact with urine. And that if the prisoners had books treated with this chemical they could piss on them, quickly throw them at the wardens, and walk out of the prison.

Their bogus organisation, Books for Prisoners, had for months been establishing a channel for getting untreated books into Portlaoise, but Malone's romances were the real deal, and his job was to bring them to Dublin. But someone (and Julian believed it to be MI5 itself) tipped off the Gardaí and they arrested Malone. Of course when they searched his bag, in reality Julian's bag, there were no books.

Jack was out on the street when William grabbed Julian's wrist.

'Go after Jack Norton and get that back, whatever it was.'

Julian sneered and went to pick up the tray.

'You are so finished,' William hissed as Julian moved towards the basement stairs.

Jack would be reading as he walked. Maybe getting to the bit where Malone has a crisis of conscience on the bus from Derry to Dublin. Was it really a sting? Were the books harmless, or did MI5 want a mass breakout to show how ineffective the Republic's security was? His bag being switched with Julian's was Malone's chance to change the plan without being blamed, but he never imagined that Julian would go to the hotel, or that Bláithín Cunningham (who clearly knew more than she let on) would get the faint whiff of something, and contact the man Julian had later seen also sniffing the books.

It was all in there, and it was dynamite. Even the bit where he said Bláithín could be working for the IRA or MI5 or even the special branch of the Gardaí. He couldn't wait for Jack to read it and come back later that evening and tell him who he had passed it on to.

The peak of the baseball cap on the man facing Julian from the bottom of the stairs was low over his face. His hands, hanging chimp-like, were joined in front of him, and his feet were apart, like those of a soldier at ease. He stepped back smartly as Julian reached the bottom step, the way a soldier might, when ordered back following individual inspection.

'I hear you've been looking for me,' the voice from Busárus in June said. It was Malone, no doubt, although he'd only seen his right-side profile that day. He looked thinner in his dark tracksuit.

Julian tried to prevent the cups from rattling.

'I hope my trousers look better on me. Time you started wearing your own,' he said, and pointed to what looked like Julian's backpack on the floor outside the boys' bedroom door. 'I'll wait out here,' he said, 'while you change.'

'Make yourself useful, put these in the kitchen,' Julian said, and pushed the trays towards him. 'It's through there,' and he pointed, although he'd have put money on Malone already knowing the layout of the hotel. It was perfect timing after the threats issued by William. He would walk away immediately instead of waiting until after the referendum party. Let Malone do the shift.

Julian's clothes were folded neatly and in sets, a pair of socks and underwear nestled inside a folded T-shirt. His jeans rolled inside a jumper he didn't recognise, and his trainers cleaned, the canvas whitened and smelling faintly of dry acid.

Malone came to lean against the doorframe. 'Nice legs,' he said when his black trousers were removed, and Julian threw them at him to be caught in the man's free hand and whipped downwards. A moment when, in a film, Malone would have rushed him and toppled him onto the bed, in anger or lust. A moment with Julian expectant, and then it subsided.

'Does Mrs McClean know you're here?' he asked. 'When are you starting?'

Malone smiled. 'Starting? In Curragh House? I don't think so. I'm for better things.' He half-sneered as he looked around the room.

'I usually go to the launderette on Thursdays,' Julian said. 'That's tomorrow; a week's washing to do. If you come back then, everything will be clean.' Why was he saying this? Even if Malone didn't want the job, why should he stay on?

'I'd rather have a bag of dirty laundry than come back to this dump.'

'Okay then, it's just in Camden Street. We could go now, but I have to be back for the teas.' He was babbling. He removed his white shirt to change into one of the check shirts he hadn't seen for three months.

'That shirt's not mine,' Malone said. 'I suppose you're just looking for an excuse to show me the rest of the goods.'

Julian didn't answer. He'd forgotten the three white shirts he'd bought in Dunnes with his first week's wages. He reached for the underpants he hadn't seen for three months to replace the ones he was wearing.

'Hey hey hey, if those are my boxers, keep them on,' Malone said.

But Julian didn't stop, and again, Malone should have advanced into the room, done something to reinforce his words, but he stayed propping up the doorframe.

'Julian, and I know that's not your real name, this ends now.

Just put the clothes in my bag,' he said, and crossed one foot in front of the other as if to show how at ease he was.

Julian pulled on his jeans and waited to feel at home. But his restored clothes did not feel right. They were nothing to do with who he now was.

'I don't see the books.'

Julian shook the still-warm trousers along the crease, rolled them from the cuffs, and stuffed them into the bag along with the rest of Malone's clothes. Any illusions he'd had about the man were at an end. This was no helpless victim. He was a self-assured thug, who was doing okay thank you, and didn't need anything from Julian. He was glad he'd named him in the article, even though he knew it would be the first thing any big-time journalist would strike out.

'The books. Concentrate. Where are they?'

'Mrs McClean had them put upstairs in the residents' library, but later I saw a man with a briefcase sniffing them, and even later I noticed they were gone.'

'I was counting on getting my books back.'

Malone would know where they were, in Portlaoise prison with the leaders of the breakout gang, or maybe they'd been retrieved by the Gardaí or MI5, depending on who had double crossed whom.

'You've done me no favours, you know. Threatening the Gardaí with Amnesty International.'

'I'll take that as a thank you then!' Julian said, and stared back at the staring Malone. 'And hopefully it'll have no impact on your future happiness.' He wanted him gone now. To have an end to the weeks of waiting for his gratitude and the two of them riding off into the sunset in search of their next adventure. He was right about Curragh House though. It was a grubby place. He'd only put up with it because he was sure Malone would be back for him. Well, that was it.

The referendum party promised to be exciting, so maybe he'd stay to be delivered of Mother Ireland at the feet of the Pro-Lifers. But then he'd be gone. He was zipping the bag closed when he heard Brendan struggling with his new bicycle on the basement area steps outside the bedroom window.

'That's Brendan. He works here. If you don't want to be seen, you'd better leave now,' Julian said.

'No, if I don't want to be seen, I'll bolt the door and your mate will go around the long way.' Malone eased himself upright and ambled towards the front-area door. The twenty seconds it took him to get there, push the two bolts closed and amble back to the room was enough time for Julian to remove his own copy of the article he'd given Jack from beneath the mattress, lick the envelope, write '*Only to be opened in the event of the death of Julian Ryder*', and stuff it into Malone's bag. He'd intended to post it to himself at home, but this was a better idea. He was clutching the bag to his chest when Brendan began banging the window.

'Open that fucking door.'

Using his stomach, he bounced the bag forward towards Malone and stared, the bag squeezed between them. Malone stood his ground, staring back without any hint of what he was feeling. Then he reached for the handles and wheeled backwards to release Julian from the bedroom.

'Be seeing you,' Julian said, and walked towards the basement door to let in Brendan. He expected, even wanted, the Gofer's usual grabbing and pushing. It would give him an excuse to explode back. He'd come off worst if Brendan hit him, but it would be worth it. When he turned back Malone was gone, in and out of his life almost as quickly as the last time. And Brendan, on his way to the kitchen, only elbowed him as he passed with barely a sneer.

Dolly Considine's Hotel

MOTHER IRELAND MAKES HER APPEARANCE

Thurs 8th September 1983, 19:30–21:45

Dolly paused on the half-landing to watch Giolla-Íosa's people create space in the crush, and allow him to get from the footpath, up the front steps and into William's capacity crowd referendum party. She clasped her hands together beneath her chest and waited for him to look up. Tonight she wanted to be ornamental and adored. To have an evening basking in the awe and respect her brother-in-law and his heir apparent, her son, would draw from the adoring crowds. The pair of them in turn silently thanking her for making it possible. She knew she would be sharing them with the smoke and the noise, not to mention the petitioners and useful influencers that Giolla-Íosa lived to work. And there would be the inevitable crisis in the ladies' toilet, drunken arguments in the Kickham Room, and needing to be on constant lookout for anything that might endanger William's favourable political promise. But she would always be able to find Giolla-Íosa in the advantageous spot he would find in the Porchester Lounge to allow the crowd to orbit around him and his attention to be taken, and given, casually, spontaneously and enthusiastically: *Ah the hard man. How are ya?*

He would be performing for her no less than she for him. And yet her dominant feeling was anxiety. No one would get the best out of her till it subsided. Mikhail Mayakovsky had laughed when she'd asked him to tone down the entertainment they'd arranged. Even William had told her to mind her own business when she asked him to 'please abandon it'. But everything about the party was her business, including William, and loathsome Julian, mincing through the crowd with the look of a boy nursing a secret and on the hunt for others. She would be like a mother hen until the performance was over, one eye flitting between Julian and Mayakovsky, and the other on her son and the party elders. Her vision swinging from distaste and dread to satisfaction and loving anticipation, and back again. She would struggle to be entirely ornamental.

Cathal was being pushed through the front door ahead of his brother, drunk of course, his face with its usual grateful-for-anything hangdog expression. She'd wait on the landing until he was squeezed through the throng and up the stairs. She'd settle him in front of the TV with his supper before she'd come down to join the fray. But when her husband got as far as William, her son put his arm around his father's shoulder and said something she couldn't possibly hear, but they both laughed, a male-bonding sort of laugh, making William turn his father towards the Porchester Lounge. Dolly's first crisis response: back to her sitting room to ring down to Sylvia: 'Soft drinks only for Mr Cathal McClean.'

She delayed to watch Giolla-Íosa being ushered into the lobby, space being made by his bodyguards and by two boys of about William's age she'd noticed recently acting as full-time voluntary secretaries and researchers, the pair of them syrupy, like double-glazing salesmen. Thank God William would never need to do any of that. He would complete his studies and enter politics as an adult, reluctantly taking on his responsibilities. *Noblesse oblige.* His family background and Giolla-Íosa's support ensuring he was ready for the task. Her brother-in-law looked up at her, waving one of the unlit cigars he'd taken to holding to help him avoid cigarettes, and spoke, his face suggesting words of encouragement, but again she was too far away to hear.

At nine-thirty, William and Giolla-Íosa, with Mrs Mitchell the Pro-Life heroine nodding between them, were waiting for the post-presentation applause to die down when, at a signal from Mikhail Mayakovsky, the lights went out and a spotlight, mounted above the bar, lit the faces of the people blocking the Porchester Lounge door and drove them apart. 'O'Donnell's Lament' on a slow wailing violin accepted the surrender of the rattle of bottles and glasses and the chatter and laughter. One of Giolla-Íosa's lackeys had to be nudged to stop the joke he was telling. Seven women in knee-length capes danced into the room. They carried swords, and Dolly had to keep her hands pressed onto the bar counter to prevent them clapping loudly to stop the performance right there.

The dancers began as a tight bunch but expanded to push the crowd apart and open a circle in the middle of the room, the spotlight following, the swords held flat at chest height with a hand at either end, hopefully meaning they were not sharp. May it please Jesus, Dolly thought. Then they turned and stood to attention facing inwards, the swords pointing upwards, their lips kissing the steel. Mayakovsky would mean something rude by it all.

Then the spotlight swung back to the door, and a wide, vulgarly painted female figure was pushed into the room. Pregnant enough to pop at any time, her arms folded over her engorged breasts, a grim determined look on her face that said to Dolly, I hope you're happy now!

The sword women shed their capes as they danced in a circle around the figure. Three of them wore short ra-ra skirts and colourful leg warmers, their shoulders padded with assertiveness. And the brown woollen stockings and long skirts of the remaining four? Did William think that's how she'd dressed when she seduced Giolla-Íosa and Cathal in 1956, when the girls in Brown Thomas's women's clothes department addressed her by name as they saw her approach? More likely it was Mrs Mitchell who was being portrayed, with her frumpy tweeds and her Aran jumper.

While the women in brown stockings danced about with joy, the ra-ra dancers poked their swords at the distended stomach of the figure. But the swords poised to penetrate were noticed by the brown stockings, who, one-on-one, began defending the mother-to-be. The remaining woman was free to lay her sword across the figure's folded arms and to caress her head and rub her back. The figure itself began to emit a wail not unlike a banshee's, which rose to challenge the music, growing louder and syncing with coloured lights that spun and flashed, until a kind of blinding, deafening crescendo caused the four old-fashioned women to turn to the figure in unison and stoop in front of her. They lifted her skirt to reveal a curled-up form encased in crinkled, blood-smeared plastic which they dragged out onto the Porchester Lounge carpet. Julian, the little fucker, his nakedness clearly visible. Causing several of Dolly's guests to cover their mouths and turn away. The music stopped and the traditionally dressed women crossed themselves and stood with their heads bowed and their swords down. The trendy women stripped Julian of the plastic sheet and lifted him to his feet. Dolly's lounge boy had provided her with the perfect excuse to finally rid herself of him. His nakedness had clearly caused offence to her guests; and even that was beside the point; it was her drinks licence that would be taken away. What had William been thinking?

'Lights Sylvia,' Dolly shouted and clapped her hands. She had to return the hotel to its normal function. Cathal was staring at Julian as if he'd never seen a penis before, and Giolla-Íosa was twitching his hands the way he did when he wanted her to know he disagreed with the party line.

But Mrs Mitchell began to clap, and she dragged her horror-struck supporters into hesitant agreement. Mayakovsky would be disappointed that his attack on Pro-Life values was being subverted by Mrs Mitchell's utter certainty in her beliefs that was well able to flip his skit on Irish motherhood into its affirmation. She'd refused to make an acceptance speech after Giolla-Íosa's presentation to her, but Mother Ireland was enabling her to speak now.

'I will not repeat the precise words, which were spoken in the vernacular, and were therefore colourfully and unnecessarily vulgar,' Mrs Mitchell said. 'But suffice to say that our loving Father has ordained that the place from which we are born is very close to where our bodily wastes emerge. It is good that we are reminded, lest we forget, that it is His works we are engaged in, not stroking our own egos. The people of Ireland have spoken. God bless us, His humble servants.'

And then she turned to Julian. 'Your appearance may have been designed to shock my friends here this evening. If so, you have failed. As wives and mothers, we see a lot of nakedness. Nakedness is good. It is how God made us. It is part of His plan for us. What is not part of His plan are the abuses to which some put that nakedness.'

Mrs Mitchell waved her right hand and one of the dancer's capes was thrown over Julian. Then she bowed towards Dolly as if to forgive her, but also to agree that her lounge boy needed to be punished.

Dolly Considine's Hotel

HELP, THEY'RE BOYCOTTING THE STOUT

Thurs 8th September 1983, 21:45–24:00

The dancer's cape covering his torso was cold and shiny against his naked skin and kept being brushed aside as Mrs Mitchel's supporters squeezed and pushed to deliver Julian from the Porchester Lounge. Some stared in angry silence, but others jeered in his face as he was passed through. The more diverse crowd in the lobby ignored him, so he had to struggle to get to the ladies. Mikhail had lifted his clothes into the space above the high, hissing, cast iron cistern before wrapping Julian in the bloody plastic sheet and bundling him inside the papier mâché figure of Mother Ireland.

'I saw it myself early one Sunday morning,' Mikhail's voice came through the toilet door. 'Every shebeen in that town was shut against me. I ended up at the brewery, and slipped past the porter to find the porter.' He laughed at his own joke, his Russian accent replaced with a hackneyed Dublin one. 'But instead I found the hop-roasting house. It was warm and the rich smell was almost as good as a pint of plain. Picture it, a conveyor belt filled with bouncing hops on their way to the ovens, and every few feet, scattered like bay leaves in a stew to be removed later, were tiny foetuses, oven-bound, to flavour the hops, courtesy of the abortion clinic in Kilburn. At least the foetuses were probably our own. Good Irish stock, adding a robust Hibernian taste to English stout.'

Scuffling sounds and shouts of outrage came through from the hall, and, independently, a banging on the toilet door. 'Hurry up for fuck's sake, I'll wet myself,' a woman shouted.

Outside the ladies, Mikhail had one arm around William McClean's neck and the other round Mother Ireland. Julian delayed to let Mikhail speak to him. 'Archetypal symbols are so important in the theatre,' Mikhail was saying to William. 'Everybody recognises and responds to them, instinctively.' He winked at Julian but did not try to detain him. 'In the Hebrew tradition two goats were taken to the temple. One was killed as an offering to their God; the other was entrusted with the sins of the community and driven out of the village. That one was called the scapegoat.'

Julian had promised to walk out as soon as the party was over. But what was to stop him leaving immediately? Neither Bláithín nor Mikhail gave a fuck about him. Malone was gone. He was on his own. He should go home to his mother and tell her everything. But instead, here he was, drained and frozen, his clothes damp from the hissing cistern, being jostled nearer and further from the bar like mindless flotsam.

'Excuse me,' Sylvia shouted at a man regaling people with triumphant and outraged referendum experiences, 'tell Flasher we need Smithwick's.'

Julian pointed at the stack of cases sitting on the floor behind the bar.

'It's all stout,' she said, an unfamiliar look of respect on her face. 'The fuckers are boycotting it.' She was being nicer to him, and he stood waiting for more, a sudden image of her as the sister he never had. 'Are you getting the fucking Smithwick's?' she shouted. The nearness of her fist backing him into people demanding their reward for protecting the rights of the unborn and setting the country on the road to pre-famine levels of population.

'Fuck Mikhail,' he said into the face of a purple-nosed man with his jacket lapels covered in pairs of tiny silver feet. 'Sliding out of Mother Ireland's belly has changed everything. I need something to do. For myself.'

Sylvia pushed three crates of empty bottles into his chest, reminding him that the counter-high stacks covering the hatch to the cellar meant he'd have to carry the full crates through the baying crowd.

'I don't give a fuck about any of this,' he told the whiskey-nosed man. 'I need my own ambition.'

People plucked at Julian's sleeves as he passed, checking the empty bottles in his crates, intent as petitioners, a fresh bottle to get them out of purgatory. 'You're next,' he sneered at each in turn. Giolla-Íosa McClean was watching him but continued to nod his head and laugh as he related a story to a woman in a fur coat standing by the open window for a little air, a shiny-suited sidekick on either side of him. His detective bodyguards were controlling the street door, deciding who was told the hotel was full and who was allowed in. Back towards the old reception desk, something about the stance and expressions of two men in short suede jackets and jeans was keeping them from being jostled by the pushing crowd. The slightly older one moved towards Julian and put a hand to the empty crates.

'We need some refills here,' he said, leaning down into Julian's face, although his glass was almost full.

'Mrs Mitchell is demanding an encore from Mother Ireland,' Julian said. 'I have to get ready for my performance.' He shook the crates of empties as he'd heard Brendan threaten, but the noise was muted in the din of the hall.

'That's what I like to hear,' the man said, and patted Julian's bum, the way a fellow footballer might, before allowing him to pass.

The key to the cellar door was missing from its nail in the kitchen. Perhaps the ghost of Paddy the Porter was renting out the cellar to men who'd picked up in the gents as he'd done when he was alive, if the story about William's grandfather was to be believed. He was about to press the intercom button for Sylvia's help when he remembered that Brendan sometimes hid his cellar key in the boys' bedroom.

'*Bold Robert Emmet, the darling of Éireann,*' a man coming out of the toilet sang as Julian passed. As usual the bedroom bulb was blown, but the streetlight let him see that Brendan's bed was lying upside down on top of his, pillow to pillow, as if fucking it, or stacked to clear a space on the floor, or to make examining the underside's innards all the easier. The shreds of torn hessian, and loose mattress stuffing, told Julian he should hope the secrets predated his time at the hotel. Scattered clothes were clogging his feet, and his shoe caught the strap of the bag Malone had taken away from the hotel the previous afternoon. A cold staccato feeling invaded him.

On the footpath above at street level, another man in a short suede jacket was staring down into the room. Julian hoped the window was too dirty for him to be seen. 'What we have here is a situation.' John Wayne's voice sounded from nowhere, his imagined projected thumbs hooked into his trouser belt loops.

'Do the men in suede jackets sipping orange squash upstairs know anything about Malone's bag, and the stuffing pulled out of the beds?'

'You're damn right they do,' John Wayne nodded, and waved a finger at him, 'and maybe your friend Jack knows why.'

'Mrs McClean barred him for making fun of the referendum party.'

'You think Judas hung about after he'd done his dirty work? Friend or no friend.'

'Anyway, he's not my friend. I just, just…'

'Yes, you only gave him your highly imaginative version of Malone's shenanigans. But now the place is surrounded with armed men in suede jackets.'

This was nonsense. Giolla-Íosa McClean always had two detectives guarding him. The other politicians would have theirs. He should feel extra safe. Except who would trash the boys' bedroom? More importantly, how did Malone's bag get back into the hotel? He should have been in Derry by now, watching his mammy's hands thrown up in horror at how grey and worn her son's clothes had become in the few short weeks since she'd lovingly ironed and folded them. He looked up at the man on the footpath for clues, confident he could not be seen, but the man leaned over the basement area railings, something menacing in his short stabbing finger motions.

Julian stepped further back into the shadows and imitated the gesture. He would remember how it was done and record it in his journal, later, when he'd found a new bulb and tidied up the room. Or at Bláithín's, if she showed up like the cavalry and whisked him away to the country.

'About time you found that key, collected the Smithwick's and went back upstairs to assess the situation,' John Wayne drawled, as if a saloon bar shootout would provide the resolution to whatever was going on.

Summer of Unrequited Love

COULD THIS BE A BONDAGE SCENE?

Thurs 8 Sept '83, 23:45

Recent aftershave overlaid the beer cellar's fermenting-empty-bottle and cloying-damp smells, and even with the thump of feet from the bar above and the high-pitched tone of a woman singing 'Faith of Our Fathers', the acoustics felt different. Could be, it was Brendan, playing with his cardboard periscope, watching women's legs through the gap in the bar above his head. Except the aftershave was not Brendan's. Julian pulled the cord and the bulb swung light through the forest of stacked crates. Everything looked normal. He locked the door to prevent drunks wandering in and moved through the disordered jumble of empty towers towards the Smithwick's corner, the aftershave smell fading as he went.

Even with the bottom of his face covered with a slash of wide tape and the black woollen hat rolled down over his forehead, Julian recognised the eyes staring up at him. He didn't allow himself to say, what the fuck are you doing here? Maybe the sight of the upturned beds and the presence of Malone's bag had prepared him for a surprise, the way a doctor says to a patient's family, I'm afraid I have some bad news.

Malone was tied up as well as gagged, his legs stretched out on the damp floor, his back supported by the stack of Smithwick's Julian wanted to get at. The questions began piling up. He rolled the hat up slowly, allowing his fingers to brush against Malone's hair, short now the way he'd wanted it to be, that first morning in Busárus. But today, Malone was captive at his feet. Powerless. The possibilities... Delaying the questions, struggling for the words to fill sentences that began who? and why? and how? Next came the gag so he could see the thin lips he remembered. A screech from Malone as the gaffer tape pulled away from his skin.

'Fuck,' he screamed, spraying Julian with saliva.

He sat on an upturned crate, waiting for a thank you and some words wrapped in the honeyed Derry accent he remembered. But except for some animation around the corners of Malone's lips, all he got was an angry stare. The tied wrists were resting on his crotch. Julian's fingers hovered, yes-ing and no-ing, no sign of the prisoner lifting them clear until, 'Do you want to be untied?' Julian asked.

'From you? Yes. Another Free-fucking-Stater interfering in things you don't understand. You see Gerry Adams and Ian Paisley on telly and think you know it all.'

Once Malone's hands were free, Julian backed away to let him undo his ankles himself. 'I just came in for Smithwick's,' he said. 'There's a run on it because they're boycotting the stout. Have you heard of Captain Boycott? He was Irish, boycotting was named after him...', his babbling reminding him of Malone in Busárus, going on about his mammy making his sandwiches and his brother not saying goodbye, while Julian had kept his mouth shut to protect his non-Swedish non-German identity. His bleached hair long since grown out.

'I don't know what your game is,' Malone said, his accent making the cliché sound fresh and meaningful. 'But I need you to get away from me before you get me kneecapped.'

Julian reached for the stack behind Malone's head and lifted down two crates of Smithwick's. 'I'm going back to the bar.' Sylvia would be angry at him taking so long. But why was he bothering? He was finished with Curragh House. This was the last time he'd be in the basement. He should collect his backpack and go look for his mother. She was probably in a bar in Phibsborough, drowning her sorrows at a Right to Choose funeral party.

'Can you hurry up? I want to lock the cellar,' Julian said. 'I have to go.' Surprised that he was talking himself back into William's party.

'You think I can just saunter out the front door? I have to wait here until they finish "speaking" to you,' he said. 'Your story better be good.' There was a touch of a flounce in the way Malone threw the final ropes at Julian's feet and began to massage his ankles to banish the red welts.

'They're so wild for drink upstairs,' an idea forming in Julian's mind, 'why don't we invite everyone to serve themselves, here in the beer cellar – *come along, free drink, compliments of the hotel*, and we'll be able to slip away while they're fighting over the bottles.' He could be at home in an hour, telling his mother all about his summer.

'The way I see it, now,' Malone said, picking his hat off the floor and using a crate to help himself stand up, 'whatever I inadvertently got mixed up in, you must have been part of the set up from the start: was it you told the Garda special branch I was an IRA courier? It was definitely you who let your bag be passed off as mine, and you who allowed the books my mother fundraised for women prisoners to go missing in action. You Free State fuck.'

'I was minding my own business when you sat beside me, remember?'

'And when I was carted off, you took my bag, impersonated me, wore my clothes, and inveigled people into asking questions about my whereabouts, even though I was released within a couple of hours.'

They were back to staring, assessing each other, the way they had the day before, except there was no doorframe for Malone to pose casually against, and his hands were engaged in getting his circulation going again.

'It's taken you two and a half months to come back,' Julian said, wanting to add, for me. But he also wanted to laugh at Malone's absurd suggestions.

'My mother collapsed when she heard I'd been picked up; I had to go home. And because of your troublemaking, every time I stepped out of the house I was followed. She had the boys round three times asking her questions, with menaces. She'll never get over it.'

'And you're back today because?' The crates of Smithwick's were beginning to make Julian's arms ache. He should get on with delivering them, but he put them on the floor.

'When I got back to my lodgings yesterday with my bag, three of the boys were waiting for me: "Where's that fucking story? We want it. Now!" I didn't know what they were talking about. But hey, they unzipped my bag and out falls the magic envelope. *Only to be opened in the event of the death of Julian Ryder.*'

Upstairs the Mother Ireland theme music had started, stopped, and started again. Her encore was taking place without Julian. Had Mikhail charmed William inside her, ready to slide out naked at the feet of his parents and uncle, not to mention the very people who in a few years' time would be nominating him for election? More likely her belly was empty.

'And then miraculously your bag returns to the bedroom,' Julian said, 'and you're teleported into the beer cellar, trussed up like a chicken.'

'This morning I was put on a bus home with a minder. He fell asleep and I jumped out at the airport and came back here to warn you; you're in deep shit.'

'And then you tied yourself up? Or did you wait until after you trashed the bedroom?'

'I was only at the basement door when I was greeted with: "We've been expecting you McGivern. Coming here is proof positive; you and Paddy Butler are in cahoots."'

It had been so long since he'd heard his old name that it took Julian a second to remember his mother would call him Paddy when he got home. Someone had gone to the trouble of finding out who he used to be.

'They think I helped you to write your lies.'

'I see things, I turn them into stories. It's hardly a crime.'

'You're either very clever or an innocent wee fucker, if you don't mind my saying.'

Julian didn't mind at all. He wanted Malone to keep talking. A few more words and he'd be inviting him to Cabra to meet his mother.

The performers' footsteps were pounding the floor above their heads and the music was beginning to reach its crescendo. Julian imagined the raised swords, the clashing and glinting in the maniacal lights. He moved to where Brendan kept his periscope, with barely time to engage the thing between the ceiling joists and focus his eyes past a forest of trouser legs, when he saw swords plunging into the papier mâché belly.

'Well, I'm glad that didn't happen to me,' he said and turned back to Malone.

'Don't you get it, you Free State twit? Whatever you wrote

had enough truth in it to upset some very heavy people. Explain to me how you can be so clueless.'

Julian laughed. 'I'm going upstairs now. You're free to leave any time you like. Former minister Giolla-Íosa McClean is in the bar as well as his brother and his sister-in-law. Not to mention the squeaky-pure Mrs Mitchell. Respectable people. The place is swarming with armed detectives. If anyone questions me, I will tell the truth, the story was put together from conversations I overheard in the bar. Anyone could have written it.'

'You've upset them, and as soon as the crowds go you'll be back down here with two broken legs, and that's just for starters.'

'You're bleeding,' Julian said. He reached up to touch Malone's forehead. Blood running from his hair. 'What's happened to you?'

Malone moved and the blood kept coming. The drops running along a joist from the Porchester Lounge floor above, and falling to where his shoes had been, sending up tiny specks of dust as it struck and was sucked into the basement floor.

'There really was someone inside Mother Ireland,' Julian said. 'I saw the swords plunging... sweet fuck, they think I was in there. I have to get out of here.'

'Shush,' Malone whispered, 'listen.' Someone was fiddling with the cellar door. Voices, indistinct, thankfully outside. Julian had left the key in the lock; they'd have to break the door down to get in.

'Open up, McGivern,' a male northern voice said, 'if you know what's good for you.'

'The boys who tied me up were talking about these old cellars all being linked together. Is there another way out?' Malone said, and threaded through to where Julian had seen Brendan standing guard in his sleep, repeating, 'They shall not pass. They shall not pass.' 'This could be the place,' and Malone stood on an upturned crate to reach between the joists to pull at the topmost row of bricks.

'Do you think you're superman or what?' Julian said, although in his story about Dolly's father this was the alcove where the body had been bricked up in its lime-filled tomb, back in the 1950s. Could there be any truth in it? What the fuck: the bricks were coming away in Malone's hands and falling onto the floor. The dust making him cough until he pinched his nostrils and pulled his shirt up over his mouth and nose.

'Here,' Malone whispered and handed a brick to Julian, pointing at the floor. Soon, enough of the wall was demolished to see there was a space behind it, and beyond that another skin of bricks.

'Hurry,' Julian said. 'That's the back row of the theatre. We don't need a big hole. Just a few inches.' The dust sticking to the blood on Malone's face made it look like he was being taken over by advancing dusty fingers.

'It's no good,' Malone said. 'The other bricks are too well laid.'

Julian handed back a brick, took one himself, and between them they began to beat against the topmost layer. After three joint blows, it moved, and soon an entire course was gone and then another. But the noises from outside the door were getting louder. More than one person kicking, and the same voice again. 'McGivern, we know the two of you are in there. Open up now or face the consequences.'

'Who's McGivern?' Julian asked, a bit breathless.

'My father's name, he left before I was born. I was named for my mother,' Malone said, and knocked three more bricks into the theatre by himself.

'That's enough,' Julian said. 'I'll give you a bunt up,' and he grabbed Malone's shoe and lifted his leg to post him headfirst through the hole, into the theatre's darkness. Then hands were reaching back for Julian and pulling him through. The last time he'd been up there, Mikhail had his hand down his pants.

'Come on,' Malone said.

'Just a minute,' and Julian spun a loose brick at the cellar bulb the way he'd seen Brendan throw his shoe at the bedroom light when he was too drunk to get out of bed. The third brick made the cellar go dark. But he was not ready to leave.

'What are you doing?' Malone asked, with very little of the previous day's cockiness. Julian wished he could see his face.

'We have to say sorry to the boy whose grave we've desecrated,' Julian said. 'I don't know your name mister, or even if you're really here, but if you are, we're sorry to have disturbed you. Maybe now you're exposed, they'll give you a proper burial.'

'For fuck's sake,' Malone said, and pulled at his arm.

Julian led the way in the dark, down the stepped seats to the front of the stage, through the tiny dressing room and out into the yard at the back, stopping on the way to take Mikhail's abandoned pork pie hat and white coat from the back of the door. After that it was easy to climb over the yard wall into the alley beyond. In less than two minutes they were in Leeson Street, the reflection of the blue lights from more than one emergency vehicle catching the windows of the corner houses facing Hatch Street.

Dolly McClean's Diary

SEPTEMBER 1983

You know why I'm writing this Julian. Although equally you will never know, because you will never read it, see it, listen to it, or even know of its existence. And yet I will pretend that wherever you are in the world, you are sitting at a teletext machine as I type, and each letter is simultaneously printed out for you. A paper copy to match my own, and recording also the hesitation between each word ..... the metronomic dots ..... that urge me to commit what has to be said. ..... if only into my diary.

I mentioned your notebooks to the Gardaí putting together the facts of the evening William died, but they failed to find them. You do know he's dead? Dead in place of you, but no less dead. If not by your hand, then by your absence, your sinful omission, as we say during the Confiteor to cover things we have failed to do alongside our sinful actions. And you failed to stop him being killed or to serve the interests of my family as you were employed to do. I don't suppose I will ever fully understand your part in the mischief that occurred, all I know is: my son is dead, and you are living. Bad cess to you.

Brendan managed to find and hide your journals before the Gardaí could locate them. And then, pretending to be someone else, tried to blackmail me. After all I've done for him, nineteen years of his lumpen stupidity. I paid him the modest sum he asked for. It was a relief to be free of him in the end.

I found a coherence and a chronology in the twelve notebooks, could see the progress from St Patrick's day through to the evening William died, your final description of him on the phone to the company sponsoring the security for the referendum party. Fat lot of good they did, might even have been involved in what happened.

In June 1962, I was nearly seven months pregnant with William, and I went down home to Offaly for a few days, mainly to convince my mother to come up to Dublin and help run the hotel during my confinement. Noreen lived in the town. My mother had known her all her life. Summoned to the farm during busy times or if someone was ill. She stayed for a year after my brother Declan died, and came back to nurse my father in his final two years. After which Mother had kept her on, letting her live-in at the house, maybe for company. We were never close; I suppose I treated her like a maid or one of the farm hands. I assume she was paid but that was my mother's territory, nothing to do with me.

Whenever I, and my advancing pregnancy, came into the kitchen, Noreen would be sitting by the Rayburn drinking tea. Now and then she'd twist around and take a sod of turf from the basket behind her, waving her hand in front of her face to disperse the smoke and ash sucked out because she opened the burner door too quickly, before throwing in the

sod and shutting the door with a clang. She spoke clearly
enough to my mother, but to me she mumbled, the way lots
of older toothless people do, although maybe she was trying to
sound like the Dubliner she thought I now was. It was always
about my father. Did I miss him? Did I remember the time he
threw someone out of the house, or the time the delegation
demanded to see him? Did I know what great respect De
Valera had for him? Once, she even asked me what I thought
had killed him, what had been the final straw.

When she was speaking to other people, her tone suggested
she was resigned to life as being the source of the cruelties she'd
endured, but she reserved a special accusatory tone for me, as if
I alone was the cause of all her woes.

On my last morning, waiting for a lift to the train station,
mother left me alone with her for ages, the two of us in silence
until she stood up and came over to the table where the pain
in my back was stretching me away from my breakfast tea, of
which I'd only taken a sip, hoping to avoid having to use the
toilet on the train. She lifted the cup, and tilting it gently over
the sink, drained away most of the liquid, careful to keep the
tea leaves from spilling out.

'Your father was a great man for having his tea leaves read,'
she said, almost without mumbling. 'A great believer in
listening to advice from all quarters before he moved to action.'

I said nothing, knowing he'd never listened to anything
other than his own impulses even when they contradicted what
common sense was telling him. She swirled the dregs round
and round in the cup with her eyes closed and then upended
the contents onto my saucer.

'I see a…' she said, the way I'd heard her begin dozens of
times before, mainly with the farm hands. But instead of going
on, she turned the saucer a little and began again. 'I see a…'
before letting out her breath, and revolving the saucer a little

more, and then again, several times, slowly so as not to disturb the pattern. 'I see a... I see a...' But clearly she could see nothing, even after so many false starts and a little cheating when she impatiently disturbed the contents to produce a new pattern. And yet she went no further.

She mumbled something as she put the cup and saucer in the sink and returned to her chair by the range. And as she sat down, she repeated the mumble, and I heard the words more clearly. 'A little corpse looking for its grave.' Addressed perhaps not so much to me as to life itself, and without any awareness of how the words might be heard by a woman well advanced in her pregnancy. She was simply recognising facts, 'A little corpse looking for its grave,' as if it was something everyone would already know about, a truth that needed to be repeated again and again, like the prayers at Mass on Sunday, especially when they were in Latin, uttered more for the sake of the ritual than for any meaning they might have.

OCTOBER 1983

Why is it to you I'm writing instead of to my son? Where is my William? I started to clear out his bedroom as soon as the detectives were finished with their searching, as if there would have been anything ..... It was you they should have ..... Shut up Dolly ..... Start again. Okay.

I started ..... with his clothes. For the Salvation Army. There'll be a bunch of very well-dressed homeless men hanging around Dublin's streets, at least until they've spent a cold wet night or two sleeping out, or have dribbled their extra strong down their fronts. A mad notion, as I threw laden hangers onto his bed, that I could start putting guests into the room. William's room, and room eleven, guest-free since before my time, a double and a single. A fresh start for the hotel. Not that I'll need much money now, my son was my greatest drain, but I expect Cathal will sink into some God-awful place where I can't rely on any contribution from him, a yellow box or a bedsit in Rathmines. They're nearly the same I suppose, except I'll have to pay for the yellow box. My misery conflicting with notions of my newly liberated life, the freedom to do anything I want, to have ideas, opportunities, fresh starts, and ultimately….. the pointlessness of it.

Sylvia fluttering at the bedroom door not sure whether to come in or not, her face contorted the way I imagine mine is when I'm passing a dry stool, until I point to the roll of black bags, and the clothes, for her to get packing.

I've read enough books and seen enough dramas to know that opening a son's bedside locker or turning over his mattress is something to be avoided unless you're prepared for shocking revelations. Condoms, porn, even gay porn and evidence – God forgive me – that the two of you might have been at it, love letters or blackmail letters to support a niggle in the back of my head that he might have had a hand in his own demise.

Smelly socks, a collection of soiled tissues, so much dust, what does Sylvia do when she is supposed to be cleaning? But the only surprise was the Star School of Motoring voucher for ten driving lessons that I gave him for Christmas. He'd told me he'd used them all. That the instructor said he was ready for his test. The test itself booked for a week after the referendum, in case he needed time to recover. The mad notion coming into my head that he knew he was going to die and saw no point in learning to drive, unless it was to steer the boat across the Styx if the ferryman was tired.

I told Sylvia to change the 'Reopening Soon' announcement on the hotel's front door to 'Closed Indefinitely', and I told her she should look for another job, and hobbled down the stairs and had a painful walk to St Stephen's Green, where I punished several people who stopped to speak to me by holding up my flattened hand at them, closing my eyes and limping onwards without speaking. I tripped over the low steel edge-protection near the bandstand and landed painfully on my right side. I was only able to stop one man from helping me by uttering a profanity I would have checked William for, had he said it – 'Fuck off you pervert' – but it did the trick and I was allowed to lie on the grass, looking at the empty bandstand, and imagining the Garda band playing 'The Wearing of the Green', of all the possible fucking tunes.

I had my second driving lesson today. Mr Lawless the teacher was very patient with me, and said I was very good for such a ….. he wanted to say fat, discoordinated, self-opinionated woman, but instead said, 'for someone who has had so little driving experience. It's almost as if you're having a refresher lesson, rather than acquiring a new skill.' In my childhood, a time when pressing pedals and turning the steering wheel took determination and muscle, some of the hands let me drive the tractor, until my father found out and swore to sack anyone who allowed it again. I suppose it reminded him of my brother's death.

I was in the kitchen, cutting a slice of ham for my lunch, holding the very knife I suppose you used when you were making sandwiches for Mayakovsky and his crew, when a thought occurred to me. I tried to wave it away by thinking how the kitchen could do with a makeover, everything cleared out, hacked back until we reach bare brick and could start again, especially on the damp. I tried to concentrate on the little mushrooms emerging from the skirting board under the back window, and the bubbly plaster filling the space between the door and the window, but the horror of it kept intruding; somewhere you are sitting with a new journal and a new pen setting down the details of the blood sacrifice you offered the hotel, your freedom in exchange for William's life. His precious blood fed through the lounge floorboards and on downwards through the dirt of the beer cellar floor into the very foundations of the building. And doubtless you are now relishing the pleasure of your freedom and anticipating the success that will follow publication of your accounts, both true and false. I see you in some fetid hovel writing, with the cold distance of some awful anthropologist, playing with titles. *The Hotel's Revenge... The Bloody Sacrifice... Her Only Son...*

NOVEMBER 1983

I dragged Sylvia with me this afternoon to buy a car. What has she to do all day except apply for jobs? She has a full licence, so I let her drive it away from the little sales compound. I've told her she must be out by the end of the month. There should be plenty of work available in the run up to Christmas. It's a little Ford Escort, blue. She drove me to Dollymount Strand and sat in the passenger seat while I stop-started up and down the beach, wondering why William had boasted about mad handbrake turns in the sand, carving out corkscrews, all the way from the wooden bridge to the massive boulder-barred dead end. Sylvia didn't like my skidding attempts, hard pulls one way shifting my bulk until I squashed her against the passenger door, and hard back sending her over onto me like a tiny child, the inner wheels digging in, the outer lifting and threatening to turn us over.

'If you drive like that on the road you'll be dead in a week,' she said, realising she oughtn't to be reminding me about death, but at least she stopped looking at her watch as if she had to be back to open the bar or make supper for the Hannifins. They've finally gone, thirty years of their whining freeloading. The house Mrs Hannifin inherited in Wexford, standing empty all these years, getting warmed up and dried out instead of them putting limits on my choices, with me at a crossroads and needing to make decisions about the rest of my life. I'm not fucking dead, you little prick.

I had a letter from Mayakovsky's solicitors today telling me that if I didn't cease and desist making defamatory allegations regarding their client's part in William's death, I would find myself being served with an injunction and a court summons. Let them, let him. It won't stop me saying my son's blood is on his hands. The whore's melt.

I've lost so much weight that I've had to buy whole new outfits. I sent a bag of stuff to the little dressmaker I've used for years to see if there was anything she could take in, so it doesn't look like I'm wearing my fatter sister's clothes. I'm not trying to slim, but it seems to be falling off me. I might have to have a check-up, ensure it's William that's causing the loss, and not cancer, or some other awful reason. I'd happily take on any cancer in exchange for another week with William. Was it you put him up to telling me he wanted his father to take a paternity test?

DECEMBER 1983

I am not staying in Dublin for Christmas. If I pass my driving test next week, I will take off on a tour of the west of Ireland. Otherwise I will book an all-inclusive Christmas break in the Great Southern in Galway, or something in Westport, taking the train down, not telling anyone when I will be back. Fuck them all.

I was barely in the door of the Westport hotel, hanging the dress (at least four sizes smaller) that I've worn every Christmas day since William was born, in the en suite, to get the creases out, when the phone rang. It was the chair of the local Fianna Fáil, Comhairle Ceantair. That's the constituency set up in case you don't know. The local TD had noticed me walking past the bar while he was consoling a distraught constituent but couldn't abandon the poor woman, even to 'staunch the flow of my surprise at seeing Dolly Considine just a few feet away in the lobby'.

'I'd have recognised her anywhere,' he was reported as saying. 'And he therefore insists that you come to Christmas dinner at the house in Castlebar. The whole family will be there, and his wife and children will be delighted to see you. The car will be outside the hotel at 1.30 precisely and will return you at whatever time you like after 6pm.'

I hung up. One way or another, Fianna Fáil played a part, whatever it was, in the death of my son. Sitting in the bar... Talking to a distraught constituent... The wife delighted to see a mourning mother she's never met, rocking up to dinner on Christmas day. That's my arse, all of it. They're keeping an eye on me. As I suppose they are on you.

And then, on the afternoon that he was killed, he came to me to say he now wanted Giolla-Íosa, as well as Cathal, to take a paternity test. That was you, wasn't it? You had such a malevolent hold over him. What did you want?

The newspapers photographed Cathal and GI on either side of my infirm mother, helping her down the church steps, noting in the caption that I was too ill to attend the funeral. I wasn't ill, I refused to go, that's all. Who was there to make me? Even my mother, 'one's Granny', as William called her, 'who'd struggled from her nursing home' didn't dare try to discuss it. Sylvia said she'd stay, but I ordered her out of the hotel. I wanted the building to myself. The first time in thirty years. Just me and the hotel. Alone, to confront she who consumes people instead of sheltering them. Woman to woman. Listen to me, I sound mad, even to myself. I sat in the upstairs sitting room with the blinds down, waiting for the hearse on its slow drive by. I cursed the hotel, and when the cortège had passed, I descended the stairs to the front door. I wondered if she'd let me leave, if she'd bar the door to prevent the last living creature from leaving. To my certain knowledge, the hotel has not been completely empty of people, me, staff, guests, even once in the thirty years since I arrived. I reached for the latch, and I sensed a reluctance, a bit of damp swelling, or the old bitch saying she would not be alone. And yet the door did open, and I stepped outside, not even bothering to pull it shut after me but moving quickly down the steps to the street and on to the student halls opposite before turning back to face her from the far footpath. 'I hate you,' I said, and walked towards Leeson Street. The tail end of the cortège, stopped outside his old school, was visible for a few moments before it processed onwards to the cemetery.

It was just a few hours before the referendum party was due to start that he offered to cancel the Mother Ireland skit. I knew nothing about the swords then, although they must have been in the building already. All I'd have to do would be to demand the paternity tests. He said I was begging him to stop it, and here he was, offering terms. Paternity tests in exchange for the sword dance. Why in God's name didn't I listen to him?

JANUARY 1984

I was still at the hotel in Westport for Nollaig na mBan – Little Christmas to you, the twelfth night, when tradition demands that the decorations be removed and the tree stripped of its baubles and put outside the house. I've always waited until the following morning, and have Brendan dismantle everything before breakfast. But the family running the Westport hotel apparently thought that this risked bad luck, that everything needed to go before midnight on 6th January. They took all day over the ceremony, with everyone who passed in or out asked to unravel the string of flickering lights a quarter turn, remove a streamer, or a bauble, or a silly miniature decoration, simultaneously (and silently) making a wish for the following Christmas. The wand-waving fairy on top being the last item to go, removed by the youngest member of the household lifted up by the porter, who then brought the naked tree out onto the front lawn, and set it alight. It was a sorry-looking sight, smouldering more than burning. I watched with my eyes streaming from the smoke, although also quite moved by the intensity showing on the faces on those gathered round and cheering. I clutched a tiny corn dolly angel I had pretended to drop into the box of decorations after I had taken my turn to remove something from the tree. I was squeezing so hard that her wings became detached, and the nail that had held them in place was pushing into the fatty part of my palm. Blood was inevitable, but I kept squeezing and squeezing until the cold, initially numbing the pain, drove me indoors, leaving other guests waving trays, taken from the bar, to fan the smouldering symbol of Christmas dead, into flames. I was surprised to see my skin was dented but not pierced. Perhaps a little disappointed at the lack of blood, that the old bird was tougher than she thought. I threw my suitcase up onto the bed and bundled my Christmas dress in without folding it. My bad luck had already been to visit me, but my decline might not be over, there might be even worse to follow if I too wasn't dismantled and out of that place before midnight.

My Mammy Was Throwing Petrol Bombs

JULIAN'S FIRST SHORT STORY, PURPORTEDLY
WRITTEN IN 1972, WHEN HE WAS EIGHT

My mammy was throwing petrol bombs at the British Embassy all evening while me and my brother Christopher were at home. We were washing up the tea things and putting them away while she was heaving milk bottles full of burning petrol over the heads of the people wedged between her and the embassy in Merrion Square. I bet she was taller than the people around her because she had her high heels on, six inches platforms, but not suitable for being stuck in the middle of a crowd pushing and shoving and baying for the blood of the British, or anyone really. But great if you needed to be tall. She might have been up on the shoulders of the man who was passing the lighting bottles for her to throw. That would be an explanation too.

I can see her bowling overarm, the base of the bottle in the palm of her hand, the bottle itself remaining upright until it leaves her so that none of the petrol spills out onto any of the people between her and the embassy.

I have never seen my mammy throwing petrol bombs or anything really. Even on Dollymount Strand last summer she wouldn't play cricket with my da and my friend Johnner's da, which would have been an ideal time to practise her skills. Instead she stretched out on the warm sand and read her book, until she took me paddling and told me about Curley's Hole in the middle of the bay, and then helped me to build a sandcastle. Which means she was in a good mood, just didn't want to bowl.

Da was in front of the telly watching the news when she came home.

'You're a disgrace,' he said, 'coming in smelling of petrol. Sitting on the bus with your eyebrows singed. An embassy is neutral ground.'

I think he meant it was like when I'm playing chasing at school and the bins are 'den' and you can't be 'it' so long as you, or any part of you, is touching any part of the bins. But you can't pick up a lid and carry it round with you. The bins and the lids have to stay put, and you run around.

'What's a building compared to the lives of thirteen people? Our people,' she said. 'Someone has to take a stand. My children will not grow up thinking I looked the other way while my countrymen were being murdered.'

She wouldn't eat her tea. Maybe it was a bit dry from being in the oven all evening. My brother gave her the plate on a tray.

'Are you not hungry, Ma?' he asked.

And she said, 'No. Well maybe I am hungry, but I couldn't eat.'

You could see Da didn't understand that; being hungry, but not able to eat. And she leaned closer to the telly, the schedule abandoned, and the news extended so we could see the embassy burning and listen to people talking about it from the studio and the outside broadcast unit.

'People will be charged over this,' Da said, 'There will be witnesses, photographs, maybe even TV footage. People will go to jail.'

'Not for murdering thirteen people in Derry they won't,' my mammy said. 'That's the real disgrace, they'll get medals.'

I didn't hear any more after that because Da told me to go up to bed. My older brother was pretending to do his homework, so he was able to stay down while I was upstairs looking out of the window to see if the redness from the fire was visible from Cabra. I didn't know which way the embassy was, but I couldn't see anything much in the sky. Maybe if we lived in a house near Johnner's on the Old Cabra Road we might see more, especially upstairs, but our house is small, even though it has an upstairs.

I couldn't smell anything funny off her when she came in to kiss me good night.

'There's a lot of people talking,' I said because I could hear them on the street. She looked out of the window and said, 'Yes.' But she didn't close the curtains like she usually does. 'Do you think I'm a disgrace darling?' she asked.

'You're me mammy,' was all I could think of to say, and I pulled the covers over my head.

'There's going to be a war,' my brother said when he came up to bed. 'Ireland will invade the north and rescue the Catholics.'

'Will Mammy have to fight?' I asked and he laughed.

'That's stupid. The army is for men. Some daddies will have to fight, but not Da.' He looked out of the window too, but he closed the curtains when he was ready to get into bed.

Epilogue

Everything was normal again in a few days, with Mammy and Daddy back at work, and me and Christopher back at school. But on the following Sunday I went up to bed and left my copybook on the table. I had written down the story of the evening my mammy was throwing petrol bombs at the British embassy. It was my first story.

When I woke up Daddy was standing over me waving the copybook and shouting. The covers were off the bed and the light was on in the hall behind him. The bedroom bulb was blown again.

'Did you write this? Did you?'

I think he said it two or three times before I was awake enough to sit up.

'Where's Mammy?' I said when I started to speak. 'Where's Mammy?'

'Did you write this about the other night?' He held the copybook close to my face but I couldn't see much without the bedroom light. He grabbed the shoulder of my pyjamas and dragged me out onto the landing. It was my copybook all right. He was shaking me, so he might not have noticed at first that I was nodding.

'Get into bed,' he said and pushed me back towards the room, the copybook flying over my head in front of me.

'Daddy's gone to England,' my brother said when he came up from the bathroom after washing his face in the morning. 'And it's all your fault.' He clattered me across the back of my head and I nearly tumbled down the stairs. But I held onto the banister and didn't fall.

Mammy asked me to show her my copybook when we were eating our porridge. And she read it. When she was finished, she said, 'Your daddy has gone to England for a little while.'

'He'll never come back,' my brother said, 'and it's all *his* fault for calling him a coward.'

Mammy kissed his head and told us both to hurry up for school.

I put in the epilogue because they always had an epilogue in *The Fugitive*. It used to be Mammy's favourite programme on telly, but I was too young to watch it and it's finished now. They have an epilogue on *Ironside* and Mammy always says, 'This is the epilogue,' because they don't put the word up on the screen, the way they used to in *The Fugitive*.

Acknowledgements

If I'm to start at the beginning, then I need to thank the children's library in Kevin Street Dublin who (with a bit of encouragement from my Mother and her Aunt Mamie) introduced me to books, the Dublin Literary Study Society (meeting in the Brazen Head pub) for fostering my interest in commentary and analysis, the People's College Dublin for helping me with my craft, Sean McCann for publishing my first three pieces in the *Evening Press*, and George Schwimmer of the Dublin Theatre Workshop for introducing me to playwrighting. All before I was 21.

Thanks must go to Kara May, whose course at Goldsmiths (University of London) was so good I repeated it, and to Jonathan Kemp and Nina Rapi of Birkbeck UoL. who challenged so many of my assumptions.

In the early '90s I started working on the story (now known as) *Dolly Considine's Hotel*. I wanted to join a writing class at the City Lit in London. I had one free day, but the only available course was for those experiencing writers' block, which I wasn't. I figured the support would be good anyway and joined. But in the session where I read from the first chapters, my fellow students liked it so much they applauded, and somehow I couldn't write another word. I abandoned Dolly & Julian. Several years later I found an agent to take on my next novel, but in spite of many months of back-and-forth comments and guidance from him, it didn't find a home. He advised me to get a new project, which sent me back to Dolly and Julian. Thank you James Lockhart-MacDonald, of Antony Harwood Ltd.

Thanks to N. Quentin Woolf and all at the Writers' Mutual sessions at the Brick Lane Bookshop, likewise to Gay Authors Workshop (GAW) who gave me such excellent feedback on early chapters. A special thanks goes to Paul Burston and V G Lee of Polari Literary Salon who not only provided encouragement but have also given me an actual goal: to read at one of their South Bank events. My other goal is to give a reading in the wonderful Gay's the Word bookshop.

I learnt a lot from the editing masterclasses run by Richard Beard of the National Academy of Writing. Richard and my fellow students put Dolly through her paces, and 'surprisingly' we have all remained friends. The Literary Consultancy (who hosted NAW) also need to be thanked, both co-founder Rebecca Swift (who helpfully told me to stop whining and to get on with it) and the present director Aki Schilz and her programme to support writers from under-represented communities.

In the mid-noughties, after a lot of rejections, I gave up trying to find an agent/publisher for Dolly and decided to self-publish. But first I had a professional development session with Eva Lewin of Spread the Word. The message I took away was that I should continue looking for a traditional publisher, which I did. On the way I had help from Holly Ainley and Linda McQueen via Myriad Creative. And more help from Jo de Vries and Emma Parkin of Conker House. I would also like to thank members of The London Writers' Café for their help and support, in particular Lisa Goll and Elizabeth Waight, and Will Amado from the Bread Matters artists' retreat in Lisbon.

Eventually I found Unbound and Xander Cansell, who agreed to publish. What is so humbling is that over two hundred supporters pre-ordered enough copies of *Dolly Considine's Hotel* to allow Unbound to publish without incurring a huge loss. To you all, I want to say a great big thank you. If I mention three individuals, it is because they read early drafts and helped to shape the story into its present form. So to you (drumroll please): Liz Bennett, Nicola Labuschagne and Ros Bentley, thank you, you are the business. Thanks to Anna Simpson and everyone at Unbound for putting up with my naivety but especially to their appointed editor Mary Chesshyre, who (Covidly safe) held my hand all the way through our months of working together; her patience and support turned close editing into a joy.

Of course, I have lots of family and friends to thank, they have put up with me, for years, wittering on about the difficulties of finding a publisher. Most of all my civil partner Tomás Campbell who has endured my grumpiness for thirty-nine years (and counting). He has always seen worth in my writing, he recognises tropes I don't even suspect, and almost never gets cross at my 'need to do a little work on Dolly'. Thanks T.

Unbound is the world's first crowdfunding publisher, established in 2011.

We believe that wonderful things can happen when you clear a path for people who share a passion. That's why we've built a platform that brings together readers and authors to crowdfund books they believe in – and give fresh ideas that don't fit the traditional mould the chance they deserve.

This book is in your hands because readers made it possible. Everyone who pledged their support is listed at the front of the book and below. Join them by visiting unbound.com and supporting a book today.

Noel Lane
Stephen Lansman
Mary Mc Colgan
Fiona McCallum
Scott McGill
Frank McMullan
Kevin McNerney
Aidan McQuade
Barbara Joan Meier
John Mitchinson
David Mooney
M Moor
Rhel ná DecVandé
Carlo Navato
Trevor Newton
PJ O'Donnell
Pascal O'Loughlin
Siobhan O'Donnell
Justin Pollard

Morgan Quinn
Hilary Rankin
Marie Renaud
Laura Richards
Julie Sale
Samantha Sale
Kim Sangster
George Scott
Kieran Scott
Ronald Seery
Rosemary Slater
David Sperlinger
Margaret Thomas
Stephen Waring
Peter Warm
Paul Waters
Ash Watson
Sam West
Grahame Williams